"*Mrs. Mike* . . . is the story of the start of young love, its growth to maturity, and its acceptance of a dangerous, hard, but enthralling life. Its level of sheer entertainment is extremely high." —*Los Angeles Herald-Express*

"It is the personality of Sgt. Mike blowing through this account like a clear breeze that gives it a refreshing quality. Everyone's dream of a cop, he was also a romantic and understanding husband, the fondest of fathers; a man of honor and humor." —*The New York Times*

"*Mrs. Mike* is an unforgettable story, not only because it portrays the deep abiding affection between a man and a woman, but because it pictures the austere beauty of a country where life is at once simple and free, yet complicated by danger and hardship." —*Boston Herald*

"The portraiture is true to life. Sergeant Mike's masculine way of talk, his ability to get on with human nature, his unending but never dramatic helpfulness, his matching the big moments with bigness, but always simply, are commonplace of men in the Force, but rare in books. The Indians are equally well portrayed. Mrs. Mike's maid, Oh-Be-Joyful, and her laconic suitor are masterly characterizations and deeply touching." —*Christian Science Monitor*

"This is a book the reader will be unable to put down until the last page is read." —*Library Journal*

The Search for Joyful

Benedict and Nancy Freedman

BERKLEY BOOKS, NEW YORK

B

A Berkley Book
Published by The Berkley Publishing Group
A division of Penguin Putnam Inc.
375 Hudson Street
New York, New York 10014

PRINTING HISTORY
Berkley hardcover edition / February 2002
Berkley trade paperback edition / February 2003

Berkley trade paperback edition ISBN: 0-425-18833-7

Visit our website at www.penguinputnam.com

The Library of Congress has catalogued the Berkley hardcover edition as follows:

Freedman, Benedict.
    The search for Joyful / Benedict and Nancy Freedman.
        p. cm.
    Sequel to: Mrs. Mike.
    ISBN: 0-425-18333-5
    1. Cree women—Fiction.   2. Nursing students—Fiction.   I. Freedman,
Nancy Mars.   II. Title

PS3511.R416 S43 2002
813'.54—dc21

                                                                2001043497

PRINTED IN THE UNITED STATES OF AMERICA

10 9 8 7 6 5 4 3 2 1

To the readers of
Mrs. Mike
who asked for this story

Acknowledgments

Claire Gerus, for making the arrangements
Susan Allison, for guiding the publication
Anne Sowards, for shepherding the manuscript
Johanna Shapiro, for her insightful literary psychotherapy
Deborah Jackson, for recognizing truth
Hartley John Freedman, for providing technical assistance
Patricia Carroll, for being there

The
Search
for
Joyful

*O*ne

THE WHISTLE BLEW. The train lurched forward. Black clouds of smoke obscured Mama Kathy and Connie. Only seconds before they had been repeating their advice and hugging me. Mama Kathy held to her belief that I was headed for sin city, as she called Montreal. I felt I was embarked on an adventure like her own, when as a young girl she'd traveled from Boston into the wilderness of the Northwest Territory. I was reversing this, going from the prairie to the big city—like Mama, starting a new life in a different world.

As I watched the land speed past in a blur of white drifts, I remembered the times Mama put us to bed with tales of her journey in the blizzard of '07. The train stalled for weeks, waiting to be dug out by snowplows. Wiping the frost from the window she looked out at hundreds of cows and steers blown across the icy fields, packed along the stock fence, frozen and dead.

When I wiped the frost from my window, the vista that greeted my eyes was smiling and sunny, the snow sparkling. I felt buoyant and excited. A call had gone out, and I had answered it. What would come of it, I didn't know.

I tried to disentangle exactly what it was that had propelled me toward this moment. Not one event, but many threads, twisted and woven together. Growing up with Mama Kathy and Papa was the main thing. There was something special between the two of them, kept alive by Mama Kathy's stories of how it had been.

"The Crees called me Mrs. Mike," she'd say, "because they couldn't get their tongues around a name like Flannigan." And I'd beg for more stories about those times. I wanted to be part of them. But the special love, the special joy belonged to her and Papa Mike. When I realized that . . . the what-ifs began. What if I was really their daughter? What if the twins were really my brother and sister?

The desire to fit in gave rise to all the what-ifs of my life. It became a game, and yet it was more than that. What if I was allowed to keep one of the kittens? What if I could go into town with Papa? What if I was a rabbit and lived in a burrow? What if I didn't have to be "included." *Included* was Mama Kathy's word. "Remember," she'd say to Connie and Georges, "Kathy is to be included."

What set me apart? We were all adopted, so it wasn't that. I didn't guess the reason because they never talked to me about it, and their love protected me from even thinking about it.

Still, I had a sense of uneasiness. In the bathtub I scrubbed my copper skin hard in an attempt to lighten it. Mama Kathy, when she understood what I was doing, scooped me up in a big towel and held me against her. "Your skin is the color of a young fawn because you are Oh-Be-Joyful's daughter. You can't believe how close we were, Kathy. She was my more-than-sister." She told me I belonged to the First Nation people and that my band was Cree. "You are Cree Indian."

The first day at mission school was my first real contact with Indian children. They regarded me with solemn black eyes very like my own. I stared at them, at their heavy straight braids. What if my hair grew long and was plaited, wouldn't it look exactly like theirs? Their skin was the same tone too, the tone Mama Kathy called sun-kissed.

The Indian children kept to themselves. They sent glances in my direction, but didn't speak to me. One girl fingered a pouch of some kind she wore around her neck, looking at me all the time. I did not return her glance; it was too full of things I knew nothing of.

At recess no one talked to me. I stood isolated and alone in the noisy schoolyard. Both sets of children, the Indian and the white, ignored me. I was marked as not belonging.

I watched the white girls jumping rope. I knew how to jump rope. I jumped better than they did. My feet never got tangled up. I continued to watch. Finally I went over to them. "I can jump rope."

Several girls giggled, the rest stared, but no one said anything. There was a short line; I joined it and waited my turn. When it came I stepped into the arc of the rope. It made a fine whooshing sound each time it struck the gravel. I jumped and jumped and never fell out of rhythm.

The Cree girl, who was called Elk Girl, contemplated me with dispassionate eyes and reserved judgment.

I wanted to know more about being Indian. I got Mama Kathy to tell me again how she brought Oh-Be-Joyful from the mission to help with her babies, who died afterwards in the diphtheria epidemic. Seven years later it was the flu, born in the dirt of European trenches, that created world-wide havoc and carried off the twins' mother and grandmother too. Mama Kathy always finished by harking back to her own children. "Mary Aroon and Ralph were taken, but the good Lord gave me you three rascals to raise." Because, when the disease was almost over and the danger seemed past, it claimed a final victim, Oh-Be-Joyful.

I didn't like this part of the story. "Tell me," I prompted, "tell me about Jonathan Forquet." And I recited along with her, "Jonathan Forquet loved her from the moment he set eyes on her. . . . Now tell who he was." I knew that too, which was what made it such a wonderful tale.

"He was your father." And we hugged each other in delight.

As she related how ill he had been, how despondent after my mother's death, a memory formed hazily in my mind. A strange Indian standing on our porch, his eyes searching me out, just me, from all the others. I was the only one he saw. After gazing at me a long time, he opened his arms.

I wouldn't go to him. I held on to Mama's skirt, but she gave me a gentle shove. "It's your father, Kathy." She chose the word well, because while I couldn't have two papas, a father was all right.

When he held me I thought of pine trees and streams, and smoky fires. He clasped me against him a long time, until I began to squirm. He turned my face so that I looked at him, and said, "I bring you a name."

That seemed an odd thing to say. I had a name. My name was Kathy.

He continued almost without pause. "I traveled a long journey to bring it. Your mother's spirit guided me to the Grandmothers." His voice was taut, vibrant. "Listen to me, child. In the lodges of your people you are named Oh-Be-Joyful's Daughter."

Oh-Be-Joyful's Daughter was my Indian name, but it had never been part of me. I wasn't that girl.

Except . . .

I think it was Oh-Be-Joyful's Daughter who showed me how to fight for acceptance at school. I used a gift I had from Mama Kathy—storytelling. Stories came effortlessly into my head, and I would spin them out for Connie and Georges during long evenings.

Most of my plots were borrowed. When I got to high school I

learned this wasn't such a bad thing. Shakespeare borrowed a lot of his plots too.

An endless source of books was Old Irish Bill. He probably had the finest collection of tattered and dilapidated books in the Northwest Territory and his own library system. You could take home up to ten books at a time, but you had to sign for them. You also had an obligation to repair them to the best of your ability. I spent many hours with brown wrapping paper, paste, scissors, and sometimes cardboard. A special satchel at our house was dedicated to Irish Bill's books.

I grew up with Kim, Robin Hood, and Long John Silver. Those afternoons when I sat on the worn couch in Irish Bill's living room, he would prepare hot chocolate, adding a nip to his— "against the cold," he would say. It was very companionable, he with a pipe, me scattering crumbs as I dunked corn bread.

Mama was a history buff and wanted us to take advantage of Irish Bill's wonderful store of knowledge. She told us she had once spent an entire winter immersed in his prized history of China, which on the flyleaf bore the inscription, "Property of the McTavishes." Georges liked how-to books, on magic and fixing things and surviving in the wilderness. He would explain to Connie, who never opened a book if she could help it, how the world ran, what was wrong with it, and how it could be improved.

Connie had her own fantasy life. Very early, about age six, she planned her wedding, "down to the last detail." A gown of billowing satin, a veil, orange blossoms—she pictured it all against a background of wedding guests. The fact that the nuptials were years in the future, and that no groom loomed on the horizon, bothered her not at all. He would appear, along with a tiered wedding cake, when it was time.

Stories. I loved stories. And stories became my passport.

I sat on a bench in the playground and began my inventions. My audience was a boy with a sprained ankle, who couldn't participate in football practice. The first tale owed a large debt to Jack London's *White Fang*. As I got into it, more and more children came to hear. My great triumph was when Elk Girl joined the group to listen to the saga of Gray Wolf.

Gray Wolf went from adventure to adventure. White Wolf was his mate and everyone knows wolves mate for life. The story continued for months, and then something impelled me to bring disaster on poor Gray Wolf. In fighting free of a trapper's snare he was shot and blinded.

I drew a deep breath wondering how he could survive in the wild. But only for a moment. It was clear to me that White Wolf came to his aid, inviting Gray Wolf to lay his muzzle against her flank and gallop through the forest with her. From then on he ran at her side. She was his eyes.

Elk Girl came up to me later in the week and put a bushy animal tail in my lap. "The spirit of the wolf liked your story. He will be your guardian."

I took the wolf tail home and examined it further. It was gray with a ring of white and one of a darker fur, a symbol of good luck, which through mysterious Indian magic would keep evil at bay.

PACKING FOR MONTREAL, I had put in my old talisman at the last moment. I was glad I had. As the silver and blue Canadian Pacific rushed on, I wondered if I would be the only First Nation person to enroll at Charity Hospital. The only First Nation person to answer the call for army nurses.

The only First Nation person.

I had faced that situation when Connie and Georges began dating. They always double-dated. Even for twins they were close. I watched them whisper together, finish each other's sentences, and laugh at private jokes. They invented a secret cryptographic code—the Twins' Code—that Georges boasted no one could break. Another signal between them was the word *tomahawk*. Whenever either mentioned the word, it meant, "This is boring. Let's get out of here." The problem was working a word like *tomahawk* into ordinary conversation.

I took it all in. I watched as they were caught up in a social life, and realized this would not happen for me. I was already in high school and no white boy asked me out. Although Randy Harrison tried to kiss me when he caught me alone behind the gym.

I took to staring into my looking glass and brooding. Was I pretty, I wondered, studying my prominent cheekbones. My eyes were large and set well apart. My lashes, long and straight. My teeth white and straight, and my mouth full, even when I laughed. My nose? What can be said about noses? Mine wasn't big, it wasn't small. It was just a nose. Did these features add up to a pretty face? I decided to ask Mama Kathy.

"Mama," I said that evening as I took down the dishtowel, "do you think I'm at all pretty?"

"Pretty?" She seemed startled. But I could see she was considering the question. "You've always been a sturdy girl. And thank goodness your health is excellent."

"Yes, yes, but am I pretty?"

"There's a look of Oh-Be-Joyful about you, but I see your father too. You have his strength."

I smiled. It was hopeless.

When Connie came in, I told her I wanted a sister walk. Connie, because she was older, saw how hard it was for me to get things out, so years ago she had instituted sister walks. A sister walk is of course only for sisters. No one else can come along, because that's when you tell whatever is on your mind.

"Connie," I said when we were halfway to the pond where a

colony of ducks and a pair of white egrets had made their home, "I want to know, it's important to me: Do you think I'm pretty?"

"Of course you're pretty."

That was a big-sister reply and it didn't satisfy me. "What do the girls at school say about me?"

"They think you're exotic."

"Exotic? That isn't pretty."

"You have a Metis French grandfather, and that strain shows. I'd guess you were Indian, but I wouldn't be sure. Let's ask Georges."

"No," I said, suddenly shy, "forget it."

I got an after-school job at the drugstore. I was stationed behind the soda fountain, where I mixed frothy sarsaparillas and chocolate shakes.

I was mixing and scooping and waiting tables while China was wracked by civil war. I barely recognized the names Mao and Chiang Kai-shek. When the Japanese set up a puppet government in Manchukuo, I was serving Coca-Colas and rainbow ice cream cones.

Two women sat down at the soda fountain and fanned themselves. Saying "I really shouldn't," they ordered double malts. A little kid, scarcely as high as the counter, undid a dime tied into a corner of his handkerchief. A couple of girls from my own grade, in circular swing skirts wearing lipstick, came in. I hardly recognized them out of our school uniform. How hard we tried to pin our middy blouses in a sexy way, emphasizing slim waists and hinting at something on top as well. When the Sisters spotted the new fashion, it was immediately abolished.

Now my classmates were young ladies, meeting boys here. Was I also a young lady?

Elk Girl came in. She had dropped out of school. I hadn't seen her in almost a year. She put money on the counter before uttering a word.

"I'll have a banana split with everything on it," she said as though we had parted that morning.

"How've you been, Elk Girl?" I asked as I sliced a banana, added three scoops of different ice creams and three sauces, sprinkled on nuts, and finished with a dollop of whipped cream and a maraschino cherry.

She followed these preparations with an eagle eye, then put her question to me. "Have you ever eaten one?"

"No," I admitted.

"That's what I thought. You fix 'em, but you don't eat 'em."

I felt uncomfortable. How did she know that, since the Depression, banana splits were considered too expensive around our house?

With great deliberation Elk Girl took out a pack of Old Golds and offered me one.

"No, I don't smoke." I was horrified that she did.

She contemplated me with the look that had disconcerted me since I was seven. "You should smoke, you know. Smoke is holy. Bet you didn't know that."

"Who says it's holy?"

"The Creator." She laughed at my expression. "Can't go higher than that." With concentration she blew a smoke ring in my direction.

I brushed it away.

"Won't your white mama let you smoke?"

I pretended to be busy counting out paper napkins and filling containers.

"Oh-Be-Joyful understood smoke."

This pronouncement shook me. What did she know about my mother?

"I live with a power woman. Sarah is very very old. She is a wind shifter and she knew Mamanowatum."

"Who's that?"

"Your mother, Oh-Be-Joyful. Mamanowatum is the way it's said in Cree. Sarah, the woman I live with, knew her, she knew Jonathan, she knew about you being born . . . and she knew what would happen."

"How? By divination? By magic?"

Elk Girl said complacently, "She looks into smoke and it shows her things."

"What things?" I couldn't help asking.

"Herself."

I frowned over the answer.

"You have to know yourself first, before you can know anything else; that just stands to reason. By the way, how do you get on with your pawakam?"

"My what?"

"Your wolf tail."

"I still have it, if that's what you mean."

She seemed pleased with this answer. "You make a good split." She carried her sundae to one of the tables and proceeded to eat with obvious relish, making sure to get every bit.

"There ought to be a law," one of the girls from school whispered in a voice meant to carry, "no ice cream for You-know-who above the fiftieth parallel."

This raised a laugh from her friends, but Elk Girl did not choose to hear. She had not come for ice cream. I knew enough about magic from my brother to know that. Georges was fascinated by things that appeared to be one thing and were in fact quite different. "The science of misdirection," he called it. Elk Girl had come because of the pawakam.

*   *   *

ELK GIRL WAS my only link with my Indian self. My only link to Oh-Be-Joyful's Daughter. She seemed to know a lot about me. I knew nothing about her, not even where she lived, except it was with a wind shifter called Sarah. Elk Girl had always been aloof, distant, and unknowable, like my Indian heritage. I decided to make her a friendship bracelet. I'd made one for Connie's birthday. It involved a lot of rummaging—tiny glass beads, seed pearls from a pair of outworn gloves, covered buttons from a torn jacket, segments of a broken watch band, strung together. I was still thinking about the possibilities of a second bracelet as I walked home from school. I wondered if I could find enough items.

Because I lived farther out than most of the kids I generally walked home alone. I turned at the sound of my name.

"Kathy!" It was Phil Dunway on his bike. Phil Dunway was the boy at school that I liked. I'd liked him since fifth grade when he stood up for me on the playground. He was a senior now, and after graduation I wouldn't see him again.

Phil caught up to me, got off and walked his bicycle. "Kathy," he said again, "I'm going your way."

I was surprised at his friendliness. At school we didn't speak. "Fine," I said. Neither of us could think of anything further to say, then we spoke at once. I laughed and took a breath. "Are you visiting someone?" I asked, because he'd never taken this route before.

"No." There was a short pause. "I just thought maybe you wouldn't mind."

Was he saying that he took this path deliberately to walk me home? My heart raced with excitement. He liked me. Phil Dunway, the cutest boy in school, liked me.

The pause between us lengthened, and I searched for something interesting to say, but could only come up with, "Lucky you, you'll be graduating in a couple of months."

"Yeah." He smiled but had nothing to add.

"So, do you have something lined up? A summer job?"

"My dad wants me to go into the contracting business with him, but things are pretty slow just now."

"You ought to think about being a Mountie. If I was a man that's what I'd be."

"I'm glad you're not."

"What? A Mountie?"

"A man." And he took one hand from the handle of his bike and laid it over mine. The wheel immediately turned, bringing us to an abrupt halt. "Can we maybe sit down somewhere and talk? If you don't have to get home, that is."

"No, I don't have to be home."

There was shade not far off, and we sat with our backs against the large oak. Phil took my hand again. "This is better," he said.

I let my hand stay in his.

"I never see you with any of the fellows at school." He threw this out tentatively.

"No. I'm not going with any of them."

"That's what I was hoping because . . ." He leaned over and kissed me. He did it very deliberately as though he had been nerving himself to it. Then he did it once more and this time I cooperated.

It felt heady. His touch awakened me to new knowledge of myself. In Phil Dunway's arms I sensed what it was to be a woman. His fingers lightly followed the outline of my cheek, my throat, and, dropping lower, my breasts.

I drew back frightened that I had allowed so much, afraid I would allow more. "I have to go."

"Can I see you again tomorrow?" he asked, getting to his feet. "Right here? Can this be our place?"

I hesitated. I wanted to, but . . .

"I'll be here," he said persuasively, "right after school. Will you?"

Words choked in my throat, but I nodded.

I thought of Phil all night, analyzed every intonation, action, and gesture. In English class I went over it all again. In mathematics I got totally lost, thinking not of square roots but of the soft, waving texture of his hair, remembering my fingers in it.

While I was still debating whether or not to meet him, I found myself there. Phil was leaning against the old oak and at sight of me his face lighted and he came forward. Without a word we put our arms about each other. This time there was no fumbling, his mouth was deliciously open and his hands sure. He continued where he had left off. He slid his hands under my shirt. I rallied from dreamy acquiescence determined to say no.

He didn't ask, just opened my shirt and stared. "I never saw a girl before," he said.

I got to my feet, pulling my shirt around me. "You shouldn't have done that, Phil."

"I'm not sorry, Kathy. I should be. And I apologize. Don't go away sore." He caught up to me. "How'd you like to go to the senior prom?"

That stopped me. I'd never been to a school dance or any other kind. No one had ever asked me. The senior prom. I'd fantasized about it forever, Cinderella at the ball.

"Well?" Phil asked. "What do you say?"

I forgot I hadn't answered him. I nodded before I could get the yes out.

"Can I have another look, then?"

I closed my eyes and stood in front of him, my face burning as he unbuttoned my blouse.

That night I took down my wolf pawakam. I felt it held the answer to my question. "Guardian," I whispered, "does he feel what I feel? Does he love me? Really love me?"

The talisman replied sooner than I expected. Sooner than I wanted. I lived a very short time in my Cinderella dream. After school the girls were whispering to each other, speculating who was taking who to the prom. Some had already been asked, and they preened themselves before the wallflowers.

I didn't say anything. Marlene was keeping count at the drinking fountain. She said, "So far, Ev is going with John Boyle, Gwen with Danny Thompson, and Cindy with Phil Dunway . . ."

She went on, but I didn't hear. I left her standing there and walked down the hall and out to the ball field where I knew he would be playing lacrosse. It was baseball season, but a bunch of the fellows got up their own lacrosse game so they could charge and block and work out their hostilities.

"Phil!" I called. "Phil."

They were taking a break, and Phil was showing off, cradling the ball. He looked up. The other boys did too. They were startled and one of them mimicked, "Phil, oh, Phil, Pocahontas wants you."

He looked at me. It was a long look. Then he turned his back, laughing.

The public humiliation pinned me to the spot. I couldn't walk away from the shame any more than I could walk away from the anger. I wanted to run, but I was chained where I was. I knew I could never tell anyone, not Mama Kathy, not Connie either.

I had brought this on myself. I had forgotten I was Indian. Remembering released me, gave me strength to walk past my classmates looking neither to the right nor the left, my ears closed to comments.

At home I got out the wolf tail and stared at it a long time. I hadn't known who I was. Now I knew. I would braid wolf hairs into the friendship bracelet.

I DIDN'T GROW up until Papa died. He wasn't sick. Something broke inside him and we couldn't get him to a hospital. It had rained for days and the roads had turned to muskeg.

I heard his voice in muffled cries, hoarse and desperate, from the bedroom.

When Mama Kathy came out she staggered against the door. I rushed to her, led her to a chair, and pushed her gently into it.

"The Luminal, Kathy. He asked for it. It's in a small silver packet in the medicine chest."

"Yes, Mama, I'll get it."

"Oh, God, the pain, Kathy. It's terrible."

"I'll get him the Luminal, Mama. It will be better."

She nodded, and I went into the bathroom, found it, and, filling a glass of water, took it to him.

The covers were knotted into a corner of the bed. Papa's eyes had glazed over like a sick cat's, sweat rolled along his face, and his body was rigid. I poured some of the water on a towel and bent over him, wiping his forehead, murmuring as I worked. "I've brought you the Luminal, Papa. It will relax you."

He was in no condition to swallow anything. A spasm bowed his body and blood gushed, splattering the wall, ejected with the same terrible force that had taken over his body.

I rushed to the bathroom for a clean towel, passing the door to my room. There, in the closet on the top shelf, was my guardian. I couldn't see it, but I didn't need to see it.

"Help me," I whispered. "Help him."

When I returned, Papa was stretched out on his back, sleeping.

I stroked his hand, his capable, strong-fingered hand. What good was his strength to him now? What good were dampened towels and Luminal, even if he could swallow it? What was needed was large decisive steps. Something had gone wrong inside. He needed stitching together, he needed an oxygen tent to help him breathe. He needed a hospital equipped to help him.

His eyes opened. He looked at me and said in a voice that I bent to hear, "You'd make a good nurse, Kathy."

Those were his last words to me. Mama Kathy came in. Her red hair was pinned neatly back; she had taken hold. I relinquished my place.

I went out and sat on the porch steps. Connie and Georges came and sat beside me. No one spoke. Then Connie gave a quavering little laugh. "You know what I was thinking? Do you remember, Kathy, when you were little, about five, I think? You use to spend hours making concoctions of dirt and grass, all mixed up with seeds and baking powder from the kitchen."

"I remember that," Georges said.

"Do you remember what it was for?" Connie challenged him.

I knew. It suddenly came back to me. I was making a medicine so Mama Kathy and Papa would live forever. "It didn't work," I muttered.

We learned it was peritonitis that took him, a burst appendix. Sergeant Mike looked after the whole province. If a job needed doing, there was Mike Flannigan of the Royal Canadian Mounted Police to do it. He was game warden, inspected traps and settled disputes. He kept illegal drugs out of his territory and was responsible for immigration violation and sabotage. And when he'd time on his hands, he repaired the telephone wires and vaccinated a village. He would turn his hand to anything, help anyone, and in the end no one could do anything for him.

Elk Girl explained it to me that night. I was exhausted, out of my head with grief, and had thrown myself across the bed without bothering with a cover. Elk Girl came in, covered me, brought the pawakam and laid it beside me, then opened the window and sat there, looking out. She stared up at the stars, and they, serene and wise, looked down on us. Elk Girl didn't speak. She didn't say that the stars were where they belonged—but they were.

WE THOUGHT IT would be a small funeral, just the family and a few friends from the town. But word was carried on the newly extended phone lines and, when these quit, by moccasin telegraph penetrating deep into the woods. People came, white and Indian, from all over the province, people we didn't know but who had known Sgt. Mike Flannigan.

The Royal Canadian Mounted Police were well represented, their scarlet dress uniforms punctuating the somber attire of the others. Among the guests was Jonathan Forquet. He came not only for Papa Mike but to stand beside Mama.

On the day of the funeral she leaned on his arm. He himself was a compelling figure, spare almost to the point of emaciation. His eyes, when he turned them on you, burned with the intensity of a soul about to leave the body, an arrow ready to quit the bow. When the prayers were finished and he spoke I could understand why the Indians regarded him as a holy man.

"This Mountie we lay to rest today arrested me, kept me jailed for a murder I did not do, refused to give his blessing to my marriage. Yet I am here from across Canada, from Quebec Province. Why? Because when I was starving in body and soul he fed me at his table. He travels now to the west where our people have always traveled. But if he was here he'd laugh in our faces. As he saw it, he did what anybody would do. His own kids died in the diphtheria epidemic, and he was still bringing soup and medicine to people too ill and weak to manage for themselves. But don't think he wouldn't go after a trap thief and bring him in, Mountie style. He was there to fight a fire, or pull an abscessed tooth. He entered our lives, one way or another. Look in your heart to see which part of him you carry."

Before he left, my father called me to him. He acted as though he had a right to do this, as though he had been here. But it was Papa. Papa was the one to oil my skates, to show me the beaver dam, to explain the migration of birds—it was Papa's lap that was always there for me.

Jonathan Forquet never bothered about me, never inquired about me. He was never part of my life. He was off somewhere being holy, preaching to unlettered Indians who were in awe of him.

Well, I wasn't in awe of him. I followed him reluctantly, my feet scuffing leaves.

He walked a little way into the woods, and the musky smell of decayed vegetation under loamy earth made me think of the grave.

He began speaking again in an intimate way, as though I was his daughter. "You have grown up well. Mrs. Mike is right, there is a look of your mother about you. There is also a look of sadness. Not only because of Sergeant Mike's death, but it has been in you, I think, a long time. It comes from the way you look at life."

"Don't lecture me. Did you find the beaver dam? Did you fix my skates? I don't even know you. And you don't know me."

"I do know you. I brought you your name."

"You show up once. One time in sixteen years. Well, you know what I wish? I wish it was my papa I was standing here with."

A slight smile hovered about the corners of his mouth. "And that I was where he is?"

I turned away.

"Oh-Be-Joyful's Daughter—"

I stopped. I wasn't used to anyone addressing me by this name.

He went on in a detached tone, but I felt the urgency behind it. "When I think of you, when I dream you, when I speak your name, you are with me. Far things are just as near. Didn't you ever feel this?"

"No. Either someone is here with me, or they're not."

"A namer is never far."

"You were. To other people you brought religion and all that, but there was nothing for me. And you can't start now, I won't let you." I was angry to find I was crying.

He went on as though I hadn't said anything, "You must remember who you are. You must learn to be joyful."

"You haven't the right to expect anything of me. Go take your good works somewhere else." I turned and ran. The joyfulness he tried to force on me seemed dreadful. At school I'm not accepted—it doesn't matter, be joyful. At work I serve sundaes I can't afford to eat—be joyful. My papa, whom I love more than anything in the world, dies—be joyful.

We didn't speak again. I was glad when he left.

Two

AFTER PAPA'S DEATH, we tried to be a normal family. We couldn't talk about Papa at first. We had to and yet we couldn't. It was Jonathan Forquet Mama Kathy told me about. I didn't want to listen because I knew I'd been unfair to him. But I couldn't stop Mama.

"When Oh-Be-Joyful died, he didn't know what to do. He went wild, gambled, made himself ill, almost died. Then he turned to religion, but he didn't find what he needed, not completely. Not until he read the teachings of Handsome Lake."

"Is Handsome Lake a person?"

"He was a Seneca prophet. Before that, like Jonathan, he was a drunk. This brought him close to death, and he experienced a vision in which it is said he was shown the braiding of all things. When he recovered, he wove the wisdom of the Seneca into the wisdom of the Christian Bible. That was in 1799. It is to this man's teachings your father has brought new life. Every second year in the longhouses a ceremony is held recounting the story of Handsome Lake through dance and recitations. Your father leads this."

And I had flared out at him, telling off the great man. Well, I didn't care how great or important he was, or what religions he resurrected. He was still an absentee father.

*   *   *

WHEN MAMA WAS finally able to retell the old stories, I felt better. I think she did too.

She told me how primitive and isolated the Northwest Territory was in the days when she fell in love with a handsome Mountie whose "eyes were so blue you could swim in them." He was about to be posted into wild, untamed country, and he considered her too young to make up her mind properly. So instead of proposing to her, he proposed to her uncle. "The storm still raging, and me standing there, my feet in a basin of hot water." There were tears behind our laughter, and we held each other and cried them.

"Your papa reached out to people in a remarkable way. For instance, Jonathan." Papa, she said, couldn't make Jonathan out. His traplines had been plundered and winter furs—fox, ocelot, and martin—stolen. Then the man Jonathan accused of the theft was murdered. In spite of the fact that it was done with Jonathan's knife, Papa did not believe him capable of cold-blooded killing. "I remember Mike telling him if he'd give his word he didn't do it, he'd release him. Do you think Jonathan would do this? No. We had to *know*, all of us, Mike and me—and especially Oh-Be-Joyful—that he wouldn't murder an unarmed man. He spent the summer in that sweltering, mosquito-ridden jail because, as he put it, he couldn't read his innocence in our eyes. . . . Yes," she pondered, "Papa was exasperated by him, but in a way he loved him."

I began to know Jonathan Forquet. I began to consider what he had said to me on our walk, and to wonder if I could get back to being happy. Not merely happy as a great many people are . . . but joyful.

Joyful is past happy. Happy is more a quiet content. Joy on the other hand is actively seeking moments when you're high on life, and if those moments aren't there, to make them, to cause them. It was the inheritance Jonathan Forquet meant for me, and for the first time I wanted his good opinion. I wanted to live up to my Indian name.

PEARL HARBOR, AND the planes couldn't get off the ground.

Pearl Harbor, and the sea sent dead to the surface like flotsam.

Pearl Harbor, and suddenly the immensity of oceans no longer protected us.

Christmas 1941. The angel from her topmost position on the tree did not signify peace on earth, goodwill toward men. Her golden wings spread over a world exploding into madness. In Canada we kept our radios tuned to the news station and scanned the daily paper.

Georges said from the beginning that when Mussolini and Hitler formed the Axis, all hell would break loose. He bought a map of the world and tacked it up in his room. A yellow arrow showed Mussolini gobbling up Ethiopia; a black arrow showed Hitler gobbling up Austria. A year later Germany, on the pretext of defending Sudeten Germans, took over Czechoslovakia. Georges pasted a black swastika on that country and put a question mark over Poland. Hitler must have had access to Georges's map, because six months later he rolled into Poland, and the word *blitzkrieg* entered our vocabulary.

"Hitler's pouring in mechanized troops," Georges confronted us, as though we had something to do with it. "And how do the Poles fight back? With horses! Can you see it? Horses charging tanks."

Mama didn't argue, that wasn't her way. "We already fought one war for democracy and found out it was for the perpetuation of the British Empire."

Georges managed a laugh. "There speaks our Irish mama."

The news supported Georges. France and England declared war.

Canada was at war a week later, although Prime Minister Mackenzie King assured us that Canada's role would be for the defense of North America. England could fend for herself. We, along with the United States, would be chief suppliers, but that would be the extent of our participation.

Headlines repeated the P.M.'s promise: NO CONSCRIPTION. "It's a relief to know that no Canadian boys will be sent overseas," Mama Kathy said.

Georges felt differently.

I argued that once the troops of the British Expeditionary Force confronted them, the Germans would be brought to heel. At the same time an irrational fear gripped me that Germany would make an end run around France and somehow rise up off our coast at Nova Scotia.

I listened to Connie and Georges debate, a rare instance because the twins were consistently on the same side in all their opinions. This time I sensed Connie was afraid.

I read the papers and was glued to the radio. Prices zoomed out of sight. We planted a victory garden. Free seed was distributed—lettuce, tomatoes, beans, and carrots. The corn was put in at some distance, because Mama Kathy insisted it impoverished the soil. In spite of these efforts, there were shortages of everything, including good news.

While I watered the garden, there were sightings of periscopes off the Atlantic coast, and an eight-year-old girl was killed in her bed by a lobbed shell. My fear no longer seemed irrational.

The North Atlantic became a hunting ground for U-boats. The liner *Athenia* was sunk by German submarines, the carrier *Courageous* lost, and the battleship *Royal Oak*. Georges made notes in the margin of his map.

The Germans didn't attempt to breach the Maginot Line. They swarmed through the Low Countries and dropped parachutists, half of which were dummies brought to add to the confusion.

France held out a month. In one of the greatest sea rescues in history, every English boat from the royal yacht to fishing smacks cooperated in evacuating 340,000 British, French, and Belgian troops through Dunkirk and other Channel ports.

Paris was declared an open city. The Germans walked in without firing a shot. On the radio we heard Churchill announce that Britain would fight on alone. "This is our finest hour," he said, while London was being pummeled by dive bombers. He vowed to defend the city street by street and house by house. Children and the aged were dispatched to the countryside. England was crying in the night.

Mama Kathy quietly joined the Ladies' Defense Society and began knitting socks. Evenings we huddled around our radio and looked at each other bleakly. For the first time it was conceivable England might lose the war.

"This is it," Georges said, "I've had it with sitting on the sidelines."

We three women, Mama Kathy, Connie, and I, stared at him mutely. He left for Ottawa right after Sunday services to join the RAF. But Saturday evening to cheer us up he gave a farewell magic show.

That brought back the famous magic show when I was seven. Georges rigged a curtain, one of Mama Kathy's blankets, strung on a wire along the living-room rafters. And he gave me a part. I was to open the curtain in the beginning and in the end draw it. We rehearsed all week. The day of the performance Old Bill came and played his Irish bagpipes. Mama baked cookies, which she passed around. Papa's contribution was to applaud. He was an enthusiastic applauder. He showed us how to cup our hands to make twice the noise. And if you jump to your feet and clap your hands over your head, it makes for a deafening ovation, especially if you add cries of Bravo!

I was seized by stage fright and when the time came for me to close the curtain, I pulled the wrong way. Of course I was only pretending to pull. Connie was actually making it move, which it did—the other way.

A huge laugh from the audience made me realize my mistake. I had ruined the show. Disgraced and in tears, I ran from the room.

Georges was after me in a flash and took me in his arms.

"It's all right, Kathy. It's like the curtain is magic and goes its own way. We're going to keep that in the show from now on."

Connie came and gave me a hug. "Are you crying because of that stupid curtain?"

"I used to be crying about that. Now I'm crying because . . . because . . ."

"Because why, honey?"

"Just because!"

She placed her cheek against mine.

This sent me into a fresh paroxysm. "Why can't I be a twin?" I wailed. "Everybody else is."

If Georges wanted to smile, he didn't show it. "It's like this, Kathy. Most people, God gets right the first time. He did with you. He looked at you and said, 'This is a good kid.' "

Georges, where are you? His hope of the RAF didn't work out. Myopia was enough to disqualify him. But he applied for and was accepted into officers' training, somewhere in England. Connie whispered not to worry, he wasn't in the front lines.

Connie would know. They had stayed up the night before he left reviving the Twins' Code.

* * *

THE WAR HAD been going on for two years. But it took Pearl Harbor to make me realize it was my war too. My war, because there was a push to corral the dark and dusky peoples of the world, to force them into labor camps—who knows, perhaps they were death camps. And my skin was copper.

I'd thought a good deal recently about being dark. In Germany the gypsies, along with the Jews, were rounded up, arrested, stripped of their possessions. Gypsies, because Hitler hadn't any Indians. But the civilized world couldn't allow the Nazis to declare themselves a master race and the rest slaves. Here in Canada we weren't all fair-skinned. We played and sang and worshipped in dozens of languages—French, Russian, Plattdeutsch . . . and Cree.

Only England, fighting alone, stood against this genocidal policy of the Third Reich. True, England had done its share of conquering the dark peoples, but it didn't enslave them and it didn't annihilate them.

Now that England was fighting for her life, and Canada too, I knew I had to act. Oddly enough, I knew what I would do. In some subterranean compartment of my brain I had worked it out. Without a word to anyone, not telling even Connie, I applied to a nursing program given in Montreal at the Daughters of Charity Hospital and sponsored by the Royal Canadian Army. The letter of acceptance lay in my pocket all week, while I got up courage to tell my family. After graduation I would be an army nurse and go overseas to join the war effort.

So this other self of mine, this dark, generally silent Oh-Be-Joyful's Daughter, stood up at Christmas dinner 1941, under another brave little tree with its dyed loops of macaroni, Papa Mike's homemade wooden ornaments, and the store-bought angel—stood up and told her family of the personal commitment she had made.

"Montreal?" Mama's cheeks flushed, and the light caught in her red hair. "You're going to Montreal, Kathy?"

"Yes, Mama."

Like a torpedo slipping along underwater, my announcement did not immediately explode. It was into silence I continued, "There's a serious shortage of nurses, and I've been accepted into a two-year course at the Daughters of Charity of St. Vincent de Paul Hospital. It's under the auspices of the army, and when you graduate you automatically receive a commission." I picked my words carefully. I didn't say I'd see action. But I would.

Connie was the first to recover herself. "It sounds like a marvelous opportunity."

"But Montreal," Mama protested. "It's a French city. To all intents and purposes, French."

For Mama this implied gambling, drug trafficking, and worse.

"The Daughters of Charity, Mama—it's a very fine institution. Ordinarily I couldn't afford the course they offer, but it's subsidized by the army."

"You'd come out of it a nurse and an officer?" I shot Connie a look of gratitude as she plunged on. "Just think of it, Mama, we'd have to salute her."

"I *am* thinking of it," Mama Kathy said, "and I know Papa would not have approved. It's sin city, Kathy. That's what he always said, full of vice, and as a Mountie he was in a position to know."

I didn't say anything. Although I could have said that he was the one who told me I would make a good nurse in the first place.

Connie intervened in her older sister way, as though she somehow sat above the fray, "This is the first time since the world was made that women are being called, asked to help, to be part of things."

"You're right about that," Mama agreed, and then made what I considered a concession. "It would mean pulling up stakes. And," she added with asperity, "it would mean Montreal."

"They say those things about any city, Mama."

"Not about Boston they don't."

Boston was where Mama was born.

"A nurse," Connie mused. "How long have you been thinking about it?"

"Since the beginning of the war, really."

"A nurse," Mama echoed, by which I knew she was thinking about it too. Then, "There must be a lot of wounded to patch together."

I jumped up from my place to hug her.

THESE WERE THE skeins responsible for my being on this silver and blue train, speeding toward what would be my life. Each taut thread played its part, but I wondered if it wasn't Oh-Be-Joyful's Daughter who gave me the courage to actually be on it. It was six years from Papa's death, and the whole world had to dissolve in chaos, blow itself apart. Clark and Iba Airfields in the Philippines had to be taken out, British air power in Hongkong destroyed, Bangkok occupied, Malaya invaded, Burma seized, Canadian boys in Hongkong made to surrender to the Japanese, and of course Pearl Harbor—for me to be sitting primly in a coach of the Canadian Pacific, looking out the window while the silver train streaked by farms, forests, lakes, and towns, the speed flattening the earth and carrying me into my dream.

I was convinced Papa knew about the dream. At the moment

of death you must see things, know things that otherwise you don't.

Classes started in less than a week. The future was open as it never had been. Connie was right, it had become a different world, where girls were encouraged to go into the workplace, share in opportunities. A career as a nurse allowed me to be on my own, take charge of my life. It was time.

I straightened in my seat, while the Canadian countryside framed itself in my window, and investigated the box lunch Mama Kathy had packed. She must have used her own ration coupons because there was a chicken sandwich. I munched with a sense of well-being.

That night I went to sleep in a reclined Pullman chair with a white doily under my head and my shoes kicked off. The porter came by with a pillow and a thin gray blanket. The engines pulsed through me; I fell asleep and woke to the sound of the rails. Sleepily I put up the window blind and was shocked to see a pressing blackness.

We had entered a tunnel. Across from me two women exchanged stories about the tunnels they hated all over the world, the worst being the New York subway under the East River. The one we were in was under Mont-Royal, a long way from fresh air and blue sky. I also did not care for tunnels.

We emerged, and there it was, stretching in every direction . . . Montreal. I looked out on broad streets, which, in spite of gas rationing, were crowded with automobiles and stolid horses pulling ice wagons, milk carts, and bread trucks. Mainly it was alive with people. I had never seen so many people. A sense of energy seemed to fill them, and they moved to a quick rhythm.

A porter came through the cars singing out, "Montreal, Montreal! Ladies and gentlemen, *mesdames et messieurs*." I was thrilled by the French even though it was all I could do to count to twenty and puzzle my way through irregular verbs.

We circled the city, approaching the station through Ouest Montreal.

The train slowed. With a last look to make sure I hadn't left anything, I squeezed into the crowded aisle and moved forward. We pulled in to Windsor Station. I stepped down portable iron stairs and caught my breath.

In school I'd pored over illustrations of the Taj Mahal and St. Peter's in Rome, but this was the most magnificent building I'd ever seen with my own eyes. A palace for trains. Elegant covered sheds for embarking and disembarking. Lofty ceilings. Commodious waiting rooms, spacious restaurants, busy offices. The concourse was like a Roman temple, with fluted columns and ornamented capitals.

And people, people everywhere, rushing, strolling, pushing, waiting in line, talking, yelling in a dozen languages. Soldiers, sailors, officers of every rank and service. Young women being kissed and kissing, both hello and goodbye. Nuns and priests robed in brown, white, gray, some wearing scarlet sashes. Children racing around, playing improvised games in all this turmoil, one lost and shrieking for his parents, another methodically banging her brother's head on the marble floor.

Some of the women were clearly not passengers. With carmine lips and matching fingernails they approached unattached males. Sin city.

I was looking for the exit, when the crowd carried me to a cigarette stand, an edifice with its own fake Roman columns and cornices. It purveyed nuts, dried fruit, gum, candy, cigarettes, cigars, pipe tobacco, knickknacks, gifts, magazines, newspapers, travelers' kits. While I stood there taking it all in, I heard someone ask for a pack of Juicy Fruit, please. I was transfixed. His voice reverberated like bass organ pipes. It was unmistakeable. I looked around. Paul Robeson, Old Man River himself.

The next second the human current carried me away, and I

saw for the first time a sailor with his sleeve sewn together above the elbow.

The city of Montreal was pushed against foothills that rose to an imposing summit. Mont-Royal, its steep slopes indicating volcanic origin, softened into richly planted terraces. At its pinnacle, rising from rock and mountain, was an enormous cross. It protected the city and in some manner, I felt, protected me.

I made my way outside, clutching my directions, and stood waiting for the tram. When it came I was told it was the wrong one. My instructions were correct, but I was pointed in the wrong direction. The conductor advised me which way to go. Unfortunately, merely crossing the street wouldn't do it. I was to go around the block and take a left at Dominion Square, which I could recognize by the Sun Life building.

A bit bewildered, I left the fortress of Windsor Station and passed the Alberta Lounge, which advertised the Johnny Holmes Band featuring Oscar Peterson, the Brown Bomber of Boogie-Woogie. Again I asked my way and finally succeeded in finding my tram not far from the Archbishop's Palace behind St. James's Basilica.

The tram came along on rail tracks with an overhead wire charging it up. I liked its reassuring noisiness, and boarded, making my way by the backs of cane seats. Straps hung suspended from the ceiling and gaudy posters warned: *Loose Lips Sink Ships*. Demonstrating this was an enormous hand with a swastika armband pulling under a ship of the line. I sat beneath "Rosie the Riveter" and laughed silently. The last few days Mama Kathy and Connie had been talking about the premium wages being offered to women by shipyards and aircraft factories in Vancouver. It wouldn't surprise me if after all they did pull up stakes.

Opposite me was an ad for Wrigley's spearmint gum, and scribbled across it in black crayon—not the KILROY WAS HERE that showed up wherever servicemen congregated, but Francophoned into KILROY ICI.

This was Mama's French city, the city founded by Paul de Chomedy de Maisonnueve. This was sin city, beautiful, overwhelming, and subtly foreign.

I glanced again at my instructions. At the third stoplight I got off and found myself facing a stark, sprawling complex stretching several city blocks. I walked along the gray stone walls trying to imagine living behind them. Were they ever breached by sun? I passed an entrance marked Emergency, and a flight of stairs with a ramp beside it for wheelchairs. This seemed a good bet. I started up, my shoes clattering on the steps and my heart racing.

Inside I hesitated. There were statues of saints in niches, and at the rear a long counter under a wooden crucifix. A Sister was stationed there busily thumbing through sheets of documents. I waited for her to notice me.

"Student nurse, are you?"

"Yes, Sister."

"You're in the wrong annex." She directed me to a smaller building partway down the street and a door marked Staff.

With fears and hopes in abeyance, I proceeded toward it. For better or worse here I was and here I would have to stay. "For the duration" had become a slogan. It was mine too: *For the duration.*

I followed a red arrow, painted on the floor, which led to basement stairs. There I paused to glance around a large bare room. Plank tables and benches were pulled out of the way against the wall, making room for half a dozen desks manned—I should say "womanned"—by middle-aged, overworked secretaries and a couple of supervising nuns. The desks were labeled A to F by little cardboard signs.

The Sister in charge was a jolly soul who welcomed me as

she looked up from a ledger. "Yes, here you are. Forquet, Kathy. You've been assigned room 212. You'll be rooming with Amanda Brydewell. The young lady checked in this morning. A double is rare. We've had to put as many as four girls in together. Your room is small, but you won't be spending much time in it. If you'll look at your schedule of classes—" Here she broke off, waiting for me to look.

But I had none.

"Didn't you pick one up at table B?"

I shook my head.

"My dear girl, if you would simply follow the arrows—well, don't stand there, get one now."

I ran over to table B. But there was a queue, held up by one well-dressed young woman who was holding the schedule as if it was a menu and she was trying to decide which entree to order. I could feel Sister's eyes boring into my back. Crouching a bit, I filched a stapled batch of mimeographed pages with a pink cover sheet.

While the Sister busied herself with my application, I checked the course list. Chemistry, Psychology, Anatomy, Biology, Pharmacology, Medical Ethics, Principles of Hygiene. Additional subjects had been added: Map Reading, Gas Warfare, Casualty Evacuation, Principles of Triage, and History of the Canadian Army. The blank spaces which at first I thought indicated free time, I saw, reading more carefully, were allocated to visiting the wards and making rounds.

I was amazed that from the outset we would have daily contact with patients. This was exciting, the best part. Perhaps Papa was right, perhaps I did have an aptitude for nursing. I hoped so. Athough we were two years into it, for me the war had just begun.

Sister Eglantine—I'd deciphered it from the scrawl on her name tag—gave me a key and pointed out the elevator. I could count on the fingers of one hand the times I'd been in one—and then there was someone with white gloves sitting on a stool running it. I pressed the up button; grilled doors opened and I stepped inside. What an amazing world this was. Trolley cars and elevators, telephones in so many public places. And if I was to believe the pictures in magazines, electric refrigerators were replacing iceboxes. What next, I wondered? Of course, hand in hand with these amazing inventions were depth charges and land mines, torpedos and dive bombers, more deadly than anything in the last war.

Standing in front of room 212 I tried to insert the key, when the door swung open. Amanda Brydewell peered nearsightedly at me. "Kathy?"

"Amanda?"

She laughed. "It's Mandy."

It was a relief to like her. I liked her pretty face, I even liked her horn-rimmed glasses. They took the curse off her being so pretty. And here I'd been torturing myself with what-ifs—

But I could see she was a genuine person and really nice, even though she'd taken the bed by the window.

"Are you a First Nation person?" she wanted to know.

I laughed at her directness. "Yes," I said, "I'm Cree."

"How exciting. I've never known an aboriginal."

"We don't paint our faces anymore," I pointed out. "We're just like anybody else."

She, it turned out, was the daughter of a prominent Toronto family. "If it weren't for the war I wouldn't be here. My family would never permit it. But I made it a point—'service to my country, doing my bit,' that kind of thing. And it won the day." Her voice dropped to a confidential note. "I suppose I shouldn't say it, I know it's terrible of me, but I love the war." Seeing my expression, she added hastily, "By that I mean of course, I love what it's done for me. Being on my own is going to be so great."

"Have you seen the schedule? It looks to me that we'll have our nose to the grindstone most of the time."

"On the other hand, there are all those young interns."

Yes, I definitely liked the irrepressible Mandy.

Sister was right about it being a small room. The furnishings were minimal: army cots, two straight-backed chairs, one desk with student lamp, and a battered dresser of four drawers. At first we divided them, but she had so many more things that I wound up giving her three drawers and most of the closet.

"The bathroom's down the hall," she said. "We share it with the entire floor. Isn't that the pits!"

Things here were regulated by bells. When the dinner bell sounded, I discovered the dining hall was the room in the basement where I'd registered. The plank tables and benches had been dragged into the center of the room. A Sister presided at each table. We drew Sister Mary Margaret, who ran what she termed a "taut ship." Voices, she informed us, were to be modulated and good manners observed. Since we were seated at the far end of the table, Mandy didn't adhere to these rules too strictly.

Before the meal was over she knew everyone. Totally at ease, she talked to the girl beside her and the one across from her and, reaching over to a girl several places removed, engaged her in conversation too. I watched with a certain wonder. Of course Mandy was a white girl among white girls. I, on the other hand, knew it was only the war that made my being here acceptable. Even so, how did the others regard me? I felt I had a friend in Mandy, but did I imagine it, or were there hostile stares and whispering behind my back?

I took my cue from Mandy and laughed along with her when she made jokes about the food. Fortunately there was a lot of it, which in some measure made up for the fact that it was very plain fare: wholesome porridge, good-for-you vegetables, and a filling potato. There was a gravy that I thought best to avoid, and bread, butter, and jam for dessert. On weekends, Trisha, who had been here longest, reported, this was varied with puddings—tapioca, caramel, and butterscotch. She was waiting for a chocolate day, but so far it hadn't come.

I was grateful to Mandy for sticking with me. We sat in the student lounge, chatting and laughing. Shedding my what-ifs, I joined in, enjoying the adventure with them.

What a nice group they were. Mandy's contribution was to say we were all in the same boat. "Not a U-boat!" they protested, laughing. Almost 400,000 tons of Lend-Lease shipments had been lost. The best thing was to joke and make light of it.

It seemed I shared in Mandy's instant popularity. What good fortune to have drawn her as a roommate. I tried to sort out my impressions of the other girls. Ruth, good-natured, with a mouth full of braces. Ellie, a bit on the plain side but with pretty auburn hair. Trisha, somewhat reserved. All starting out like me to help in this global emergency, to test our wings as persons, to take flight. This was a good place, I thought, to start doing something I hadn't succeeded in yet—being Oh-Be-Joyful's Daughter. The banter and small talk continued until the second bell.

AT NIGHT, CONSCIOUS of a Sister patrolling the corridors, we whispered from one bed to the other. Mandy was an only child and had had a nanny. Imagine! A child to have her own servant. And of course as a teenager she hadn't worked. No drugstore for her; she sat on the other side of the counter. She and I would never have met if not for the war. Her father was a corporate lawyer, and they lived in a two-story house and did not, I'm sure, associate with Indians.

She was right about one thing: the war forced you to think in bigger terms; it brushed away prejudices and there was a feeling of equality as all were needed to pull together. We talked so late that it seemed I barely closed my eyes when the morning bell got us up. In robe and slippers I went down the hall to the bathroom. I was stopped by a piece of notepaper tacked to the door. WHITES ONLY.

Shock imploded in me as though I'd taken a depth charge. I ripped the paper from the door, balled it, and, entering the bathroom, threw it into the wastebasket.

"What was that?" Trisha asked, with a mocking grin.

I turned on her. "The Cree," I said, speaking slowly, articulating carefully, "do not speak ill of anyone. They may take their scalp in the night, but they do not speak ill of them."

The other girls watched from a distance, in an uneasy clump.

I continued in the same tight voice, "I will just say this one thing. I intend to stay here and become a nurse."

Mention of our common goal broke the spell. To my amazement the girls crowded around me, stumbling over words in their anxiety to get them out, assuring me all together that they were behind me a hundred percent. Trisha, I noticed, slipped out to remove a similar sign pasted on the drinking fountain. I saw her crumple it in her hands. I went back to my room, my heart still pounding, still turning the incident over in my mind.

I didn't tell Mandy, but by lunch she knew all about it. "I'm so proud of you, Kathy, for standing up to them. And most of them don't feel that way, you know."

"I don't really care how they feel, as long as they don't interfere with my plans." I heard myself say this and thought, Wow! a new Kathy. I felt a flush of excitement. Was this new Kathy possibly an aspect of Oh-Be-Joyful's Daughter, which had eluded me such a long time?

"Tell me about First Nation people," Mandy was saying. "I really want to know, to understand."

I couldn't. I didn't know that much about them. I disappointed her by having a white mama and papa and a white brother and sister. "The twins have lighter hair than you do."

Mandy's questions set me thinking. It was too bad to know nothing of the traditions of my own people. If I was to be persecuted as an Indian, I should at least understand why.

Three

OUR FIRST CLASS was a lecture, and we trooped into a large auditorium. There was a brief swearing-in ceremony, at the end of which we were told we were now privates, subject to the rules and regulations of the Royal Canadian Army. Our grades would be monitored, and we would have to maintain a passing average. But on graduation we would be commisioned as second lieutenants. I was conscious of a new feeling, pride and a sense of responsibility.

The assembly was turned over to Mother Superior, who welcomed us, first in French, then in English. The audience settled into respectful silence.

I hadn't realized she was a small woman. Strength and energy seemed to overflow and escape her body.

She paused to look us over with piercing black eyes. When she had made her assessment, she launched into the body of her speech. "The history of nursing in Canada is in a very real sense the history of women in Canada. Marie Rollet Hebert was the first woman to provide nursing care. In 1642 another woman, Jeanne Mance, established the first hospital here in Ville-Marie.

"Our order, the Daughters of Charity of St. Vincent de Paul, eventually added an orphanage and dispensed free health care, funded in part by philanthropy, but mainly through a brewery and a freight company that the Sisters organized and ran themselves." She paused, daring us to laugh. No one did.

"The next hundred years saw nurses trained to serve as administrators, doctors, surgeons, and apothecaries. Canadian nurses first came under fire in the Riel Rebellion."

I pricked up my ears at the mention of Louis Riel. I knew from Papa that my mostly French grandfather, Raoul Forquet, was his lieutenant. But I judged it would be as well not to mention that here. The past was very much part of the present in these cloistered walls. It would be prudent not to trumpet the fact that I was the granddaughter of a revolutionary.

"By the last war," Mother Superior continued, "more than three thousand nursing Sisters served as officers. They were stationed in England, France, and Belgium, and around the Mediterranean. Forty-seven died under combat conditions."

She paused while this sank in.

"Because you young women are to be serving in a wartime situation, the entire program has been accelerated. Instead of the normal three years, it has of necessity been compressed into two. And if you inspect your handouts, you will note that instruction in military matters has been added to the established nursing classes. It will require diligence and hard work on your part, but it is our hope that you will follow the tradition of your chosen profession with the honor and dedication that is the standard for the Daughters of Charity. I ask you to remember that the eyes of your country are on you and on this institution."

Although I laughed and joked about it afterward with the others, the sense of awe remained. I explored a bit on my own, trying to memorize the layout of the hospital. Plaques on the wall each carried the name of a donor, and one, I noticed, honored a Brydewell. Was that my roommate's father or grandfather?

The second lecture of the day took place after lunch and was given in the same hall. I tried, as I had last night at supper, to count heads. My best guess was there were around sixty aspiring nurses. We filed in and took our seats with a buzz of anticipation. The lecturer was not only a medical man, but a distinguished professor at McGill University. He strode onto the podium, a white-haired gentleman obviously brought out of retirement. "One of your young interns," I whispered to Mandy.

He greeted us pleasantly and stated that he was going to commence with a test, "which is by way of determining both your courage and your observation. Now then," he continued smoothly, "I have before me a beaker of urine. Observe it closely."

No one ever in my memory had used the word *urine* in public. It was indicative of coming to grips with the functioning of the human body. Which of course as a nurse I would have to do.

"Now," the professor's voice filled the auditorium, "please watch carefully because I am going to ask each of you to come to the podium in turn. At which time you will do exactly what I am about to do. Observe." With that he dipped his finger into the vial of urine, then brought the finger to his mouth and sucked it.

A murmur of horror went through the room. Ignoring it, he invited us in the most cordial terms to come up by rows and repeat the experiment. Like stricken sheep we mounted to the podium and one by one dutifully filed past the urine in its clear glass receptacle and imitated his actions.

Each in turn, wincing a bit, stuck her finger in the urine and with a final shudder licked it. When my turn came I immersed my finger and, repressing a gag reflex, proceeded to lick the substance off.

When we returned to our places the professor rocked back on his heels and, brushing aside his white coat, hooked his thumbs in his waistcoat pockets. "Well, young ladies, you deserve an A for courage, but an F for observation. I stuck a finger into the urine right enough. But it was the finger next to it I put in my mouth."

A gasp followed this announcement. Mandy and I looked at each other and burst out laughing.

There was more hazing from second-year students, whose chores we ended up doing, including bedpan duty. But I was not again singled out. The story of the Whites Only incident had spread through the hospital, and it won me, if not friends, at least respect.

THE HOSPITAL WAS a massive network of services. There were the pre-op and post-op patients, on which everything from appendectomies to bowel resections were done. There was a trauma center and a burn center. Of course, as first-year students we weren't allowed near the serious cases unsupervised.

My first job was to clean the needles and syringes that had been used during the day. Our limited supply of autoclaves was strained past capacity by the influx of new cases. We had to fall back on the old-fashioned procedure of washing instruments in ether, then plunging them into boiling water. But, as I discovered the next morning, making rounds under the careful eye of a doctor, the ends could become plugged. When I jabbed the needle into a patient's arm sometimes nothing came out. This was unpleasant for the patient and for me. I guessed that the problem was the hard water I'd washed them in. So I did what Mama Kathy would have done—after dinner I went outside and collected snow. Melting it took a long time with very little water to show for it. And I didn't get to bed until after the bell.

However, I had soft water in which to sterilize my needles, and next day when the resident had me start an IV, my needle glided in smoothly without sticking. Afterward, the girls wanted to know my secret. When I told them I had gone out and collected snow, they said I was crazy.

I had collected snow before. When I was little I made ice cream by taking Mama Kathy's vanilla and shaking it into newly fallen snow. Thinking this, I realized a week had gone by with no word from anybody. Just as I began to worry, a whole packet of mail arrived, two letters from Vancouver and one without stamps, meaning armed forces. I was most surprised hearing from Georges. Georges dear—I remembered him in his magician's cape (which was Mama's apron worn inside out but with a Georges flair), waving one of Papa's good dress handkerchiefs and, over his protests, making it disappear. Georges, Georges, can't you make the war go away? Georges dear, where are you? North Ireland with the 80th? Libya? Egypt?

Mama Kathy and Connie were embarked on their own adventure. Mama had consented to pull up stakes after all. They were in Vancouver machining spare parts for planes at thirty-six dollars a week. With wages like that they could put by for the rainy day Mama was always expecting.

But there was sad news as well, the kind that was in almost every letter these days. The Clacks' youngest son had volunteered and was missing in action. I paused a moment to remember his pleasant, freckled face and readiness to laugh.

Then turned to the lively descriptions of life in Vancouver. They had found a comfortable apartment, but with no growing thing about. Mama had lugged in a flower box, in which they planned to raise a tomato vine. Down the street in the schoolyard a section had been set aside for a communal victory garden where they donated what free time they could.

I felt the love behind the ordinary sentences and drank in every word. Both Georges and Connie asked if I'd heard from the other. I knew how hard it was for them to be apart.

My own free time was Sundays and a half day on Saturday. Mandy and I went to the library at the first opportunity to find out about Indians. We carried several volumes to the table; Mandy sat on one side, I on the other. My tome started back in 1763 when the Crown laid claim to all unoccupied land.

I leaned across to Mandy and read the paragraph in an undertone, adding, "The Indians, being nomadic, didn't occupy any land at all."

"So the Crown took it all. Pretty neat if you can get away with it."

"Oh, they were fair—according to their lights. Indians were allowed the *use* of selected lands. 'Selected lands' is code for reserves. And here's something they don't teach you in mission school: even today the Indians don't hold legal title to their reserves."

"I tell you what," Mandy said. "When we've finished off the Germans, we'll go to Ottawa and march on the Canadian government, make them give it back."

"Here it tells about the welfare system instituted for the aboriginals. Instead of justice—handouts."

"That fits with what I'm reading. Two and a half times more poverty among Indians, three times the prenatal death rate."

"But they're starting to fight back. Listen to this. It was proposed in one of the tribal councils that they stop thinking of the money as charity and call it rent, rent owed them on the land."

We'd done enough digging for one day and absorbed all we could of Indian rights. Mandy was hungry, and when she mentioned it, so was I. We splurged on sandwiches and a soda.

"In school," Mandy said thoughtfully, "I remember reading how the tribes escaped extermination in the States by fleeing to Canada, where they were discriminated against but not slaughtered in those terrible Indian wars."

"You don't have to fight a war," I responded, "if you can get it all with a forked-tongue paper."

We didn't go back to the library. Mandy had other things to do, and I didn't like the feelings of anger and resentment that had been stirred up in me. That was no way to be joyful.

The next fortnight I was assigned to blood draws, which entailed going up and down the rows of beds taking blood, smearing the plasma onto glass slides, and labeling and keeping them straight. The second-year nurses complained at this acceleration of our training. We had been promoted from bedpan duty much too fast, in their opinion.

The number of patients on crutches distressed me. They were so young, these boy-men without feet or legs, the lucky ones in casts. I watched my chance and slipped into the stock room to try crutches myself. I spent half an hour swinging about on them. At the end of that time I was exhausted and my armpits were sore. As a result I sewed additional padding onto those waiting to be used, and sprinkled them liberally with baby powder.

Mandy kept a diary in her underwear drawer. It had a vellum cover and tiny gold chain and key. I wondered what she said about me. I think she was disappointed that I wasn't more fun, that I had my nose in a book all the time.

At night, instead of chatting, I sat late, memorizing bone and muscle structure for hands and feet, and I was working on the neck. There were no plots or stories in these books, but after a while I managed to weave the charts and graphs into tales of saving lives.

Besides Saturday half days we students had all of Sunday to allow for church attendance. This, I often thought as I turned the pages of my hymnal, is the sin city Mama Kathy worried about.

Mandy was asked out a lot. Several times we double-dated.

But I had the feeling that it took a good deal of manuevering on Mandy's part. I was invariably self-conscious and uncomfortable and finally persuaded Mandy that I preferred a good book, or listening to Frank Sinatra and the Andrews Sisters, or studying French by puzzling my way through *Le Devoir*. Also I was familiarizing myself with the big bands, Tommy Dorsey and Benny Goodman. They set your feet tapping—that is, until they broke off the music for news flashes.

General MacArthur withdrew to Bataan. They used the word *withdrew* but it didn't fool anyone. It was a retreat, a rout, and the rich oil fields of the Dutch East Indies fell to the Japanese. They took Singapore and the struggle was now for Java. In the Java Sea on February 27 we lost five warships in a seven-hour battle. The Japanese sustained slight damage to one destroyer. By March 9 the last Allied troops in Java surrendered.

I gave up reading the papers. It didn't do to think of all those young men dying horribly out there on unknown beaches or winding up in ward B without faces, without limbs. They put their lives on the line and it wasn't enough. We were losing, losing badly—over six million tons of shipping in the Atlantic and endless square miles of territory in the South Pacific.

A new load of wounded were brought in from ships sunk in the North Atlantic, some off our coast. The protective attitude the Sisters had endeavored to maintain for us new girls was a thing of the past. We were, you might say, posted to frontline trenches and found ourselves in the thick of things.

The first time I was called on to hold down the head and shoulders of a patient in the throes of a gastric bleed, whose body contorted and whose blood splattered my uniform and my shoes, I almost passed out myself. Instantly I was in the little back bedroom, and it was Papa. Somehow I managed to stay on my feet and, afterward, in the bathroom, splash water over my

face. I dabbed at my uniform and shoes, making a solemn resolution as I did. A resolution I broke the very next day.

I was present at an amputation. It was all right when the
form was swathed by a sheet, but then a mangled leg was steril-
ized and a surgical saw—which was nevertheless a saw—bit
into flesh and began to cut. I swayed on my feet . . . that wasn't
a human being under the drapes . . . this wasn't happening to a
human being. The room swirled. I passed the bandage roll I was
holding to the person next to me and raced for the bathroom.

I slammed the door shut and leaned against it. The gastric
bleed, now this. At the first sight of ligaments and tendons, I'd
given way. I hadn't the stuff to make a nurse. I couldn't look at
dismemberment in a cold, professional way. I'd blown it.

"Don't feel too bad, Kathy."

I hadn't noticed Sister Eglantine washing her hands in the
corner.

"Compassion is very important in a nurse. The very best
nurses have it in good measure. If you can look for the first time
on an amputation unmoved, you're not much of a human
being. And you have to be a human being first."

I took my hands from my face. Sister Egg, the girls called her,
because she was a good egg. Short, dumpy—everything about
her could be drawn with circles, even to her rimless spectacles.

"It comes in time," Egg continued, "standing up to it, seeing
it for what it is, a lifesaving procedure."

"You think, in time—?"

"My dear, if I were a betting woman, I'd go right down to the
East Side and I wouldn't stop till I got to the funeral parlor on
St. George. But I wouldn't go in there. I'd go next door to the
basement and take a seat at barbotte and roll my dice, and I'd
wager everything on you—your guts, your gumption, and the
fact that you'll make a fine nurse someday." She folded her

hands over her stomach and grinned broadly. "How's that for confidence?"

Sister Egg swept away self-doubts. She had seen girls come and go. She knew. She knew the ones who would make it. "Besides," she said, "it's really the fault of the accelerated program. Ordinarily, a first-year student would not be exposed to such a drastic procedure. But there's no help for it. It's the war."

This seemed reasonable to me. With renewed confidence I went back to the surgical area and stood up to the lecture on professional conduct I received from the surgeon, Dr. Bennett.

To prove to Sister Egg she had not been wrong about me, I took to reading to my amputee patient. It turned out he was British. He told me he didn't want to go home. He couldn't face the pity and especially the way they would try to hide it. "They'd be so damned understanding," he said.

I discovered he was fond of poetry—"To hold infinity in the palm of your hand, eternity in an hour." That evening he had a hemorrhagic discharge under the skin. Dark purplish areas became less as I applied compresses, but I still shuddered at the twenty-three stitches with which the leg came to an end. ". . . Eternity in an hour," I repeated to myself.

Mandy was busy weekends, so I took to going to the movies with Sister Egg. We went to the old Roxy Theater, the Palace, and Loew's. Like me, Egg could never get enough. We sat through double features, short subjects, Fox Movietone, and Pathe newsreels.

The newsreels were hard to watch. Wounded stacked like cordwood waited to be moved to aid centers. Suffering looked artificial on young faces. They were my own age and younger.

Another clip showed the result of the blitz in one London back street, a dazed grandmother emerging from an air raid shelter. She walked a block to her home. It wasn't there. Nothing was there. Then she spotted something, a pan, a little bent but still serviceable. She began to sift through the rubble, saving a torn quilt, a cracked mirror from her life. I chose this time to get popcorn. Egg didn't comment on these absences, but nothing got by her.

We only had a single movie theater in my out-of-the-way home in Alberta, and I didn't go on a regular basis as I did here. Weekly I blew my nose through hopeless romances and parted lovers.

Egg leaned toward me in the dark. "Go ahead, you're entitled to a good cry. After all, we don't permit you girls to show emotion no matter what lies under the bandages you unwrap. This is one way of crying for the boys on the ward."

Bull's-eye! I hadn't known it myself. How had Egg? She had lived three times longer than I, and behind her childlike face was a world of knowledge.

Then I caught her before the lights came up, dabbing at her eyes. "We're two of a kind," she admitted. "But don't blackmail me with the girls."

We enjoyed a good cry, but we laughed too, at the Schnozz and the antics of Jerry Colonna. I stored up prat falls and slapstick situations for the moments I dressed a septic arm or wrote lies for the British boy who had lost a leg. Although there were others in the same condition, I suppose I empathized particularly with him because he was so far from home. And then of course I'd been there when it happened.

Our long winter was almost gone, and one Sunday in early March Mandy suggested ice skating at Berry Pond. I was glad to fall in with the idea, especially as the first thaw would bring an end to a sport I loved. This was a typical Montreal day—cold. I double-dressed, hoping to keep warm that way. Mandy put on two sweaters under her skating outfit but, twisting and turning before the mirror, decided the extra padding made her look fat.

But Mandy was more complicated than anyone gave her credit for. Before we left the room I was wearing her best and warmest sweater.

It was good to be outside, good to leave the hospital behind. We ran down the stairs, our skates over our shoulders, and walked briskly, swinging a free arm, making footprints in the crusty snow that was starting to soften under the sun. We blew our breath before us in frosty puffs.

There were already quite a few skaters on the pond. "It looks like a postcard come to life," Mandy enthused.

We dusted off one of the logs that had been pulled up as improvised bleachers, and sat down. Then began the job of fastening on the skates. Mandy was finished first. Her skates belonged to her, while mine were borrowed. As she waited for me, Mandy studied the skaters. "Look," she exclaimed, "there's that cute intern that transferred in last week. Robert. Robert Whitaker II."

"How do you know? Have you met him?"

"I looked at his application—a picture is enclosed, you know. I'm not so nearsighted that I can't spot a good thing. You have to admit he's attractive. Six feet tall, from Nainaimo on Vancouver Island, son of Dr. and Mrs. Robert Whitaker. He's twenty-six years old—"

"And he's had mumps and measles and his tonsils out," I snapped. Now I understood the reason for this excursion. "How'd you know he'd be here?"

"You're not angry, are you? I overheard Dr. Finch giving him directions."

I finished tying my laces and stood with a bit of a wobble. I'd been on ice since I was three, but this was the first time this year. I followed Mandy and cut myself a nice line to the middle of the pond, tried a turn, then several. It was exhilarating—only, my teeth were cold. Other people get cold ears and noses. With me it's teeth, and as far as I know they don't have tooth-muffs.

I realized I was here simply as window dressing, and I watched Mandy's manuever with interest. Her plan was simple. She skated backward and plowed into him. They both wound up sitting on the ice. She begged his pardon and introduced herself. Robert Whitaker II or III or whatever hadn't a chance.

Skating straight for me, they came to a T-stop, and I was introduced.

I liked him. And I certainly saw why Mandy did. He was nice looking and had a great build.

"Imagine," she said, "Robert's joined the hospital staff!"

"Really?" I tried to sound as though I were processing new information.

They glided away to "The Skater's Waltz." Mandy looked marvelous. Her cheeks were pink with the cold, and her smile dazzling. I fought down a twinge of jealousy. Sometimes it's hard being the roommate of the prettiest girl in the program.

I lowered my head into the wind and, with my hands clasped behind my back, took a racing stance and zoomed twice around the pond to their once. It was invigorating to be on ice, with your toes and your teeth freezing.

They came alongside. "Robert's invited us for hot chocolate."

Steamy hot, it opened a path of warmth inside. Robert told us he came from a large family, two brothers and a sister. "My dad's just a small-town doctor. What there is has to stretch. So I mostly worked my way through school, did KP at the frat house, drove an ambulance, got by on a scholarship. You know, scrounged. Managed one way or another."

He got by with Mandy too. She had met her intern, and from then on they were very thick. She kept saying it wasn't serious, but it looked to me that it was. She spent every available minute with him.

The nursing staff was constantly being rotated and I was transferred to what I was told was a responsible job, but one I didn't like as much as it had nothing to do with nursing. While I preferred being on the wards and felt I did more good there, I realized of course that someone had to receive medicines and store and dispense drugs. I discovered the job was largely a matter of keeping records. We were short on supplies and once, when we ran low on disinfectants, were told to add salt to water and use it. Before my time there'd been some kind of scandal regarding drugs and they were very security conscious, doing everything by the book.

Shortly after I'd logged on, the driver of a lorry came in with boxes and crates which he began piling in front of my desk.

"You have to sign for it, miss."

The voice had an odd lilt, almost an accent. I looked up into eyes that could have been my own, except they were crinkled in laughter, and were in fact joyous.

I smiled back into a face as dark as my own. The driver, in spite of army fatigues, was Indian.

He had apparently craned over and spotted my signature on the papers before me, because he said, "Right here, Kathy."

I tried to remain businesslike. "Yes," I said, taking up a pen.

"What's your Indian name?" he asked.

"Oh-Be-Joyful's Daughter." It came out spontaneously, as though that's who I'd been all along.

He nodded. "That's a beautiful name. What band are you?"

"Cree."

"Cree? You're a long way from home. I suppose it's the war?"

"Yes," I said, "it's the war," and returned his receipt.

He shoved it into his pocket but didn't go. "Are you always here at this hour?"

"For a couple of weeks."

"Then I'll see you again." This time he got as far as the door and came back. "I forgot to tell you my name. It's Crazy Dancer."

"Crazy Dancer? Is that really a name?"

"I'm a delight maker, you know, a clown."

I must have looked puzzled.

"I see you went to mission school and had a white man's education. You don't know about our people, do you?"

"Well," I hesitated, "I did go to mission school, but . . ."

"That explains your not knowing. But don't worry, I'll teach you."

"Teach me? Teach me what?"

"To be an Indian." He gave a quirky smile and left.

I looked out the window and watched him below in the parking lot. He moved to an inner rhythm as though he scouted along rushing streams and wild forest places instead of back alleys. He swung lightly into the driver's seat. I could see he was a dancer, a crazy dancer.

I suppose it was what he said about being Indian, but I couldn't get him out of my mind. My impression was that he possessed a kind of kinetic energy. Was he handsome? I wasn't sure. Would Mandy think his nose too high-bridged? It was an aquiline nose compared to the flatter noses of whites. But in any culture his face was arresting. In those few seconds a dozen moods had sat on it. He said he was a clown; I believed it. His mouth was ready to smile, his eyes to squeeze together in laughter. Yet there was dignity, almost a haughtiness in the way he carried himself.

Had I imagined more than was there? My Indianness was a part of me I had never explored. And Crazy Dancer wanted to teach me Indian things. I found I was looking forward to the next delivery of medicines.

I'd had an unusual relationship with young men—that is, none. Or practically none. Mostly it was fending off patients in the ward. If they weren't too ill or distressed, they were full of banter and a kind of flirting talk. After all, they were young, they were young men. They were fond of telling me all the things we would do when they got out of here. Once they were up and around, it would be dinner out and then we'd take in a movie, and then . . . And we would both laugh at the innuendo, confident it would never happen.

These fantasy romances were accompanied by an attempt at hand-holding, and frequently my patients essayed more. All this phantom attention was bittersweet. Some of the boys were nice looking, and some persuasive. Others were pathetic and I was careful not to draw away. But at night when I closed my eyes many times there were tears on my lashes because I was playing my old game *What if. . . .*

MONTREAL, MAMA KATHY'S sin city, was a wartime city, filled with soldiers and sailors, some on leave, some waiting to be shipped out. Guys were always trying to pick me up. But they'd try that with anything in skirts. Once by a drinking fountain I was tempted. The sailor was cute and had a nice smile. "Here, let me hold your hair back." I walked away.

But I was disturbed by my reaction. When I analyzed my life, I had to admit it was lonely.

Two days later Crazy Dancer piled more boxes in front of my work station. "Hi!" His smile possessed his face.

"Hi," I said.

"Oh-Be-Joyful's Daughter," he continued formally as though he were proposing, "I have borrowed a car for Sunday. Will you go with me to a drive-in movie?"

"Yes," I said, without hesitation.

"One o'clock white man's time. In the parking lot."

"All right."

"Kathy!" The sisters moved about so quietly you never knew they were there. Sister Magdalena had come around the bend of the hall. "We're waiting for these items. Haven't you checked them yet?"

Crazy Dancer, not at all abashed, stared at her curiously.

"Well, young man, haven't you wasted enough time?"

"Perhaps, if you mean clock time. But there are other kinds."

He would have left then but Sister detained him. "What kind of time are you referring to?"

"Personal time."

"What a strange young man," she said when he was gone.

"Oh, I don't know, he's Indian," I said airily.

THE DRIVE-IN MOVIE was in the country, and the gas coupons must have cost a bundle.

"It's probably our last chance. The rumor is that they're going to black out the city," Crazy Dancer said.

I'd heard that too and was glad they'd held off. I'd never been to a drive-in and was curious. There were dozens of spaces. You drove into one, dropped your money into a slot, and were hooked up to the picture. Instantly the sound of a love scene flooded the car.

"Haven't you ever been before?" he asked.

"No. It's strange—the sound right in the car with you. You feel as though you're part of the movie."

"Actually"—he hesitated briefly—"the movie isn't that important."

"It isn't?"

Crazy Dancer draped an arm casually over the back of the upholstered seat, and gradually lowered it to my shoulders.

I moved nearer the door. His other hand dropped to my thigh.

"What are you doing?" I said, pushing him away.

"What everybody in all the cars are doing." He reared back and gave me a penetrating glance. "Don't tell me you don't know what drive-ins are all about?"

I looked wildly around at the other cars. No one was watching the movie.

"Stop right there, Crazy Dancer. Because if you don't, I'm going to walk home."

"All I had in mind," he protested, "was, you know, a little making out. You don't mind a kiss, do you?"

"It depends," I said tentatively.

"One like this maybe. . . ." And he pressed me so close that I felt the door handle in the middle of my back.

I sat straight up. "If it comes to this kind of holding and this kind of kissing . . . it's not going to be in a borrowed car. And don't tell me you're being shipped out and before the week's over you'll be at the bottom of the ocean floor."

Crazy Dancer regarded me with grave eyes, but his mouth was laughing. "How well you make my argument for me."

I asked, suddenly frightened for him, "Is it true?"

He shrugged. "Who knows?"

We sat and looked at each other, while lovers vowed vows in our ears. I felt ridiculous sitting there, while all around us . . .

"I'll take you back," he said, and put the car in gear.

When we arrived at the hospital parking lot, he didn't open the door, but continued to sit there. "If you didn't make out with me . . . ," he said slowly, reasoning it through, "does that mean you don't make out with anyone?"

"I feel like an idiot," I said. "Any other girl would have known when you suggested a drive-in."

He was still unraveling a skein of thought. "Would you call what we had a disagreement or a fight? With a fight you can kiss and make up," and he shot me a glance.

"A disagreement," I said emphatically. He looked so disappointed that I reached over and gave him an emphatic kiss. Then, jumping out, ran for the nurses' entrance.

$\mathscr{F}$our

THAT NIGHT AS I lay on coarse hospital sheets rinsed in disinfectant, I wondered at myself. I had said one thing and then turned around and undid it in a moment. Why had I kissed him? And what would he remember, the lecture I'd given him or the kiss?

I knew, of course, and hugged myself in the dark as I listened to the litany Mandy insisted on most nights. I didn't mind her going on about Robert Whitaker because I'd found out quite by accident that she'd had the chance to room with someone else but elected to stay with me. That obligated me to hear more examples of her young intern's sterling character. As she enumerated his peerless attributes, I thought—Crazy Dancer has none of those. In the first place he hasn't a proper kind of name. Robert Harley Whitaker II, now with that name one could be a banker, a trial lawyer, the head of a corporation, an admiral in the navy, or the first-rate surgeon he would become. Someone named Crazy Dancer couldn't aspire to any of those positions.

"Robert's such a gentleman," Mandy went on.

I laughed inwardly at the thought of Crazy Dancer being a gentleman.

"And he dances divinely. . . ."

Ah, here we were on common ground. Or were we? I visualized Robert Whitaker with Mandy on his arm doing a box-step

fox trot; I could see his black polished patent leather shoes
treading lightly.

What did Crazy Dancer wear when he danced? Probably he
painted his body and wore a corn-husk mask and bells on his
ankles and moccasins scuffing the earth and maybe a breech-
clout. This time I laughed out loud.

"What are you laughing at?"

I could see Mandy was offended so I changed the subject.

ANOTHER NIGHT LATER in the week, with our window wide open
and spring in the air, Mandy whispered from her cot to mine.
Robert had three tickets for Delormier Stadium. They were
hard to come by and expensive. So when she urged me to go
with them I was tempted. I figured out I would have to miss
three Saturday movies to see a game. But I was pretty sure
Crazy Dancer would show up, so I said no. It crossed my mind
once or twice to wonder how Robert was able to afford such
things. Supposedly he was a poor boy from a poor family. But
somehow he seemed always to have money.

Toward the end of the week we had another bed-to-bed talk.
Mandy had gotten to know a lot about Montreal. Robert was
alert for any local color and passed it on to her. There was a section in the French quarter that no respectable girl would ven-
ture into. Certain hotels rented rooms for twenty minutes at a
time all through the night. The town, according to Robert, was
wide open—sports betting, lottery tickets, chemin d'fer, bac-
carat, roulette, blackjack, craps, and barbotte. While even the
war failed to put an end to drug smuggling. But the Daughters
of Charity of St. Vincent de Paul said their novenas, sang their
prayers, and kept sin away. They attempted to do the same with
the wounded and dying—but they kept coming.

I had expected to hear from that crazy Indian, Crazy Dancer.

I hadn't. Mandy too was without a date for Saturday night, as Robert had been preempted by Dr. Finch for an evening at his home. "To meet his ugly daughter." Mandy made a face and mounted a campaign to get me to go with her to the canteen that was set up in a high school gym. "It's not the Victoria Rifles' Ball or the debutantes' coming out or even the St. Andrew's Annual, but for heaven's sake, Kathy, it's all there is, and I don't want to go alone."

I agreed, mainly to get some sleep. Next day I discovered she wouldn't be alone, Ruth was going too. Mandy lent me a flowered scarf to dress up my outfit, and we started off.

Harsh unhooded lights revealed an upright piano, but no visible player. A handful of servicemen hung around a couple of card tables. They held paper plates with potato chips and not much else. A Crosby record was wobbling on the phonograph.

We stood uncertainly in a bunch. Two sailors homed in on Mandy. I didn't blame them. Mandy was the girl next door, or at least what they wishfully remembered the girl next door to be.

Ruth, on the other hand, was self-conscious about her braces and the cheap silver fillings, which she was replacing out of her meager army pay. Her main worry was that Mr. Right would come along before she was finished. Each Saturday morning she spent at the dentist, returning with all sorts of dental horror stories including the one her dentist told on himself. The reason he had chosen that particular profession was because as a kid his wisdom teeth came in at an angle and stuck right through his cheek.

Ruth had joined us with a great deal of perturbation, afraid she would be asked to dance and afraid she wouldn't. She'd be asked, was my guess, because if she neither laughed, smiled, or spoke she was quite attractive.

Tonight, hopefully, she'd find something other than teeth to talk about.

I put my arm through hers. "Let's get some potato chips."

We started for the tables, but another sailor approached and, with a grin and a few mumbled words, invited Ruth to dance. One glance of panic in my direction and she was whirled away. I held to my course—at least I was going to have something to eat. This time it was a soldier, Canadian army, who came up to me. "There's beer in that wash bucket," he said.

I hadn't noticed the galvanized pail sitting under one of the tables. "No, thank you." I wasn't sure whether he was offering it to me or not.

"Want to dance?"

"All right."

It was a pretext he didn't bother to make too convincing. He held me too close and talked incessantly. I was glad the record was almost over.

"My name's Ed."

"Mine's . . . uh . . . Trisha." I don't know why that name came to mind. I guess the Whites Only sign still rankled.

"Look, Trisha, we've got to go someplace, get out of here."

No, I wasn't the girl next door, I was the girl you took to the nearest drive-in.

"I'm . . . meeting someone." I gulped and looked around for Mandy. I could see she was having a good time, and I didn't want to stand there explaining, so, mumbling that I was going to the restroom, I slipped out. The strains of the newest song on the Hit Parade followed me: "Saturday Night Is the Loneliest Night of the Week."

The next day I was in the middle of a nightmare. That same soldier showed up, the one I'd danced with. I couldn't believe it. I heard him at the front desk asking for Trisha.

There was nothing for it but to intercept him. I plastered a stern look on my face and approached.

The look was wasted. "Trisha!" he bellowed. "I'm so damned glad to see you. What happened last night? Had a devil of a time finding you. I asked all over."

"Did it ever occur to you I didn't want to be found?" I made it as frosty as I could, and anyone else would have backed off. But this guy was impervious to nuances, subtleties, and, I suspected, a hammer over the head. Sister Mary Margaret, trying to be helpful, asked if we cared to step into a private room.

"No," I said as he said, "Yes."

At this moment Trisha herself appeared. "I heard someone was asking for me?" This was addressed to me, as she had already taken Ed's measure. His name had come back to me, and I attempted an introduction, but Trisha was sure the soldier was my revenge, and poor Ed was totally confused by two Trishas. I threw up my hands and left.

I heard later through the grapevine that they had straightened things out to their mutual satisfaction, and ended by going out together. Maybe I did have my revenge.

I WAS MOVED to the trauma center. Duty there drained the life out of you. I saw terrible things, great ragged holes opening in layers, receding deep into flesh.

Sister Egg saved me. Egg was a mother hen to us girls. She caught me in the hall. A severe look lay over her normally good-natured expression. In a clipped, businesslike manner she said, "Kathy, no questions. You are to come with me."

Good heavens, what now? I tried to think which rule I had inadvertently broken as she bustled me out of the building.

"No need to be so somber, Kathy." She burst into smiles. "We are embarked on an expedition to save the caterpillars."

"To save the caterpillars?" I echoed, thinking I hadn't heard correctly.

"Yes, in the park, right across from the elementary school. I fill in teaching the fifth grade part time and I learned to my dismay that the science class is coming tomorrow to collect caterpillars. They intend to chloroform them, stick pins through them, mount them—need I say more? I decided to get to the park first and hide them. And I thought . . . well, I chose you as my coconspirator because I know you have a kind heart."

I laughed until tears came into my eyes. This roly-poly little nun and I made quite a team.

"Tell me, Kathy, am I a good judge of character?"

"The best," I assured her. And when Sister Eglantine, with a guilty look around, got down on all fours, I did the same. The hunt was conducted on hands and knees. We investigated grass blades, wildflowers, small branch stems, leafy shrubs. I made the first find, a lively black fuzzy one journeying along a sunflower stalk. Into Sister's basket it went. Sister found the second and third. It was hard to see the green ones, but I saved several, millipedes I think they were, with so many feet you couldn't count them. It was fun to outwit fifth grade science. It was May and the sun slanted in broad stripes along the grassy floor and, when I squinted, hung in prisms of color.

I needed that day with Sister.

THE NAVAL WAR had turned into a debacle. Wolf packs stalked our shipping in the North Atlantic, mostly sloops, World War I destroyers, carriers with obsolete aircraft, and, it was whispered, insufficiently trained crews. The way it worked, apparently, was that when a U-boat spotted a convoy, it would radio Brest or another French port the Germans had taken over, and word would go out to all the subs in the area. While the original wolf tracked the victims, the rest of the pack converged at high speed, often being refueled and resupplied on the high seas. The packs no longer limited themselves to cutting out stragglers or picking off isolated vessels. They engaged the cruisers and gave battle to the entire convoy.

I read the lists of missing and dead posted in the window outside City Hall and listened when I could to the CBC shortwave in the lounge. It broadcast not only from London but the war fronts. From these sources it was apparent that the losses were dreadful.

Human remnants of these engagements wound up on our wards. To cheer myself I concentrated on the cartoons in the Sunday supplement: a Mountie astride a sinking U-boat, another U-boat about to be devoured by a grizzly bear, and Adolf Hitler with a startled look running from a wild-eyed moose, who had just bitten out the seat of his pants.

It was necessary to laugh when you could.

I didn't know how true that was until Ruth tested positive for TB. This was a test we had to undergo every six months, but it was looked on as routine. Ruth's X ray, however, showed a lesion on her left lung. She was immediately isolated, and her roommate was moved out.

Sister Egg roved the corridors shaking her head and muttering to herself. This was not an unusual sight. Whenever things didn't work out as Egg thought they should, she could be seen roaming the hallways and arguing, whether with herself or with the Lord, no one was sure.

First-semester grades were due to be posted, and, condemning myself for being so selfish when my friend wouldn't graduate at all, I nonetheless kept checking the bulletin board. So far, nothing.

I'd left a patient propped up in bed reading, so I returned to monitor his IV, and my heart pushed into my lungs. A screen had been placed around his cot. I became queasy—I knew what that screen meant.

I came closer and stared at the blanket-covered form. A corpse has very prominent feet because that is the only part that humps up. It wasn't possible. I'd just been down to the basement and back. Finally I got up courage to pull back a corner of the blanket.

It wasn't my soldier but someone I had never set eyes on before. That shouldn't have made it better, but it did. The trouble was, when I started to laugh I couldn't stop.

Mandy found out that in order to play this gruesome joke the senior girls had brought up a stiff from the morgue and simply moved my patient to another room. That evening there were amused glances directed at me.

Why had I been the victim of such a cruel prank? Trisha and Ed had become a twosome, so it wasn't that.

"You goose!" Mandy couldn't contain herself any longer but burst into whoops of laughter. "It's an honor, reserved for whoever gets the highest posting. That's you!"

All thought of grades had been driven from my mind. Mandy took me by the hand and dragged me down to look at them. Kathy Forquet topped the list. Classmates shook my hand, kissed me on the cheek, hugged me. I had been awarded the highest distinction.

MIDWEEK OF THE second week, and I still hadn't heard from Crazy Dancer. Perhaps the kiss hadn't meant anything to him after all. Saturday came and went. Sunday came and went. I decided to forget there was such a person.

I was scrub nurse on a laminectomy, with Robert assisting. When it came to the delicate manuevering in the lumbar spine, Dr. Finch indicated that Robert was to take over. Finch lived in one of those grand houses on the upper reaches of Mont-Royal, and I'd heard his wife was high society. This morning he was definitely hung over, and I was relieved that he let Robert close.

It was reassuring to watch Robert at work. His fingers were quick, deft, and he tied off the bleeders in style.

Good going, I smiled over at him. He was a first-rate surgeon. Mandy would be pleased at this assessment.

There was something else on Robert's mind, however. As we disposed of masks and gloves and washed up, he said, "Incidentally, I've made some inquiries and found this outstanding TB sanatorium in Arizona."

"Arizona!"

"I know. It's expensive. But we want Ruth cured. And they have a great record."

I hadn't heard anything past *expensive.* "How expensive is it?"

"For a year? Several thousand."

"The Sisters could never raise anything like that, even with the doctors contributing and us adding our pennies."

"So," he said with a shrug, "Ruth dies."

"Oh no, good heavens, no."

"There may be a way," Robert said, "if we get Egg on our side." He paused.

"Well, go on."

"You stand in with her. So you should be the one to broach it to her."

"Broach what?"

He smiled a devil-may-care smile. "Bingo."

Bingo was strictly illegal, as was any form of gambling. I stared at him.

He went on imperturbably, "The Sisters don't have money. Bingo is the only way."

"Organize a bingo night here in the hospital? They'd never go for it."

"You're talking about Sisters who ran a brewery. Besides, it's to save Ruth."

They *had* run a brewery. They were pretty tough-minded ladies, and it was worth a try, especially as Ruth was not taking it well. We had all visited her at different times, using reasonable precautions, of course.

"I'm in a state of suspended animation," she had greeted me, explaining that she didn't feel at all ill, didn't even have a cough, and her sputum samples were negative.

"Stop complaining," I said, and we both laughed.

I'd brought a box of chocolates, and she hunted through it for those with soft centers. She was the kind of girl who could put it away and still remain thin as a rail. Her penchant for sweets, however, might have accounted for all those fillings. She mentioned the fund. "I don't have much hope of it," she admitted. "I don't see how they can possibly raise money for a first-class institution like the one in Arizona."

Robert's institution had been investigated by the Sisters. They were impressed, and started a fund in Ruth's name. I'd overheard the Sisters discussing it. It seemed they had all made their contributions, all but Sister Eglantine, who not only had failed to put up her share, but to date hadn't paid anything. "Not a red cent."

Mary Margaret hastened to add, "She didn't refuse."

"No," Sister Ursula conceded. "But we have yet to see the color of her money."

When they toted it up, including pledges by the doctors and staff, even if Egg's contribution equaled the rest put together, it fell woefully short.

That afternoon, Robert and I approached Sister Egg, laying out our suggestion with a good deal of trepidation.

"Bingo?" She regarded us with an enigmatic expression, one that could be interpreted as anger, shock, or possibly dismay. But it must have been her spectacles that reflected these emotions, for she went on to say, "What an extraordinarily good suggestion!"

The fist I had balled my hand into relaxed. I relaxed.

"How do you propose we go about it?"

That, naturally, was why Robert was there. "There are certain elements in this town," he said, "who would be happy to set it up for us, once they understood it was in a good cause, of course."

"Of course," Sister agreed, looking pious. Looking pious is part of a nun's training; they can do it at the drop of a hat. "God works in mysterious ways—" Sister Egg could always be counted on to come through with an appropriate saying—"his wonders to perform."

"Amen," said Robert.

THERE WAS A note at the nurses' station for me. Crazy Dancer had been by, and Sister said he'd written it on the spot. I saw I needn't have worried about that kiss—he was just as confused as I'd been. The note said:

Dear Oh-Be-Joyful's Daughter,

I think I've figured it . . . certain things that aren't okay for me are okay for you. If that's right, it's okay by me. I've got a surprise to show you, a motorcycle. She was a mess when I bought her, but I've been working on her all week, and she's purring like a bobcat. Let's take her out. How's Sunday? One o'clock in the parking lot.

Best regards,
Crazy Dancer

I was smiling before I came to the end. That's where he'd been, working on a motorcycle. A motorcycle was a good idea. Nothing much could happen on a motorcycle. Besides, tomorrow was Sunday. It was going to be a wonderful day.

*   *   *

IT WAS AND it wasn't.

Services had barely ended when Crazy Dancer was in the parking lot. It was one o'clock sharp. Mama always said Indians were never on time. But he was.

"There it is," he said with a proprietary gesture.

I looked in the direction he pointed. The motorcycle was a three-wheel job and had been polished to a high gleam. It was obviously homemade, and what had been a toolbox was converted into a seat.

"Is that for a passenger?" I asked.

"It's very comfortable. I tried it out."

I wanted to ask, "Is it safe?" But he was so pleased with himself that I couldn't.

"Once," he said with a flourish, "an Indian brave would have come on a fast buffalo pony. But this is now. How do you like it?"

I barely hesitated and said gamely, "I can see you've put in a lot of work on it."

"I have. It hardly takes any gas."

"Really?"

He patted the seat to encourage me. "Try it."

"I just sit on it. Is that it?"

"And hold on."

"To what?"

"To me."

"Oh." I sat gingerly.

"Does it seem all right?" he inquired.

"Oh yes."

"Are you comfortable?"

"I'm fine."

"Good." He threw a leg over the saddle and grabbed the

handlebars. "If I go too fast, or you want to stop or you get cold, just holler in my ear. I can hear you."

"You're sure?"

"I'll start up the motor and we'll see."

He did and it was loud. I leaned close to his ear and yelled, "Crazy Dancer!"

He turned, grinning, and the next moment jumped hard on the pedal, kicking it into action.

With a roar and a shivering jolt we leaped forward.

Once under way, the engine transferred its reverberation to me, throbbing through my body. The wind in my face was glorious, my hair flew out behind like a banner. My eyes teared but I made slits of them, taking in the rushing meld of buildings, cars, trams, signs, people. Nothing had its own identity, but blurred into and became part of everything else.

Crazy Dancer and I escaped the city, crossing the Jacques-Cartier Bridge and speeding into a softened landscape of greens and blues. We were riding at the sky, penetrating vast openness, mounting the clouds. It was intoxicating.

Crazy Dancer's waist was my security, that strong, slender waist that I fastened my arms around and clung to.

"Okay?" His shouted word streamed back to me. In answer I hugged him tighter.

We continued to sail along, then something happened to the steering. The motorcycle wobbled. I felt him lean to one side for balance, then tense. I laid my face against his shoulder and braced myself. Crazy Dancer made a last minute effort to spin out and away from the tree.

We struck.

The motorcycle went one way, Crazy Dancer and I another, for I hadn't let go of him. We slid along a grassy embankment and landed in one heap completely intertangled.

Crazy Dancer turned in my arms. "It was to make you joyful," he said.

I intended to say, "Yes, of course," but what came out was a sob.

I saw the concern in his eyes. Indian eyes are not expressionless as I'd often been told; they showed every bit as much concern as blue or brown. "You okay?"

I nodded. "It did make me joyful. I loved it."

"I know what the problem is. By changing the toolbox into a seat I raised the center of gravity. It's too high, I couldn't control the steering. The road turned, but I couldn't force the machine to turn. Are you sure you're all right?"

"I'm fine, just shaken."

"You'll be all right then. I'm going to have a look and see if I can get her going."

He got up, limped over to the machine, whose wheels had only now stopped whirring, and dragged it back to the tree for closer examination. "Well, we popped a tire, number one." He stood the bike up and started the motor. With infinite care he moved the shift lever. A horrible grinding noise came out, but it didn't seem to worry him too much. "Stripped a couple teeth off first, but second seems okay." He laid the bike down again. "The tire I can fix. To patch it I need to pry it off and remove the inner tube. Now, let's see what I can use for a patch." While he looked in the toolbox part of the seat, I rolled my sweater behind my head and made myself comfortable.

"Crazy Dancer, you were going to teach me Indian ways. Remember?"

He shrugged this off. "No one wants them anymore."

"I want them. At least I want to know about them. You said you would. First off I want to know how you look when you're dancing."

"I paint my body different colors, sometimes black and white. My hair is in horns twisted with corn tassels."

"Yes, I thought so. I thought that's how you'd look."

"I've made my diagnosis," he said, looking up. "I got to operate. I'm going to make a patch from that bit of rubber on the seat. Lucky I got a lighter so I can melt it and make it adhere. Lucky I left room for the compact bike pump in the bottom of the seat." He waved the pump triumphantly. "Cost me two bits extra, but I'm glad I made the investment."

"Tell me why you dance."

"Oh, that." He was busy with the rubber, heating it. "I dance because that's when the power floods into you. You seem to be just fooling around, but it's more than that. A clown acts silly, he acts in a contrary manner. He jokes and mocks, even at sacred rituals. You get people laughing and they start thinking in new ways. I teach like that, by bad examples."

"I don't know if my mind is Indian enough to understand. I think I do, but I'm not sure."

"When people question things, that's when they make changes."

"Yes, I see. Your crazy dancing is powerful medicine."

"That's right. You heal the spirit and that sometimes heals the body. Take me. I enter the house where the person lies ill. I have my mask on. I jump about, blow ashes on the sick person. The best kind is nicotiana from inner bark. Cedar is good, it purifies. Sometimes instead of dancing I get someone to play games with me."

"You play games? How does that get anyone well?"

He seemed surprised. "The life force is in motion. Kickball is a good way to release it, or kickstick—even making a patch."

"Don't you have medicines?"

"Of course. But first we put the heart of the healer in sympathy with the spirits. Then we give medicine. Bear gallbladder is strong against poison. Skunk oil is good for sore throat. Rub on grease from a wild goose for cramps or stomach pain. If you can't get a goose, duck is pretty good. Moose and beaver soups boiled with milkweed or red mulberry poured through wood ashes is strong against rattlesnake bite. Brings down the swelling. Even better, if you can catch the snake, cut it up and put it on the wound. Sure we got medicine."

"It all sounds very strange to me and I can't believe it does any good."

"What do you expect? You can't learn to be an Indian in one lesson." He regarded me quite soberly. "Are you sure you want to be an Indian?"

"No, I'm not at all sure."

"You are like me, stuck between worlds. That's why I joined up."

"That doesn't make sense. They're fighting over countries you don't even know about."

"My reasoning is this. I offer my life and perhaps my death in their battle, so I've won a place in white Canada. I have a right to it."

"Well, maybe," I said, not convinced. Privately I thought he would have to scrub at his lovely copper-colored skin harder than even I had and that in the end it wouldn't do any good.

"Will your unit be called up?" I asked.

"Who knows? For now we're detailed to drive lorries and keep 'em running. . . . There"—he straightened and patted the seat of the three-wheeler—"this should get us back. Let's give it a try. I thought we'd start at the top of that grade."

He dragged the machine over to the hill, and in one of those swift movements typical of him had the motorcycle in an upright position. Straddling it, he kicked up the motor. "Listen to that," he exclaimed, "purring like a bobcat."

I approached somewhat reluctantly. "So it was the center of gravity?"

"That's right—when it's too high, the motorcycle wants to steer itself."

"But you won't let it?"

"Now I know this habit, I'll hold it down. Perhaps a regular two-wheeler is better."

"Personally I like four wheels. It seems more stable."

"Four wheels? You're talking a car. You don't like cars."

"Under the right circumstances I like them."

He looked dejected. "A car eats gas and I only have a green ration card." To reassure and persuade me back to the motorcycle, he pointed out a gray and white feather attached to his key ring. "Don't be afraid. The spirit of this bird protects us."

"He must have looked away for a moment," I said.

But Crazy Dancer had his own interpretation. "He reminds me not to try to fly like him, because this is only a machine."

I mounted, my arms once more around him.

To reassure me, he explained his plan for reconnecting with the road. "We're going downhill in neutral and at the bottom shift into second. We'll have to get up to thirty or thirty-five or stall, so hang on."

It was like a runaway roller coaster, but I hung on and we made it.

Crazy Dancer took the ride back a bit more cautiously, because while the motor purred like a bobcat, there was an occasional hiccup.

We stopped at a drugstore for ice cream. It reminded me of the one back home, but this had small round marble-top tables and wire-backed chairs. "I used to work in a drugstore."

"You did?"

"Yes, only it wasn't fancy like this."

"I bet you made good milk shakes."

"I did."

Two white kids came in and were served ahead of us. Crazy Dancer didn't say anything but went to the counter and gave our order there. When he came back he said, "I'll leave a big tip."

"Why would you do that when they ignored us?"

"It is a contrary lesson, one of my bad examples. It makes them think, Why would he have done that? And they will feel bad that they don't deserve it."

I couldn't help laughing at his logic. "Oh, Crazy Dancer, I don't think so."

"My backward examples work. After all, I cracked us up and yet here you are having a malted with me. How do you explain that?"

"It must be your strong medicine."

He laughed, delighted. "Now you are sounding like Oh-Be-Joyful's Daughter."

When we drove into the hospital parking area there were several people about. They sent curious glances our way, taking in Crazy Dancer and his machine. I didn't care what they thought. I'd had a good time. I was happy. In fact I was joyful.

"It will be better next Sunday," Crazy Dancer said.

"Next Sunday?"

"Yes, when you come with me again."

"Crazy Dancer, you forgot to ask me. You can't just assume things, you have to ask."

"I did ask," he said. "Do I always have to use words?"

"Yes, you always have to."

He looked with a very sweet expression, I thought, into my eyes. "Will you come with me Sunday, in the Moon When the Pony Sheds?"

"Yes, I will."

Five

HE CREPT INTO my mind at odd hours during the week. I had a suspicion that he seemed as unconventional to his own people as he did to me. But I liked the unexpectedness of him, the honesty. And I was touched by the fact that he hadn't tried even a kiss. He was feeling his way with me.

He lived by inner laws that perhaps I would never understand. The thrust of everything he did was to bring out the harmony in things. That made him a religious person. And I was reminded of my father, Jonathan Forquet. But Crazy Dancer's God was in everything, in motion, in doing, in being.

A clown, he said, made you think in new ways.

I hunted up Sister Egg to see what she thought.

"That God is in everything? St. Eckhardt in the sixth century wrote extensively on this very point. But scholarship isn't necessary. You just open your eyes and look."

"I'm so glad we think alike. Would you go so far as to say His spirit is in dancing and even soccer?"

"Dancing and soccer? And lacrosse, I suppose? Well, now let me see. God enjoins us to be happy. And since we are happy when we do these things, I would say yes. Definitely yes."

I could have hugged her, I was so pleased.

* * *

THE LAST FEW days Mandy was, as Mama Kathy would have put it, a bit off her feed. In anyone else it wouldn't have been notice-able, but I lived with her, and Mandy, usually open about every-thing, now was abstracted and jumped when I spoke to her unexpectedly.

I didn't pay much attention at first. I told myself she'd had a quarrel with Robert and they'd make it up.

That didn't happen. She continued withdrawn and uncom-municative.

Finally, I blurted out, "Mandy, what is it? What's wrong?"

She shook her head. "It's nothing."

"You're not yourself. Something's happened. Can't you tell me?"

"It's nothing. Really. Just a problem Robert and I have to work out."

It was a polite way of brushing me off, but I persisted. "Is Robert pressuring you to, you know . . . go all the way?"

That made her laugh and for a moment I thought things would be all right. "Oh, Kathy, you are funny, so full of good old-fashioned homespun morality. Robert and I have been sleeping together almost from the beginning. Oh, I know good girls don't. But the war's changed all that. It showed us we have to live in the present."

There was a pause, which I didn't know how to fill, so I put my arms around her. I felt her sag. With a complete change from boisterous confidence, she crumpled.

"You don't think less of me, Kathy, do you?"

"Of course not. It's just that it didn't make you joyful."

"I *was* happy. For a while it was wonderful. It still is, only . . ." She stopped herself and when she continued it was more carefully. "Robert's sensitive, you know. You wouldn't think it, a big, strapping guy like that. But he is. I keep telling him a doctor can't take everything to heart the way he does. He empathizes too much with his patients."

Whatever was bothering Mandy, it was not Robert Whitaker's concern for his patients. I wasn't any closer to knowing what was going on than I had been before.

Sunday came. I dressed with care and scrutinized myself in the mirror. I wanted Crazy Dancer to be proud of me, to think I was pretty. I was in the parking lot at exactly one.

He must have been going on Indian time. He was late.

I watched various vehicles pull up, and leave again. A half hour dragged by in this way before it occurred to me that perhaps he wasn't going to show up. There was a sick spot in my stomach that expanded as minutes passed and it became increasingly obvious that he wasn't coming.

With a last look around I turned on my heel and went to my room.

Who did he think he was to treat me like this? He couldn't have forgotten. He had deliberately stood me up. In some recess of my being I still expected I would hear from him. He'd have some excuse, some story. And I didn't intend to listen, no matter what.

Monday there was no word. Nothing.

When Mandy invited me to go with her and Robert to Harry Sharp's, the casino that everyone talked about but that wasn't supposed to exist, I decided I'd go.

Mandy rarely asked me to join them, and I felt this might mean she was ready to take me into her confidence. Besides, in the mood I was in, I rather looked forward to investigating the darker side of Montreal. And Harry Sharp's casino was as close to Mama's sin city as I was liable to get.

For the occasion Mandy lent me a dress. It was a floaty chiffon in pale yellow. I wished Crazy Dancer could see me in it. I repressed that thought with annoyance.

"You look ravishing, Kathy." The prospect of a nefarious evening brought color back to her cheeks and the old animation. "Have you any money?"

"Not much. Will I be needing any?"

"Well, there's no use going to a gambling casino if you don't gamble."

"You're right," I said. Where and how could I come by money? There was the money I saved during the week for movies, and I might borrow a similar amount from Sister Egg. I shut out of my mind Mama Kathy's reaction to such a scheme.

I knocked on the door of Egg's room. "It's for an emergency," I explained.

The casino was on Cote Street, which everybody called Luck Road. All the swank places in Montreal were subterranean, and this cavern exploded in light and sound. Rapid French struck us from all sides and seemed to accelerate the more plodding English. Other languages intruded. People joked in Russian, laughed in French, and whispered in Armenian. One man wept bitterly in what sounded like Bulgarian or some other Slavic tongue, and seemed on the point of suicide, but allowed friends to restrain him. It was Dante's inferno mixed up with carnival.

The decor was elegant but far from tasteful. There was a crystal chandelier, a gaudy jukebox in conflict with it. Boxed palm trees were scattered about, and, in their shade, spittoons. The floor was marble, disfigured by black heel marks. At one end of the bar an enormous fresco beamed down on us of a woman in extremely high heels, garters, and a feathered boa that covered some essentials, but not all. The room was ringed by rows of slot machines, and people congregated around them. Gaming tables, however, were the focal point from which all other activities radiated like spokes of a wheel.

The crowd around the tables was as eccentric as the room. A conglomeration of expatriates from a dozen countries waved their money, collected chips, and placed their bets. I had a strong feeling they were not what they seemed, that nothing here was. The well-dressed gentleman with goatee, who resembled a French banker, I was sure I had seen driving a cab. It was carny time, and people dressed themselves in their wishes, their dreams.

I was one of them in my borrowed finery.

There were floor-length gowns and women in slacks. Among the men, zoot-suiters in the drape shape with the reet pleat and the stuff cuff mingled with starched ruffled shirtfronts and cummerbunds.

The closeness of the room intensified the sensations my nose picked up—brilliantine, that was a definite smell. It came from a head in front of me that glistened with it. The man turned a hawklike face in my direction. He wasn't looking at me, but at Mandy. It was an insolent look, bold and— He noticed I was observing him and ducked into the maze of people.

Expensive French perfumes were at variance with those picked up in the dime store. The atmosphere was invaded by stogies and cigarettes. Belinda Fancytails from Havana were advertised. They sold everything here.

Sharp's casino imitated both the discreet establishments of Nice and the flamboyance of Las Vegas. Mandy held onto me. We had somehow gotten separated from Robert and were scrutinizing the crowd for him. I followed a strobe light picking out face after face. There in an alcove was the man with the brilliantined hair and hawk face, talking to . . . I thought it was Robert, but the light moved on. When it completed its circuit and swung back, there was the hawk still in the alcove, but alone, nursing a drink. Someone called, "Frankie, *c'est va?*" and he answered with a smile and a wave of the hand. The smile was unpleasant. One front tooth lay on top of the other, giving him the appearance of a wolverine.

"Here's Robert," Mandy called.

Robert had found us and put an arm around each. He was perfectly at ease. Indeed he was at home in this frenetic strobe-light jungle that pierced you with drums and syncopated music intoned by a beautiful black singer.

"How do you like it? Exciting, huh?" I nodded numbly as he pointed. "Over here they're shooting craps. The dice have to bounce off the rail for the throw to count. If they don't, look out, some thug is apt to chop off your hand." One player was talking to his dice, beseeching them. A woman was kissing hers. Everything was extravagant, exaggerated.

"And over here, Montreal's own game, barbotte. You'll find it played in any alley for penny stakes—and here for enough money to buy all the buildings on the Place d'Armes."

He herded us over for a better look. "It's the stupidest dice game ever invented: five winning combinations, five losing, nothing else counts. A strictly even chance, minus the cut of up to five percent the house skims off on each roll. Played with tiny 'peewee' dice, easy to shave. No skill, no strategy, no technique whatsoever—just plain dumb luck."

Crowded around the table were a raucous and ill-assorted bunch of frenzied gamblers, some dressed to the nines, one who looked as though he'd slept in the bus station. This man, unshaven and reeking of cabbage, was rolling the dice, a mad gleam in his eyes.

"That's Marcel. They call him Magister Ludi, King of the Games. He has more luck than any living person, of both kinds, good and bad. You should have been here last week when he came in without an overcoat. He pawned it for six bucks, lost that stake in two rolls, scraped his pockets for all the change he had on him, lost that, and finally panhandled nickels and dimes from the spectators to make a last two-dollar bet. He won. And won again. Walked away at closing time with more than seven thousand dollars. He bought a new wardrobe, paid a year's room and board in advance at some fleabag inn, and he's back tonight losing the rest."

Making room for the vultures who wanted to savor Magister Ludi's bankruptcy, Robert finally brought us to a table where he was welcomed by players and croupiers alike.

"This is my game," he announced. "Roulette. *Le rouge et le noir.*"

Through the din I heard the croupier calling numbers and colors, the French words an invocation.

"So, little ladies," Robert adapted his manner to the place, "what is your pleasure? What will it be? Red or black? Even or odd? Columns? Rows? Or thirty-five to one on your lucky number?"

"You go ahead, Robert," Mandy urged. "Kathy and I will just watch until we get the hang of it."

"No," I declared. When the pony sheds! Where did he get off, standing me up? "Place your bet, Robert. And I will too."

"Kathy!" Mandy was as amazed by this new side of me as I was. "Are you really going to?"

I laughed and repeated her words back to her, "No use going to a gambling casino if you don't gamble."

"A woman after my own heart," Robert encouraged.

"In that case . . ." Mandy followed reluctantly.

Robert stepped up to the roulette table and placed his chips on Black. The croupier barked his warning call, the gigantic wheel spun, sending out sparks of light, and the money was raked away. Bettors lost and bettors won, their winnings added to the piles in front of them.

I picked a person with a mountain of chips before him, a gentleman with a malacca cane adorned in mother-of-pearl. The handle unscrewed, and out came a small flask from which he refreshed himself in moments of stress. He seemed to be the luckiest one there, and when he put his chips on Red, I emptied my purse and placed the first and last bet of my life.

My last, because after it was explained to me in French that the house accepted only chips, not cash, and the croupier with a resigned expression exchanged my money for a small, very small pile from a store he kept for ignorant females—to the relief of impatient gamblers and a crowd of kibbitzers the lighted wheel could be spun again, the winning number proclaimed, and the long arm of the rake descend to capture three weekends of movies and Sister Egg's ten dollars.

It was gone in under thirty seconds, including the conference with the croupier. The gentleman with the malacca cane barely paused to resupply his hoard. I couldn't do this. Mine was gone. Forever.

I realized a rather dull evening stretched before me. I should have patronized the slot machines, where I could have drawn out the excitement. I realized I was wrong about Mandy too. She didn't seem ready to confide anything to me. Perhaps I'd been mistaken, and there was nothing to confide.

So I amused myself watching as the strobe lights traversed the room, spotlighting one client after another. An elderly woman with a figure like a girl's, who wore both slacks and jewels, a large bald man, who squinted at the light and waved it angrily away—then the light found Mandy. She was watching Robert a few feet away at the roulette wheel. There was an odd expression on her face. When Robert was picked out, I was struck once more by his relaxed, self-confident manner. Was he too much at home here? That might put Mandy's expression into context—it was worry. Or was it fear?

I laughed at myself and inhaled the disgusting smell of brilliantine. With his back to me and shielding himself from the strobes in a row of slot machines was the one called Frankie. He was also watching.

He was watching Mandy.

I DROPPED BY to see Sister Egg with the first of my repayments, and she gave me two letters. I tore open Crazy Dancer's first. A letter from a sister can wait.

> *Dear Oh-Be-Joyful's Daughter,*
>
> *I was transferred, they'd only black it out if I said where. But I'm in Canada, at least for now. I found an engine and a couple of carburetors in pretty bad shape here too.*
>
> *I'm writing so you won't forget me. I do not forget you. Let me know if you miss me, and how much. I miss you a lot.*
>
> *Sincerely yours,*
> *Crazy Dancer*

There was a P.S., an army post office number where I could write him. On this he abbreviated his name to just Crazy.

I glanced away smiling. He hadn't stood me up. He thought of me, just as I thought of him. He missed me—a lot.

"Good news, Kathy?" Sister Egg regarded me contemplatively.

"Oh yes. From someone I didn't expect to hear from." I had to look away from her gaze to hide the fact that I was out-of-all-proportion joyful.

And she was rewarded for being her good egg self with wonderful news. The Reverend Mother had quietly quashed the bingo scheme. But at the last minute when Ruth was about to be separated from the service and dispatched, not to Arizona but to some inferior institution, one of the radiology technicians admitted she had accidentally splashed some drops of hypo on the film. At the time she hadn't realized what had happened, and only later associated the accident with the diagnosis of lung lesions that had showed up on Ruth's X ray.

I don't think Ruth herself could have been more elated than Sister Egg. "A girl with an appetite like that I knew couldn't have tuberculosis."

I had opened the letters in inverse proportion to their importance. Connie's was the most thrilling.

> . . . *Have I mentioned Jeff before? We've been going out quite a bit. Of course I've been going out with other people too. In fact, Mama Kathy made a boyfriend list to tease me. When I saw his name on it, I immediately took it off. I told Mama that he was simply a friend. I think now what I meant was—he was in a different category than the others. You've guessed what I'm trying to say, haven't you?*
>
> *We're engaged, Kathy. Engaged to be married. I can hardly believe it myself. I'm so in love. Someday you'll know the feeling. . . .*

I stopped reading and hugged the letter. What if "someday" was now? What if I too—?

I carried the letters back to my room and waved them at Mandy. "What do you know—my sister, Connie, is in love."

At this announcement of mine, her eyes filled with tears.

I looked away, pretending not to see them. Whatever it was, she kept it to herself.

I wrote Connie immediately, trying not to let any of the uneasiness I felt about Mandy come through. While I was enthusing to Connie, saying how happy I was for her, I kept remembering how happy Mandy had been. Love, I thought, must be difficult.

More about the romance came the next day from Mama Kathy. Jeff, according to her, was perfect for Connie. And she put in details that Connie didn't bother with. He was a stress analyst who worked in the same plant as Connie. His job was on some sort of experimental aircraft. It was very important work. In fact, it struck me that everything about Jeff began with a superlative. He was very handsome, very talented, very important. I wondered how Georges would feel about this *very very* person who wanted to marry his twin.

I was answered in the next mail delivery. Georges, in a hasty scrawl, wanted to know a lot more about "this Jeff character."

Like pups from the same litter, we three were headed in different directions.

Mama's world had brought me far, given me an education and a profession. But it didn't accept me. And, what was worse, didn't admit it didn't. As a student nurse I had gained respect and the confidence of the Sisters and my fellows. During working hours I was on an equal footing, there were shared jokes, friendly remarks; I was included. Mama always said—*Kathy is to be included.* Here, at the hospital, my uniform was a badge of admittance. Out of it, my status disappeared, and I wasn't included except once or twice as an afterthought. That's when I remembered how much kindness can hurt.

Looked at fairly, Mama's white world had prepared me, as few Indian girls were, to take a place in it. But had I left room for joy? Happiness I long ago rejected as not good enough—it must be joy that lifted you up to the skies. Joy at seeing, feeling, hearing, joy at being in the world. Joy became my prayer. The only prayer, Sister Egg tells me, God wants to hear.

So each day I remind myself I am Oh-Be-Joyful's Daughter, and look for a piece of joy to take to bed at night. I seize on a cloud lighted by a sinking sun, or the pattern in a leaf, or the reds and golds autumn brought, and wrap myself in it before sleeping.

But in the morning I have to face the pain, the useless bravery and hopeless courage in the wards. I couldn't get the ulcer case out of my mind. The ulcer broke through to the stomach, and a naso-gastric tube was used to suction it. That afternoon the patient died.

Not "the patient." *Ralph. Ralph died.* I was hiding from his name. You can't allow names, they make it too real.

No one expected him to die. It was a shock. I kept reviewing the plasma drip I'd been responsible for. But that had gone routinely. I could think of nothing I could have done to keep him alive. So I played a game of dominoes with cot 14, remembering to call him Bob. The dominoes were bone, not wood, and the clicking sound gave him a great deal of pleasure.

"Is there any strategy to this game?" I asked. "It just seems to be matching ends."

Bob's answer was a grin. "You got to beat me before you complain about it being too easy." Midway in the game he said, "No holding out. If you *can* play, you got to."

I gained a new respect for the game. It was like life: you have to play if you can play. And those pieces that were sidelined? You had to forget them and go on.

THE WAR ITSELF was a morass of contradictions, fought from the fogs off the Grand Banks of Newfoundland where wolf packs hid, to the sands of el-Alamein with Rommel falling back to Tunisia chased by Anderson's First Army. Massive German reinforcements arrived, and the battle seesawed.

I don't think in Washington, Ottawa, or London they really knew how the war was going. A victory here offset a defeat there.

Outside Stalingrad German troops were mired by winter. In the Pacific Admiral Halsey mounted an offensive against an island I'd never heard of—Guadalcanal. U.S. and Aussie troops attacked the Japanese in Burma and drove them out of Gona.

Recently there were German prisoners among our patients. I found it difficult to even approach them. There they lay, looking like everybody else. They didn't wear the blue-gray uniform of prisoners, with the large red circle in the middle of the back, a target in case they tried to escape. No, they were in the usual white hospital gowns.

They might look like anybody else, but they were responsible for the shrapnel cases, the amputees, the boy with infected shell fragments in his back. One of them might have killed the Clark boy. And what about cot 19? It was not impossible they had had a part in John's face being shattered, or the abscessed jaw in the corner, with yellow streaks seeping into the fibers of the dressing. They were Nazis, the horde that overran Europe, occupied Paris, bombed London.

The senior nurses were slow in answering their calls and more and more it was left to me. I tried not to think that even now their comrades were trying to kill Georges. Lying helpless on army cots they were just more broken bodies with the same fear-filled questioning eyes. Yet when they cried out, it was in guttural words I didn't understand.

They didn't ask anything of us, there were no requests. It was clear they found their position a peculiar one. While they themselves had been captured, they knew—*we*—knew that in the broader theater of the war Germany was the victor. Everywhere land was taken, ships sunk, populations driven into camps. They must wonder why we inferior peoples didn't recognize that we were conquered. Why didn't we give up and admit defeat?

It must rankle to be so dependent on us.

However, I was a nurse. I administered morphine and pain medication to these examples of the "master race," handled syringes, turned them to avoid bedsores, changed linen, gave baths, and shuddered at their wounds. I couldn't help it. They suffered.

Cot 5 had developed pneumonia. His breath came in weak rales, and it was obvious he was dying. He was very young, eighteen or nineteen. At the end he reached out groping for something, someone to hold on to. I gave him my hand. The name on his chart was Kurt. I was afraid to say it for fear the sound of my English voice would frighten him.

He murmured something in German. "Gott."

That we agreed on. "Yes," I whispered under my breath, "God will look after you."

A second later I closed his eyes and a tear of mine fell onto his face. That's when I found out it was as hard to lose a German as a Canadian or English boy.

One of the men on the ward, with chest injuries and third-degree burns on his hands, thighs, and abdomen, had been picked up from a U-boat. "I would have let him drown," Ruth said bitterly. She had lost an uncle in a U-boat attack.

More than I hated wolf packs and Hitler I'd begun to hate the war.

Whether this burn case would survive to undergo a lengthy series of skin grafts was questionable. We had extracted numerous shards of metal, and were giving palliative treatment. He'd lain motionless in a coma for a week exuding the faint smell of decay accompanying extensive burns and made no better by overlying disinfectants.

I was changing the dressings when his eyes suddenly opened and he looked at me. Gray, thoughtful eyes.

"I hear English voices. Am I in England?" He spoke a cultivated English, better than my own.

"You're in Canada," I told him. "Montreal."

"I always wanted to see Canada."

"Don't try to talk. You're going to come along fine now, but you've been quite ill."

He nodded and slipped, not into coma, but into sleep.

He must be an officer, I decided, to be so well educated, to have such a command of English. I'd forgotten his name, so I flipped the cover page of his chart—Lt. Erich Helmut von Kerll.

I was busy for a while in the other wards, but before I left the floor I looked in on him. He had come around but didn't remember our conversation. He once more wanted to know where he was.

He looked at me and saw me for the first time. "Very kind of you," he said, "an enemy and all."

"You're a patient," I said firmly.

"Very kind," he said again.

I checked the chart of the next bed to make sure he'd been given his evening medication. When I turned back the lieutenant was asleep.

I looked in on him the next morning. He was asleep and his vital signs were stable. His fever, however, remained high and he was continued on intravenous feeding. While I was adjusting the tubing he woke and asked for water.

"It isn't allowed." Nevertheless I brought cracked ice, put a little in his mouth, and passed a chunk across his parched lips. He tried a joke. "Florence Nightingale was some other war, wasn't she?"

I smiled at his attempt.

"What's your name?" he asked.

"Kathy."

He seemed disappointed. "I thought you'd have an Indian name."

"I do. Oh-Be-Joyful's Daughter."

"Remarkable," he said and fell asleep.

EARLY THE NEXT morning before going on duty I stopped by Lt. von Kerll's bed. The night nurse had not carried out her instructions. The edges of his abdominal burns were adhering to the dressings, and it was necessary to moisten them and peel them away. No matter how gently this was done, it was an agonizing procedure.

He grit his teeth. While he said nothing, he sweated his gown through. Gingerly I got him into a fresh one.

"Oh-Be-Joyful's Daughter, I think you don't intend to let me die. I think you intend to get me well."

"I'm going to get you well," I said with resolution.

"I feel much better and I'm hungry."

"That's good news," I said, wondering what I could feed him at this unorthodox hour. Breakfast preparations were not yet under way. Then I thought of the nurses' station—they always kept something on hand. "I'll try to bring you a cup of broth."

I did bring it, but by the time I got back with it he was sleeping. I looked down at him with a pleased warm feeling. The stench of decay no longer hung about his wounds. He was resting comfortably.

RUTH HAD A date and asked me to take her shift in the wards that evening.

When I came on duty Erich von Kerll was awake and slightly propped up in bed. Beside him was soup and a glass of juice, neither of which he had touched.

"Aren't you hungry?"

"I wasn't. I am now."

"Good. What will you have first, the drink?" I held it to his lips. "Now for the main course," and I ladled a spoon of potato soup into his mouth. He took three or four sips then put his hand up.

"Enough?"

"Yes, thank you."

"You'll be able to sleep now. Shall I put the light out?"

"I knew you before, when I was just lying here. I knew when it was you adjusting the machine, changing plasma bags, giving injections, taking my pulse."

"Did you?" I said, trying not to show how touched I was. "I've often wondered if comatose patients don't comprehend more of what goes on around them than we think."

"Yes. Well, I did. When I was in the water I thought, this is when Brünhilde, or one of the lovely Rhine Maidens is supposed to take my hand and lead me to that Vallhalla reserved for warriors. Instead of a maiden of light, waves of oil rushed into my mouth and washed my eyes. And there was fire on the water."

I had forgotten, I allowed myself to forget he was off a U-boat. I recoiled, I couldn't help it.

He read my expression, stiffened, and a look of whimsical grief passed over his features. "I was second mate on the U-186. Our kill was nine merchant ships, two of them Canadian, and a corvette."

I compressed my lips.

Why had he said that? Why remind me we were enemies? I walked from the room.

Six

THE CHRISTMAS SEASON was a busy time here. The saints' days were observed by extra services. I mailed packages to Mama Kathy, Connie, and Georges. Books this year. *A Christmas Carol* for Connie, a beautiful *Audubon* for Mama, and a life of Houdini for Georges. Mandy and I exchanged presents; she gave me earrings, long and dangling. I loved them, although I couldn't imagine where I would wear them, or with what. I found a pretty little pin for her. The Sisters clubbed together and gave every girl a white prayer book.

The Sisters had been persuaded to allow a dance to be held. There were a few regulations: absolutely no liquor on the premises, the affair to be chaperoned, and the hours posted.

We girls, delighted at the prospect of a party, made a trip to the closest woods and brought back fir branches and sprigs of holly. We strung popcorn and macaroni and colored them with leftover cake dye, then turned our attention to the hall.

The tree was symmetric, tall and gaily trimmed with ornaments, some of which dated back a hundred years, and at its base the Sisters laid a crèche. The holy family was represented, the shepherd, the wise men, all the animals, and of course in the manger lay the Christ child, while over him an angel kept guard.

I was reminded of the angel wrapped in newspaper a year ago and wondered when the family would be gathered under it again.

I decided to bring a strand of popcorn to the German burn case. He'd undergone a second skin graft and I had not behaved in a professional manner, stalking out as I had. After all, I told myself, it's Christmas. So I went to the foot of his cot.

A tent was arranged to keep the covers from his body. He lay quietly. I thought at first he was sleeping, but his eyes were fixed on the ceiling.

"Merry Christmas," I said, holding out the purple chain.

He turned his head. "Merry Christmas, Oh-Be-Joyful's Daughter."

"You remembered my name."

"Yes, but I haven't had much occasion to use it. I drove you away. My outburst the other day—it came from anger that I can't always control. Anger that I'm caught up in events, tossed this way and that, and find myself a prisoner. The anger spilled out at you simply because you were good enough to talk to me. I am sorry. Can you forgive my boorishness?"

"I don't even recall what was said. My impression was that you were in pain."

"Pain." He shrugged impatiently. "Pain is no excuse."

"No," I said, "just an explanation. . . . You looked so thoughtful when I came in. Were you thinking of home?"

"We generally go skiing. Afterward there's eggnog and Brandy Alexanders with your feet in fur-lined carpet slippers, lolling in front of a fire, roasting chestnuts. Yes, I was thinking of home."

"We used to roast chestnuts too. That was part of our Christmas."

"I begin to think," he said slowly, "that the world is more alike than different."

"And war is old-fashioned and outmoded, and no one wants it anymore."

"No," my German enemy agreed, "no one wants it."

I tied the purple popcorn to the lamp and wandered into the basement to see if anything still needed doing. The staff was assembled and the hall was beginning to fill with groups of sailors and soldiers.

The music started, Sister Ursula at the piano and Dr. Goodwin playing a bass fiddle. In contrast to a few unhappy experiences at school, here I wasn't permitted to sit down. These boys wanted a girl to hold, to talk to. They told me about Maryanne, Aggie, Marie, Patty. The name of the girl kept changing, but they were the same girl.

Dr. Bennett was deep in an analysis of the war. He was explaining to Sister Mary Margaret the psychology behind the latest battlefront moves. "Hitler's egomania is beginning to work for us. He has fine generals, Rommel, for instance, a real professional. But the little madman doesn't listen to him. He doesn't listen to any of them. He knows better. Mark my words, that's the flaw in his character, the fatal flaw that's going to win us the war."

Once Dr. Bennett noticed me, there was no escape—he had found a new victim for his thesis and whirled me away. Dr. Bennett was one of those doctors whom the war had brought out of retirement, energized and given renewed purpose. We had only taken a turn or two when he was tapped on the shoulder and relinquished me to . . .

Crazy Dancer.

I made an effort to keep my feelings in check and said lightly, "This isn't happening. It isn't real."

"It is possible," he conceded, "to dream someone else's dream. But not this time."

"Are you here for an hour, a day, forever?"

"I'm here for the Christmas party." And he swept me into new patterns.

"I didn't know you knew how to ballroom dance. I thought you only danced with a corn-husk mask braided into horns, and stripes of paint on your cheeks."

"I can dance anywhere, anytime, anyplace."

The music called our feet and insinuated into our bodies. Crazy Dancer and I touched a star together.

The Christmas star on the tree was cut twice from silver paper and placed at right angles to itself so that the intersection made it appear to have another dimension. We stopped in front of it, breathless.

"I have a Christmas present for you." He rummaged in his pockets and came up with the gray and white feather off the motorcycle.

"You can't give me this, Crazy Dancer. It's your protection."

"You hold it now for both of us."

"You're sure?"

"I'm sure. That's why I came. I'm only here on a Christmas pass. I came because of what you wrote."

Desperately I tried to recall, to mentally scan my letters. Sometimes you write things you wouldn't necessarily say. Had I signed any of them, "Love, Kathy"? I didn't think so.

He jogged my memory, "The part where you said you missed me. . . ."

"Oh." I was relieved. "I did miss you."

"Missing," he said, "is a powerful wish. You wish someone is with you. Right?"

"Yes. . . ."

"So I came," he finished triumphantly.

I had to laugh at his absurdities. He was a clown who made very good sense.

Mandy, curious about him, dragged Robert over to meet Crazy Dancer.

"I know you already," Crazy Dancer told her. "Sometimes it was you who signed for supplies."

"Of course," Mandy said, placing him. "I thought you looked familiar. Are you posted back here now?"

"No. I came for the dance."

"You came to Montreal for a dance?"

Crazy Dancer shrugged. "—I'm a crazy dancer."

"Come on." I guided him toward the soft drinks and away from Mandy.

The dance broke up promptly at midnight with the traditional "Good Night, Ladies" waltz, and I went with him to the coatroom, where he got into a wool cap, muffler, boots, and a fur jacket. "The cold doesn't have room in the city to spread out. It's pushed together by all the buildings ... and look what it makes!" He led me to the door and opened it.

Sudden cold, and I burrowed into his furs. There descended flashing bolts of color. The sky, prismatic, rained down pulsating sheets of light. We were part of the changing flamboyant purples, greens, and golds as they illuminated us.

"Don't forget to miss me." He left with a kiss that for me would always be part of the aurora borealis.

GRADUATION FOR THE senior class and the arrival of new student nurses marked my first year.

One of them arrived early. There were special circumstances attached to Emily Champlain coming a week ahead of the others. Emily was a small, dark, serious-minded French Canadian who had been reared by the Sisters of the Sacred Heart in their orphanage. She was past eighteen and they didn't know quite what to do with her. The war had placed a strain on their facilities and space was at a premium. Our nuns were appealed to and here she was.

The only experience she listed in her application was a summer working as an aide in a rundown mental institution for women.

Emily, as it turned out, was my first trainee. Since she had worked around schizophrenics, catatonics, and cyclomaniacs, it was decided to try her in our closed ward. This ward was intended to be a way station in which servicemen broken in mind were evaluated and sent on. In reality it was almost impossible to place these patients, as all suitable institutions were filled past capacity. So the Sisters accepted that the Lord meant this final burden for them, and took it on with what grace they could muster.

Matron Norris, a rather formidable person in her midfifties, was put in charge, and the closed ward became hers. She shared it grudgingly with the psychiatrist, Dr. Bloom, who visited whenever his schedule allowed, which was not too often. Matron Norris used him in lieu of the bogeyman: "We don't want Dr. Bloom to see this behavior, now, do we?" At times she simplified it to: "What would Dr. Bloom think?" Dr. Bloom was a strict Freudian, and I sometimes wondered if a childhood trauma could possibly be at the root of the disintegration of a soldier found cradling the torso of a buddy who had no head.

At any rate I was nominated to work alongside Emily so she wouldn't get into trouble. I showed her around. There was a large room and screened-in porch with bars, as well as a corridor dormitory and bathroom. Seeing these young men, listless, vacant, subject to sudden flashbacks, going suddenly manic, was enough to unnerve the most stable among us. I sized up Emily with some concern. She was so young, just a kid.

"I think the two of us will be able to manage a shift," I said cheerily. "What do you say?"

She looked a bit uncertain, taking in a soldier who roamed about agitatedly, berating an officer for calling in an airstrike using wrong coordinates. I pointed out a burly orderly posted at the door. "As a rule, Matron handles any disturbance. But—"

"*Mais oui*, it was *le meme*—the same—where I worked before."

"As a rule," I assured her, "everything goes along pretty well. The patients themselves are very helpful at times."

She nodded her neat dark head. "They have a way of knowing which will burst out, harm themselves, attack the others."

I was surprised at this insight, and thought she was probably right. "You like nursing, don't you?"

She brightened at once. "Oh yes. The Sisters at the convent always said, 'Take pride in your work. You cannot be a good person if you do not take pride in your work.' "

I nodded absently. She reminded me of myself a long time ago, last year in fact.

Matron Norris sat us both down and outlined our responsibilities. We were to patrol the rooms together and keep on the move, settling disputes, dispensing medication, in some cases feeding—the spoons in this ward were sometimes bitten through, their handles twisted or missing altogether.

Emily raised her hand, as though in a classroom, for permission to speak.

"Well?" the matron asked, not at all pleased by this interruption.

"At the Hotel des Femmes," Emily began in a small voice.

"What are you saying? Speak up, girl."

Emily cleared her throat and looked to me for support. But not knowing what was on her mind, I had to let her go it alone.

"At the Hotel des Femmes where I worked before, they gave the patients the responsibility."

"The patients!" Matron had heard quite enough. "My dear

girl, the line between staff and patients is never to be blurred. I want you to remember that." She concluded the interview by saying that any violence on the ward was to be handled by the orderlies. If additional help was needed, there were the MP's. "On no account are you to involve yourselves. Is that quite clear?"

We sat before her and nodded dutifully.

"Oh, and Kathy, as the senior member of the team, I hold you accountable." She dismissed us with "Have a nice day."

But I felt out of sorts. It didn't seem fair to put me in charge and, at the same time, hem me in. Perhaps that's why I listened to Emily.

She hesitated, trying to gauge my reaction in advance, then plunged in, once more relating her experiences at the Hotel des Femmes. "The patients were given responsibility, *n'est-ce pas*? They themselves broke up fights, and did other useful tasks like . . ." She pondered it. "Like mend the radiator. Your radiators do not function properly," she ended triumphantly, as though that proved her case.

"No," I admitted ruefully, "they certainly don't."

"*C'est très froid*," and she shivered in her old patched sweater, but the next moment she was all business. "The matron Norris did not talk of suicide. Can we talk of suicide?"

"We try to keep watch on those patients that are acutely depressed," I said uncomfortably, "if that's what you mean."

"But someone, now and then, kills himself anyway. No?"

I admitted that happened. "We can't be everywhere."

"That is where the other system would help. We appoint a patient to watch. Each watches the other. *C'est meilleur*, two watchers instead of one of us. And those who watch, it gives them esteem of self."

"Importance," I said, liking the solution. But there were several big ifs. Matron for one. And the patients themselves for another—could we trust them? "We *are* terribly short-handed," I conceded.

Emily watched me struggle with the problem. "We'd be taking a chance," I said. "Matron Norris is old school, strictly by the book. If she found out, she'd put us on report. . . . It isn't that she isn't an excellent nurse," I finished. "She is."

"*Je comprends.*"

I knew she did, because her face assumed unhappy lines, and it helped me make up my mind. "Of course, the way I look at it there's no use bothering Matron with such a scatterbrained idea. But we can talk the plan over with the patients and see what they think of it."

"Oh, could we?" The mobile young face exuded sudden joy. The joy touched me.

I only hoped she didn't burn out. I had seen enthusiasm such as hers fade after a few weeks. However, Emily's underground system was worth trying. It didn't hurt anyone and it freed us for tasks we rarely got around to in the locked ward.

The men endorsed the plan whole-heartedly, partly, I think, because it was not officially sanctioned. But in spite of its adoption and even with Matron's disciplined calm, there were certain frenetic times on the ward, such as meals, baths, and bedtime. The bathroom in particular was a place of chaos. Lightbulbs were often smashed and the mirrors soaped, graffitti appeared above the urinals, and there were water fights. Matron always sent us in together to tackle the bathroom.

This evening cot 26 stuffed something into his mouth and was choking on it, so I bent him over and whacked his back. I hated leaving Emily alone and listened for any disturbance. But things sounded normal. My patient finally brought up a three-day-old dinner roll he must have hoarded under his pillow.

I got him into bed and hurried down the corridor to the bathroom.

Shock stopped me at the door. Emily Champlain had our resident catatonic arranged as a towel rack. His rigidly outstretched arms, which were impossible for any of us to move manually, were draped with towels for the men coming out of the shower, and his turned-up palms were soap dishes.

As luck would have it, Matron Norris had chosen this moment to conduct Dr. Bloom on one of his periodic inspections.

At the door she turned catatonic herself, and the good doctor, cyclomanic. He found his voice first and thundered, "How can you treat a human being this way?"

Emily looked stricken. I was about to come to her defense. It wasn't necessary. An eerie voice, rusty from disuse, came out of the towel rack. "On this ward, Doctor, everyone does his job."

At Matron Norris's request I was transferred from duty in the locked ward. I missed working with the innovative Emily and wondered how the patients would fare without the "system." I learned later that Emily herself lay low, but a patient committee met with Matron Norris and argued quite rationally that wartime conditions required wartime solutions. She acceded to patients' demands and reinstated a modified form of "responsibility therapy." I think she got as much pleasure hoodwinking Dr. Bloom as we did hoodwinking her.

THE NEXT MORNING I returned to my old beat and was checking the linen closet with Sister Magdalena, when through the open door to the ward I heard raised voices.

The patient next to the German lieutenant was on his good elbow talking to, or rather *at* von Kerll. Until last week we had kept the prisoners separate from the other patients. But casualties were coming in so fast that we were overwhelmed, and put newly admitted wounded wherever we could find a bed.

A French Canadian sailor, invalided from the Mediterranean

theater, was being treated with sulfanilamide administered every four hours. He had responded so well that now here he was belligerently continuing the war.

"*Certainement*, U-boats are floating coffins, *c'est tout*. They're slow torpedo boats on the surface, slower underwater. Slower than a tug in harbor. Once you're submerged, you're pinned down, the easiest target in the world."

The German lieutenant started to defend his submarines, but the sailor cut him off, to heap scorn on the whole German war plan.

Sister Magdalena asked me to pay attention to the linen count, and insisted on adding those in my arms to the ones in the closet. "It doesn't seem to tally," she moaned, and went through it all again.

Meanwhile I tried to glean something of what the sailor was taunting von Kerll with. ". . . And your great Fuehrer with the Charlie Chaplin mustache, what does he know about strategy? He was a corporal in the last war. Okay, so you made a cemetery out of Russia. Winter's here. You know what a Russian winter did to Napoleon. Seen a paper lately? Well, the Russkies have what they call a 'scorched earth' policy. *Vraiment*, they're retreating, but they don't leave so much as a blade of grass for you Krauts. No electricity, no water, no food, no transport, not even a mule. They wreck their own rolling stock, and your trains don't fit their tracks. I'm telling you it was a celebration for us when the little corporal opened the Eastern Front."

Von Kerll retorted that the Axis didn't need Moscow. Capturing the Ukraine meant capturing Russia's breadbasket and controlling the oil reserves of Eastern Europe.

I had enjoyed our sailor giving the German what for. But now that von Kerll was matching him argument for argument, the Quebecois lost his temper. He cursed, first in French, then English, finally he tried German. But von Kerll laughed at his accent.

He became so infuriated that I thought I should intervene. Enough was enough. I left Sister Magdalena in the midst of matching sheets with pillowcases and marched in. "Able Seaman Duprez, I want to know what this means, fraternizing with the enemy."

"Fraternizing?" he sputtered and became so indignant that I was afraid he'd burst open his stitches. "I was just telling that Jerry officer how it really is, *non?* And which way things are going."

"You did a fine job. But now it's time for your shot and a little rest." I pulled the bleached muslin curtain along its track between the beds.

He wanted to continue his voluble defense, but I gave him a glass of water along with a lecture. "You get so worked up you're apt to do yourself damage. Lie back, that's it, and take it easy." I administered a hypo and read to him until he fell asleep. Then I went around to the other side of the curtain to see how my prisoner patient was doing.

I saw he had started a letter and put it aside.

"Can I give you a hand with that?" I asked.

"Yes," he laughed, "a right hand." His own had deep lacerations produced by metal splinters that penetrated the burn. "I'm afraid I'm awfully clumsy with my left."

I picked up the discarded page. "How stupid of me, it's in German."

"I'll start again in English."

"Who's the letter to? Your wife, your girl?" The question was routine. I asked it of everyone.

"I'm not married. At least I showed some sense there. Actually the letter is to my mother. To tell her I'm well and no part of me is missing. That's important. Mother sets a great deal of store on appearance. If I'd been maimed, or if my burns had reached my face, I don't think I'd go home."

"I'm sure you're wrong about that. There was an English boy, an amputee, who felt the same way. It was quite a struggle for him. But when he was discharged, he went home."

"He was brave, braver than I. But then he didn't have to confront the daughter of an Austrian vice admiral. You see, my mother's family is old. By comparison my father is an upstart. When I was a child we used to vacation at my grandparents' estate on the Bodensee. Austria is a land of lakes and that is the largest. Great bathing and boating."

I don't know when it stopped being routine—as he talked I could see a blond boy in a sailor suit wandering the shore, pitching stones, seeing how many times they skipped. More pictures formed. Novels from Old Irish Bill's library, romances by Wassermann, Thomas Mann, and Romain Rolland furnished the background. Gracious hotels looking out on ski runs, summer homes on the lake, picnics aboard the family yacht. And the daughter of this house, I imagined her too. Bobbed hair, of course, after the latest fashion; she'd be quite a beauty. Her little boy longed to climb into her lap, but no one took liberties with Elizabeth Madeleine Hintermeister von Kerll.

"Heinrich, the old gamekeeper, used to take me fishing. Have you ever had rainbow trout? Pike and grayling too. The finest fishing in Austria."

"You're Austrian? Not German?"

"We were annexed in '38, in preparation, I see now, for the war." He stopped, and went on again in an altered voice. "March eleventh at ten in the evening. On the thirteenth Hitler announced we were a province of the German Reich. You can see why. We are the third-largest producer of crude oil in Europe. And we have a modern airport at Wien-Schwechat near Vienna. You don't have to look further than that. The Nazis tore up our constitution. We became a German satellite overnight."

"But Hitler is Austrian himself, isn't he?"

"The house painter?" He snorted. "Yes, he is Austrian. So are the cattle in our barn, if being born on Austrian soil makes one Austrian. But the heritage is something different. Our Academy of Science goes back to the Middle Ages. Architecture, poetry, music, the Vienna waltzes and operettas of my grandparents' time. The Burgtheater is the best German-speaking theater on the continent, and then there's the Viennese Staatsoper, the state opera. Music was born in Vienna. Haydn, Mozart, Schubert, even the moderns, Schoenberg, and Alban Berg. And our museums have a wealth of Old Masters down to the cubist painter Oskar Kokoschka, who naturally has fled. But that's Austria, the heart and soul of her."

My mind had caught further back. All thought of a little blond boy throwing stones into the water disappeared. "It was a plebiscite," I said.

"What?"

"A month after the Germans took over Austria there was a plebiscite. Austria voted to go along, voted for the—what is it called?"

"The Anschluss." His voice had dropped so low I could scarcely hear him. The next minute he rallied. "You have to understand. It was called a plebiscite, it was supposed to be the will of the people. The will of the people was to live, and that was the only way we could manage it."

"Still, you left that part out."

"You're right. I apologize. I wasn't deliberately misrepresenting. I wanted you to see Austria as she had been, as I know her."

He spoke so sincerely that I relented a bit. It had not occurred to me that not all Germans or Austrians supported the war, that some, like Erich, were caught in its net.

In the days that followed, his Austria became very real to me. Years of reading . . . Schnitzler, Franz Werfel, Mann's magic mountain down which lovers skiied, made it easy to close my eyes and see a line of sloping meadows and craggy peaks rising behind them, smell forests of beech and larch, and the many streams sparkling their length like unwinding ribbons. To see the mighty Danube moving lazily, a water bridge from Germany to the Black Sea, where the snow of the valleys and the snow of the streams met.

He spoke of *Grunderjahre*, the good times, his life a procession of nursemaids and governesses, whom he ruled with the quick easy charm of his class. When he was nine a tutor was found for him, a tutor who was strict and knowledgeable in science and mathematics.

It had been decided, probably when he was in his first little sailor suit, that, like his father and grandfather, he would be commissioned in the navy. It was easy to picture him sailing his toy boats from the shore of the Bodensee.

The next time I dropped by to check on the malfunctioning Quebec heater in ward B, I found my two patients arguing violently about the war—this time it was the American Revolutionary War. Von Kerll was vigorously defending Benedict Arnold, who he claimed had been unforgivably snubbed, passed over, and insulted by jealous fellow officers.

"No excuse," Duprez declared hotly, "for stealing a cannon and bringing it with him when he defected."

I could see they enjoyed these mock battles so much, I was sorry to see the sailor go. His infection was cured and he was discharged, gleefully promising to visit von Kerll and keep him up to date on the number of U-boat coffins sunk.

I continued to keep my eye on the Quebec heater, which definitely needed surgery, and received further accounts of von Kerll's magical childhood. That bygone era was so glamorous, so far removed from anything I'd ever known. He had been at the Olympic Games in '33, heard Hitler officially declare them open, watched in amazement as the black American, Jesse

Owens, sprinted to victory leaving the champions of the master race to eat his dust. "Only my father's warning glance kept me from exploding in laughter."

He talked of skiing in Cortina. Remembering the hot spiced mulled wine drunk afterward by a blazing fire was his way of dealing with skin grafts. I sat and listened because I knew the pain he was in. He told of climbs he'd made. "Class five-nine," he said with a touch of pride. "And at night, in one of those isolated mountain huts, sometimes I'd practice my English on a Brit, American, or Aussie. There's a special camaraderie among climbers. The nationality doesn't matter, just the mountain. The same goes for sailors."

With Erich it always got back to the sea.

"The sea runs in my veins like blood in other people's. In fact I am amazed to hear the way U-boats are referred to, as though they are inherently evil—We don't stand to, we *lurk*. We don't cruise the waters, we *infest* them like some sort of vermin. We don't pursue, we *stalk*."

His grin invited me to smile back. But I couldn't. U-boats did infest, they did lurk and stalk—and kill.

"Even aboard a sub, things aren't what people imagine. It can actually be enjoyable. I remember one occasion, patroling in the St. Lawrence." I gave a start. That was right here, home base.

He went on; perhaps he hadn't noticed. "I've been on it when we took a pounding from aircraft. But this particular day it was so quiet and peaceful that we cruised on the surface with the hatch open. To breathe fresh air was marvelous. And there was a tranquility over the scene.

"It was a crisp autumn morning, very early—about five or five-thirty. I remember a little cabin among pines, smoke curling already from its chimney. The captain called to me from the bridge, 'Looks like home, eh?' At which the engineer pipes up,

'In my hometown the baker lived in a little house just like that. He used to make Brötchen.' "

Erich looked over at me. "You've got to taste Brötchen sometime, it's a roll, very crusty. Freshly baked, it's part of the traditional German breakfast. . . . Slipping along between the banks of the St. Lawrence, that's what we thought of, not of war, not of pursuing or being pursued—but of those warm morning rolls and a mug of coffee or hot chocolate."

"You make it sound so normal," I said grudgingly. "A Sunday morning outing on the St. Lawrence. And torpedoes at the ready?"

"I'm just trying to say that one side isn't all white and the other totally black."

"It *is* totally black. Look around you at this ward."

This silenced him.

His dressings needed changing, all three, abdomen, thigh, and hand. No matter how delicately I went about peeling off the saturated gauze, his breathing quickened, and in a flood of words he began speaking of a great winding staircase with marble balustrade, along which slipped that shadow boy peering down at the party below—"I would sit still as a mouse on the stairs, looking into the music room while they put on amateur theatrics or a musical evening."

The dressing was off now, and he spoke more calmly, telling me that when he was older, he himself played at these concerts. He must play very well because his face softened and took on a distant expression when he spoke of music. "I wonder if I'll ever get this arm back to where I—" He broke off.

"Of course you will. You'll be starting physical therapy. If you're conscientious your arm will be as good as new."

But there was another skin graft to undergo, and to distract himself from the agony of the aftercare, he said very rapidly, his finger indenting the sheet, "I've made a study of boats. Boats of all kinds. But it's the history of the submarine I find most remarkable. Even the idea of a ship proceeding underwater is remarkable, don't you agree?"

Before I could answer he raced on. "Da Vinci designed an early prototype. But then, he designed the first of everything. The sub I like best is from the thirteenth century. Someone submerged himself in a huge glass bottle."

This effort was more than he could sustain. He converted a groan into a laugh, but he had to talk if he wasn't to disgrace himself and cry. "The first suggestion that came near being practical was when William Bourne, an Englishman, considered completely enclosing a boat and rowing it under water. That was never built. It was another forty years before a craft was actually constructed that could be rowed fifteen feet under water."

"What was that like?" I stepped back to let him know I was finished.

He drew a deep breath. "What was it like? Greased leather was stretched over the ship's frame with close-fitting flaps for the oars."

"Those early inventors must have asked themselves what-if a million times."

"What did you say?" he asked, puzzled.

"Nothing." I was suddenly embarrassed. For I had been thinking how extraordinary it was that an Indian girl from Alberta should come to know the history of early submarines. Too bad that fantastic ideas such as glass bottles had to end in worldwide war and destruction.

Seven

WHEN I GOT back to my room Mandy was sitting on the edge of her bed waiting for me. "You're late again tonight, Kathy."

"You're a fine one to talk. I haven't seen you back here this early in weeks."

"What have you been doing?" It was not said casually, but in an accusatory manner.

"Nothing. Writing a few letters for the men."

"For a particular one, don't you mean? An officer off a U-boat. Kathy, you're spending too much time with him. People are beginning to talk."

"That's nonsense, you're imagining it."

"I'm not. It was brought to my attention and not in a nice way either."

I couldn't believe what I was hearing. "Mandy, if you're talking about Erich von Kerll, he's a patient. He can't use his right hand, so I'm writing home for him. I don't think I'm breaking any international laws or codes of conduct."

"Still, you must consider how it looks."

"I don't care how it looks. I consider it part of my duties as a nurse. Besides, what I do on my own time is my business."

"People are talking, Kathy."

"Let them."

"Have it your way. Knowing you, I know there's nothing wrong with it. Still, it does seem funny, spending so much time with a German."

"He's not German, he's Austrian."

"Big difference," she said with a shrug. "Besides, why be mad at me? I'm just trying to be a friend, letting you know what the scuttlebutt is."

"I'm not mad at you. I'm just telling you not to pay any attention to that kind of petty gossip."

Was it the reflection in Mandy's glasses that gave her a speculative look? "He's the third bed on ward B, isn't he?"

"Yes," I said shortly.

"I thought so. The good-looking one. No wonder they're talking."

Was he? Was he good-looking? I'd been afraid to make such an assessment myself.

"Don't pretend you hadn't noticed." Then a note of real concern stole into her voice. She was no longer passing along other people's opinion but focused on her own. "You've got to remember, Kathy, he's European. Austrian, German, it doesn't matter. They're a lot more traditional than we are."

"What do you mean, traditional?"

"I guess I mean bigoted. I don't want you to be hurt, Kathy."

"Because I'm Indian? Is that what this is about? Mandy, you are so wrong. Things aren't on a personal basis."

"Are you sure?" She peered at me intently and there was no way I could any longer misinterpret the anxiety of her glance.

"Mandy, you think I don't realize the difference between Erich and me? His grandparents have an estate on the Bodensee. It goes right down to the water's edge. He had his own sailboat when he was nine." I stopped abruptly. "I'm not crazy, Mandy."

"But you *are*. You're reckless, like me, when you love. So I had to make sure you weren't edging that way."

Her glasses looked a little misty to me. I diverted her with Erich's stories of early submarines. "Did you know they once sent someone down in a bottle? Then they tried rowing along the bottom."

She started laughing when I told her about the model they built with wheels to roll along the ocean floor. "There's an American version too, the *Turtle*, in the shape of a walnut standing on end."

I had succeeded in distracting Mandy and making her laugh. But I took seriously the fact that I was the subject of criticism. Did they think that while U-boats were sinking our ships, drowning our men, I had been discussing submarine warfare with an enemy?

I was horrified that such an interpretation had been put on our talks, and I searched my mind. Had I been guilty of indiscretion? I felt confused. At the same time, angry. I was not doing my country any harm. Who did I hurt by absorbing the life of an Austria that didn't exist anymore? I had only been listening to an outdated chapter of history.

As for Mandy's fear that I was becoming interested in him—of course that was nonsense.

I WENT AGAIN after chapel Sunday to visit Erich, but I didn't offer to write letters and I didn't stay long. Just long enough to let whoever was concerned know I wasn't intimidated by gossip.

And long enough to settle the question of his appearance for myself. His features were finely drawn, yet there was strength in them. His light brown hair fell forward over his forehead in a boyish manner. But his mouth was set in too hard a line as though he was watchful and on guard. I suppose he was. After all, he was a prisoner and an enemy. And yes . . . he was good-looking.

Why hadn't I noticed that immediately? Or had I, and not wanted to complicate things by thinking it? It took a world war for my kind and his to meet and talk. And I mustn't forget it.

I began to doubt that it had all been as innocent as I pretended. Had I been attracted to him from the beginning, in spite of professional ethics? In spite of a chasm of differences between us?

Mandy had been a friend after all, and quite right to point out the danger I'd been headed for. I would keep this and every other visit short and impersonal and never speak of submarines again, even if they were thirteenth-century glass bottles.

He watched as I straightened the things on his night table, gave him medication, and turned to go. "Must you leave so soon?" He hurried on, I think to prevent my leaving. "I received a Red Cross package today. Amazing when you think of all the frontiers on both sides it had to pass through."

"Was it from home?"

"My parents received the customary letter from submarine command: 'missing in action.' "

"What a shock that must have been. I'm so sorry."

He regarded me levelly; his gray eyes held a question, but he didn't ask it. Instead he said, "I've been awarded the Iron Cross."

"Oh." I could hardly congratulate him. The pause was awkward. "It must be a relief to your family to know you're alive."

He nodded. "I wonder if they'll get the letter you wrote for me before the war ends?"

"I'm sure they will."

"I don't know. I haven't seen a newspaper or heard the radio since I've been here. We were supposed to be winning the war. It was supposed to be over by now. Is it possible that we will lose? I never considered that might happen. What would it mean for

Austria? Would my father's party, the old Social Democrats, regain its position, I wonder?"

His talk of war and politics made me nervous. "Is there anything I can do for you before I go?"

He pulled himself from revery to the present.

"Are you meeting someone? A young man? Is that why you're dressed up and look so pretty?"

"Goodbye, Erich."

"Kathy, I'm sorry. Please forgive me. I haven't much to do except lie here and think. I think about you a lot. I wonder what it's like to be an Indian in Canada."

"Not now, Erich."

"Is your young man white or Indian?"

"I don't have a young man. He's Indian," I said over my shoulder as I left the room. I was so flustered that I ran into Sister Magdalena. "Sorry," I muttered.

IT WAS UNSETTLING to have claimed Crazy Dancer as my young man.

Was that how I thought of him? But I hardly knew him. In fact I very much doubted that anyone could know him. And my mind rocketed between two worlds. The only thing they had in common was that both were insubstantial. The pictures in my mind were of an idealized courtly life on the shores of the Bodensee, where Erich played American jazz records till morning. Which didn't stop him clicking his heels and bowing over the hands of ladies. These fragments broke and distorted as pounding moccasined feet trampled them into shards.

But it isn't possible to have a meaningful relationship with someone you see only intermittently. And it had been almost four months. Spring was trying to burst out of its frozen straightjacket, buds were thrusting tentatively but the coldness of the air nipped them back.

It was grand walking weather, and I returned to my room for a sweater. A walk would help clear my mind. I had to sort out my feelings, put things in order. But when I returned to my room it was to find a crisis. Mandy didn't know it was a crisis, but looking at her I knew instantly.

Mandy was dabbing hydrogen peroxide on her hair.

"What are you doing?" I asked, taking the bottle from her and checking the label.

"I thought I'd put some blond highlights in my hair."

"Mandy, this isn't that kind of peroxide. It's medicinal."

"I guess you're right. It hasn't made any difference."

"Just wait," I said.

In half an hour bleached white streaks appeared. Mandy flew about the room tearing at it as if she could tear it out.

"What will I do?" she wept.

"Sit down," I said, and began to brush her hair from underneath where the peroxide hadn't penetrated. The strands blended and, to finish the job, I set her nurse's cap on her head.

"Oh, Kathy," she exclaimed, surveying herself in the mirror, "you saved my life."

I smiled at her extravagance.

"At least you saved me from a tongue-lashing by Sister Ursula."

I agreed that was quite likely.

I took my sweater from the hook on the back of the door and went for the walk I'd decided on earlier. I got as far as the parking lot, when there was a cacophony of sound as a car horn was depressed again and again. I looked over at the distraction and saw it was aimed at me. I stood still, my mind not registering what I saw.

Crazy Dancer leaped from a decrepit car, leaving the door ajar. "Is it you? I can't believe it."

"I came for our date."

"What date?"

"The one we made last June, the Moon When the Ponies Shed—" He burst out laughing. "I put in for a transfer, and it finally came through."

He looked so jaunty standing there that I joined in the laugh. "I was just thinking about you, and you turn up."

"Were you thinking that Christmas was a long time ago?"

"Something like that."

"I was thinking the same thing."

I walked over to the car. "What happened to the motorcycle?"

"You said you wanted four wheels. So I made a trade."

I surveyed his acquisition somewhat dubiously.

"It's in good running condition," he assured me.

"What about gas?"

His face lit up—he'd been waiting for me to ask. "It doesn't run on gas. Well, just to get it started. Look at this."

I walked around to the driver's side with him. He opened the hood and pointed out a nest of metal tubing and what looked like a second carburetor. "It runs on a mixture of kerosine and gasoline. Mostly kerosine. There's a separate throttle that feeds the kerosine into the engine."

"It won't explode, will it?"

His smile was teasing. "Do you still have the gray and white feather?"

I nodded. "Well, as you say," I conceded, "it has four wheels."

He came around with me while I got in, then walked back to the driver's side. He fiddled with the controls and the engine started up. It sounded just as an engine should and I hoped it would behave like one.

Crazy Dancer shifted his feet. "Here we go!"

As we pulled out of the parking lot I asked, "And it's running on kerosine?"

"You bet."

"Why doesn't everyone use such a device?"

"It's not legal."

I absorbed this a moment, then said, "You're very good at adapting the white man's inventions."

"Pretty good," he admitted.

"You should meet Georges. He likes to fool around with motors, but he isn't as good as you are."

"Georges is your brother?"

"Yes, he's Connie's twin."

"You didn't tell me they were twins."

"I didn't?"

"Twins. Did you know that everything of importance in the world is a twin? Rain is the twin of sun. Mountains the twin of valleys. Hot is the twin of cold. Good the twin of bad. Which is he?"

"What do you mean, which is he?"

"The good or the bad, the left-handed or the right-handed?"

"They're both right-handed."

"That can't be. The right-handed bring berries, fruit, and flowers to the world. The left-handed, nettles and briars. The right hand made all the animals except the grizzly. The left hand made the grizzly to kill the rest of them."

"A fairy tale!"

He shook his head. "Twins balance the world."

"The world doesn't seem very balanced to me."

He looked troubled. "The Grandfathers never dreamed this world. Perhaps it is as you say, fairy tales."

He seemed so dejected at this possibility that I said, "I didn't mean *everything*, only that my twins are both right-handed."

"Perhaps," he probed the question, "it is different with white twins." This explanation restored his spirits.

We were driving past some of the ugliest scenery I had ever seen, acres of nothing but railroad tracks, freight cars, and switch engines.

"Where are we?" I demanded.

"These railway yards are what keeps Montreal in business, and fed also."

We were bound, he told me, for Ile Perrot at the confluence of the St. Lawrence and the Ottawa, with only primitive and deserted dirt roads.

"You picked a rough place to drive."

"No," he said, "it's for you to drive." He stopped the car and insisted I change places with him. "It's your turn," he encouraged.

"I don't drive."

"I thought so. I was testing you out on some of those curves back there."

"What do you mean?"

"I purposely came up to them too fast. If you drove, you'd automatically press your foot to the floorboard like it was a brake. And that's your first lesson. You don't speed up approaching a curve. You speed up *in* the curve. That way centrifugal force gives you more traction, especially if the curve is banked."

I thanked him for the lesson and wondered what was next. It turned out the second lesson was to get the feel of the car, know where it was on the road.

"Most drivers haven't the faintest idea where their wheels are, how close to the shoulder, how close to the dividing line. They make left turns too flat, and they can't back into a parking space unless it's the size of an eighteen-wheeler because they don't know where their wheels are."

I began to protest. "This is supposed to be a fun date." He

replied there was nothing more fun in the world than driving, if you knew what you were doing. He said it was like dancing, only with wheels instead of feet.

I made a last attempt to get out of it. "If I'm going to learn, it ought to be on a regular car, not one with two gas pedals."

He brushed this aside. "Start the engine on gas, and all you have to worry about is the kerosine pedal. The trick is to go slow, stay in first, and know exactly where your wheels are." To practice this he fished out of the trunk some beat-up highway cones swiped from a construction job, and laid out a mille miglia on that country road.

Crazy Dancer was right. It was fun doing a slow-motion ballet with an automobile, knocking over cones in the beginning but finally squeezing through them. Until I got the hang of the clutch, I achieved some nasty jerks and stalls. However, I braced myself against the wheel and had the satisfaction of seeing Crazy Dancer get the bumps. He took it gamely, encouraging me with a soft patter of praise, and only when we were headed for a boulder did he grab the wheel.

"A little practice in the city, and you can get your license."

He came by the following day to give me a short course in engine maintenance and how to hot-wire the ignition in case I forgot my keys. We disassembled and reassembled the two carburetors half a dozen times and checked the tubing before he was satisfied. The fuel pump was the next order of business, then how to jump-start a dead battery. Belts and hoses were Crazy Dancer's particular joys, mainly because on this jalopy they were always slipping, wearing out, or leaking.

At the end of the session, with dusk settling in, he sent me back to take notes and draw diagrams. I'd become pretty good at this in my anatomy course and mentally substituted engine parts for body organs. The fuel pump was a heart. Air intake and carburetor were bronchi and lungs. Transmission was muscle, and electrical system, nerves.

Our next date I showed Crazy Dancer my sketches. He was delighted and gave me a crash course in sectioning and dimensioning. I got covered with oil and the muck under the hood, but that wasn't much different from an operating table.

To crown my success Crazy Dancer announced I was ready for the last and final test. It turned out this was to drive an army truck, which a buddy of his had parked up a side street. Other than the fact that everything was outsized, I had no trouble. My reward was a big hug and an old grease-stained race driver's cap which he set on my head.

Back at the wheel of his own car, he drove us out to the Ile Perrot.

"You know," he told me, "I think you are three things: a spider, a turtle, and a lark."

"Is that good?"

"Very good. A spider is industrious. *You* work all day at the hospital. A turtle is wise. *You* ask questions. A lark is sweet singing and happy. *You* are Oh-Be-Joyful's Daughter."

"Yes, but I have to remind myself that I am. That I should try to be."

Crazy Dancer thought about this and did not like it. "No, trying won't do it. You *let* yourself be joyful."

"And if I'm not?"

"Then I'm here to help."

He waited expectantly for my answer. "I don't know, Crazy Dancer. We're so different."

"And so alike. We are more alike than you think."

"I was raised white and I'm trying to learn to be more Indian. You were raised Indian and you would like a piece of the white world."

"I like their cars and their motorcycles. I like engines. But the whites themselves? Sometimes I think they hate everything. They hate the animals and move into their hunting grounds. They hate the forests and cover even the grass, paving it until not a blade shows. They hate water, and spill oil and wastes into it. They even hate air and make it thick with smoke."

"They make war on everything," I agreed.

He nodded sagely. "It is the reason we have two souls."

"People have two souls?"

"You didn't know that? One is linked to the body. The other is your free soul, the one you send into dreams."

"I was sent a dream once, when Papa Mike died."

"Did you know that a soul can get lost in a dream?"

In spite of myself I felt alarm. "Is that true?"

"Sometimes it runs away on purpose. Then a shaman goes after it to bring it back."

"I can understand why it would run away. You can dream so many more beautiful and interesting things than just the ordinary everyday things around you."

Crazy Dancer frowned at me with a stern expression. "Nothing is ordinary. Nothing is everyday. You need practice in how to look. I have taken you to where the forest comes down to the sea. Let's walk awhile and I'll show you what I mean."

He stopped the car and gave it a little pat. "It did well, don't you think?"

"Yes, very well. You could patent your invention—if it were legal, that is."

He walked ahead of me. Here on the island the trees seemed to grow from bald rock. "We make an earth walk," he said. "I will teach you how to look. First, at this." He rubbed the frost from a boulder with his sleeve. "Once I found a shell in its deepest crease. At one time, I think, the sea covered it. And over here"—he sprang lightly, rock to rock—"here is a tracing, an imprint in the granite itself, made by a piece of fern in the before time. Observe the pines: each has its own pattern on its bark, made by winds, snows, rains, and flowing sap. See the down-drooping needles of the hemlock and the straight spurs of the pines. Now see last year's nest in that one."

"Where?"

Our feet crunched on the last snow patches. At the edges they were melting.

"Where I'm pointing. It was a martin's. Now," he said, "close your eyes and listen to the voice of the forest. Hear the buzz of gnats, the crickets' chirp, the deep note of the bullfrog, the rustling of baby quail. That raucous cry is a jay. These sounds tell you that the forest belongs to anyone who can see and hear and breathe it."

"Is that true for the whole world? How rich I feel!"

He threw back his head and laughed. When he lowered his face to mine, I was conscious of him as I never had been of anyone before. Tamarack, pine, and hemlock were part of him, and a man's scent. I knew I was going to be kissed in a way I never had been kissed.

My eyes closed. Somehow I knew his closed too as he tasted my return kiss. For my arms had gone around him. My free soul climbed out of me into him.

When he stepped back we looked a long time at each other. Each was thinking, Is this the person I love? I wanted it to be Crazy Dancer and he wanted it to be me. But was it?

"Let's go back," I said.

On the return trip we were both rather silent. That kiss I think had been as much of a surprise and shock for him as it had for me. And he too was trying to evaluate it.

He took me to the nurses' entrance but didn't kiss me again. I thought he would, but he didn't. Of course, he was Indian; he had never heard of the custom of the goodnight kiss that white girls granted white boys when they had a nice time. I remember Mama Kathy telling Connie, "Some boys try to persuade you they're entitled to more, but they're not. They've had the pleasure of your company."

I laughed at this, knowing Mandy had allowed Robert much more than the goodnight kiss. Before I was even in the door I was looking forward to next Sunday. And, what was best of all, all week I was Oh-Be-Joyful's Daughter.

For some reason the rich images Erich Helmut von Kerll stirred my imagination with no longer made an impression. The childhood he spoke of seemed remote and alien. In fact it seemed a bit artificial. Winters he skied at Cortina del Ampezzo just across the border, where the Hapsburgs' hunting lodge had been. In his parents' time it was turned into a fashionable hotel. He described the tiled stove going to the ceiling with beds built into it on either side to keep warm on winter nights, and fluffy eiderdown quilts to snuggle into.

It was vivid, as portraiture is vivid, but no longer real. A good book was more alive, and at night I turned pages, reading after lights-out by flashlight. Still, I enjoyed Erich's account of the Lippizaners, which he rode in the fall. I could picture him stiff in the saddle, hard hat on his head. I'd seen a picture once in a magazine, a red jacket with black velvet collar, silk ascot, and shiny boots. He'd have a riding crop under his arm.

Then I pictured Crazy Dancer, bareback, bare-legged, hair flying, laughing wildly. And I placed myself behind him, holding him tight as I had on the motorcycle. That motorcycle had had some good features after all.

"You seem so distant," Erich said, "so far away—so happy," he added ruefully.

This brought me out of my daydream reminiscence. "You'll

be pleased to know that you're doing so much better that the doctors are thinking of releasing you."

"To prison," was the morose reply.

"It's not a prison. It's a big warehouse that they've converted into a detention center. Lots of prisoners are coming in now. Italian as well as German."

"More than before?"

"Yes, many more. If you count all Canada, there must be thousands."

"So many? Has the tide shifted, then? I don't ask you," he added hastily. "I speak to myself. It's the damn second front, the Eastern Front, just as that little French Canadian said. I am a patriot, Kathy, a good Austrian. Yet if it would shorten the war, even to lose is acceptable. . . . *Gott im Himmel*, my father would shoot me like a dog if he heard me talk this way. And he'd be right." He turned away and flung his arm across his eyes.

"I'm sorry, Erich."

He turned back then, the same unhappy smile on his face. "Tell me about yourself, Kathy. What's it like to be an Indian in Canada?"

"You asked me that before."

"Did I? Oh, God, I don't want to be stuck in a warehouse full of Nazis."

"The war won't last forever, and you'll be going home."

His smile had disturbed me, but now that it was gone there were deep lines in his face. "If you meant to make me feel better, you haven't."

"Sorry."

"That's because the hard part will be not seeing you."

"Thank you. That's very nice."

"I didn't say it to be nice. I don't speak from politeness. I look forward to your visits. They're the only thing I have to look forward to."

"I must tell you I've been criticized for spending so much time with you." I had spoken impulsively. If I could have taken back my words, I would.

He regarded me with an intent probing expression. "And yet you do. Why?"

"Your stories. Mama Kathy used to tell me stories. Then I took over and told them too. But yours are much more interesting. I can picture it all—so elegant, so far removed from my own life or anything I know."

"And that's it?"

"What do you mean? Of course that's it."

"You'll have to forgive me," he said hoarsely. "I'm in love with my nurse. Just like all the others. How many offers of marriage have you had?"

I laughed, but I knew underneath we were both serious. "Less than a dozen this week," I joked, realizing it sounded forced, that I was trying too hard to keep the conversation to something we could manage.

He tugged at a black onyx ring on his finger, pulled it off, and put it in my hand. "In case I don't see you again."

There was a diamond centered in the onyx. I drew away, leaving the ring between us on the covers.

"Think of it as a war trophy, like a German helmet."

"Don't be cruel," I said, closing my hand because he had picked the ring up once more.

"Don't *you*," he whispered.

I turned away and somehow got out of the room. It wasn't until that evening I found the ring in my pocket.

WHEN I CAME on duty next day I discovered Lieutenant Erich von Kerll had been discharged to the general war prisoner population. I flipped through his chart. The skin grafts had taken, and the areas on his hand, thigh, and abdomen were healed.

I didn't know what to do about the ring. I'd planned on returning it to him that morning. Now I didn't know what to do. I couldn't send a valuable ring through the mail. But I didn't know when or even if I would see him again. Connie had described her engagement ring to me in detail, a raised center diamond surrounded by chips, one for each month they had known each other.

A soldier was brought in suffering from shock and internal bleeding. I transfused two pints of whole blood. And so it went.

I grabbed a bite of lunch with Mandy. I told her about the pneumonia case. We'd had to do a tracheotomy on him, and, as Dr. Bennett closed, the patient stopped breathing. "I wrote a letter for him last week, Mandy. He lived on the Bodensee."

"I thought he lived on a farm with his mum."

That gave me a jolt. Why had that slipped out? Why had I mentioned the Bodensee?

No one expected him to stop breathing; he hadn't seemed critical.

The EKG went flat. I willed him not to die.

The floor was mopped, the mop ran over my shoe. Linens were changed; doctors continued rounds; nurses dispensed medicine; cot 9's body, covered with a sheet, was lifted to a gurney. I helped in this and watched it wheeled out the double doors. It was happening in another plane, another slice of time. I wanted to take it up with Sister, complain to staff . . . no one should die when they're nineteen.

By 3:30 my feet hurt and my back ached, and there were still two hours to put in. When my shift finally ended, I decided to forget supper, fall into bed, and sleep the clock around.

Someone was sitting in shadows in the corner of my room. "Don't put on the light," someone said.

"Mandy?" I asked uncertainly.

A shaky intake of breath answered me.

"Mandy." I crossed the room to her. She lifted her face and even in the dim light I could see her cheek was swollen and discolored, her eye puffing and closed.

I was so shocked I couldn't speak.

"I hate him."

I think that's what she said, for she could barely articulate.

"Who, Mandy? Was it Robert? What happened?"

"I'm in terrible trouble, Kathy."

"No, you're not, I won't let him near you."

She shook her head and began crying. "It's not that. It's me. It's what I've done. Oh, Kathy, I'm going to get pitched out on my ear."

"What happened?" I asked again.

She tried to tell me, backed up and started again. My heart turned stone cold: It had to do with drugs. Mandy had been stealing drugs.

She was telling it between dry, hacking sobs, but I already knew. She'd tried to back out and he'd sent this goon after her.

"There was a message from Robert. I was to meet him. We always meet in the park, and he knew I took this shortcut through the alley. Well, this, this man sprang out at me. He had a stocking cap over his face, but I think he might be one of those guys that hang out at the casino. I thought he was going to kill me or rape me. Kathy, no one's ever deliberately hurt me before. He punched me to the ground. . . ."

I tried to calm her. "What about the drugs? When did you start taking them?"

"It was such a stupid thing to do. It started with this osteomyelitis case, a patient Robert had grown fond of. I told you how he empathized. Well, he thought the boy needed more medication than was being prescribed. And the boy himself carried on. Nerve damage, you know, there's no pain like it. Robert kept after me to pinch a couple of grams of morphine. So, stupid me, I saw an opportunity and took some. I thought it was just that once, that the boy would get better and not need it, or . . . you know, die.

"But Robert came to me again. I didn't know what to do. I told him it was too risky, but he kept on and on about it. Finally I agreed and looked for another chance. I was almost caught. Sister Mary Margaret came in unexpectedly and I hid behind those sacks at the back of the storeroom. I was so scared. I swore never to do it again. But Robert convinced me it was humane, the right thing. Only, only . . . the boy was transferred to a neurological center in Boston.

"Robert didn't tell me; I heard the girls talking. That's when I realized—the boy had nothing to do with it, or very little. It was money. He'd lost money, he told me that much, and he borrowed. Kathy, I'm sure it's those people at the casino. They won't stop at anything. They're pressuring him to repay. I know that's what it is." She choked on tears. "Maybe it started with the boy, I don't know. But it's over the gambling. He'd never had money before, and he threw it around. It's my fault too, I didn't ask where it came from. . . . Then the tide turned. He started to lose. He knows how rough those people play and he's terrified. That hurts the most—instead of confiding in me, he sicked this lowlife on me."

I didn't know how to comfort or reassure her.

"They suckered him in, Kathy."

Sin city, Mama had said. "Could you describe the man who did this?"

Mandy shook her head. "I told you, he had a stocking cap over his face."

"But height? Weight? Was he French?"

"Medium height, medium build. And as far as being French, he didn't say anything."

"So there's no way you could identify him?"

She hesitated. "By his hair. He smelled of hair tonic."

"Brilliantine," I said, placing him.

"I'm so ashamed and so frightened," Mandy said into her hands. "Do you think the Sisters will find out?"

I hesitated, but there was no avoiding the truth. "When they take inventory the count won't match."

Of course Mandy knew this. Elongated moments passed between us. Then she began speaking very fast. "I thought maybe you'd fudge it for me. You know, *make* it come out. I hate to ask, but I don't see any other way."

"No, Mandy, I won't do it." I saw immediately that she had expected to talk me around. She'd have to have come from my background to know what being a nurse meant to me. It's not only a career. It's having a place in the world.

"Don't refuse. Don't say no, Kathy."

"I'm not even on that service. It's been months since I worked in the dispensary."

"They're always short-handed. You could request it."

"And then alter the books? No, Mandy."

Another pause filled with unuttered argument. "I'd do it for you."

"Then you'd be very foolish. What I *will* do is get to work on this face of yours. We need ice to bring the swelling down."

"No." She drew away from me. "Either you're my friend and help me, or you're not."

"You're not thinking straight, Mandy. They'll come after Robert again. He can't stall. He's got to pay up. And the only way he can do it is through the drugs. He's going to sic this Frankie on you again."

"Frankie?" Her hand grasped mine in a paroxysm of fear.

"Yes, the name came back to me. There's no question that's who it is. The brilliantine gave him away. I saw him huddled with Robert at the casino."

"I remember. Every time I looked up, he was watching me. You really think he'll come after me again?"

"If you don't give them what they want, yes, I do."

"Robert knows I won't continue."

"He doesn't know anything of the sort. He knows that this one beating didn't force you into it. The threat of more might."

"And he'd be right." Mandy grabbed both my hands. "I couldn't go through this again. Kathy, I loved him. That's the worst part, that Robert is behind this."

I could see the croupier bending forward, raking in the chips, *le rouge et le noir.*

Eight

A TRAVELING FAIR was in town. A few stubbled fields had been transformed with whirligig rides that featured a Ferris wheel and calliope. On the Ferris wheel Crazy Dancer held my hand. On the rocket ride he put his arm around me.

The best part was having our picture taken sitting on the moon. Crazy Dancer studied the small strip of pictures carefully. "Many older Mohawks still won't have their picture taken. They believe that this"—he waved the pictures—"can catch their soul." His voice dropped to a whisper. "If that's so, then I give mine to you and keep yours in return." And he divided the pictures between us.

We strolled past tents and sideshows arm in arm. He bought us cotton candy that dissolved into sticky pink sugar as we ate them down to their paper cones. We passed along a row of flag-draped booths, the Canadian Red Ensign, the French Tricoleur, the Union Jack, and the Stars and Stripes. Crazy Dancer stopped to throw balls at a target of moving ducks. We walked on arm in arm. It was almost dusk. No lights were allowed to show, and the carny was closing down. I hadn't realized we had left it behind until we were surrounded.

A gang of French Canadian toughs began taunting us from behind one of the outlying wagons, telling us to go home to the reservation. One of them came toward us. I saw to my horror he had a gun. He was quite drunk and, going up to Crazy Dancer, kept sticking it in his ribs and telling him to fork over his money.

Crazy Dancer pretended not to understand his accent, and asked politely if he would mind repeating what he had said. The guy repeated his demand for money, but Crazy Dancer only shook his head. "Sorry, I still don't understand. What is it you want?"

The gun was twisted in his side. "Money, you dumb Indian. Money. You understand money, no?"

Crazy Dancer seemed to make a great effort. "You lost money? In that case we must look for it. Where can it be?" And he jumped on top of a packing case and peered through the slats. "Not here." Then, throwing himself at air, he did a complete somersault, landing on a side rail that had been stowed out of the way on top of the crates. He walked this backward, pretending to look to the right and then the left for money. He felt in his own pockets and shook his head. "Not there."

A series of flips landed him on the roof of the wagon, and the next second in the midst of the dumbfounded trio. Pulling off the cap of one of them, as though he still looked for money, he exchanged it for another cap, ramming the first on a totally different head. They stared blankly at him. Crazy Dancer pirouetted madly, cartwheeled exuberantly, and, uttering ear-splitting Mohawk war whoops, began to weave in and out, behind and in front and through them.

"This guy is *fou!*"

"Berserk."

"Crazy, man, he's crazy."

"I'm out of here, *tout de suite.*"

"Crazy Dancer," Crazy Dancer announced, taking a bow.

There was no applause. They ran, and I was still shaking from the encounter. "What a performance. My God, you really can dance. It was unbelievable. When you yanked off that guy's hat I thought it was the end of us. But why didn't you give them money? Wouldn't that have been easier? They might have killed you."

"It is a lesson from when I was young, that many times if you do not recognize evil, it goes away. Just as they are going now."

"So you *did* understand what they were saying?"

"The gun in my side made it very plain." He waited for this to sink in. "Sometimes you ignore evil," he explained. "Sometimes you dance to calm it down, and sometimes you make a game and ask evil to join in."

When I asked Crazy Dancer how he knew which to do, he replied, "How do you know which medicine to give?"

"The doctor writes a prescription," I started to say—when it struck me. Crazy Dancer was the prescription for Mandy. It was Crazy Dancer, crazy and fearless, who would bring Frankie into line.

"I need a favor, Crazy Dancer."

"It's not every person I've sat on the moon with," he replied.

I told him about Mandy, all he needed to know. "Her boyfriend had her beaten up, and she's afraid the same goon will come after her again. Could you stop him?"

He considered this only a moment. "In the days of the buffalo a warrior like me would take his hair, a trick we learned from the French."

"And today?"

"Does he work at the hospital?"

"No. He hangs out at the casino. His name's Frankie."

Crazy Dancer clapped his hand to his forehead. "I know him. He stinks of hair tonic. This will be a pleasure," he added. The relish of his tone alarmed me.

"I hope you'll be careful." I said this, wondering if I should have involved him, because I knew very well *careful* was not in his vocabulary.

A PERSON BURST into our room, a person whose tight curly hair glistened with brilliantine. No men were allowed on the floor, but here he was, disheveled and wild looking, yelling. "Call them off, call them off and we're quits."

I reached out and put my hand on Mandy's arm. She had to stand her ground. She had to face down her attacker.

But I was the one he confronted. "Call off the shadows," he said distractedly, "and I'll do anything you want."

"I don't know what you're talking about."

"Oh you know, you know all right. Indian shadows dancing on my walls, and drums and bells clanging in my head. But when I open the door no one is there . . . nothing is there. I might have thought I'd dreamed it, but this is real enough." He took a tomahawk from under his jacket. "What do you say? Is it yours?"

"No."

"Don't give me that. It's real and it belongs to a real person. No ghost."

"You're right about that."

"Then you know who it belongs to?"

"Yes," I said.

"And it's no ghost, no shadow? It belongs to someone who's going to use it."

"Maybe not. If he uses a tomahawk on you he goes to jail. If he uses ghost dancers there will be no mark on your body."

"Look, this could all be in my head. I don't care whether it is or not. I want it to stop."

"It will stop if you don't come near Mandy or threaten her or let her be threatened again."

Frankie, for that's who it was, fingered the edge of the toma-hawk. "This is the end of it?"

"It can be if you stay away from her."

"I woke up this morning with this thing beside my head on the pillow. I don't know how it got there. I don't know how he got into my room. That crazy dancing was bad enough, a war dance with godawful screeches. But a shadow is just a shadow. I figure the tomahawk is something else, it's for killing, and that now he's threatening to kill me."

"I would read it like that," I agreed.

"But it's over? The Indian magic or whatever it was is over, right?"

"It's up to you."

"If it's up to me, it's over."

BUT IT WASN'T up to him, not entirely.

I was about to monitor a labile blood pressure when I discovered I'd left my watch in my room. I went back for it, to find Mandy there.

She still showed the effects of the beating and refused to be seen, giving out that she had a bad cold. My watch was on the dresser, and, as I fastened it on, the door opened a crack, then more fully, and Robert was in the room. He took one look at Mandy's face and sank down on the bed looking as though he would cry.

"I didn't know. I swear to God, Mandy, I didn't know."

Mandy swayed on her feet. She seemed almost to believe him.

"Of course you knew," I said. "You're the one that set the thing up, that had that pervert waiting for her."

Although he answered me, Robert didn't take his eyes from Mandy. "Nothing physical was supposed to happen, nothing like this. Believe me, he was just supposed to let you know they were planning a little accident for me if I didn't come up with the drugs. They've done it before. They like traffic accidents, that's their thing."

"Oh, my God, Robert."

"The hell with them. Let them plaster me all over the sidewalk. I'd rather have that than—than what happened to you. Mandy, please don't hate me or despise me."

"It was so brutal, the way he grabbed me."

"Oh, God." Robert put his face in his hands. "I'll kill him for hurting you. I'll take that little sneak apart."

"He kept hitting me and punching me until I was on the ground."

Robert lifted a stricken face. "He didn't . . . assault you?"

"I was making too much noise, screaming and crying. No one ever hurt me like that before. You don't even beat an animal like that."

"My poor girl. I don't expect you to forgive me. I'd no idea— why, I'd lay down my own life for you, Mandy."

"You may do just that if you don't come up with the money," I interpolated, because it seemed to me Mandy was ready to rush into his arms. And that was one spectacle I didn't want to witness—*Mandy* comforting *him*.

We three looked at each other in silence, trapped in complexity we didn't want to face.

At last I said, "It isn't only the hospital, the army could be involved."

Robert groaned. "If I could keep you out of it, Mandy, I'd confess my part in a minute and get it over with."

"How could you keep me out of it? I'm the one that took the drugs. Besides, if what Kathy said is right and the army gets to know of it, you'd be court-martialed. It's wartime—they could shoot you."

"Not a bad idea," I said. "But I doubt they will."

Robert turned on me. "Oh, you doubt it, do you? Well, all I know is I've got a great choice: to be run down in the street or face a firing squad."

Mandy, stifling a sob, wound up in his arms after all.

When he left, Mandy let me work on her face, and I was able to bring down the residual swelling with ice. Her "cold" improved, and she resumed her duties.

CONNIE'S WEDDING WAS approaching, and I'd written that I couldn't come. But she telephoned. I heard her ask, and I couldn't say no. I decided on the spot to borrow the money. After all, it was my sister.

The trip was accomplished over a weekend. I traveled, one of the few women, in a train jammed with servicemen on leave or posted to the west coast. The conductor put me up front where he could keep an eye on me, and I kept my nose in a book.

Mama Kathy was at the station. I recalled it later in almost snapshot highlights. Her arms around me made me remember the Kathy I had been. At the church I met Jeff and liked him. He was a big man, sandy colored. Hair, mustache, eyebrows all the same neutral shade.

It was just an impression because Connie was in the priest's private chamber. I stopped at the threshold when I saw her. Mama Kathy had made Connie's childhood dream true. The gown was the one she had described to us for years, the waist tucked with invisible stitches, the scalloped neckline, the filmy skirt cascading over satin. How often had I heard it described! The bouquet she carried, the orange blossoms for her hair—all matched the fairy tale.

I fastened on the beautiful dangling earrings Mandy had given me. The chords of the organ meant a final kiss, and I went with Mama to take my place in the pew.

It played out exactly as it was supposed to. It was her day. Twenty years later, and the groom and tiered wedding cake appeared as if by magic.

IT WAS AN unusually busy week. I must have passed and repassed the nurses' station a dozen times. Sister Ursula came looking for me. "Kathy," she said, "Colonel Boycroft wants to see you."

"What about?"

"It's Colonel Boycroft," she repeated.

This was it. Colonel Boycroft was someone you saw when a complaint had been lodged against you, or you were brought up on charges. Even the room was oppressive, it seemed to close in on you. The colonel, from behind a massive desk, sent a keen glance in my direction. Nothing escaped him, not a strand of hair out of place or a pinned hem you hadn't had time to sew.

He began amiably enough. "Well, Nurse Forquet, you've done very well here. I understand you are in the graduating class. Is that correct?"

"Yes, sir," I said and waited.

"We've all watched your progress with pride."

"Thank you, sir." The more he went on the more nervous I became.

"The reason I asked you to come in is that something disturbing has transpired. Was it last May you did your stint at the dispensary?"

"Let me see, yes, it was . . . ," I was saying on one level. On another I was thinking—It's caught up with Mandy.

"We have just inventoried our accounts and made the unfortunate discovery that the written record and the supplies on hand do not tally."

"You mean some of the medicine is missing?"

"Drugs, Nurse Forquet. This is about drugs."

My heart was pounding. "There isn't a possibility of a mistake in the records?" I asked.

"I wish there were. They've been gone over meticulously. Naturally suspicion falls on those that had access. Now, if you've any knowledge of this affair you'd do well to tell me about it."

I shook my head.

"It's only fair to warn you that the matter is now under official investigation."

"I didn't take the drugs, sir, if that's what you're thinking."

"I'm not thinking that at all. However, everyone who had access this past six months is under suspicion."

"I see, sir," I murmured, because he seemed to expect me to say something.

"My personal belief is that the matter will turn out to involve some outside source."

"Yes, sir," I said briskly, and left his office with a more hopeful attitude. An "outside source" was none of us, but a vague phantom figure to pin the theft on. It seemed to me a good solution. And I turned my attention to my upcoming graduation.

I knew Mama had spent every cent she had on Connie's wedding. I knew they couldn't come, but I wrote anyway. I was glad Connie had her wedding. I remembered how dream-like it had seemed, but I knew Mama Kathy had worked behind the scenes to match it to Connie's expectations. Only Georges was missing from it. But he was showered with descriptions, as we all wrote blow-by-blow accounts. Connie enclosed pictures and a piece of wedding cake.

There were very few times in my life when I was reminded that I was poor, and even fewer that I cared. But for this occasion wouldn't it have been wonderful to send everyone tickets to come to Montreal? What a fine time I would have had showing them the city.

I was graduating six months earlier than originally planned. The ambitious program combining nursing with military training, casualty evacuation, army discipline, all that, had not been feasible. So the military part was postponed, to allow us to become nurses. After graduation we would report to Ottawa to receive a concentrated preparation for battlefield conditions.

The year and a half had passed, one day so like another. Routine melded it together. The faces changed, the names changed, but the cot numbers didn't. The work gradually became more specialized, more intensive, and the responsibility had grown, but it wasn't that different from my first days. Now graduation was only a month away. After that I had no idea what my life would be.

Mandy and I had long conversations on the subject. We agreed that we wanted a posting overseas. After our strenuous apprenticeship we thought it should pay off with actual combat service. Mandy was keen for the Pacific theater. She wanted to see coral sands and palm trees, and experience warmth in winter. It seemed a likely prospect, as the Americans were retaking island after island. But the European front was seeing some of the most hard fought battles of the war. One thing Mandy and I were determined on, we would stick together.

I had sealed up my letter when Mandy came in breathless and flustered. "I just heard, Kathy. They've apprehended someone. But it's all right," she hastened to assure me, "the girls say he's an outsider."

"You mean there really is someone?" I'd convinced myself that Boycroft had tossed that out as a cover for letting things drop. Apparently I had misjudged the situation, and he had no intention of letting it drop.

"Outsider or not," I said severely to Mandy, "we can't let some innocent person—"

"It won't come to that. He's the wrong man. They'll discover that and let him go."

"Maybe," I said, but I knew from Papa Mike that the law could stumble as badly as the rest of us.

"Anyway," Mandy concluded, "Boycroft wants us in his office."

"What, again?"

"Trisha and Ruth too. And maybe some others."

Trisha and Ruth were already there, looking scared and guilty. In real life, I thought, people play their roles backward. The more innocent you are, the guiltier you look.

"Now then," Boycroft began, "it's been brought to my attention that you four were all on duty at one time or another during the tenure of Charlie Smith." He was observing us closely.

Each in turn denied she knew any Charles or Charlie Smith.

"What about you, Kathy?"

"Charlie Smith? I don't know any Charlie Smith either, sir."

"I thought you might. He's an aboriginal. Drives one of the trucks for the army vehicle pool."

"Oh," I said, breaking in on him, "*that* Charlie Smith. Yes, I know him. Surely he's not under suspicion?"

Boycroft tapped the surface of the desk with his pen. "You know what a private's pay is. He had opportunity and motive."

"And he's Indian," I finished for him.

"Now see here," he said, suddenly flustered, but the next moment regained his composure. "That has nothing to do with it."

"Yes, sir." I saluted. The other girls were staring at me. "I'm glad to hear you say so, sir."

This was the point at which Mandy would speak up. She would say something like, "It's Robert Whitaker II you want."

She didn't.

She didn't say anything.

Boycroft dismissed us.

Mandy joined the other girls, forming a small knot in the hall. I ran past them to our room and got the wolf tail from the back of my closet.

"He doesn't have the right kind of name," I whispered into the fur. "The one they call him by, Charlie Smith, won't stand up in court, it won't stand up against Robert Harley Whitaker II. They need to find a guilty party, close the case, get it off the books. A poor Indian called Crazy Dancer fits the bill. You've got to help him."

I heard Mandy at the door and shoved my talisman back on the shelf.

She came in.

"What is the consensus?" I asked. "That the Indian did it?"

She didn't answer.

Without Mandy to back him up there was only Crazy Dancer's word, the word of an Indian.

And if I implicated Robert, put the blame where it belonged? But again it was a question of names, who he was and who I was.

"Mandy, you've got to speak up. Crazy Dancer did you a good turn. You owe him, Mandy. For God's sake, Mandy, you owe yourself the truth."

She regarded me stonily.

Apparently Mandy and I had nothing to say to each other. And this was the friend I wanted to share a war with.

I MADE ROUNDS in a preoccupied fashion. If I gave testimony, I saw what the consequences could be. We were both Indians, weren't we? Probably in cahoots. For an army nurse to aid and abet was a serious offense. Was that what I had done? How? By putting ice on Mandy's cheek?

On my way to breakfast Sister Magdalena stopped me with the usual refrain, "Colonel Boycroft—"

"I know—would like to see me."

The stiflingly small room held the same young women, but I was scarcely conscious of this. I focused with every sense in my body on Crazy Dancer. He was standing there, looking debonair, even genial. Boycroft, I'm sure, had been affable. And Crazy Dancer would have expanded on his answers. Especially when the girls came in. Had he told about doing a shaman dance? Poor, vulnerable Crazy Dancer. He had no idea how serious the white man considered this, and probably figured that since they were on a wrong tack, the whole thing would blow up in their faces.

Each of us in turn was asked to identify Mr. Smith as the private who delivered the medical supply shipments.

"Yes, he's the one."

"It's him."

I too nodded in the affirmative and uttered, "Yes."

Surely Mandy—But looking at her, she appeared cool, restrained, and in perfect control. "I'd recognize him anywhere" was her contribution.

When it was too late, when a pair of uniformed MPs came in and took out handcuffs, I could see realization set in. This wasn't a game. These people were going to take him into custody, arrest him.

Up to now Crazy Dancer had avoided looking at me, afraid I would spoil his fun. Now, with a bewildered glance he sought me out.

My eyes fell before his expectant glance. His wrists were clamped behind his back, and he was marched from the room.

Mandy was waiting for me in the hall. "Don't worry about Crazy Dancer. It's just to throw them off the track, delay things while we think what to do. I know I can count on you, Kathy. I never doubted your loyalty."

I pushed her roughly into the storeroom.

"As it happens, you're right. I am loyal. But my loyalty is to Crazy Dancer. If you think I'm going to let Crazy Dancer take the fall for Robert, you're wrong. It's Robert's mess, and one of you is going to clean it up. If you don't go back in there and tell Boycroft the truth, I will."

"You're sticking by him because he's Indian."

"There's also the fact that he's innocent," I reminded her.

"That's why it isn't as serious for him as it is for Robert. For Robert it means court-martial—maybe even . . . You can't ask me to do it."

"I'm not asking. I'm telling you, you have to."

"I can't, Kathy. I simply can't do it."

In a way I was proud of her not being able to. Of course she couldn't. She loved him.

"And what about me?" she went on. "If I tell on him, I'm dragged in."

In spite of myself I almost smiled. I had never known Mandy to put herself second before.

"After all, I'm army too. What if I'm sent to prison? I'd die. My family would die. They would never get over it."

"I think they would." But mention of her family shifted my thinking, and I struck out in a new direction. I remembered the Brydewell plaque in the hall. We shouldn't leave her powerful, influential family out of the equation. "You've given me a clue. Your father's a lawyer. You've got to phone him, level with him."

Mandy recoiled in genuine horror. "You don't know him or you wouldn't ask me to do such a thing."

"It's the only way. I'll place the call for you."

"You mean right now? I tell you I can't."

"You can."

"All right, I *won't*. I'd rather die."

She had repeated that once too often. "If that's your decision, very well."

Mandy shot me a wide-eyed glance. I could see she was struggling. But there was no question, we had to have help. And there was no one else.

"All right," Mandy capitulated, "place the call."

We went into a vacant office, and she guarded the door while I dialed the number she gave me and handed her the phone.

It was her father's office, and she was passed through a receptionist and a secretary. I stood beside her as she cleared her voice. She began by asking how everyone was, including the dog. Then in a rush of tears the whole miserable story poured out.

She listened intently to her father's reply. He did not modulate his voice, and I heard enough to know his decision was final.

Mandy hung up and looked at me. "I hate you."

"He isn't coming?"

"He is!"

Mandy walked away without another word.

I had nothing to say. I had answered the appeal in Crazy Dancer's eyes. What else could I do?

NEXT DAY MR. Brydewell arrived. He was the eye of the storm, a gentleman used to having his way. Jurors must have felt this and quailed before him—judges too. He came in, trailing an expostulating Sister who was explaining that there was an adequate waiting room on the floor below, and that gentlemen were not allowed. . . He paid no attention but demanded that we accompany him to the office of the Mother Superior.

Colonel Boycroft was already there. The size of the room and the opulence of the appointments, in such contrast to his own cramped quarters, seemed to diminish his authority. There was no armed guard at the door, but the nun who acted as receptionist was as formidable.

Brydewell was quite at ease in these surroundings. He neither threatened nor bribed. Addressing Reverend Mother with deference, he said how delighted he was to meet the head of an institution that his family had been connected with for years. He let her allude graciously to the gold perpetual donor plaque, and even managed a disparaging gesture.

Turning to Boycroft, Brydewell mentioned his own service in World War I, and dropped the names of a couple of majors and a general. When his daughter telephoned, relaying the salient points of this unfortunate incident, the first thing he'd done was inquire into the reputation of the officer in charge. And he could report quite honestly that he heard fine things about the colonel's integrity and fairness. At which point his mind was much relieved.

Brydewell accepted a cordial from the hand of Reverend Mother, and continued. Regarding the matter at hand, a confused and totally incorrect version had been bruited about. It misrepresented the circumstances grossly. Regrettably, his own daughter, while in the care of the good Sisters and on his, the colonel's, watch, had been abused and physically beaten into taking a part in this wretched affair.

Without mentioning the word *lawsuit*, the implication was there. He left no doubt he considered the hospital extremely remiss in its supervision. If not exactly *in loco parentis*, the institution had a responsibility for young people who volunteered to serve their country. The fact that the true criminal was a member of the hospital staff and most particularly an army doctor placed the armed forces in an awkward position as well.

Mother Superior listened attentively, offered no defence, gave no advice, and rendered no judgment. However, she radiated a benign atmosphere of reconciliation, so that at the end of the interview both men understood each other perfectly, set down their drinks, and shook hands with great cordiality.

I felt dazed. I didn't know exactly what had happened.

When I got back to our room, Mandy was packing. "They won't let me graduate. After all the work I put in. Isn't that the pits?"

I put my arms around her. "Mandy, you don't know how lucky you are."

She shrugged this off. "My dad isn't going to do anything for Robert. He told me he deserves what he gets. The only good thing to come out of this is they're releasing Crazy Dancer."

"The only charge they could have held him on was being an Indian."

"Kathy, I wouldn't have let anything really awful happen to him. I intended to come forward if, well, you know, if things got worse."

"I believe you, Mandy. You always were soft-hearted."

"Soft-headed, you mean."

"That too," I agreed.

At lights-out, after the final bell, I heard her bed creak. I reached out my hand, but she wasn't there.

I sat up. I could discern her by the glimmer of moonlight. She pulled her skirt on over her head, got into her coat, and came, shoes in hand, to the side of the bed.

"I'm going home with Dad in the morning. And in the morning they'll arrest Robert. But it isn't morning yet."

GRADUATION!

The day came at last. But neither Mandy or I would be seeing palm trees. I'd had an interview with Reverend Mother, in which she asked me, after I finished the three-week officer training course, to return to the hospital as nurse instructor. The position was traditionally offered to their top graduate, and she thought I would be of most service helping train the new crop of student nurses.

I didn't mind. With Mandy gone, the adventurous aspect was gone too. To me war was simply a vast ravening horror that mutilated and maimed. Where I confronted its carnage made no difference. If I was wanted here, here I would stay.

The line of graduates, of which I was a part, straightened in anticipation as Mother Superior welcomed the audience, which consisted of the Sisters, a few ambulatory patients, and a sprinkling of friends and family who happened to be local. I was conscious of the gap beside me where Mandy would have stood.

Poor Mandy, no one spoke of her. They had reprinted the program, erasing her name. I rearranged the yellow roses in my hand as the line prepared to move. This hard-won day, the day I had looked forward to for a year and a half, was not the wonderful, exhilarating event I had hoped for. There was no one here for me. I hadn't expected there would be, but I felt a twinge thinking of Mandy, thinking of Mama, Connie, Georges. I had hoped Crazy Dancer would be in the audience. But he wasn't. The long line began to move.

Then I saw him. Crazy Dancer must be going on Indian time because he was late. This didn't embarrass him in the slightest. He came down front and took an aisle seat. People noticed and pointed him out; the drug debacle was fresh in everyone's mind. And the entire hospital was following the court-martial of Robert Whitaker II. The sentiment that predominated seemed to be: "I hope they throw the book at him."

But that didn't happen. I'm sure that Robert was not the first young officer to stand before an army court, humbled and repentant. The fact that it was wartime loomed large in determining judgment. The accused was a surgeon. They needed surgeons. Especially in North Africa where Rommel was pounding away at Monty's Eighth Army. It was explained to Robert that there was such a thing as hazardous duty, and if he were to volunteer for it, that would go a long way toward squaring things.

Crazy Dancer appeared unaware that he was a subject of interest. He had come to see me graduate. And as I stepped up to receive my diploma from Mother Superior, I felt a surge of— not happiness, but joy. I was Oh-Be-Joyful's Daughter.

With a whoop I sailed my cap into the air, and Crazy Dancer caught it.

I DIDN'T SEE him until Wednesday, which was odd. He never came on a Wednesday.

I ran out to find out what was up. "It's Wednesday," I said.

"A good day," he replied, "to visit my mother."

"Your mother?"

"Yes, I think it is time. She is a whirlwind of a woman, on the council, into politics, and, besides that, a recognized power woman. She will make the blanket ceremony over us."

"The blanket ceremony? Isn't that . . . ?" I stopped, confused, wishing I hadn't started that sentence, hoping he would finish it.

He did, in a straightforward way. "Yes. It is the way we in the First Nation pledge ourselves to each other."

"A marriage. You're asking me to marry you?"

"I am, and in all the ways possible: with Guiche-Manitou looking on, in a courtroom with a piece of paper, in a Catholic church with a priest."

Crazy Dancer loved me. And I experienced the same joy I had

when he showed up at graduation. Joy is a feeling that wraps you and lifts you like frosty breath in the air.

But now Crazy Dancer was saying something else. "I want to know that you are here for me when I come back."

My joy bent like a stalk about to snap, and I waited, knowing, but waiting anyway.

"They called my unit up. We are being shipped out in two weeks."

So this was the way it was to play out. I wasn't going overseas, but he was. I'd seen what shells and shrapnel did, I'd seen the pattern of abscesses under ulcerating skin, I'd dug out fragments of metal, probed for spent bullets.

Crazy Dancer said gently, "I see by your worry for me that you love me a lot. You do, don't you?"

"Yes. We traded souls when we sat on the moon."

"And you will go with me to my mother's?"

"If that's what you want."

"It's the way I planned it," he confided. "I sold the car and bought two bus tickets. There's a short walk at the other end, a couple of miles. You won't mind, will you? Because it gives us the price of a dinner out and we can take in a movie. *The Great Dictator* with Charlie Chaplin, how does that sound?" he concluded happily.

I explained to Crazy Dancer that it would take a day to arrange things with the Sisters.

Nine

THAT NIGHT, THE night before I was to get married, I tried to remember—did he actually say, Will you marry me? Did I answer, I will? I smiled and held my talisman against my cheek. This was the last night I would go to bed alone in a narrow virginal white cot. From now on there would be someone beside me, someone waking up with me. I didn't think it would seem strange, because it was Crazy Dancer, and I felt at home with Crazy Dancer.

I was drifting into sleep, and in my dream there was a feeling of loss, as though I had misplaced something. At first I thought it was Mandy I missed. Suddenly, the hairs of my guardian seemed to crisp and stand erect, as they processed a recollection I didn't want . . . making his cot up with hospital corners, settling another patient into it, answering the bell that had been his and no longer was. . . .

Elk Girl said very distinctly into my ear, "What about the onyx ring?"

"It's a keepsake," I said to Elk Girl. "He said so himself . . . a war trophy, like a German helmet." In the same breath he'd said, "I'm in love with my nurse." We kidded about that, they were all in love with their nurses. We took care of them, talked to them, listened to them. Of course they loved us.

My dream shredded into the calm gray fields of sleep. Some time later I looked into thoughtful gray eyes. Elk Girl laughed a harsh laugh.

"It didn't mean anything," I told Elk Girl.

"That's good," Elk Girl said. "Because it wouldn't be very smart to marry one man when you're in love with another."

"It would be a terrible thing to do," I said indignantly. "And I am not in love with an enemy soldier. What kind of girl would fall in love with a German?"

"An Austrian, a gray-eyed Austrian," Elk Girl reminded me.

"I was glad," I told Elk Girl, "when they moved him to the prison ward."

Elk Girl regarded me skeptically.

I reached out my hand to her, knowing it wouldn't touch anything. "It's Crazy Dancer we should be talking about. It's Crazy Dancer. Ask the forces you talk with to look out for Crazy Dancer. They're sending him overseas. Don't let any harm come to him."

Elk Girl continued to regard me with that same unnerving look. "He's in danger all right, but not from enemy fire. Friendly fire is more deadly. It is you yourself who will wound Crazy Dancer and kill his spirit."

"Never! I'd never do anything to hurt him."

"You're marrying him, aren't you?"

Elk Girl faded. She wouldn't stay and listen. So it was Crazy Dancer himself I told. The next morning in the parking lot I said not hello but, "I love you."

His eyes shone, and the spirit in him shone. I set down my suitcase and showed him the guardian wolf tail.

"He travels with us?" Crazy Dancer asked. "Good. He will help us find our way between worlds."

When he kissed me I realized again how far joy is past happiness. Joy is a whole new ball game.

We had a chicken dinner at a colonial-looking restaurant. Afterward we went to the Chaplin film. At first I laughed along with the rest of the audience as I watched Chaplin and his Hitler mustache go through the silly antics of a buffoon. But the laughter dried up. I resented Hitler being portrayed like this, whacky and nutty. One was thrown off guard, no longer afraid. Yet we must be afraid; I was afraid. This fool had reached into the life I was beginning with my young husband, and . . . and God knows what would happen. Separation, that was for sure. He didn't seem to worry, but I did. The thought of being injured didn't bother him. To him bodies, like jalopies, could always be fixed.

Sometimes they could. Sometimes. The film was still flickering on the screen, when I whispered, "Can we go?"

"You want to go?" He was amazed. He'd been having a good time.

Once we were outside the theater I attempted to pass it over, "Instead of watching other people's lives, I want to get on with ours. I want to meet your mother."

"I'll tell her you prefer her to Charlie Chaplin. She'll like that. She says movies are a drug they feed the people, like the old Roman circuses."

"She must be quite a character."

He nodded, agreeing with me. "She's small and her voice is gentle. But she has the soul of a warrior.—Tell me," he added, squeezing my hand, "why in God's name are we talking about my mother?"

We traveled most of the night, and slept sitting up in the bus, holding hands.

Starting a day with Crazy Dancer beside me brought it home. Someday, when the war was over, that was the way it would be.

"Good morning," he said.

"Good morning."

"So this is married life?"

"Don't forget. There's a war to get through first."

He dismissed the war with an impatient shrug.

Our stop seemed to me the middle of nowhere. We freshened up in a filling station and for breakfast had Cheez-its and candy bars.

It was his country we were in, and he pointed out rivers and streams, crest lines and valleys. "I've hunted partridge through this area from the time I was thirteen, and I recognize it just as you would recognize furniture from your house. . . . An old bureau with a chip in the third drawer, that would be where the old elm has fallen. Or a scuffed leather armchair, that's the hill to your right, where there's evidence of landslide."

"Would you want to live near here, once we've set up housekeeping?"

He seemed surprised at the suggestion. "I'm at home anywhere. It all belongs to me, remember?—and to you," he added generously.

Grabbing my hand, he twirled me round and round until we couldn't stand any longer but fell into the grass. We didn't try to disentangle ourselves, but lay with the sound of a cricket in our heads and the sun on our bodies.

I loved his body. It was athletic, supple. He lay against me, relaxed, content it seemed with the tip of my ear. But a second later that wasn't enough for him, he made demands that swept us into other patterns. We met on the other side of our bodies.

Crazy Dancer laid the flat of his hands against my shoulders to push himself away. "We must save this magic for our wedding."

"Just remember that," I said.

We proceeded to the village, a poverty-stricken place with rows of subsidized houses, all small, ugly, and the same. I stole a look at Crazy Dancer. Standing at the edge of these hovels he hugged himself. The proprietary smile on his face told me he was the richest man I knew.

Children appeared from nowhere. We were surrounded by them, noisy, laughing, shrieking kids who shouted his name and pulled on him to get his attention.

"Johnny," he said, recognizing one and hoisting him to his shoulders. And then, "Charlie, you've grown a foot." Charlie was caught up in his arms. A third hooted with pleasure and tugged at his pant leg. Crazy Dancer was considerably slowed in his approach and went forward like a walking bush of birds.

The houses came awake, heads appeared at windows, doors opened. An Indian woman came up to me, and her smile reminded me of someone. Of course—Crazy Dancer.

"The prodigal son has returned," she said in fluent English with a trace of French accent. "And brought me his bride."

He was repeating my name to his mother and to neighbors who gathered around. "Oh-Be-Joyful's Daughter." He said it with pride.

For the first time in my life I had the feeling of wholehearted acceptance, as though I too had come home. I realized of course that the special fondness with which Crazy Dancer was regarded had been extended to me. His choice, his woman, would have been loved no matter who she was.

His mother, Anne Morning Light, like mothers everywhere, insisted that we eat. There were several hasty conferences at the door, and small packages of food passed in. With so many contributions we did not simply eat, we feasted. Morning Light watched with obvious pleasure as we devoured cakes of maize with maple syrup, sausages, and potatoes. Quietly, people slipped into the room and took places where they too could enjoy our enjoyment.

As we ate, Crazy Dancer extolled my many accomplishments to his mother. And what did he mention? Not that I was a fully qualified nurse. Not that I would receive a second lieutenant's commission in the Canadian army. Not that I stood at the top of my class. The thing he was proudest of was the skill he had taught me. "Oh-Be-Joyful's Daughter is a whiz with cars. She knows engines like the back of her hand." And on and on, reflecting the times I'd given the right snap to the wrench in changing a tire while he sat on the curb giving directions, or jimmying the door with a coat hanger while he laughingly dangled the keys out of reach.

I don't think Morning Light knew exactly what to make of this unexpected talent. She smiled and began telling us of the wedding ceremony that would be carried out this very day. There were to be readings from the Gaiwiio, the "good words," followed by draughts of strawberry juice, for it was in the month when strawberries ripen that Handsome Lake was sent his visions.

Morning Light must have given some signal, for the people there sprang into action. We were taken, I by the women, he by the men, to be bathed and purified for the marriage. The ritual was explained to me. It was to be according to the longhouse religion, and again I heard the name Handsome Lake. And coupled with it, Jonathan Forquet.

"My father," I said.

"And her namer," Crazy Dancer added.

This produced an astounding reaction—utter silence.

Then, here and there, someone reached out a timid hand to touch some part of my clothing. I felt my own skin prick with awe. Was I really the daughter of such a venerated figure?

"In this day," Morning Light told me, "Jonathan Forquet is our prophet. The Great Spirit has entered him. He is a holder of Gaiwiio. His mission is to keep the Six Nations People together, to interpret the calendar in the old way of Handsome Lake. He relates the myths and teachings of those times to the present, to show us how to live in a white world. We are dreamers and shamans, and we must understand this. While we fight for autonomy, for reparations, for simple recognition, we must never lose our spiritual selves."

"I know," I muttered, "he tells you to be joyful!"

The small brook wound not too distant from the village. There my clothes were removed, and I knelt with Anne Morning Light and several girls in the water, which they splashed over me, laughing.

I splashed back.

"But we're not getting married," they protested.

"Then you should," and I splashed again.

In this way I was prepared for the blanket ceremony. I thought of Connie and the armful of white roses she carried and the orange blossoms for her hair. "Something old": the dangling earrings from off my ears. "Something new": a lovely brooch Mama bought for her. "Something borrowed": a garter one of the girls at the factory contributed. "Something blue": the ribbons trailing from her bouquet.

My bridal gown was also white, the softest white deerskin imaginable.

The slow padded sound of drums shook from my head the strains of Mendelssohn's wedding march. I was led deep into the woods to a natural glen where people were assembled.

I had no one to give me away. But an Indian woman gives herself away.

The drumbeats increased. I saw the ceremony was to be danced inside a large wheel that Anne Morning Light had drawn in the dust. I stepped inside the circle. Crazy Dancer threw a feathered prayer stick that struck quivering in the ground. With a cry he leaped after it, landing beside me. There were bells on his ankles. Stars had been drawn in the dust, and the sun and the moon and many animals. Our feet danced them away. Making an act of power and an act of beauty, a blanket was laid over our shoulders. We surrendered our shadows to each other. He held mine, I held his.

Crazy Dancer carried me to a hut that had been erected close by in the glade. It was freshly built of sweet willow boughs. The floor was draped with skins, and, tossed against them, my old wolf tail.

The flap was lowered, the world left outside.

Crazy Dancer took off my white deerskin dress and held me naked on his lap. "There are parts of your body that I love more than I should."

"Which parts?" I whispered back.

"Here"—he opened my arm—"the soft part opposite the elbow. And here"—with a finger he closed my eyes so he could put a kiss there too. "And your woman parts, which are so mysterious to me." He explored them, telling me as he did so the difference between white and Indian lovemaking. "I've heard white guys say there are forty positions for sex. They're wrong, it's one beautiful dance, and the lovers flow from one to the next, and on and on, like this and like this . . . ," and I thought I would swoon from the exquisite torture-pleasure that we knew, and relinquished to know again.

Church, flowers, orange blossoms, and an organ . . . they were for Connie, not for me. I had stepped inside the wheel of life.

Food and sweets and drink were brought to our door, and left outside for us.

Afterward, Crazy Dancer told me our honeymoon lasted three days and three nights. For me it was something outside time. When it was over and we were once again back in the world, I still moved like a dreamer.

Morning Light handed me a small bucket, and I went with her to cull wild rice that, she explained, grew in the shallows of lakes and ponds. "It is called spirit rice. No one plants it. It just grows."

It was early fall but the weather was summery, and there were marsh marigolds, lupins, and I spotted pasqueflowers, all growing in profusion.

Tucking up our skirts, we waded along the edge of a small estuary. The water was still, almost mirrorlike except where we broke the surface into ripples. Anne Morning Light shook her head over Crazy Dancer's participation in the white man's war. "It comes of sending him to school. I wanted to teach him myself, reading, writing, some mathematics, and lots of history. But he wanted school, so I warned him, if they find out you're literate you'll wind up in the army someday. And that's what happened."

"I wouldn't worry about him. Crazy Dancer does what he wants to do."

"I sometimes think the Mohawk man is born with an extra gene for fighting. They want to get in on the fighting, no matter who's fighting or on which side. Why should we fight the Germans? They never oppressed us. The British did. The French did. And especially good old Uncle Sam. But Crazy Dancer laughs at all that. He thinks he can leapfrog over problems, put together the white man's machinery, and then they'll have to deal with him, man to man. I tell you it's a dream. It won't happen."

"I don't know, Anne. Things change. Maybe Crazy Dancer can help them change." And I remembered the afternoon Mandy and I had spent in the library. As I felt in the water for the clumps of rice, ripped them up, and began to fill my pail, I recalled my own indignation. I saw that Anne Morning Light's sympathies lay with those who advocated independence from the British empire for Canada, and self-rule for the Mohawk/Iroquois nations. I wondered to what extent one chooses one's wars. Or did the wars choose you?

I don't think we had worked an hour when I noticed a canoe with an outboard motor headed straight for us. It was hardly recognizable as a canoe, its prow standing almost vertical in the water. Of course. Crazy Dancer! He came in where we were, jumped out, grabbed me, and plunked me down on the floor of the canoe.

"We haven't finished," his mother shouted.

He laughed, pulled the cord, and we started up. I leaned out, laughing too, and waved goodbye to Morning Light.

"Was I right? Did my mother treat you to the local political scene? She's such a gentle, quiet person, you wouldn't believe how she challenges rules and anything she thinks racist and oppressive."

"Good for her."

"I don't know. I've had to get her out of jail twice. Once for blocking a doorway, and once for disrupting an official meeting."

"She's fighting for the rights of her people. I admire that."

"I don't know what happened to the way women used to be."

It was a mock complaint, to which I replied, "It's the war."

THE VILLAGE SEEMED to have changed, and in some subtle way even the noise of the children was ratcheted down. The effect was almost that of watching a shadow play. A play of the death of an old chief.

It was Crazy Dancer's mother's uncle. On the way to his cabin Crazy Dancer told me, "Sacred Arrow sent a dream. He wants me to show him the other side, put him on the path to the Grandfathers."

I walked beside my husband, proud that I was to share in sacred ways.

We joined a dozen or more people crowded into the small house. The old man's bed had been moved into the living room to accomodate these well-wishers.

I thought he looked reasonably well for someone on his

deathbed, but Anne, who had caught up with us, whispered, "His generation still believe they can choose their time of death. It's one of the few freedoms they still have."

Sacred Arrow was glad to see Crazy Dancer and, shoving away several small children who tumbled about him, clasped him against his chest in a strong embrace. "I will tell you more about the dream I sent you," he confided. "Three angels came to me. They carried bows and arrows in one hand and in the other huckleberry bushes, and their faces were painted red."

I would never have recognized from this description that these beings were angels. Which led me to speculate that an angel must appear to the dreamer in a form the dreamer would recognize.

"These three angels told me," the dying man went on matter-of-factly, "that this is a good time to make the sky journey. They told me to dream this news for you." He patted Crazy Dancer's hand. "Thank you for coming. I am in luck to have you here."

"Make the trip in these." Impulsively, Crazy Dancer stripped his moccasins from his feet and fitted them onto Sacred Arrow's.

This signaled a new phase and the shaman took his place beside the old chief and began extolling his life, recalling the fine deeds he had done and bringing to the attention of the Creator his many acts of kindness and bravery. This commentary was intoned to the accompaniment of drums.

We listened respectfully for a quarter of an hour. Then, returning to his mother's home, Crazy Dancer prepared for the responsibility laid on him by beginning a fast. "I must howl to the earth, and dance the map of the other world."

"But you don't know it yourself, do you?"

"That's why I thirst and fast. I must be pure so the knowledge will be given to me."

Toward evening Anne Morning Light returned with me to

the old chief's house. By now they had lit a fire in the cookstove, and it was swelteringly hot. Benches had been hauled in and the men sat around chewing tobacco. Tin cans were scattered here and there on the floor as spittoons, but one old-timer, more proficient and more accurate than the others, spat directly from half across the room into the round stove opening. It wasn't a hundred percent, though; a glob of tobacco juice sizzled on the lip of the stove. Children kept running in and out, banging the door. A dipper of water was passed to the dying man, but he waved it away.

The audience waited, I assumed, for the dance to begin. But Crazy Dancer didn't come as a dancer, he came to the accompaniment of mud-turtle rattles, which were pounded on one of the benches. He burst in like thunder, knocked over a bench, rushed to the stove, and, reaching in, scooped up a hot coal which he tossed from hand to hand.

Then, dropping it, he grabbed up handfuls of coal dust and began sprinkling everyone with it. "He is sending the Great World Rim Being on his way," Morning Light whispered. From her tone of voice I imagined this must be the devil. It was a good idea to send such a being far away from where a good man dies.

I watched Crazy Dancer's shadow on the wall. Anne said against my ear that it was the Doorkeeper's Dance. Twirling, leaping, he seemed at times to fly. At others his feet pounded the earth, and he crouched—only to find strength to spring up again. He was a flame of the fire itself, dancing through that night and the next day and the following night. The morning of the third day Sacred Arrow died. He died quietly behind closed eyes.

The children continued to play around the corpse, but Crazy Dancer changed his rhythm. With his feet in the death dust of this world, he led his uncle to the shadow world. Now that Sacred Arrow was traveling west in his moccasins, his obligation was at an end and he danced to lighten the hearts of those who grieved, especially his mother, who was the old chief's favorite niece. He jumped around and clowned and made faces. He was a delight maker and the children laughed their delight while old people blew smoke on him. But in seventy-two hours he'd had neither food nor rest. Still the drums beat. And still he danced.

That was one second; the next he collapsed on the floor, his heaving sides the only indication that there was life in him. I reached him first, going down beside him and laying my head on a rapidly pounding but steady heart. I raised my head, smiling. This man of mine had the heart of a grizzly. A glass of water was put in my hand and I tilted it against his lips. He opened his eyes at once, and they asked, "Have I done well?" Mine replied, "You were wonderful."

We returned with Anne Morning Light to her house, and she busied herself being a mother. She brought food and, when we had finished eating, wrapped up what was left for our journey. Before letting us leave, she cut Crazy Dancer's hair. I understood it was a sign of respect for his uncle. Crazy Dancer had grown up in this house, learned to dance and have fun here, learned the ideals of loyalty to the band and the family. And learned, I could tell by the attention to me, a guest, the strong Indian sense of hospitality.

Going from a wedding to a deathbed seemed ominous to me. But my feeling of premonition was not shared by any, least of all by Crazy Dancer. First Nation people danced and celebrated, almost without differentiation, the milestones of life. Death was simply a further journey.

The kids started a ball game behind the house. Perhaps the old chief stopped a moment to watch.

Anne Morning Light saw us off with something called moose

milk, a homemade drink that had much the effect of bathtub gin. One swallow and you felt as though your eyeballs had come loose.

She took Crazy Dancer aside and told him he had chosen *chaiwootcha*, a good woman. I felt a rush of gratitude toward this sweet-faced scrapper, who thought I would be good for her son. She let us go with the assurance that she would dream us. Dreaming, Crazy Dancer told me, connects the world.

We left, swinging our arms and with a light step. He pointed out kinnikinnick, a little evergreen shrub growing by the side of the trail, whose leathery leaf, when dried, was their usual smoke.

"When we get back to Montreal," he said, "we will marry in a church and get that piece of paper."

The truth was I already felt satisfactorily married. I felt the excitement of our lovemaking and, underlying it, the comfortable feeling that we got on like a pair of old shoes.

"I never worked for money," he said unexpectedly, "only at what I liked."

"I know," I teased. "If it had a carburetor, you loved it."

"If I'd known I was going to be in love with you, I would have worked for money."

"You're poor because you chose freedom," I said stoutly.

"But you'll have nothing now but government checks, and they're not much."

"Whatever they are, they're more than I had before."

He stopped walking and looked at me intently. "There is sadness in you. Is it because I'm being shipped out? Because I can promise you no Nazi bullet has my name on it." He laughed. "They never heard of Crazy Dancer. So I'll come back."

I smiled and said nothing. I had seen some of the boys who came back. Their body parts were disposed of with other wastes. To deflect the conversation I told him a story. Crazy Dancer loved my stories.

"This is a true one," I began, because Indians love true stories best and generally begin their tales that way. "It happened last year, on Sister Egg's birthday. You probably noticed there's a marble statue of St. Francis of Assisi inside the main entrance to the left of the staircase."

"Yes, I've seen it."

"It's large, isn't it? I mean, more than life-size?"

"It's large all right."

"Well, we wanted to play a trick on Sister Egg, she's our favorite Sister. We thought of it as a sort of birthday present. So we set about moving St. Francis to the other side of the stairs, the right side."

"But it must weigh a ton."

"That's exactly right. The idea of the joke was to get a rise out of Sister Egg, have her cry out, 'A miracle! A miracle!' I must tell you it was very hard work. We rolled a rug around St. Francis and fastened it with belts. Then with a jury-rigged winch we loaded him onto a piano dolly. It took forever, but when we finally manuevered the saint into place and un-wrapped the rug, he looked as though he had always been sta-tioned there.

"When Sister Eglantine came down the stairs, she noticed nothing, so *we* rushed out, shouting, 'A miracle! A miracle! St. Francis has walked to the other side of the staircase!'

"Sister Egg stood stock still, then went up to the statue and examined it, shaking her head in puzzlement. 'Well,' she said finally, 'he was in his old location a hundred years. I imagine even saints want an occasional change of scene.'

" 'But,' we chimed in, 'it's a miracle, Sister. Shouldn't you notify Rome?'

" 'The only miracle,' she said, 'is that none of you girls got a hernia.' "

en

NOW WE WERE back in Montreal things that should have been simple were difficult, and ultimately impossible. We had stayed longer than we intended. After all, one could hardly hurry a man's dying. But it did not leave time. There wasn't time to arrange for the church until a week after Crazy Dancer was due to sail. Of course, we didn't need to rent the church itself. I suggested the little vestibule off the Father's office. But there were other weddings scheduled, and several baptisms. Time grew short. And suddenly there wasn't any.

"It doesn't matter," I said. "We'll do it when you come home. Connie will be the matron of honor, and you'll get to meet Jeff. And Georges will be best man. You and Georges will be great buddies. And our mamas will meet and not know what to make of each other, and like each other. And they'll both be proud."

He listened with his head cocked in a look of skepticism. "It sounds good, but it doesn't sound real."

After he left, I remembered his saying that, I remembered how his face had clouded over. It sounded like fantasy to me too. But why shouldn't it happen like that? By then the war would be over, and my family would come. And Anne as well. Why did our wedding seem so misty and unreal?

His orders were waiting. He was to sail on the large troopship in the harbor. The only thing he said about that was, "I don't want you going down to the pier and waving."

So I didn't.

We didn't say goodbye. We found a cheap room to rent. But since we wanted it for consecutive hours of day and night, we paid a ransom for it. It didn't matter. It didn't matter that it looked out on an alley, and trash, and empty beer cans.

In the morning I found he had filled my shoes with flowers. I put my arms around him. With his cheek to mine, he couldn't see the sudden tears. That's how his sweetness affected me. We put the flowers in a water glass and admired them. "Look, even when they're the same variety, their faces are different."

I made him breakfast of things that didn't have to be cooked, and did the same for lunch. Dinner was a short foray, and then back to our cave. We had a whole marriage to pack into a couple of days. He washed my hair. I gave him a back rub. We lay on top of the bed and made lazy love. He pulled me down on the floor and we made frenetic love. I showed him the Twins' Code. "Always let me know where you are."

The idea of a code intrigued him, and he coded a love letter to me on the spot. "Every fifth word . . ." he said as he worked laboriously with a pencil stub.

He taught me Mohawk love songs and war chants. We sang the crazy tunes we heard on the radio:

> *Three little fishies*
> *And the mama fishie too,*
> *They swam and they swam*
> *Right over the dam.*

He told me he understood nursing because he had delivered puppies. "I put this soft, clean muskeg moss under the mother. It's absorbent. We use it to diaper babies. You never see an Indian kid with a sore butt."

I agreed that modern medicine could learn a lot from First Nation people.

Next thing I knew I was confessing one of my childhood tragedies.

"I don't have a birthday. Not really. I was born in the forest somewhere. The closest thing I have to a birthday is the date Mama Kathy and Papa signed the adoption papers, August second."

"No," he decided, "that's not when you were born. You were born when we were married."

And so it went, down to the last minute.

He gave me a cheery grin when he left. There were no important last words. Crazy Dancer walked out of the room and closed the door.

I jumped up, ran across the room . . . and stopped. I didn't open the door. I didn't look after him.

It was my turn to close the door on our little room. It was necessary to take a short walk before returning to the hospital. As far as anyone there knew, I had just taken a leave. They knew nothing about my marriage. That was a good thing, as that part of our plan hadn't worked. In their eyes I wasn't married. Later, when I could talk about it, I might tell Sister Egg. But not now. It was too close, too dear, and too painful.

In the little chapel on the hospital premises I found the sanctuary necessary to reenter my life. One prayer I repeated again and again. "Don't let the Germans discover there is such a name as Crazy Dancer."

Back in my room I wrote my first letter.

Dear Crazy Dancer,

Guess how long you've been gone? An hour and fifteen minutes. There are so many things I didn't get around to telling you. Elk Girl, for instance. She gave me the wolf pawakam when we were in grade school. Then somewhere in middle school she dropped out. She is a very strange person. She has powers. Sometimes I dream her.

I stopped. My thoughts had taken me down a wrong avenue. Elk Girl had said some disturbing things about our marriage. I crossed out the part about Elk Girl and started my letter again.

I went about my duties writing letters in my head. At night I got down on paper the thoughts I'd had during the day. Silly things, like the time Connie, Georges, and I spent the afternoon gathering bright stones to outline the garden path. We soaked them overnight to bring out their colors. In the morning we hurried to look at our acquisitions. They were gray and ugly, all color leached out of them. Why didn't he write?

Of course he couldn't. He was stuck on that damned ship. I wondered if he'd remember the Twins' Code. Of course he would. Every fifth word represented a letter and he could spell out where he was. If I knew that, if I had a setting to put him in, it would be easier.

Everyone complained about the mail. It came when it came. I told myself I'd probably get a dozen letters all at once. I woke in the morning, my face wet with tears.

By noon there was an extra on the street, the news was all over—the troopship that left our harbor ten days ago was torpedoed in the North Atlantic. All hands were lost. How could a German torpedo find Crazy Dancer? Then I remembered, he was listed as Charlie Smith.

My soul, my being, that inmost self fought the printed word, the many words that buzzed about me in the hospital and on the radio. I rejected them. I rejected the possibility that he could be dead. He wasn't dead—he'd promised me. We'd gone under the blanket together. I'd know if anything had happened.

Then I recalled the tears on my face.

I wonder if the dead know they're dead. Maybe they just keep on, frozen in their bit of time, doing the same things in another reality. I kept to my schedule. If anything, I was more efficient than before. The only thing I had to be careful of was the concern I read in Sister Egg's eyeglasses.

"You're working too hard, Kathy."

"No, I'm not."

She shook her head, and I could tell she wasn't satisfied. "Hear anything from Mandy?" she asked.

"No."

"And what about that young Mohawk, the one who used to pick you up in those odd conveyances?"

"Oh, him. He went away."

"He was called up?"

"He's dead," I said. I jammed my hand in my mouth, but it was too late. The word was out.

Egg took both my hands in hers. "Sit down, Kathy. There. Now tell me."

"He was on his way to the war. He didn't even get there. He was on that troopship."

"Oh, Kathy. I think you were fond of him?"

"There's a big wad of undigested feeling stuck in me."

"My poor girl. How difficult it must be."

"I loved him. I loved him, Sister. But what good was it, our loving each other? No good at all, it didn't mean anything."

"Of course it did. Love is the dearest feeling there can be. You were fortunate to experience it, and so was he. If he knew your love, you gave him a great gift."

I fumbled in the pocket of my uniform. "Here. Here he is. We're sitting on the moon."

She didn't take the picture from my hand but bent over it. "Imagine that," she said.

I replaced the snapshot carefully.

"He was a fine-looking young man."

Was, was, how I hated that word.

"You are right, Kathy. Keep busy."

She must have passed the word on. The charge nurse kept me hopping. Once I snapped back, "Can't you see I already have two patients to clean up?" Instead of reading me out, she gave me a look of such tender concern it almost broke my heart. "I'll send Adele in to finish up," she said. "By the way, there's an Indian woman asking for you at the front desk."

It was Anne Morning Light. She had a telegram.

The telegram should have come to me. But of course the Canadian government didn't know about our marriage, and if it had, would have taken no notice of a couple of dumb Indians under a blanket.

Anne Morning Light soothed me with stories of Crazy Dancer as a boy. He had always been fiercely independent, disappearing into the woods for days at a time. He had a ragged paperback, *101 Ways to Live Off the Land,* and built his own wigwam in the woods behind their house. His father made good money as a structural steel worker on high-rise buildings. "He danced too," Anne told me, "at the end of a girder, twenty stories up. He died in an accident. Not falling—a Mohawk never falls. And not from the machinery—machines never betray a Mohawk. No, he did something much more dangerous, he joined the union."

Thinking of that death brought her son's. She broke down, and in that cold, antiseptic, whitewashed waiting room I tried to comfort her. Together, we mourned our loss.

"I don't suppose you're pregnant," she asked.

"No."

"A baby, now. Some part of him. That would have been a comfort."

When she left I went with her. Sister Egg arranged it. It didn't matter much where I was or what I was doing. I moved through empty spaces. Sounds reached me, though, and scenes passed before my eyes. The sun was warm, the sun was good. I registered that. I knew everything that went on around me, yet it was remote, an alien universe.

I took accumulated sick leave and moved in with Anne Morning Light. We didn't so much live together as side by side. We no longer talked or tried to comfort. We knew it was no use.

I went to the stream where I had been bathed and prepared for my marriage. No laughing girls now, no splashing water. The water was still except for a small eddy. I followed it and came to where the ghost rice grew. For a moment I saw his upended canoe, heard his laughter.

I turned away and started back. Here in this forest he had shot partridge, walking softly. If a blade of grass bent, it straightened. And no leaf rustled as they did under my feet. A spring in his step carried him this way where I plodded past the bureau drawer and the rocking chair—those familiar logs and burnt stags and broken boughs. They furnished the world of his growing up.

But looking at them I felt nothing.

"Kathy," Anne Morning Light said to me that evening, "your healing is not here. My healing lies in a return to my life. I'm going to Quebec. They're holding a protest rally for a Mohawk who is under a sentence of death."

"What did he do?"

"It was harvest time, he went back home to bring in the crops. He didn't run off, he didn't hide. The military police knew where he was. They picked him up in his fields."

"Poor thing," I said. "He didn't understand."

"No, he didn't."

"Well, I guess I'll go back to the hospital. It was very good of you to have me—"

Anne shook her head vigorously. "You're not ready to go back to nursing. You need nursing yourself."

I persuaded her I didn't. I persuaded her I was fine. When she left I sat down and didn't get up for hours. Night came and still I sat there. The dark invaded my mind.

Everything was nothing, and nothing everything. Why had that never been clear to me before? I thought not of what I would do, only what I would not do.

I would not go back to the hospital.

I felt I was treading the obverse side of the moon. Vast, dark, hollow. I wandered it. I walked it. Even when I did ordinary things like buying a train ticket, I was wrapped in it. If someone spoke to me, I replied. If they smiled, I smiled back.

But I kept treading the pockmarked face of the moon's far side. Our feet had dangled over the edge, he'd had his arm around me.

Outside, the world rushed by. In the morning, from the train window, I watched the sun come up. It tinted everything a delicate salmon color like the inside of a seashell.

The sun did not come up in my head. It remained dark there.

They called Montreal . . . I made no move. I wasn't going to Montreal.

The train hurtled along. My dark mind looked at the bright fields. My dark mind reached for him. It was one of those soul-shattering moments when it strikes you again, as hard as the first time—I will never see Crazy Dancer again.

He was dead.

Accept it, his mother had told me.

I didn't want to accept it. We hadn't invented a code that would tell me where he danced now.

The darkness grew and blotted out thought, blotted out possibilities, blotted out hope. I musn't trust hope, or possibilities or thought. The far side of the moon is bleak.

The porter woke me, gently repeating, "We're here, miss. . . . Your stop."

Why had I bought a ticket for home? Mama Kathy and Connie were in Vancouver. No one would be here.

Yet it was comforting to recognize—a fenced pasture with the fenceposts leaning and the strung wire sagging—a tree with its center closed over an ancient burn. The tree grew around the black, charcoal wound and continued to live. But when you destroy the center of a person, that isn't possible. Besides, the person may not want to go on. Definitely doesn't want to.

I trudged along the road. I was going home.

No one was there.

I walked all morning and most of the afternoon. I'd forgotten to eat. I felt dizzy and the sun also turned black. When I got to my house, the door was open, so I went in.

Elk Girl surveyed me critically. I wasn't surprised to see her. I didn't ask what she was doing here.

"You look terrible," she said, and put me to bed.

I slept, not through the night, but through several nights. Whenever I opened my eyes Elk Girl was there. She sat beside the bed and did quillwork. "How long have we known each other?" she asked when she saw my eyes open, then answered her own question, "Since we were seven."

She spooned something that tasted of swamp and cattails into my mouth. "Didn't you ever wonder why I was your friend? Why I singled you out? Why I bothered?"

I knew I was not required to say anything. Besides, I couldn't rouse myself, it was too much effort.

"It's because of who you are," she went on.

Who was I? I waited to hear.

"Oh-Be-Joyful's Daughter, the only child of Jonathan Forquet. He came from the mountains and the forests, from the rushing river and the holy places to bring you your name. And with the name he brought you a special gift. He brought you Gaiwiio, the good messsage."

Clang went the gates of memory, memories that were not mine. They danced just out of reach and beyond recognition. I closed my eyes and slept.

Minutes passed, perhaps hours. Elk Girl took up where she had left off. "Do you want to begin at the beginning of the world, or in the middle with George Washington?"

She herself made the choice. "The Great Spirit has an evil twin. Whatever the Great Spirit makes is wonderful and perfect, and the Evil Spirit comes along behind him and tries to destroy his creation. But he is not strong enough to undo it completely—only partly. For instance, currents. At the beginning of the world currents flowed in both directions at once. There was the *coming* side of any river, and the *going* side. So that you paddled your canoe either way without effort. Evil Spirit tried to eradicate currents altogether, but he was only able to do it one way. And so on until we come to George Washington.

"The Evil Being Who Lives on the Rim of the World, in January, five days after the new moon following the zenith of the Pleiades, whispered into George Washington's ear. And General George Washington ordered a scorched earth policy against the Iroquois for siding with the British. They fled over the border into Canada, miserable and starving. Among them was a Seneca named Handsome Lake."

I turned my head away. I didn't want to hear. I had been married according to Gaiwiio, Handsome Lake's "good words." The trouble was they led to my father. My father who was no part of my life.

But her voice droned on. "Sick and without hope, Handsome Lake turned to drink. And he died."

I drifted off with the uncomfortable feeling that was not the end of it.

When Elk Girl continued it was in a declamatory chant. "My great-grandmother was a witness to his death. She was there and saw it. And she dreamed it into me as I now do to you. "

The wooden planks under my feet became a dirt floor. Against the wall, bowed figures mourned an incantation. The man stretched on the bed was not Handsome Lake. For one heart-stopping moment I thought the features were those of Crazy Dancer. But when I knelt, I saw it was Jonathan Forquet. His nostrils were stuffed with ground tobacco leaves. It had been a long time since he had breathed.

I walked with others to the dirge of voice and drum and stopped where they stopped, at a desolate knoll. The grave had been dug in preparation and the wrapped body of my father was laid into it. In the distance a wolf howled.

On the third day the Gaiwiio was recited.

The howling wolf came close. It was white. It went to the grave site and began to dig. It dug and dug. Finally it dug down to grave clothes. But my father was not there.

With a single impulse we turned and there on the summit of a nearby hill was Jonathan.

The people gasped and knelt in awe. Their voices broke and they shrank back afraid.

I was afraid.

He raised his hand in blessing. "I have come from the sky road to bring you a new world. Gaiwiio is old, but I bring it new and full of hope. The prophet Handsome Lake has made known

Jesus's warning—not to follow the way of the money changers, the white men, but to take from the before times of our people and mix this with the best of the white world, giving thanks to the new moon that will arrive again in January."

I woke from my vision hardly able to breathe.

"Did you see?" Elk Girl was almost dancing with excitement. "Did you see the death and rebirth of Handsome Lake?"

"It wasn't Handsome Lake. It was my father."

Elk Girl dug her fingers into my shoulders. "You're sure? It was Jonathan Forquet who came? Your father?"

"It was my father I saw dead. It was my father I saw buried."

Elk Girl covered her eyes and fell on the floor.

"And when the wolf dug up the grave clothes, it was he who stood on a hill and spoke."

Elk Girl said from the floor, "Well, that's clear enough." She got up, straightened her skirt, went to the washbowl, and poured water over her hands, face, and the back of her neck. Then she patted her hair in place. "Finish the soup I brought you, Oh-Be-Joyful's Daughter. We must go."

I pulled back as though I had been scalded. "No! Not to my father."

"He has sent us his pawakam."

"No. He abandoned me. I don't care how great a man he is, I can't forget that. I can't forgive it."

"Kathy, you think he hasn't been where you are now? He had to choose between being your father and being father to the rest of us. People come to him from great distances because he has found the answers that are withheld. He has woven the sayings of Handsome Lake into the wampum of life."

It was a bus journey, and we went in the morning. All day and that night we dozed, conscious when the bus slowed that we were passing through cities. Edmonton, Saskatoon, Regina, Winnipeg, Thunder Bay. In Sault Ste. Marie I heard a town clock strike thirteen. On we went, North Bay, Ottawa, Montreal. Quebec I had always thought of as the end of the world. It wasn't. We rode past it into a scruffy countryside, but old-growth forest could be seen in the distance. We got out at a poverty-stricken little town, and had lunch at a place called Ma's. I had two eggs sunny side up. Elk Girl took her breakfast into the kitchen and had a long confab with the Indian who worked there. I had been silent the whole trip and she was put out over this. But I wasn't able to pull myself out of that dark place.

She returned from the kitchen and said in a businesslike manner, "Jimmy Longbow will take you the rest of the way."

"You're going to leave me here?" Somewhere in the world I was sitting on a stool eating eggs, but where?

"You're the one Jonathan Forquet wants to see," she retorted.

"Wait," I said as she turned to go. "Do you think he really did die?"

"Of course."

I looked after her, no longer sure which was dream and which reality.

Jimmy Longbow handed me a walking stick with a leather thong he had fashioned himself and we started out. Before too long we were in the forest I had seen from a distance. The cool autumn air trapped between pines was pungent. The trees went down to the edge of the river.

My guide melted away. There was no need of him. Jonathan Forquet was at work in a clearing. Before him, lifted on a rack, was a canoe; another was pulled up on the beach.

He put down a tool, and, coming toward me, took my hand and looked deeply into my face. He knew. I could tell that. He knew about Crazy Dancer, and that he was dead.

"I don't know what to do," I burst out.

"Sit down here on this stump. First you will have a cup of water."

He watched me drink with a look of satisfaction. "You did the right thing. You can always come to your"—I thought he was going to say father but he said—"namer."

I stole glances at him as I drank. He seemed not to have become older but to encompass youth with age. "What are you doing?" I asked, indicating the two canoes.

"This is my workshop. I make canoes."

"To sell?"

"Of course to sell. How else is a man to live?"

"You're known as a holy person. In India a holy person collects alms and is fed by the community."

"Why should I accept charity when I can make canoes?"

He took me to a small pine lean-to whose chinks were padded with moss. "Sleep here," he said, showing me a pile of furs in the corner, "and tomorrow you will help me and I will try to help you."

Like a child I obeyed my father.

When I woke I could hear the teeth of a bandsaw. I emerged and came closer, inhaling the aromatic scent of birch bark that had been freshly peeled and rolled in large paperlike layers. Its outermost crust was chalk white, deepening to a buff color.

"Paper birch, cut from high on the tree. I strip it off in a single sheet early in summer."

"What wood do you use to make the frame?" I could see he was pleased at my question.

"A hard maple or cedar. This is cedar I'm shaping now. This piece in my hands will be a gunwale. But I've run out of water. It has to be kept wet."

I picked up the pail beside him and, going down to the river, filled it.

He nodded thanks without pausing in his movements. "Pour the water into this trough," he directed.

I did this, wondering if he remembered the way we had parted years ago, and the cruel things I had said. He placed the cedar strips to soak, making them malleable for bending.

"The ribs too," he said, placing shorter strips to soak. "And lastly, the stem. On other boats that would be a keel, but on a canoe it simply divides the building of it."

We left the construction pieces of cedar soaking and went in to breakfast. He pulled apart a home-baked hominy loaf, which we ate with honey and berries.

"When he died," my father said unexpectedly, "it was your death too."

My eyes filled with tears and I nodded.

We went back to work.

The afternoon was spent fastening the gunwales together in the outline of a canoe. "Tomorrow," he said, "we will put on the skin."

Work stopped when the light faded. Jonathan brought out a pipe and sat in the doorway, smoking. He had laid the guest breakfast before me; I saw it was up to me to rustle the other meals. Dinner didn't look too different from breakfast—berries, a substantial slab of hominy grits, which I essayed on his stove, cooking it with what I thought was bear grease. I topped it off with goat cheese.

We ate in silence, but it was a comfortable silence. Companionable.

"Did you ever die?" I asked.

He nodded over his pipe. "Yes," he said, considering each word. "The doctors told me that I did, that my heart stopped."

"And you were really dead?"

"Yes."

"And the rest, that people say about you?"

"People believe what they need to believe."

"I see. And that is the stuff of myths and legends."

He continued to smoke.

By the next morning our framing was pliable and bent easily, assuming a graceful outline. Together we unrolled the birch bark and lashed it to the ribs.

"Do you see the true beauty of birch? How the grain runs around the tree rather than along its length? That enables us to sew the sheets together." As he spoke, he mixed something with the bear grease brought from the cabin.

"What is that?" I asked.

"For caulking. Pine gum and spruce resin with fat."

The afternoon was spent raising the gunwales to the proper height and binding them to the stem. "Canoe building goes much faster today. Today I rely on Phillips screwdrivers. Not that there is a single screw in the finished canoe, but for temporary bracing there's nothing like them. Bandsaws and jigsaws are a lot faster and more accurate than stone implements. The roots of a living thing are in the past, but the buds open in the present and bloom in the future."

"The present is empty," I said, "and I can't even imagine a future."

He didn't say anything.

It was a day in which we waited for the wood to dry. My time was spent sewing. My thread was made from the cores of spruce roots by patiently scraping layers of skin away. Jonathan came over, presmably to check my stitches. They were small and even, as though sewn with fine silk thread. I was proud of them.

Looking over my shoulder, Jonathan said, "Your mother was an orphan."

My regular stitching went awry.

"She was raised in the cold, severe atmosphere of a mission, but her name was a message from dead parents that she was to be joyful, Mamanowatum. So she knew very well the burden she laid on you when in the spirit world she whispered to the Grandmothers—who passed the name to me."

"My life is in shreds, Father. I can never know joy again."

"I haven't finished my story," my father chided me. "Oh-Be-Joyful grew up behind those repressive stone walls. When small children were punished, she relived her own punishments. She began to break the rules in order to be banished to punishment row. This was a dark storeroom, where children sat on a wood bench and cried. When Oh-Be-Joyful contrived to be shut in with them, she told stories and joked and played finger games. Punishment row became the happiest place in the mission."

My father's story was finished, and he went back to work.

What had he been trying to tell me? That even though I could no longer feel joy for myself, I could create it for others? My stories were dried up in me, I had no jokes, I knew no finger games. If anyone still cried in punishment row, I would say, "Move over."

Another day and another night. My father showed me a collection of miniature canoes in a shed out back. They were six inches long, beautifully made and signed by him.

"White man's enterprise?" I asked.

"Of course." A rare smile lit his face. And I realized that the present held an occasional flash where someone else connected with you.

The caulking, when we reached that point, took a great deal of time as it underwent repeated inspections. Jonathan was a scrupulous and careful craftsman. I was reminded of one of Sister Egg's aphorisms: "What's worth doing is worth doing well."

"The ribs," Jonathan said, "give it strength and make it sea-worthy."

Prebent and wedged tightly against the birch bark, they formed the hull of the canoe.

Two weeks from the day I arrived we stood back and looked at a lithe and capable boat.

Without saying anything my father took me to the edge of the river. It was as though he felt I had earned a vacation, and this was it. We stood looking at bright pebbles which the water magnified. The current was slow, but in the shallows a runnel had formed, quick moving, rushing on.

Jonathan picked up a small piece of bark. He tossed it into the fast-flowing channel. Our eyes followed its course as it breasted ripples and was carried along. "That was you when you came here," my father said.

"But where will I wind up?" I was concerned for the small piece of bark. I hadn't been concerned about the world at war or the protesters Anne joined—but I was worried about the fate of that tiny piece of bark.

"It doesn't matter where you wind up," my father said, "as long as you are in control. Do not let yourself be carried like that bit of wood, who has no say in the matter, and gives no direction, but allows itself to be swept along, it doesn't know where or how."

"But what can it do?"

"Why, dip a paddle in the water, steer a good course."

"And what is a good course?"

"It is different for each of us." And with that he returned to the canoe. I thought it was finished. But it seemed there was more caulking, and ornamenting and invocations. I made myself comfortable on a tree stump, pulled my sweater more closely about me, and watched. With the completion of the canoe my visit was at an end. I wanted to leave him something, so I picked a bouquet of wildflowers. Vines and vivid poppies and the season's last white columbine.

When several hours had gone by, he took a rest and sat down beside me. I handed him the flowers. "I don't know what this coarse yellow one is, I'm afraid it's a weed."

"There's nothing wrong with weeds. Weeds are generally tougher and stronger than flowers. Take you, you are tough and you are strong."

"Then I am still Oh-Be-Joyful's Daughter?"

"I call you that. And someday you will grow into that name."

"Because I am a weed?"

"Yes. Because you are a free-growing, strong weed."

He had a parting gift for me as well, a couple of the miniature canoes. "Give them to your friends."

"You don't want me to keep them?"

"No." He handed me a scroll of birch bark, plain and unmarked. "This is for you. Make it into anything you like."

Eleven

I RETURNED TO Montreal and the Sisters of Charity a whole person. I missed Crazy Dancer. I missed loving him and being loved by him. I missed the life we never had. But the wasteland inside my heart was gone.

I PUT IN for overseas duty and went through a three-week equivalent of boot camp, during which I got my knuckles rapped by a forceps for being slow to hand the operating doctor a scissors and practiced battlefront hospital sterile precautions, including Lane's technique of two gowns, two caps, and two pairs of gloves. When the site was prepared, you stripped off the outer layer of clothing to immediately begin the delicate work in a sterile environment.

There was also strenuous physical training: chin-ups, push-ups, hiking with twenty-pound backpacks, map reading, revolver practice, setting up and dismantling tents, how to wriggle under barbed wire and set fuses. Other hardening activities included firing .303s, with a ferocious recoil that banged you on the shoulder. A brief course in prevention and treatment of malaria and other tropical diseases, and we were posted.

The weather that a month ago still held traces of summer

had become a Montreal winter. But my life, which had teetered at the world's rim, was given back. Like Oh-Be-Joyful in punishment row, I would try to snatch other lives from the brink if I could. For this I needed to be in the thick of things, although with the German conquest stretching from the west coast of France to the east coast of Greece, it was difficult to judge just where that might be. Presumably, however, the Royal Canadian Army would know, and I left it to them.

When I said goodbye to Sister Egg, I had no idea where I was headed. She took the crucifix from her neck and with a mumbled blessing placed it lingeringly in my hands. "If you get the chance, Kathy, ask His Holiness the Pope to bless it."

That was her way of telling me she thought it was Italy. This seemed a good judgment call. Our new class of Liberator fighters had given us air superiority in the Mediterranean and the 4th and 16th German Panzers along with an Italian division had withdrawn from Sicily, while Palermo was taken by Patton's forces. This amount of activity made it more than likely that I would be handing Sister Egg's crucifix to the Holy Father.

An old World War I tramp steamer had slipped into harbor under cover of dark. It listed crazily to port and rode low in the water. I sent up a small prayer, "Not that one."

But it was that one, and at 0300 hours, still in the dark, with a light snow falling, embarkation began. Reinforcements were marched aboard, supplies loaded, heavy equipment stowed, and last, as my cold teeth testified, nine nurses, recruited from several hospitals in several cities.

"I'm going to the war you never got to, Crazy Dancer."

The companionways were narrow, and the ship listed so badly we could hardly keep our footing. The steep metal ladderlike stairs which we climbed down resembled the entrance to hell, as the further into the bowels of the ship, the hotter it became.

Three stories down we reached our quarters, bunks crammed in so tight you couldn't sit up without banging your head.

The ten-day crossing was not to be a picnic. We had started to unpack our few belongings when an explosion rocketed through our quarters, throwing us against our bunks. Were we under attack before we'd left the harbor?

Whistles blew, restraining a general rush to reach the deck. Order was restored, and much to my relief we were taken topside and marched off, our sailing deferred for three days.

"What happened?" I kept asking. I was billeted back at the hospital and heard on the radio that the ship next to us, a fishing boat out of Halifax, blew up. Her boiler had exploded.

We embarked in broad daylight on another ship, which looked to be a good deal more seaworthy. The same nurses were there and another three had been added. Far from being confined to quarters, we were pressed into instant service dispensing tablets to seasick recruits. We were not immune either; one of our number, Carol Smyth from Nova Scotia, was stricken. I shepherded her up the sequence of ladders to the deck and fresh air. Manuevering her to the rail, I told her to hold on. With people retching, throwing up, and moaning to all sides of us, I felt a bit on the queasy side myself and took my own advice. I held the rail, breathing in gales of good, brisk salt air.

One of the nurses told me that a friend of hers had made the crossing on the *Queen Elizabeth*. "Imagine. They flew her to New York, and it was luxury all the way. You sank into carpets inches thick, there was scrollwork and gilt and mirrors everywhere. And a grand staircase and ballroom. The staterooms were fabulous, each with private bath. And the you-know-what looked like all the other chairs. They were cane with red velvet cushions, and she went around trying to lift the seats of three or four matching chairs before she found the right one."

This was decidedly not the *Queen Elizabeth*, or even the

Queen Mary. Typical of a winter passage, the seas were rough. But the rolling water under us and the spume that lashed us were invigorating. And the sight of the twin smokestacks of our corvette convoy, reassuring.

Meals were hearty affairs with no concern shown for civilian rationing or delicate stomachs. We joined the officers' mess, and it was a cheery company. A rufous-haired young doctor speculated on two things throughout our voyage, my virginity and our destination. The latter, I think, was rather generally known, as a chorus of "O Solo Mio" went along with dessert. Why the time expended on tropical medicine I don't know. When I asked this question I was told, "There's your way, my way, the right way, and the army way." Which was all the answer I ever got.

In the morning there was a briefing. We were to be put ashore at Naples, which was completely under Allied control. A map was pulled down which featured a red line labeled GUSTAV drawn across the waist of Italy. These were the German entrenchments, anchored at Monte Cassino. With a pointer the briefing officer indicated a CCS, Casualty Clearing Station, set up on grounds that the Fiat Company had used as R&R for its employees. There was, we were told, heavy fighting at Mignano, just south of Cassino, and we would in all probability be asked to establish an Advanced Dressing Station in the vicinity.

I would be in the midst of it, right enough, and what-ifs crowded my mind, including what if I died. For some reason I had not considered this a serious possibility. But by the time we pulled into harbor, tension had mounted. The constant din of Dakota flying ambulances taking the critically wounded to hospital ships for evacuation to England, and the sight of the destroyed docks brought home the reality of war. The Bay of Naples was a rusting junkyard. The piers had been targeted at various times by both armies, until they were nothing more than enormous chunks of masonry, broken, upended, leaning crazily into partially submerged ships, toppled trucks, and an airplane wing sticking half out of the water.

In order to disembark we jumped onto a platform of planks laid across the hull of a wrecked cruiser, then scrambled into tenders and were brought ashore, where we were taken by jeep to the clearing station.

Impressions revolved with the speed of the jeep. Mt. Vesuvius, stark, rising from distant plains; houses crumpled in disorderly piles in the street, making it necessary to swing onto the sidewalks or cross the middle of a piazza; disabled staff cars, a stripped-down tank, wrecked vehicles of all kinds; the cry of gulls mixed with the sound of scratched gramophone records blaring a dozen songs into a cacophony of noise.

Our driver seemed to make no effort to avoid mowing down groups of drunken soldiers, part of the army of liberation, I supposed. By some miracle no one was hit. There were Off Limits signs everywhere, but, as far as I could see, they were ignored.

We pulled up in an area cluttered by tents arranged in rectangular groupings. Hand-lettered signs hung at the entrances: O.R., RESUSCITATION, X RAY. And several larger tents marked WARD A, WARD B, and so on. A kitchen, an officers' mess, a patients' mess, two QM tents, a dispensary, and a linen tent. Aside from the fact that it was all under canvas, I was going to feel at home.

We were issued rain slickers and hard hats, assigned a tent, and turned in. Throughout the night, planes took off and landed, sirens wailed, and at 0400 hours we came under bombardment. I grabbed my hard hat and jammed it on my head. I slept in it the entire time I was in Italy. A deadly whistle pierced the air, the ground shook, and we got under our cots, calling to each other periodically that it was okay, we'd make it through, and other inane remarks to prove we were alive. This was important to prove, especially to ourselves. Nearby an explosion ripped the air, there was sharp pain in my ears, and for the next few hours I was stone deaf.

From among the veteran nurses here since Sicily, two groups of Field Surgical Units were assembled and moved out as we "slept."

A series of small, sharp flicks in various sections of my body started me scratching. I had never experienced bedbugs. It was worse than the bombing raid. I tried my insect repellent against them, but they were impervious.

In the morning we were broken into teams and stood out front waiting for transport. This was particularly uncomfortable, as a light snow was falling. Where was the Mediterranean sun? I guess it doesn't come out in January.

The jeeps didn't arrive. There was a snafu of some kind. We never did know what it was. However, an officer appeared to tell us we were dismissed till 0200 hours. Three hours to explore Naples. What unbelievable luck.

I set out in the direction of town, but the first vehicle that came along stopped for me. I thought for an instant that the driver was Indian like me. He was Indian, but not like me at all. "I'm Gurkha," he explained, and then, curiously, "What are you?"

"They call us Indians too. I'm a First Nation person from Canada."

"How amazing that we meet here in Italy."

"Yes," I added, "in the middle of a war."

"That part is not surprising. We Gurkhas are the best mountain fighters in the British Empire. We come from the Himalayas," and he laughed deeply into a thick curly beard. He assured me this was the famous Route 6, the Via Casalina, one of the two major highways leading eventually to Rome. Hannibal, if I remembered correctly, traversed it a few millennia ago with elephants. Now it was clogged with transport of all kinds—tanks, trucks, staff cars, road-clearing equipment, and long rows of wounded being passed in stretchers down the grade. Civilians waved, threw flowers and kisses. It was hard to believe they had been implacable enemies just a few short weeks ago.

The atmosphere was almost one of carnival, American servicemen distributing chocolate to ragged little street urchins, and dwarf women vendors shrieking, "Hello, Joe!"

My Gurkha friend refused to drop me off. "These are mean streets," he said, "no place for a woman alone." He turned into cobbled alleys so narrow pedestrians had to flatten against the sides of buildings to let traffic pass. This was my first European city, and I was amazed at how primitive it was, how different. The buildings built into each other, the wash strung across the street and over the traffic, kids everywhere, ragged, ragged little waifs, some with shoeshine boxes.

My driver told me he had been shod. "Like a horse," he said, "in one of these streets by one of those rascals. I ask for a shine, but he tells me the left shoe needs resoling. Before I know what's what, he takes out these nails half an inch long, I swear. He rips off the old sole, slaps on a new one, trims it to fit with a wicked-looking blade—right on my foot. Then come the nails, bang, bang, bang, into the bottom of my shoe. I thought he was going to crucify me, starting with my feet."

He pointed out a pair of ten-year-olds eyeing us from an alley. "You have to watch out for these little beggars, they're multitalented. They also steal anything that isn't fastened down."

I suggested we stop for a bite at one of the small curbside restaurants that didn't look as though it would be too expensive. "You can park the jeep right there and keep an eye on it."

He agreed readily enough, but refused to leave the jeep. "Not fastened down," he pointed out. He warned me against expecting too much of the restaurant. "There's not much food in

Naples. If we're lucky there'll be a little pasta, cheese, and some of those sweet rolls, *taralli*, they call them."

I brought some out to him.

The proprietess, a handsome woman with a flour sack tied about her, discussed the entire menu with me, although she knew I didn't understand a word. With many smiles, she explained why each item listed was not to be had. I also wound up with the delicious *taralli* tarts.

For dessert she disappeared to emerge fifteen minutes later with an enormous bouquet of flowers. In the rush of Italian that went with them I caught the word *liberatore*. That's how the people here saw us, as liberators.

I kept checking my watch. There was time to look into the bookstore across the street, if my Gurkha friend was not in a hurry. I saw he was taking a siesta, so I went across to the shop. Bookstore was hardly what it was. They sold guitar strings, maps, tourist guides, and rather pretty jewelry, locally made.

I bought the map, and a bracelet for Connie, not trying to figure out lire, just dumping all my Canadian change on the counter and hoping to get something back. I didn't. My Gurkha friend deposited me at base camp by 0200 hours, where I was assigned to the 7th British Army Brigade, Royal Sussex battalion.

Things moved expeditiously from then on. We were loaded into a truck and I found myself back on Route 6. We passed the little alley we'd discovered this morning, and the *ristorante*. We ourselves must have resembled a rather gray line dusted with snow that followed alongside the Rapido Valley. The ground here resounded with the deep menacing sound of distant mortars. It was borne in on me that we were here to take from the Germans the barrier where they had dug in, variously referred to as the Gustav Line and the Hitler Line. The core of this natural mountain barrier was Monte Cassino. The Fifth Army had taken the Mignano Gap and Monte Trocchio. Morale was high. It was thought we'd win Cassino by the end of the week.

But I had studied the map I'd bought at the little bookstore. "Why do we need Cassino?" I asked aloud.

A dozen voices explained it was the gateway to Rome.

The final sacrilege: "Why do we need Rome?"

It turned out that Rome wasn't actually strategic, and the Americans had wanted to bypass it. But Churchill was determined on Rome, principally for its symbolism. At least, that was the word that filtered through to us nurses. So, as part of the Royal Sussex, it was Cassino.

Our vehicle, which had been slowed almost to a standstill, now lurched to a complete stop. With a muttered curse, the driver jumped down to see what was going on up ahead. He walked along the side of the road. The explosion wasn't that loud. But mixed with a human cry it was inhuman. The man was splattered with white chalklike dust and blood. A mine had taken his foot off. People came running up. They seemed to know all about this kind of thing. "It's a *Schuh* mine. Nasty little buggers."

Our driver was lifted into the truck. We put on a tourniquet and gave him morphine, and he was passed back down the line for return to Naples.

An MP approached, asking if anyone present had an army vehicle driver's license. No one spoke up.

"Can any of you drive a goddamn truck?"

"I can, sir." Oh, Crazy Dancer, what have you got me into?

I slid into the driver's seat and rejoined the convoy proceeding into the foothills of the Apennines, going north. There were scattered cypress here, myrtle, and a few stunted pines. Beyond these, vineyards were planted with veins of cold blue lava running through them.

The country rose steeply to a mountain grade. We came to another traffic jam. In order to let a tank company through they rerouted smaller vehicles onto a secondary road through the hills, though to me it seemed more rubble than road.

Italians didn't bother with such things as guardrails, or perhaps they had been torn off. On one side of the narrow lane my side mirror clipped daisies off the bluff, on the other was a drop of a thousand feet into the valley. How close were my wheels to the unseen edge?

The palms of my hands were so wet I had to wipe them one at a time on my uniform. All this while we were climbing, but it became steeper, and I shifted into low.

Then, horror of horrors, an armored personnel carrier appeared, coming at me from around the bend. I was going up, they were going down—they had the right of way. I and those behind me would have to back all the way to the bottom.

I put the truck in reverse and crept backward, my huge antagonist honking at my slowness. The very size of the vehicle coming at me made me consider squeezing onto the shoulder so he could pass.

"Come on, lass," the driver shouted. "The war'll be over at this rate."

I held my breath. I prayed. Where were my wheels? I inched backward into the tight elbow and heard the shrubbery scratch the fenders.

The personnel carrier passed us, the driver and a whole row of soldiers giving me the V sign for victory.

"Please, God, no more vehicles."

And we met no more.

We reached the pass without incident and started a gradual descent. The quality of the air changed, becoming moist and fragrant. Pines were replaced by larch and beech. This was the Liri Valley, but we merely passed through a small corner of it before once again climbing narrow back roads. Our goal was to establish an aid station in the vicinity of troops who had bypassed

Monte Cassino and would be attacking from the rear while the main force of the British Eighth Army kept up the pressure from the front. At least that's what my passengers were speculating, now that they had somewhat recovered from our first casualty.

The guns that pounded the earth were only a few miles away. I was waved to a stop, then directed to the Field Surgical Unit up a side road, cut so recently that the backhoe was still at work a hundred yards ahead and there was a smell of turned earth. We piled out of the truck and I saw immediately that this was not the standard Advanced Dressing Station with the equipment I had been taught to employ. Except for what we had in the truck we were on our own. When I sat down to catch my breath, my fingers knotted up as though they were still clutching the steering wheel. The light snow had turned to rain and we made it a first order of business to set about erecting tents. This was one instance where my training paid off.

But casualties started to arrive before we were finished.

A convoy of wounded, and the tents were at the bottom of the truck, disassembled. Hurriedly we unpacked disinfectant, plasma, sulfa powder, morphine, penicillin, needles of all sizes, scissors, basins, bandages, cotton wadding, syringes, urinals, folding cots, blankets, sheets, towels, disassembled operating tables, anesthesia equipment—it was amazing what came out of that truck. Finally, under it all, canvas and poles, where some unknown quartermaster, God bless him, had stowed it.

A matron already on the scene had appointed herself triage officer. Priorities one and two were those so badly wounded they must be treated on the spot, with priority one reserved for the men who might possibly be saved. Priority three was for first aid, where bleeding could be controlled, broken bones temporarily splinted in bivalved casts, pain somewhat alleviated. These patients were evacuated to the general hospital. Walking wounded just sat there. Some bravely pitched in and helped fetch and carry.

Traditionally, the leading principle of medical practice in combat is rapid evacuation. The wounded are picked up by stretcher bearers and brought to the unit medical officer, who gives them the minimum attention necessary and passes them on to an ADS, Advanced Dressing Station, where more facilities are available. From there they are transferred to a CCS, Casualty Clearing Station, which is a small emergency hospital where urgent surgery can be performed.

Here, however, the whole carefully planned system was out the window. The bad roads, flooded valleys, constant enemy fire, and the severe nature of many wounds made normal evacuation impossible. Our Field Surgical Unit provided surgical services right at the front, using the generator that came out of our truck.

Surviving members of a tank crew dug privies, "six-holers" we called them, potato sacks piled between them for a semblance of privacy, but they were only waist high.

In back of the last tent was a row of stretchers holding those that hadn't made it. All through the night we kept adding to their number. The burial detail didn't arrive until noon.

Thank God there was already an operational kitchen and warm soup, enough to go around. I know it saved my life. Pea and carrot soup with a little onion will always be a special memory for me. I sat down and drank it slowly while the *ack-ack* rasped from the valley floor.

Restored, I went to help set up the field transfusion unit. To add to our problems, the rain turned to sleet. Our main task now was to get everyone under canvas. We actually hauled up the ward tents over the patients. We spread tarps across the mud and called them floors. The cots sank and we had to do our nursing on our knees.

I encountered a case that at the Sisters' hospital would have been assigned "locked ward." He was waving his rifle about in a wild way, and I was afraid he would shoot himself or someone else. I had to wrestle him for it. The barrel was slippery with blood, but he wouldn't let go. "It jammed," he said over and over, "the damn thing jammed on me."

One of the walking wounded helped me pacify him.

The bright spot was that penicillin was delivered in quantity. It worked miracles and I thanked God for it.

My first sight of Major Farnsworth, the senior surgeon, was with a mop in his hands, trying to mop up the standing pools of blood and rainwater that collected on the canvas floor of the tent so he could keep his footing at the next operation.

I took over for him. He acknowledged this with a brief nod. You didn't get to know people if you could help it. I did ask, however, about the high incidence of eye and head injuries. "It's the topography mainly. Bullets and mortar fragments ricochet off the flint rocks and boulders into eyes and faces. Get used to it."

By the time we had been there three days, we were beginning to function properly. Then orders came through to move. It was like untrimming a Christmas tree. Putting it together, decorating, that's exciting. Undoing it is something else. But we disassembled and packed and tried to get it all back into the trucks, and even retain a vague memory as to where we'd put various items.

The line crawled forward and after perhaps forty-five minutes we rounded a bend.

There was Monte Cassino standing before us like a wall, and, on top of it, the famous monastery. From great ravines, rocky ledges, fierce slopes and jagged crests the dark escarpment rose stark, majestic. We had toiled our circuitous way to this point, and it loomed above us, sheer granite.

I stared in awe. Holding it, the Germans commanded an unobstructed view of the Liri and Rapido Valleys, the mountain pass of Abruzzi, all the way to Monte Trocchio lying like a beached whale along the Rapido River.

Looking at the featureless gray face of Monte Cassino, I asked, "We are going to take that?!" I watched shells hit and splinter on rock, the fragments spraying out in all directions. For days I had been seeing the consequences—raw gashes where eyes had been, skull fractures, depressed scalp wounds. A fly could not get up this formidable precipice, and yet our boys, under German field glasses and German guns, had tried and would try again. And I would give them morphine when I couldn't do anything else.

I continued to stare at that great mass. No trees. No cover. It was absolutely bare. No way to throw up protection. On it one was exposed, and under it, a target—as we were now. I thought of the slow Allied progress, hill after hill, pass after pass, a river to cross, and, at the end, to be met with this. I didn't see how . . . looking back on it, I still don't see how. This was Monte Cassino.

We began to unload, setting up behind the first shelter of rocks we came to, only a few hundred yards behind our forward troops. Our orderly, who was also our cook, provided everyone with a laugh. Yes, even here, in these circumstances, it was possible. We heard a dog howling, and Stan went to investigate. He came back carrying a large German shepherd, left behind by the Jerries because he was wounded. Stan classified the dog priority one and made room for him in the critical care tent. We couldn't spare a cot, but a lot of the boys didn't have one either. And in all other respects the dog was treated as well as anyone. Since he only responded to commands in German, Stan claimed he'd taken the unit's first prisoner of war.

We soon saw why we had been repositioned at the front. By morning the sky was silver with Flying Fortresses, followed by wave after wave of Mitchells. Shells fell all around us, and tracers occasionally zigzagged toward our tents. The din was con-

stant. Everyone yelled, yet you couldn't hear a thing. Our own
people were hit. Nursing Sister Lander was carrying a basin of
sudsy water. She was hit in the back; the shell fragment went
right through her and struck the basin with a ringing tone as
she dropped dead.

Wave after wave of shells, punctuated by machine-gun fire,
the scream of rockets. Waste bags soon held arms and legs, even
fingers. Injured arrived on stretchers, or on the back of a corps-
man. The corpsmen, sometimes ridiculed by new recruits for
their reluctance to bear arms, were worshipped on the battlefield. They snatched the wounded from beneath streams of arc-
ing tracers, from places tanks couldn't go.

I noticed several of the fellows I'd patched up back on active
duty. We worked as fast as we could but boys held their wounds
together with their fingers, waiting for attention. Others clawed
at infected areas. Burn cases lay and screamed. You could go
mad. Some did, and wandered away, only to be picked off by
enemy fire.

A few feet to either side, that's all it took to feel eyes from
the monastery watching. The weather had taken sides and
become a partner of the Germans. The mercury dropped, the
snow turned to thin sheets of ice covering the rocks. Fog settled
in, and the airstrike that was supposed to soften up the enemy
for our forward push was called off. Our troops attacked with
no air cover. The fog became wispy, then stringy, and in some
places cleared. They were thrown back.

Most of our mechanized equipment was useless. Our tanks
couldn't climb these boulders, while below in the valley our
vehicles, from personnel carriers to ambulances, were mired in
mud. The Germans had opened a dam, flooding the plain, turning it into the kind of muskeg we have in Alberta after a chi-
nook. The only means left for resupplying us in this forward
position was by pack mule. So much for modern warfare. We

would have had no plasma, no penicillin, and no morphine if not for the mules. As it was, they forgot to send batteries for our radio, and all communication was cut off for two days.

It was clear that the first concerted offensive for Monte Cassino had ended in a complete rout. Allied headquarters finally realized that Cassino was not simply the next range to be taken. It was the anchor of the entire German defense.

What were the boys thinking, whose limbs filled our garbage cans? It was hard to meet their eyes, hard to keep up one's morale, hard to keep our patients from freezing. It was below 30°F and a captured German, who had fought on the Russian front, declared this was worse.

Scuttlebutt had it that there'd been an amphibious landing at Anzio. From there Allied troops were to fight their way through the Germans, and come to our aid in a pincer movement.

It was a brilliant plan and must have looked good on paper. But it didn't work. They ran into the same seasoned German troops our forces had been up against, and had all they could do to maintain their beachhead. I began to think the war fought with globes and pulldown maps bore little resemblance to battlefield positions, and that much of their cleverly worked-out strategy was obliterated by what actually happened, as men tried for handholds on icy slopes and cover where there was none.

All I knew was that the formidable natural fortress before us, was still before us three weeks later, and, according to a report I helped Dr. Farnsworth fill out, we had lost over 1,600 men simply trying to stay where we were.

And where was that?

It did no good to think these thoughts, but they kept coming into my head.

Twelve

REINFORCEMENTS ARRIVED, THE 2nd New Zealand Corps under General Freyberg. They were to break into the Liri Valley, swing around, and attack Monte Cassino from the north while we tried again from the southwest. Of course, they never got together on the details.

Orders came from General Mark Clark's staff at Naples to capture Colle Belvedere, a ridge partway up Cassino, take it at any cost, give no quarter. We heard that this threw our General Tuker into an apoplectic fit. "Blasted idiots. Don't they know it's already held by the Free French?" He muttered strings of curses for several minutes before gradually subsiding.

News came that the Germans had mounted a counteroffensive at Anzio. Far from being able to help Cassino, our forces at Anzio were fighting for their lives. This did nothing to improve General Tuker's temper. He took it out on his pet hate, the monastery. "Like the eyes of an oil painting, it follows you. No matter where you are, there it is, looking down at you."

Another directive from General Clark's headquarters had a curious effect on him. The fury that had swept him before was nowhere in evidence. He internalized it, became calm, became frostily correct, became the prototype of a soldier and a gentleman. As though he were ordering a taxi for the theater, he had his driver fuel up his car for Naples.

"Why in the world," I asked, "is he going to Naples? Is it to shoot Mark Clark?"

The corners of Dr. Farnsworth's mouth twitched, and he came as near to smiling as I'd ever seen him. "That would be an acceptable solution."

Before the hour was out, Tuker was back. He was driving the car himself, with the corporal slumped beside him. We helped bring the wounded man in and set his broken arm. The general marched back and forth just out of earshot and unburdened himself to Dr. Farnsworth.

"Nurse Forquet."

I turned, to be told I was driving General Tuker into Naples.

"There are no drivers available," Farnsworth explained. "But I've heard you're an ace with anything that burns petrol."

"Well, I—"

The general looked me over. "You'll do. Let's go, Lieutenant."

Once on the way, he dropped his abrupt manner and offered me tea from his canteen. Then he withdrew into his own somber thoughts, indicating that I was to do the same. The drive south on Route 6 was in striking contrast to the way up. The engineers had cleared and repaired the damage, wrecked vehicles had been towed away or rolled over the side, bomb craters filled and paved, and, wonder of wonders, they had drawn a yellow centerline.

On the other hand, there were the tanks that never reached us, the abandoned trucks with boxes of supplies from soap to bandages, and presumably batteries. All the things we so desperately needed.

When we entered the outskirts of the city, the general began to talk. "There's no way to take Monte Cassino and not the monastery. I requested Fifth Army Intelligence to furnish all available information regarding it. The answer came back promptly. They had none. Nothing at all. It sits atop Monte Cassino, but they had no interest in it. Whether it is occupied by a German garrison no one thought to enquire. Although it has been a thorn in our side from the beginning, no one bothered to discover if the building has been reinforced over the years, and if so, with what."

I kept my eyes on the road. I didn't know how you replied to a major general.

"Therefore," he said, "this trip into Naples has become necessary. In the middle of a battle it is necessary for me to stop everything and go to the library. That, young woman, is exactly where we're headed, the library!"

I hope we get there, I answered silently. Following his directions, we'd left Route 6 and were prowling about in some corner of Naples, totally lost. But generals have plenty of practice in map reading. He calmly spread out a colorful assortment of road maps, on his lap, on my shoulder, on the dash, and got us to the library ten minutes later.

I helped him pull down volumes as old as the librarian, who, once he understood our mission, brought out ancient compendiums from storage. One was in English, and from it I absorbed a bit of the history of the Monte Cassino monastery. Founded in the sixth century by St. Benedict, the monastery was almost entirely rebuilt in the sixteenth and seventeenth centuries, and converted into a fortress in the nineteenth. The only entrance was by a narrow, low archway of stone blocks, each thirty-five feet long. The walls were a hundred fifty feet high, of solid masonry, ten feet thick at the base, and faced with cream-colored Travertino stone. It comprised a cathedral, a seminary, a fully equipped observatory, and a college for boys. Its famous library ran the entire length, with workshops for paper making, illuminating, and bookbinding.

The general sat at a table and made notes. An hour and a half later he closed the last reference book and looked over at me. "I would be pleased if you would dine with me, Miss Forquet."

I gulped only once. "I am hungry," I said.

Outside there was an American four-wheel drive parked next to our car.

"Take that one," he said.

"But—?"

He waited, looking at me quizzically.

"Yes sir." Military necessity, I would say to any American MP who tried to arrest me, a general at Cassino needs a four-wheel drive.

I liberated the American vehicle, hot-wiring the ignition as Crazy Dancer had taught me. This was more like it!

The general had invited me to dine, and dine we did. We were escorted with bows and compliments to the best table in the best restaurant in the city, whose only wall was bolstered by sandbags.

"I don't suppose the menu is to be believed," I said, looking over the elaborate bill of fare.

General Tuker chortled and read aloud such specialties as duck, prime rib of beef, and Yorkshire pudding. I craned to see. These items were indeed listed in a flowing, calligraphic hand.

I looked at him questioningly.

He was delighted to inform me, "Stocked from the senior officers' mess. We have the food, they have the atmosphere."

"What a great idea," I said approvingly as I looked out over the bay. It was a magnificent panorama. Perched on a hilltop, we were unable to see the pulverized destruction.

Wine with the meal, and my tiredness floated away. Alongside the roast beef and Yorkshire pudding was the best pasta I'd eaten before or since, made with mussels, calamari, prawns, and scallops baked in a mushroom sauce. By the second glass of wine I forgot I was dining with a major general and commanding officer of a division. He was a fascinating conversationalist, a scholar, and author of several military treatises. I wondered what he would have to say about Cassino after the war. I hoped he could report that we'd won it.

Over claret he discussed the problem of the monastery. "A thousand-pound bomb, even if well placed, would be quite useless."

"It's a shame that such a beautiful old building must be destroyed at all. You don't suppose the monks still inhabit it? Are you certain they were evacuated? And what about the art treasures and documents?"

"The Germans are good about sparing art and documents. About the abbot and any remaining monks, I don't know. They may have also given shelter to refugees. It's quite possible. And someone thought there was a deaf-mute servant. In any case we'll give notice before we attack, broadcast a warning."

Our American transport got us back to the front in record time.

OUR TROOPS HUDDLED against winter snow turned to slush. A grayness lay over the mountain like a scrim. Below in the valley it was no better: the marsh was a sea of mud. The depressing landscape matched the uncomfortable circumstances in which the waiting men found themselves. They were too miserable to sleep or read. Water was rationed, as it had to be brought seven miles by mule, so shaving was out. Although one enterprising soldier was using the dregs of his tea to moisten his stubble. Several men had settled down to writing letters home. Most sat and stared at the monastery. Everyone knew by now that its total extinction was imminent. We had been told officially that reinforcements in the form of the 4th/6th Rajputana Rifles were on the way. Two more battalions of Gurkhas held the valley.

The objective was point 953, a promontory close under the defending walls of the monastery. It seemed an appalling route to me, but then, as my friend had told me, the Gurkhas were renowned as mountain fighters. Somewhere, although they had not yet arrived, was a company of Maori sappers, also known as New Zealand's "wild Irish." Their job was to remove those deadly *Schuh* mines with which the place was strewn. This was difficult, as they were simply little wooden shoeboxes with a minimum of metal, making mine sweepers all but useless, while the snow hid them from visual detection. When they did show up, the Maoris were a cheerful bunch. They didn't bother with salutes, but waved smilingly at their officers.

With the addition of so many troops the plan must be to attack simultaneously, again from the southwest and the north, a route that had been chiseled out by the Americans in the first, failed attempt that preceded my tour of duty here. But with the seasoned Indian division backed by the 2nd New Zealand, it was felt we had a chance. The wait now was for all these forces to get into position. If they attacked with strong air cover it might work. I frequently checked the sky—slate and gray, but no shielding fog.

I heard engines and glanced up. Not the Mitchell medium-range bombers we were expecting but Flying Fortresses all the way from Africa. Weren't they early? The troops from India had barely arrived, and the New Zealanders weren't in position yet.

The planes, dipping slightly, flew directly at the monastery. The bomb bays opened. Were the monks still there? Were they kneeling at the altar chanting the antiphon of the Blessed Virgin? The explosions sent up tremendous clouds of brilliant orange, punctuated by smoke and dust shot through with yellow flashes. Had they finished "Beseech Christ on our behalf" before those words were swallowed in this unchristian baptism?

When the smoke cleared, there was a murmur from the troops. It was a miracle. The monastery stood. Seemingly, it had not been affected by this first deadly run. A second pass, and a third. It stood, with no discernible damage. At 1400 hours it was the turn of the Mitchells. As each successive smoke cloud dissipated, the pounding began to show. The windows appeared larger and their frames were jagged. There was a fissure in the walls, and the roof was beginning to look uneven.

Then, as I watched, the west wall of the building collapsed. I remembered the refugees—had they knelt and chanted with the monks? Tuker had mentioned a warning salvo. But there was none. The planes had appeared too early out of the sky.

Demolishing the monastery was only part of their job; they were to provide air cover for the assault. But when the monastery crumbled, they considered their mission accomplished and left, with Tuker shaking an impotent fist skyward.

The fury of the bombing had been fury in a vacuum, wasteful and tragic. That beautiful centuries-old abbey was gone.

The planes had gone too. Whether deliberately or not, Air Command had not been given the full picture. The monastery was the target, they wiped it out, they left. Air cover was not on their agenda. Too many generals, too many egos vying for headlines back home. Egg would have said, "Too many cooks spoil the broth."

Planes or no planes, the attack was ordered, and hell opened before my eyes. They moved out, two platoons, the third following in reserve. They crawled silently along Snakehead Ridge toward point 953. The men set their feet so as not to dislodge a stone or stumble. It was easy to turn an ankle carrying a heavy Bren gun or a flamethrower.

The Germans opened up. Withering fire caught the climbers in the open. Machine guns, mortars, grenades—and mines, the area had not been properly cleared of mines. The rubble that had been the monastery now provided ideal cover for German gunners.

Our men were picked off. Stretcher bearers began bringing down the wounded. I passed among them with gauze and morphine. The Rajputana Rifles reached what looked like a belt of scrub. Instead, it was a thicket of thorn, breast high. I began pulling them out of wounds along with shards of barbed wire. I had never seen such vicious lacerations.

Their colonel was shot through the stomach and lay looking up at me. I stopped the bleeding. The morphine was used up. We were short of basic supplies. I had to watch him die. There was one Gurkha stretcher bearer who again and again climbed over those exposed crags to bring in another fallen shape. He must have made sixteen trips into that inferno. This time he was halfway back when the soldier at the other end of the stretcher was hit, and fell, barely fifty yards from me. I rushed out and grabbed his end of the stretcher. He struggled to his feet and tried to help, but ended up leaning on my shoulder. Somehow, the Gurkha and I brought them both in.

The Gurkha nodded at the chaos we had just left. He was asking for my help, and I went with him. A barrage of mortars exploded around us. When it cleared sufficiently to see, the man we had come after was dead. The Gurkha signed that he had spotted someone farther on, but by now I was confused as to where I was and where our lines were.

A shape loomed out of the dust. Another stretcher bearer—only something was wrong. He was wearing the wrong uniform. I stood still, grooved into the rock I stood on. He'd have to kill me, of course. Instead he said, in passable English, "You're lost?"

I nodded. I couldn't speak.

"That way." He pointed. "South of that rock. That's where you want to be."

"*Danke schön,*" I whispered, hardly getting it out.

"English?" he asked.

"Canadian."

"Good luck," he said, and disappeared in the other direction.

"Good luck—" But he had gone.

My Gurkha, who had stood silent and motionless during this exchange, told me such meetings between the lines were not uncommon. Unofficial, unsanctioned, it nevertheless happened as both sides respected a mutual low-level grunt truce and evacuated their wounded.

The attack was repulsed, and the Germans held on to the Gustav Line. It was almost three months later that our forces took Monte Cassino.

I REMEMBER HEARING several wounded praying in Polish. I had come to recognize these brave fighters in their long gray-green coats. They had lost their homeland early on, but now, as the Germans retreated, they had hope for the first time. The final operation itself was spearheaded by a Canadian corps under Major General Sir Oliver Leese. The way it played out, as I heard afterward, Leese, by taking and holding the Liri Valley, strengthened us at Cassino. The combined pressure breached the German defenses in a number of places, and allowed the Americans to push up the coast, while the British entered the valley. Cassino, that great wall, fell to the Polish Corps May 18, 1944.

The Germans could not withstand this concentrated drive and gave way even in the Alban Hills. The road to Rome was wide open.

Many times in these last months my hand strayed to Egg's

crucifix, which I wore inside my shirt. On the same chain was tied a gray and white feather. I thought of Crazy Dancer at the most unexpected moments. I think because I expected to be dead by now, and I wanted him to guide me as he had that old chief. I wanted to walk in his moccasins.

It was haphazard, I felt, whether one survived this madness or not. It depended on such things as going for a drink of water or scrounging up more morphine, or deferring getting the bandage rolls that were needed. You were or you were not in a certain place when the shell made a crater of it. Nurse Lander could have asked someone else to dump the basin. Nurse Lander could have stayed in Canada and not volunteered in the first place.

Funny, I didn't know where in Canada she came from, or even her first name. All I remembered—she was the one who kept everybody's spirits up, the first to wade into the mud and help with the plasma. She didn't hesitate to drag a dead soldier to the burial row, her blond hair flying. And her own body had been added to the pile. I hadn't had time to think about her until now. I thought about the German stretcher bearer too. I hoped he'd survived.

I stroked my feather and Egg's cross. I'd been kept alive and relatively sane. Soon I would be entering the Eternal City.

DAYS LATER WE were strung out on the road to Rome. It was a victory march, but probably not recognizable as such. We were a straggling line of exhausted, dirty, exultant beings. Of all the conquerors that over the centuries had taken Rome we were certainly the least likely and the most ragged. Our vehicles were in no better shape than we were. How we could have used Crazy Dancer! Overheated motors, clogged fuel lines, blown tires were the norm. Sooty, blackened, fed a vile mixture of gasolines, they rolled on.

I was driving again, simply because it was assumed I would be. When we got to Rome I planned to apply for a proper army vehicle license. In the meantime I was part of the long line wending its way, with a recalcitrant sun showing itself occasionally.

Then the engine sputtered, the jeep bucked under my hands and came to a stop.

"Get that thing off the road."

"Yes sir." I outranked him, but on the road those directing traffic have ultimate authority, even over generals. Besides, we nurses had never had time to learn army protocol, and it wasn't expected of us. I jumped out of the jeep and with the help of a couple of MPs pushed it into a field of cauliflowers. I opened the hood. Thanks to Crazy Dancer I had seen enough engines to recognize that a wire from the distributor had burned through. I borrowed the foil from a pack of cigarettes a soldier had dropped out of line to inhale. I twisted the ends of the wire around each other and splinted them with bits of foil.

Getting back into the jeep, I tried to start it when a sudden explosion racked the column ahead—where I would have been if the jeep hadn't acted up. A land mine sent pieces of trucks and people showering down. Something penetrated my body.

I thought it was the sound. I didn't realize I'd been hit. But the flying metal fractured my right elbow, all three bones, humerus, radius, and ulna. I was taken back to the same casualty station I'd helped set up. I pleaded with Dr. Farnsworth, who was still with us, to operate there and then. I had seen him perform miracles in the field. Otherwise, it would mean being airlifted to London, and a circuitous route home.

Farnsworth, bless him, agreed without argument, commandeered a surgical nurse, and woke up our anesthetist. My elbow was x-rayed, and he went to work, asking me if I minded baling wire.

"Doctor," I said, "I'm wearing a crucifix. Would you mind taking it to Rome with you? The Pope needs to bless it. And when he does, it's to be sent to Sister Eglantine, Charity Hospital, Montreal, Canada."

"Don't fret," he said. "It's as good as done. I'm sure His Holiness will not refuse a good Anabaptist."

Before the anesthetist clapped the mask over my face, I saw the bolt intended for my elbow.

THE HOSPITAL SHIP was hazy. I'd get used to the roll and then it would start to pitch.

I remember nothing of the crossing. I was in and out of morphine dreams, in which I had tumbled off the world and was trying to climb back on, but the globe rotated and I couldn't manage.

The ship's chief medical officer bent over me, explaining in a kindly voice that I would not in the future have the use of my right arm. "Oh, and practice your signature with your left hand."

A nurse without the use of her right arm?

I FOUND MYSELF a patient in ward B, one of my own wards. They'd put me at the end and curtained it off for privacy.

I didn't like being a patient. Still, I think it should be a requirement for every nurse and doctor. You see things from a different point of view. For instance, the bedpan. The position is antithetical to human beings, but tied into an IV stand it's difficult to get up and take it with you into the bathroom, which was what I did.

Sister Egg popped in every day to scold me. "You're giving us so much trouble, Kathy, that I know you're better."

I confessed to her my fear over the loss of movement in my arm.

"You've seen enough to know what therapy can do. We'll bring you right along."

I redoubled my efforts, squeezing a ball in my hand when I was too tired to do anything else.

The strangest thing about being back from the war was that no one wanted to hear about it. I tried innumerable times to convey my impressions of the other nurses, accounts of the roads, the scenery, what it was like to be under bombardment, how we went about setting up a clearing station, triage, evacuating priority-three patients, having dinner with a major general—bedbugs. So many things. They'd piled up in me with no opportunity to assess them. Even Egg was too busy to listen. Civilians, I thought, deliberately shut out the war. And I remembered myself—hadn't I always gone to the ladies' room or to buy popcorn when the Movietone news showed hospital ships unloading wounded? It was too much to absorb, too much grief, too much anguish, and no frame of reference.

But it was too bad. Because along with the horrors and the glimpses of hell, there were some wonderful things about the war. The way wounded men hauled unconscious buddies into the station. Nurses and doctors forgot the civilian pecking order and helped each other with the most menial duties. Frontline combat erased rank, sex, and color. Not once in Italy did anyone question my copper skin.

A joyous note in the midst of this sere landscape, a package arrived and out tumbled Sister Egg's crucifix and a note from surgeon Farnsworth. He had indeed marched into Rome, and an audience with the Pope had been arranged. The Pope was highly interested in the Anabaptist service and blessed the crucifix on the spot.

The pupils of Sister Egg's eyes rolled up out of sight. It scared me until I realized it was sheer ecstasy.

My arm was becoming more flexible, but I had a long way to go before it could be considered usable. Egg made a mark on the wall. I was ambulatory now, and only the incapacity of my arm kept me from working. I walked my fingers painfully up the wall again and again, morning, noon, and night, aiming for Egg's mark. At times I'd flinch from even starting.

Then it happened: one glorious day my fingers crawled up the wall and touched the mark.

I went flying to Sister. She looked at me calmly through round spectacles and went with me to verify my performance with her own eyes. "Excellent," she said, and made a new mark higher than the first by a good six inches.

Two weeks later my arm was almost well. Follow-up X rays showed that Dr. Farnsworth had been as good as his word. There was the bolt, hammered into the humerus, and the baling wire twisted around the fragments of the two forearm bones. Twenty years down the road arthritis might set in, but the best preventative was to build up the muscles and exercise them daily.

This prescription was exactly what I wanted. I took up my duties as though I had never seen Maj. Dr. Farnsworth mop the blood from the tarpaulin floor, as though I had never performed Miller-Abbott suctions at midnight under flashlights when the generator quit, or transfused with wrong-size needles—the only ones I had—or looked into eyes of anguish and seen eighteen-year-olds meet death calling for their mothers, or had an enemy wish me good luck on the field of battle.

My father had put me back together. I had been able to manage Monte Cassino. Now I must do the same for my life.

Thirteen

SOME DAYS LATER there was a melee at the prison compound, the result of a knife fight. I was told to scrub for an emergency amputation, and received the shock of my life. The draped body on the operating table was that of my friend, the Austrian lieutenant, von Kerll.

Dr. Bennett shook his head and muttered, "I don't know if it's worthwhile trying to patch this Boche up."

My training took over. The surgical nurse swabbed the wound and debrided it. I prepared the tray of sterile instruments.

"Somebody had it in for him," the doctor continued. "As I reconstruct it, there must have been more than one. They tried to slit his throat. During the course of which his leg was pinned, and someone went to work on it. The guards heard the commotion and dragged this fellow out. I don't know if it was in time. He's lost four pints of blood."

Involuntarily I checked the plasma bag. A moment later I asked, "Does he have to lose the leg?" I had to ask, even though I'd seen enough of this kind of carnage to know.

The other wounds were superficial. Someone, as the doctor said, had tried to cut his throat, but the slash missed the carotids. I remembered what Crazy Dancer told me about slashings. Dogs bite, it is the wolf that slashes. I deliberately sent my mind off on this tangent, while they took the leg just below the knee. It was a long operation. But at least Dr. Bennett had a sturdy wood floor under his feet and wasn't trying to keep his balance on a bloody tarp. I helped pack the wound, and began to dress it.

"He's a strong fellow. He should make it."

I liked Bennett. He hated working on the Boche, as he called them, but always did a meticulous job, and somewhere during the operation he forgot they were the enemy and began rooting for them as patients. By the end he had employed all his skill to see they made it. They usually did.

I walked alongside the gurney. How could I tell him? I'd almost rather lose my own leg. But I couldn't let him hear it from anyone else.

I remembered his initial relief at finding himself in one piece. It was on account of his mother. What kind of mother was she? She should rejoice that he wasn't at the bottom of the ocean. I reined in my thoughts, as I had taught myself to do. There were fewer and fewer places I could send them.

A student nurse and I accomplished the transfer to the cot. Then I went to wash my face and calm down.

I washed my face, but I didn't calm down. I dreaded the moment he would open his eyes.

Of course, when he did, he didn't realize. I was checking the glucose drip when he spoke quite distinctly in English. He said, as though continuing a conversation, "It must have been a *Zaunkönig*. It shrieked past, exploding my eardrum. The floor heaved, the sides of the ship buckled, lights flickered and flared up. Then nothing. It was dark. I remember this vile taste washing into my mouth. I was floating in an oil slick." He grabbed my hands. "Are they going to strafe us here in the water? Or leave us? Better have it over with." And he switched to German.

Bending over him I said soothingly, "What about the Rhine maidens? The Valkyries protect the ocean-going warriors."

"They didn't come. I called them, but they didn't come."

It was as I thought, he believed he was waking from his first ordeal, that he was just now off the U-boat.

I stopped by ward B again before going off duty and stood a moment by his bed. His sleep was restless, and he murmured, perhaps cursed, in German. I didn't know what he said, but I wanted him to wake up.

No, no, I didn't. I dreaded his waking up.

Erich wasn't lucid until the next day. I came by at noon to check on him. He was lying quietly, resignedly staring at the ceiling. It was a featureless white ceiling. "Kathy," he said in a very gentle tone, "you're here. So it's all right."

"What's all right, Erich?"

"I dreamt I wasn't in the hospital at all, but in prison. Gott, I thought. . . . But you're here. So it must be all right."

I hesitated. "You *were* transferred to the camp. Don't you remember?"

"So it's true?" He closed his eyes, and his jaw set. "It was better to be floating in waves of oil. That was better than . . ." He made himself stop.

We were both silent. It was Erich who finally spoke. "It wasn't yesterday you were sitting beside me? It was months ago?"

"Yes. Eighteen months."

There was a pause while he absorbed this. "And how have things been for you?" he asked politely.

I tried to match his tone. "I'm still doing business at the same old stand."

"And how is that young man of yours?"

"Dead." The word lay between us.

"I'm afraid to ask anything more. I suppose it was the war."

"A U-boat attack," I said, slowly and deliberately, without mercy.

A vein in his neck throbbed. That was all.

Why had I done that? Why had I punished him, I asked myself when I was out in the hall. He'd had no part in it. It wasn't his fault. Cassino, the monastery, it wasn't his fault. Yet it was, it was. He'd been awarded the Iron Cross. They don't do that except for direct kills.

I recognized that I was not in control and ducked into the bathroom, took several successive breaths, and steadied myself. If I didn't go back, someone else would tell him.

He didn't look at me when I came in but turned his head away. He was very angry.

"Hello again," I said, with professional cheeriness. "I thought I'd look in on you once more. Is there anything you want?"

He tried not to ask, but it broke from him. "My leg, if you wouldn't mind. Something for the pain. There's a cramp in my calf."

I deliberately massaged the wrong leg, hoping to get him to realize, to focus.

"The other one, the left. Just at the knee and below." It was that terrible phantom pain, where severed nerve ends scream, and nothing can be done about it.

"If I can just shift you a bit in bed, that sometimes relieves it." I slipped my hands under his shoulders, straightening him. "Any better?"

He smashed his mouth together rather than answer. But he was turning over in his mind what I had said.

"Your young man—when?"

"Soon after you were transferred."

"God, it's a filthy war."

"He called it fish-hearted."

"Fish-hearted? I like that. It's a damn, filthy, fish-hearted war. Will it ever be over?"

"Yes. We're going to win."

"But," he protested, "the Third Reich was to last a thousand years. Hitler was to overturn the Treaty of Versailles, restore the Teutonic spirit, Saxon myths, Skaldic poems, the Hanseatic code written on stone in runic rhymes. *Sieg heil!* With his great sword Gram conquers the giants and the dwarves. Ravens dine on the flesh of his enemies, swans pull the chariot of the sun across the sky— Kathy, give me something for the pain, or I will break down and cry like a child."

I counted my heartbeats. Then I said, clearly, distinctly, and with emphasis, "Which leg is hurting?"

"My left, I—" He stopped.

He knew. Oh, God, he knew.

I listened to the minutes on the wall clock. I'd never been conscious of them before.

"They *had* to take it off, I suppose?"

I was startled to hear him speak so calmly. "Yes, it was practically severed when they brought you in. It had to be done to save your life."

"I see. To save my life." He laughed shortly.

The charge nurse tapped me on the arm. "Cot 14 is asking for you."

I didn't want to leave him like this, but he had withdrawn to his own private hell.

I wasn't able to look in on Erich until the following morning. He seemed deep in thought, but when he saw me smiled deprecatingly, as though too much had passed between us and he was unsure of himself. "It was good of you to come by. Thank you."

"I wanted to, Erich."

"I'm afraid I took the news rather badly. It's one of those situations that don't come up often. I didn't know how to handle it. But I'm getting more used to it now. At least I think I am. I can talk about it, at any rate. And there's something I want to ask you."

"Yes?"

"It's about that British boy, the one who lost his leg. He didn't want to live afterward, did he?"

"No," I said truthfully, "he didn't."

"And then later, when he grew accustomed to it, he didn't want to go home. And he got you to write letters for him, saying he was slightly wounded but on the road to recovery?"

"Yes. Yes, he did. Oh, Erich, I'm so sorry. But it won't make as much difference as you think."

He held up his hand. "I'm not interested in all that. I'm sure they have marvelous prostheses these days. And I know the crutches will only be temporary, until the wound heals. I don't care about that. I'm not interested. I want to know about the British boy. I am interested in him. Did they amputate both legs?"

I shook my head.

"Just one? Which was it? Do you remember?"

"The left."

"Like me."

There was a pause before the uncomfortable interrogation resumed. "Where was the leg taken off? Below the knee? That's where they took mine, isn't it?"

"Yes, yes. But what's the use of—"

"A lot of use. A lot. It's very helpful."

He closed his eyes, and I began to hope he'd drifted off to sleep, when he said, still with his eyes closed, "You wrote letters for him, telling the lies he wanted the family back home to believe."

"I did, but I never sent them."

His eyes opened with a queer, bright, penetrating glance. "You didn't send them? Oh, Kathy. You are very much Kathy, aren't you? Or are you sometimes Oh-Be-Joyful's Daughter? What's it like to have two names?"

"Why don't you ask me something I can answer?"

"All right. Will you write letters home for me, Kathy? And tell them the same lies?"

"If I don't have to send them."

"No. You have to send them."

"But don't you want to know the rest? The British boy changed his mind. He went home, Erich. And he sent me a snapshot, taken at his wedding. It had a happy ending."

"I'm not interested anymore in the British boy." And he turned on his side, away from me.

WITH THE WAR going strongly in our favor, it seemed an odd time for a prison break. Yet one morning sirens screamed and searchlights crisscrossed a sky which was just lightening. I dressed hastily to hear the news. Sometime in the night five German prisoners cut through the barbed wire and escaped. One was captured almost immediately hiding in the granary, and returned. The hunt was on for the others, with snow-tired vehicles, a ski patrol, and dogs.

Before the day was out the remaining four were recaptured, one of them shot and killed.

The excitement produced a complete dislocation in hospital procedure. But I continued my careful supervision of Erich's progress. He was at a critical stage. Physically he was coming along, making an adequate recovery, but he totally rejected his body. The lack of interest he had expressed in the English boy extended to everything. I also was banished, everyone was, everything, including life itself. I'd been in that place. I knew it well.

However, the escape triggered something in Erich. I didn't realize at first when I found him pale and clammy, that it had anything to do with the breakout. His respiration was so quick and uneven that I was alarmed and decided to send for the resident, but Erich put out a hand and stopped me. "Please tell me," he said. "Who was killed? Was it Norbert? Norbert Freund?"

"Yes, I think that was the name. Did you know him?"

"He's the reason I'm here, the reason I don't have a leg."

"I don't understand."

"There's a clique, among the prisoners, of hard-line Nazis. They were suspicious of me from the first—I didn't give their stiff-armed salute at the mention of the Fuehrer's name, I didn't join in their songs of the Vaterland. So I was ostracized. That suited me fine.

"I judged from the influx of new inmates that the war was going badly for us. And this was confirmed—the arrivals were boys of fifteen and sixteen, called up, taken out of school. Old men were among them, the Volkssturm, who were the home guard, air raid wardens, they also wound up here. You can imagine the anger, despair, frustration at being out of it, while comrades, brothers, sons, fathers are dying."

"That explains the timing of the escape attempt," I said, pleased that he was taking me into his confidence again. "Everyone was asking, Why now, when it all seems to be winding down? But that explains it." I hesitated, then asked something that bothered me. "Do you feel that way, Erich?"

"Of course. My countrymen are being killed and maimed. At the same time I can't help wonder—when it's over, what will Austria's fate be? Will the Allies stick by their promise that the old Social Democratic Party and the constitution be restored?

Or will she suffer reparations as a defeated enemy? I don't know. It could go so many ways."

I pressed him to tell me what led to the knife fight.

"A couple of weeks ago, during the exercise period, I slipped into one of the small warehouse sheds to write a letter. I was sitting on the floor, my back against a sack, piles of boxes in front of me. A small group of men detached themselves from the others and stole in, one by one. They didn't notice me there. I realize now I should have stood up, made my presence known, and left. Even then it might have been too late. As it was, they began to discuss an escape."

"They planned the whole thing in front of you? You knew it was going to happen? Why didn't you say something?"

He gave me a long look.

"That was stupid. I'm sorry. Of course you couldn't."

He continued, assuming a detached tone. "One of them took out a cigarette butt. Another jostled him for it, and it dropped. In retrieving it, they spotted me. That was it. They tried to kill me."

"But you wouldn't have said anything. You didn't say anything."

"Because I wasn't a Nazi, they didn't credit me with being a patriot. To them it's the same thing. They don't understand the code that for four hundred years my family has lived by."

Perhaps they didn't understand, but I did. The nuances he saw, the distinctions he made, were those of a thoughtful man who rejected the fanaticism, yet embraced and loved his country. Even now with the war going against him he saw not only defeat but hope. It was a beginning, and I, who had made so many beginnings, saw that my job was to help him come to terms with his disability.

As far as I knew he had never looked at the amputation, and when I tended it, cleaned it, applied lotion, he looked away. If he could have left his leg in my care he would have.

It was time. I handed him the washcloth. He looked at me inquiringly. "I've already washed."

"You haven't finished."

His eyes followed mine, traveling the length of his leg, coming to an abrupt stop below the knee. "No," he said, "I can't."

I waited.

"I find it repulsive."

I waited.

He accepted the washcloth, clenched his hand over it, and, in a single angry gesture, made a pass over the stump. "There. Are you satisfied?"

I took the lotion from the table.

"What's that?"

"It's the lotion I rub you with. You have to start doing these things for yourself, Erich."

"Why?"

"Because the less scarring, the better success you'll have with the fit of the prosthesis, the more comfortable it will be, and the longer you'll be able to wear it."

He grit his teeth and, looking at the ceiling, pressed the lotion into his palm, and made a swipe with it across the wound. Most spilled.

"It's a start," I said. "We'll try again tomorrow."

The next day when I came, he took the washcloth from me and applied it assiduously to the wound. Then, reaching for the lotion, rubbed that in thoroughly. "Did you know," he was talking very fast, not letting himself think about what he was doing, "that D minor is Mozart's key of fate? He was composing the string quartet K421/417B while his wife was having a baby in the same room. You can hear her cries in the music, then the sudden forte as the second octave leaps to the minor tenth. An uproar in the thirty-second bar of the andante quiets to piano. The child is born."

"That's beautiful," I said. "You can pretend the string quartet is playing while you try the parallel bars." I got him to his feet and handed him crutches. Having so recently gone through therapy myself, I knew the physical pain, the emotional ups and downs, but I was living proof of its benefits, and I was determined that Erich should be restored to a normal human being in spite of himself.

He swung along beside me down the corridor. When we came to the therapy room, he confronted the bars, let the crutches clatter to the floor, and negotiated the space between bars by hopping and swinging his arms. What a superb athlete he was. Never once did he grab the bars for support.

I was ready with the crutches at the other end. The effort had exhausted him. He was wet with perspiration, and I insisted on a wheelchair for the return trip.

He didn't like me to show concern. If he'd had a bad day, he was sure to cover it up. But I got to know these ploys. He would talk music then, or philosophy or poetry. "Listen," and he quoted,

" 'You are like a flower, so chaste and pretty and pure. I look at you, and worry strikes me in my heart. It seems to me as if I place my hands on your head, praying that God will keep you so pure and pretty and chaste.' "

He looked at me with a distant smile. "The Nazis burned Heine's poetry, every scrap."

"Who would want to destroy such a lovely thing?" I asked.

"You are very *schön* yourself, Kathy."

"*Schön*? Isn't that thank you?"

"Thank you is *danke schön*; *schön* by itself is pretty, very pretty."

I gave him his pain medication.

"Why didn't you tell me that while I was in prison you'd seen action?"

"I don't know. It didn't seem relevant."

"Not relevant to be shipped to Italy, to have gone through Cassino, to have been wounded? Kathy, what happened to you happened to me. What you saw I saw, and the men locked in the psychiatric ward saw. It's relevant, Kathy. Believe me, it's relevant."

The day Erich stood for the first time with his artificial leg, a change came over him. Once on his feet he said, "I begin to imagine I am a man. I don't imagine I will do snowplow turns again or a downhill schuss, but the world is definitely meant to be grappled with from a standing position."

I laughed and agreed.

But now the parallel bars were an agonizing obstacle course. He faced them daily and marched along between them, not reaching for them, not even touching them, but, after a step or two, collapsing.

I always caught him. That was my job and I did it. Then one session in the therapy room, it all came together. His strength, his sense of balance—he walked unaided.

He turned to me in triumph. I shared it with him. He didn't want to go back to bed, but sat on the edge of it. "I no longer feel that terrible sense of *Weltschmerz*." He smiled and translated, "World weariness."

"I know."

"Kathy, you fought right alongside me. I wonder why."

"I'm your nurse," I said, and went about the thousand and one duties that called me that morning. I had asked myself the same question, but always backed away from it as I did now.

Now that I had gotten him this far along, discharge and prison lay ahead. A man with one leg was vulnerable, and given a second chance would that same fanatical clique of prisoners succeed in killing him?

I went with this problem to Egg.

She looked over a mound of work. It didn't matter how high it was. She always found time for me.

"Kathy, I've been so busy I've hardly seen you."

"Sister, can we save another caterpillar?"

She laughed. "Love to."

"Well, then." I sat down and told her my struggle to bring the Austrian amputee to the point where his life seemed worth living again, only to throw him once more to the Nazis.

"Oh, dear." Egg's eyebrows shot up in consternation. "But how can we prevent it?"

I'd been waiting for that question. "We're so short-handed, and he couldn't escape. He couldn't very well limp out of here, even if he wanted to. We could use him in a dozen different capacities. So why not make him a trustee?"

Sister's glasses regarded me keenly. "Well, now," she said, "let's see what we can do."

ERICH WENT TO work for the nuns with a will. He managed his artificial leg with the skill of a skier, and was on his feet for hours taking on the heaviest tasks. Egg in particular was delighted with him. He upended and moved garbage cans, stowed cots, carried the mail sack in, and became our general factotum.

His quarters were an unused storage room, into which he crammed his old cot and a single chair. He added a bookcase, which he built himself out of a couple of bricks and a board he scrounged from somewhere. It was soon stocked with second-hand books the Sisters picked up for him in lieu of wages. I was not surprised to see a copy of Heinrich Heine's poems. I was surprised at a treatise on elasticity.

"Why would you be surprised? I'm an engineer."

"You are? I didn't know that."

"I have a degree, but the war came and I never made use of it."

Another volume also puzzled me, *The Last of the Mohicans*. "Now why would you be reading that?"

"It's a wonderful book. My favorite when I was thirteen. Did you ever read it?"

"I don't think so."

"You'd remember if you had. It's on account of this book that I didn't mind too much winding up in Canada. I always thought I'd like to live in blue sky country."

"You'd miss the city," I said, "the libraries, theater, music."

He laughed and his voice lit with enthusiasm. "I'd live in the forest, but I wouldn't be a hermit. I'd come in for an evening on the town, as the Americans say." He bent toward me. I was sitting on the floor and the door was open. This was something the Sisters insisted on. Propriety was in this fashion assured.

"In all this time I haven't seen you wear the onyx ring. Do you still have it?"

I flushed. "I should have given it back to you before."

"But why? It's yours. I gave it to you."

"I never accepted it. I couldn't accept it. It's too valuable."

"You talk as though it's a Draupnir, Odin's self-perpetuating gold ring from which nine new gold rings drop every ninth night. But this is only an ordinary black onyx ring. I would like to see it on your hand."

"You would?" I asked, suddenly feeling a strange admixture of things.

"You know, *Liebchen*"—he had taken to calling me that when we were alone—"it might even be possible . . . my boyhood dream of living in the wilderness, fishing, trapping, being close to nature. That kind of life must appeal to you too, it must be in your blood."

"Yes." And the few days I had spent with Anne Morning Light obliterated the little storage room. I'd been bathed and purified there, I'd been married. The honeymoon tepee of willow, the soft skins—Crazy Dancer filled my heart and my being. What was I doing here! I stumbled to my feet and without explanation rushed back to my room.

I hardly slept that night. "He's dead, he's dead," I told myself viciously. It was only a year and some months—too soon to allow myself to be involved, even mildly, with anyone. With Erich, sometimes I forgot this. I forgot to hurt. What kind of person did that make me? Was I woman first, and person second? I got out of bed, stood in front of the dresser, and raised my eyes, looking at my reflection in the oval mirror.

I saw a woman. Young, dusky, and yes, attractive. I continued to study my face in the glass. *Schön*, he'd said, means pretty.

Deliberately I opened my top bureau drawer. I had wrapped the ring in tissue paper. But a gray and white feather lay on top of it. I put the feather with my wolf tail guardian at the bottom of the drawer and unwrapped the ring. Onyx—black, hard, polished, the diamond not large but magical. As I held it, colors shifted in its depths. The movement in its center made it seem almost alive. I put the ring on the second finger of my right hand. The innocuous hand. My left hand was bare. Indians don't exchange rings.

Crazy Dancer was no longer in the same world with me. I was young and I was "*schön*," and someone thought enough of me to give me this beautiful ring.

I was conscious of the ring all morning, although no one noticed it. Or if they did, didn't comment.

I ran into Erich by the laundry chute. We each had a load of soiled linen to send down to the boiler room where the wash was done. He saw the ring immediately. But he said nothing.

At noon he caught up to me in the cafeteria. "Let's take our lunch outside," he said.

I fastened my sweater and followed him into the grounds. We sat on a low stone wall and unwrapped our sandwiches.

"It seems," he said, "that the American and British are at the Elbe, only sixty miles from Berlin. It's over, Kathy."

"Yes, I think so."

"And I'm not going back. Not like this. Not as a cripple."

"Erich, no one would imagine that you . . ."

"Not in the fore part of the day. But you know how it is. The damn thing starts to pain me. If I fight it, a sore develops, and the next day I'm a one-legged man on crutches. So, around four in the afternoon I unstrap the prosthesis. My mother generally entertains at that hour—you know, the local dignitaries, perhaps a visiting virtuoso—and I'd be expected to be part of the soiree."

"You've gone through a war, Erich. You have an engineering degree. Get your own apartment, make your own schedule."

"There speaks the new world. The obligation of centuries doesn't rest on you. You're free, independent, young—in a free, independent, young country. Kathy, I want to be part of that."

"You mean, stay here?"

He reached over and wiped a speck of mustard from my mouth. "Stay here with you," he corrected.

"But—" Too many what-ifs tumbled about in my mind.

"I want to transfer the ring, that I'm very happy to see you wearing, to the proper finger. In Europe the wedding band goes over the vena amoris on the middle finger of the right hand. That you're wearing it at all must mean something. Does it mean you feel for me some part of the love I feel for you? That is the question. I've loved you from the moment you changed my first damned plasma bag."

I tried to interrupt, to stop him, but he wouldn't have it.

"How could I speak? How could I say anything? I was the enemy, a defeated man, a prisoner. But things have changed. It would seem for the worse, but maybe it wasn't for the worst. I lost my leg. I thought that meant my life as well. I hoped you'd forget the surgical scissors, leave them so I could cut my wrists. But then I took a more philosophical view. I realized that committing suicide isn't really the first reaction. First you want to kill everyone else." He laughed.

I had tears at the back of my throat, but he could laugh.

"Don't you think that's an amazing insight? I do. I think it's pretty funny. And of course, once I thought that, killing myself was no longer an option. That's how a sense of humor saves us sometimes. Still I knew I wouldn't go home. But that was a negative. Now I see the positive side."

"Which is . . . ?"

"Staying here. Making a new life in the new world. I want it to be with you, Kathy. The things we joked about could actually be true, couldn't they? Please," he said, and put his hand over mine, "make it true. Marry me."

The next moment I was in his arms and we were both crying. Then I pushed myself away. "We have to think, Erich. Can this possibly work out?"

"Kathy, I've done nothing but think about it."

"But there are things you don't know. I'm married. I was married."

"What?"

"Yes, to Crazy Dancer. We were married in the Indian way. It was a blanket ceremony. The Canadian government doesn't recognize it, of course. But I feel married."

"But Crazy Dancer's ship, the troopship that left in the harbor here, was sunk by a U-boat. You told me that. He died at sea."

"Yes, that's true. But I still feel married."

"Of course. I understand. The commander, and Rudolf, one of my shipmates—I can't think of them as dead. I keep remembering conversations. Questions come up I want to put to them. When they're gone suddenly like that, you can't make yourself believe it."

"That's how it is," I said, seeing the plains of Romagna, seeing Nurse Lander, hearing the ping on the wash basin. "You don't quite believe it."

Erich watched me with concern, with apprehension. We had gone through the same things—he'd said that.

"When you were in prison, I found that I missed you. . . . And when I came back from Cassino and you were in my care again, it just happened. My mind and heart are still scrambling to make all sorts of adjustments."

"I'm trying to understand what you're saying, Kathy. You missed me—that's what you said, isn't it?"

"Yes . . ."

"That's enough. It means you have some feeling for me. What? Fondness? Love? Could it be love, *Liebchen?*"

Gray eyes looking into mine. "Yes, yes, it is love. I love you, Erich."

His embrace was total, and my starched nurse's cap fell on the ground between us.

Fourteen

OUR PRIVATE REALITY, the one that from that moment encompassed us, gave way to a public occurrence. April 12, 1945, Franklin Delano Roosevelt died. The world stood still and tried to absorb what this meant. But if the Germans hoped the shock would paralyze the forward thrust of Allied armies, they were mistaken. The Russians, pushing from the east, were poised to take Berlin. Montgomery on the west was trying to beat them to it. Hitler, it was said, had gone to ground in vaults under the city, while above him in the streets there was hand-to-hand fighting. Another terrible rumor that everyone believed because it was so unbelievable was that Hitler, paranoid, watching everything collapse around him, turned on his own people: Many Berliners sought safety from Allied bombing in the railroad tunnels; it was said Hitler ordered the water sluices and valves opened, and drowned them by the hundreds.

Rumors piled one on another. A few days later the story was bruited about that Hitler had married his mistress, Eva Braun, and died with her in a suicide pact, after first poisoning his dog and watching the effect. May fourth, German forces in the field surrendered to Montgomery. The formal document of surrender that ended the European war was signed and witnessed May eighth at Eisenhower's headquarters in Reims, in the presence of French and Russian delegations. Ike, who had just come from viewing the mass graves of Treblinka where men, women, and children were reduced to jutting ribs and pelvic bones, refused to shake hands with the German general. This was no civilized war, and he refused to confer civility on it by a handshake. Americans are great. I love them.

Wild celebration in the streets of Montreal. The great bells of Notre Dame pealed out over the city. The hospital flew the yellow and white flag of the Vatican alongside the Canadian Red Ensign, the Tricoleur, the Union Jack, and the Stars and Stripes. Patients sat up in bed and blew horns and paper favors that unrolled. Everywhere people joined arms. Strangers kissed and sang. Radios blared "La Marseillaise." Bars stayed open and there were free drinks. Erich picked me up and twirled me around, and we both ended on the floor. We stayed where we were, laughing and kissing.

"I'm no longer a prisoner," he said. "I marry you as a free man."

"Hurray!" I shouted.

But when he had a chance to think about it: "It's bad the Russians hold Berlin, after what we did to them at Stalingrad and Moscow."

He cheered considerably as it came out that Berlin would be divided into two zones, and Vienna into four. The *Standard* ran an interesting article revealing that Roosevelt and Churchill had met here in Quebec Province in August of '43 and again at the Octagon Conference September 11, 1944, in which a plan was developed to limit Russian spoils. The editorial page predicted that the Americans would mop up the Japanese in short order. The world would be at peace.

"We lived through history," I said.

"And contributed to it," he replied bitterly.

But this was not the time for bitterness. The future, which

had been on hold, was suddenly here, open, and ready for us. We felt the wonderful hope that filled the air, it spilled into our personal lives. Anything was possible. All the what-ifs could come out of the shadows.

We were happy, so filled with new confidence that I didn't want the slightest cloud to mar our wedding. "You must write your parents," I said to Erich. "You must tell them everything, explain your decision, tell them you are getting married to an Indian girl and starting a new life."

He agreed. He too had enough happiness to share.

Neither of us mentioned our coming marriage at the hospital. Though Erich was no longer a prisoner, he was Austrian, and feeling didn't die easily. However, Mama Kathy had to know and, if possible, attend. She, and Connie and Jeff, and Georges if he was back. It would be a wonderful reunion. After Papa died, our telephone had been discontinued. We couldn't afford one. But Mama had moved back home and wrote proudly that a phone line had been installed. It was as though I stepped into a new era.

I felt quite cosmopolitan as I laid out my dimes and placed a call to Alberta. There was no answer from the other end. I was about to hang up when her voice came through the wire. Unmistakably her voice, yet altered. There was no timbre in it, and before knowing why I was asking, "Mama, are you all right?"

I heard her tell me Georges was dead, but it didn't register.

"He was killed two days ago, after the surrender. He was moving from his quarters at Bletchley Park, crossing a field on his way to say goodbye to a friend. And, you know, they're renovating everywhere, trying to clean up the rubble. There was an earth-moving machine working above him. It triggered an unexploded bomb, and the building he was walking by gave way."

I love you, Mama, I love you. Even that I couldn't say. My dimes were used up. I continued to sit in the phone booth.

I sat in the public phone booth and tried to make sense of things, collapsing buildings, dying two days after the war ended, never coming home. Thank God Connie was married and had her own life. Still, I know she thought of herself as half a person. I remembered Georges from the time I was very little. I remembered he made shadow pictures for me on the wall, a rabbit whose nose twitched, a long-necked dinosaur that changed into a giraffe when I got scared. I remembered his magician's hat, and that he had made reality disappear and replaced it with his own. Please, please. Make this reality go away, make it disappear.

I walked back to where Erich waited.

"Well," he asked, "can they come?"

"No." I didn't tell him. I was afraid he would try to comfort me. For things that make no sense there is no comfort.

I DIDN'T WANT to be married in a church. That belonged to another young man, and young woman.

I put on my best dress, and Erich bought a beautiful spring bouquet of jonquils and sweet alyssum, which I carried, trying not to remember the flowers I once found in my shoes.

For the occasion he borrowed the onyx ring. "On our first anniversary you'll have a gold band," he promised.

We were married before a justice of the peace in a civil ceremony, one the dominion of Canada recognized. Since we were in Canadian jurisdiction, the ring went on the fourth finger of my left hand.

There was no one to stand up for either of us. I hadn't called Mama back. I hadn't the heart. Erich had been part of the German war machine responsible for the fact that Georges would not be coming back. I wasn't sure she would feel that way, but she might. And I didn't want any cloud on this special day.

I didn't know Erich had rented a motel room. It was the first of the surprises he'd arranged. "I'm going to dress you like an Austrian bride. Look," and he produced a pair of lace curtains from Mother Superior's room, that were supposedly in the wash. He draped one around me in a sort of flounce. The other, a bridal veil, he fastened to my hair with bobby pins I produced from my purse.

He stood back and surveyed his efforts. "The hair is not right," he said critically. "It needs to be up. And, you know, poofy in front."

"I know how to do that," and I imitated one of Mandy's coiffeurs.

He was delighted. "You look like a grand duchess," he said, and wound flowers in my pompadour. I broke one off to put behind his ear. Then we bowed to each other, linked arms, and waltzed around the room. Every time he made a turn he fell down, me on top of him. This occasioned a glass of claret, which was part of his surprise, and a song.

He started with "The Blue Danube." I contributed the latest Bing Crosby hit, "Don't Fence Me In." He took over with *"Röslein, Röslein, Röslein rot, Röslein auf der Heiden."*

He was shy about making love because of his leg, but a sheet tossed lightly over us, and who knew. Who knew, who cared? When he called me *Liebchen* the great Nordic god Thor strode the moment, sweeping us to a Valhalla of storm and ecstasy. We clung to each other. The onyx ring, on my left hand now, said, You are one.

THE SURPRISES CONTINUED. Next, our wedding breakfast. He had paid the manager's wife to shop for and cook the meal, which he assured me was in the finest Austrian tradition.

"There," he said, sitting across from me, while between us was spread bacon and eggs, pancakes, potatoes, and a lavish frosted roll. "Now I feel married." The coffee was steaming hot, and ladled into it, a mountain of whipped cream.

Erich's final surprise was to produce Mandy. She gave me a big hug and kiss. "Getting married agrees with you," she said, "you should do it more often."

Out of her nurse's uniform she looked like a pinup girl fresh off a Petty calendar. Erich, it turned out, had phoned and persuaded her to come after swearing her to secrecy.

"I'm not in touch with anyone from the hospital," she told us. "But Robert made it back. We're engaged," she said, answering my unasked question. Then came a defense and justification of him, which, while it failed to change my opinion of Robert, made me like her even more.

"You can't believe what that boy went through. He was posted to North Africa with the 8th, just west of Tobruk, the Gazala-Bir line. And it sobered him down, but good. Do you know it's absolutely true that the enemy—" She stopped self-consciously. "Excuse me, Erich. But it's got to be said. They didn't pay the slightest attention to the red cross clearly painted on top of the hospital roof. They strafed everything. Patients were killed and one of the doctors."

"He was with the 8th Army?" Eric asked. "That means they were up against Rommel."

"That's right. The Boche—the Germans," she corrected herself, "held everything from Alamein to Tripoli. The conditions were impossible, a dead horse right outside the building swelled up and gave off an awful odor. The hospital ran short of supplies. Especially water. The patients weren't bathed. Can you imagine, Kathy? Everyone stank, and everyone had heat rash. I mean, they sweated all day and slept in their clothes at night.

"And the birds! That was the other thing, birds flew up and down the corridors, and dogs prowled between the beds licking up anything on the floor. Can you imagine working under those conditions?"

She apparently had put out of her mind that volunteering for these conditions saved his skin. However, I said temperately, "As long as he came out of it okay. So you're engaged?"

"Oh yes. He even got a commendation. And that went a long way toward smoothing things over with my dad." She went on to expound a bit of Mandy philosophy. "Have you ever noticed that when things are meant to be, everything falls into place?"

Not for everybody, I reflected, pushing back thoughts of Crazy Dancer and Georges, and the Gurkhas, trying not to remember British, New Zealand, and Maori boys left on the mountain. Mandy went on. "A surgeon friend of Dad's is retiring and he bought the practice for Robert."

I saw what she meant about things falling into place.

"I don't intend to stay in the nursing profession," Mandy was saying. "You have to be crazy to work that hard. Besides, we're planning a family. We want three children, a boy, a girl, and—whatever. What do you two want?"

We looked shyly at each other. Oddly enough we had never discussed children.

"A whatever," Erich told her.

Mandy treated us to a dinner at the Hotel Windsor, and pulled me into the ladies' room to say, "Remember our first quarrel?—well, almost a quarrel. I told you people were talking about the time you were spending with Erich, and I advised you to cool it. I'm so glad you didn't pay any attention to me."

I hugged her, thinking this was the reason I loved this flighty, irrepressible girl. She was genuinely glad to see me happy. She was a friend.

Back at the table she explained for the second time that

Robert couldn't be here. She filled in the picture by adding that he was assisting at a rhinoplasty.

"That's a nose job, isn't it?" Erich asked.

It turned out the practice was in plastic surgery.

"But Mandy," I couldn't help exclaiming, "he's such a talented surgeon. You mustn't let him waste his gift."

Mandy set down her fork and stared at me in her nearsighted way. "I knew you'd say that, Kathy. Every time I'm with you, you change my entire life. That's exactly what I said to Robert, feeling just like you when I said it. But he's not only doing the rich and infamous. Three days a week it's reconstructive work on vets. You remember those 'serviceable' faces we gave them on ward A?"

It was hard to apart from Mandy. I didn't know when I'd see her again.

Later that night I sneaked Erich into my room, and under the covers. Money for another motel evening had run out, so in whispers we planned our life. One of the first things Erich did was to apply for Canadian residency. That made it all seem real. The little blond boy in the sailor suit pitching stones at the edge of the Bodensee, a future Canadian citizen.

We worked on a vita for him to mail to various architectural firms here in Montreal and Quebec, listing his schooling and credentials. With his degree in engineering this seemed a good route to try. We worried about the backlash he was almost certain to encounter. But when we thought about it soberly, it didn't seem that a one-legged Austrian naval lieutenant and an Indian woman who didn't know much about being Indian would do too well trapping and living off the land.

He would, he decided, start as a draftsman. "First I'll draw the blueprints, then I'll design them, and then . . ."

"And by then you'll be a world-famous architect and own the company."

"And go into politics," he concluded.

"Politics?" I was impressed.

He seemed a bit embarrassed. "That's the way I would have wound up if I'd gone back to Austria. In my family it's expected."

"Well, here nothing's expected. You do what you want."

After Erich was almost discovered in the hall making his nightly excursion to my room, we rethought our secret marriage and came to the conclusion that we should tell Sister Egg.

HAND IN HAND, we stood in front of her desk. She looked up with candid, round, nearsighted eyes, framed in glasses that mildly distorted them.

Before she could verbalize her question, Erich took my hand and stretched it toward her. Since our marriage I wore the ring on my right hand, on the vena amoris, which pleased Erich— and no one else suspected.

"What's this?" Sister asked.

"We're married," I said, wiggling my fingers so the small diamond flashed.

Egg rose from the chair to make the sign of the cross over us. Her round child's face was flooded with joy. "Bless you. Bless you both." Then, sinking back in her chair, "Imagine, a romance here, within the walls of this old building. It is absolutely delicious to think about. And you love each other very much?" She looked from me to Erich and back again.

"Very much," he assured her. "We love each other very much."

"Good. Good. That is very good. It is also good not to broadcast it. There is very little forgiveness yet for the war. I myself don't want to know anything officially." And she recited one of the little aphorisms for which she was famous. "Never trouble trouble, till trouble troubles you. Now," she said expeditiously,

"I will take soundings, ferret out the lay of the land, and let you know when it's advisable for you to make your announcement."

"Isn't she something?" I said to Erich that night under the covers. Sister Egg, heaven knows under what pretext, protected us by changing floors with Sister Magdalena. Even with this added security, we still laughed with our heads under the covers, and when he hummed Austrian folks songs, it was with his lips against my ear.

We found out all sorts of things about each other. He had mixed up the names of colors when he was little. He thought blood was green. And I told him the story Mama Kathy used to tell me, that when I was little I insisted on dressing myself, and the year I started school wore my dresses backward so I could button them.

"Kathy, Kathy," he said. "You were always Kathy."

I told him about my blue-eyed papa. "Mama used to say his eyes were so blue you could swim in them."

Finally I was able to tell him. I hadn't planned it, it just spilled out, the pent-up agony over Georges. "The reason no one came to our wedding is that I never asked them."

"You didn't? But I thought—"

"I know, the phone call. Erich, Mama Kathy just had word. Georges is dead. Two days after the war ended." I was able to cry now, so harshly that my body shook. Now I wanted his comfort, now I could accept it. We had grown close.

What to do about Mama Kathy had been troubling me. I'd been married for six weeks, and she didn't know about it.

Erich resolved the dilemma by saying, "The best thing to do now is just show up."

"You mean, go back to Alberta? That's where she is now."

"Yes. We'll save for it."

I hugged him for having such wonderful ideas.

*   *   *

WE SENT OFF the first job inquiries. Acceptance would bring independence. We could find an apartment, set up housekeeping, and openly acknowledge our marriage. But we worried.

Since Egg had not reported back to us, I could only assume that she still felt a tide of opposition, and did not judge even my job secure. Especially now, with prisoners repatriated, half the cots were empty in many wards. The pressing need for nurses was past. We were treating mainly chronic conditions. Aside from service-related cases of malaria contracted in the South Pacific, hookworm picked up in the Philippines, and an eye condition brought back from the Libyan desert, there were largely civilian disorders, the usual appendectomies, fractures, and infections, and Dr. Bennett had a cholecystectomy scheduled. The hospital was no longer on a wartime footing. I could easily be replaced. So for the moment we left things as they were.

A letter came.

I recognized the handwriting, and something inside me shriveled.

Crazy Dancer.

Crazy Dancer had written me this letter. I looked at the postmark. It was yesterday.

My fingers went at the envelope like a ravening thing, fumbling in their haste. I could only get it open by tearing jaggedly. I didn't read it. I picked out the important words: *Meet me . . . two o'clock in the afternoon . . . Canadian Pacific station.*

After taking in the gigantic fact that he was alive and had written this, I read it. Slowly, word for word.

I was in such a turmoil I couldn't think. An initial rush of joy was extinguished by an avalanche of emotion. Chaotic, undecipherable. My God, what had I done? Marry in haste, Egg would say, repent at leisure. Mama Kathy said a year was a decent interval, a year to mourn the dead.

A year for the dead to rise up again.

It had been wartime. Things happen fast in war. Life, death, it was all on a different scale, a different timetable. You acted or the moment slipped away.

He was alive! Dear, dear, wonderful Crazy Dancer. The first spasm of joy should have been what filled my heart. Instead it was twisted with fear. I thought of Erich, who had wanted to open his veins with my surgical scissors. Green blood, I thought hysterically.

Half formulated recriminations attacked me from all sides. They pounded my head. Was I married to two men? Had I destroyed all three of us?

I had not consciously gone there, but I was standing in front of the chapel. I didn't go in. I was damned, cursed. There must be some evil in me that had brought this about. Why hadn't my wolf guardian protected me? Perhaps he was angry with me for leaving my Indian self behind. My only possible justification was that it had all come about through love. At that moment Elk Girl's dream warning returned to me. She had said I could wound Crazy Dancer, and when I denied it, tossed back cryptically, "You're marrying him, aren't you?" Friendly fire, she called it.

My soul hid from black dancing eyes, and from gray thoughtful ones. What had I done?

I SCRIBBLED A note to Erich. I told him I had a headache. I did. Instead of turning in, I walked. My thoughts kept pace with me. The only explanation that fit, he must have been a prisoner. But the telegram—lost at sea. And the newspaper—TROOPSHIP SUNK WITH ALL HANDS.

I don't know where I walked. Mont-Royal loomed above me. Buildings seemed to lean in on me. It was hard to breathe.

Thoughts I didn't want to remember seared themselves into my head.

At some hour I threw myself into bed. Tomorrow when I saw him—what? At two o'clock in the afternoon he would know I hadn't waited for him.

I avoided Erich all morning. I knew his routine, so it was easy to do. At twenty of I left for the station, that great hub of the CP Railroad. Wealth from furs and mines had built a nineteenth-century palace. The railroad tied the land together and made it a country. Who had told me that? Of course, it was Erich. In a few moments I'd be trying to explain about Erich.

I could see the tracks now. The train would be coming into view, blue and silver. Knots of people craned for a sight of it. Baggage carts rolled past, porters directing them. The air vibrated. The crowd strained forward. The juggernaut appeared, snorting as its tail followed. I pressed myself against a marble pillar. I heard a mother trying to explain to a son why there was no third rail. "It's a diesel." But he felt cheated of the third rail, the deadly one. They spoke in French, "*Mort.*" I saw him. There he was! Crazy Dancer! I wanted to run up to him, kiss him, hug him, laugh with him. I clung to the pillar, hardly able to keep upright.

He stood still and looked around. He's looking for me. I'm right here, Crazy Dancer. But I didn't move.

There were so many people. I saw him look through them, past them. Streams of passengers that the train disgorged funneled to either side of him. Then he saw me. An electric charge passed between us.

He covered the space in a second. The next I was in his arms, being held and holding. He murmured my Indian name over and over, "Oh-Be-Joyful's Daughter."

I couldn't say anything. He put me at arm's length and looked long and lovingly into my face.

I had to speak. I had to tell him. "I thought you were dead."

"But they didn't know my name, remember? None of their death devices could be marked for me."

"There was no word. You didn't write."

"I wrote. . . . You never got a letter?"

I shook my head. "The ship you were on, the troopship, sank with all hands. That's what they said: with all hands."

"I was never on it. There was an officer waiting for me. They assigned me to a special engineer detail."

"You were never on the troopship?"

"Not that one. The ship I was on was a floating repair shop. They put me to work fixing defective torpedoes. We were attacked off the coast of France, rammed by a U-boat. The ship broke up. You can live six hours in the waters of the North Atlantic, did you know that? Anyway, I was picked up by the Resistance, and hidden in a farmhouse. I wrote you all this."

"Crazy Dancer, I'm so happy, so grateful that you're alive. But I'm married."

"Of course you're married. That's one of the first things we'll do, have the wedding in the church; our mothers will sit in the first pew and cry. It will be beautiful."

"You don't understand," I said.

"I do. I understand how bad you felt to think I was dead. But I'll make it up to you, beginning now. Let's get out of here, go someplace where we can be alone."

"Crazy Dancer, you didn't hear me. I'm married."

The dancing lights went out of his eyes. They returned a blank stare. "Go on," he said.

"I thought you were dead."

"You said that."

"I thought you were dead," I said again.

"Oh-Be-Joyful's Daughter, tell me what you have done."

"I married someone, a patient. See?" I held up my hand with the onyx ring.

"Black," he said. "A black wedding." Then, "But you were married to me."

"You were listed as dead. Your mother brought me the telegram."

"And your heart said nothing? Your heart didn't tell you it was a lie?"

"I didn't know. I had no way of knowing. And there was no word from you."

There was a pause that couldn't be filled.

"You might have waited," he said simply.

Yes. I might have waited.

I felt his hand over mine, firm, dark, sinewy. "Never mind," he said. "It's done. Over with. We'll forget it."

I looked at him, bewildered. "What do you mean, forget it?"

"You made a mistake. I can understand it . . . you thought I was dead." The life that had been extinguished lit his eyes once more. "I forgive you." With that he gathered me into a strong embrace.

I managed to get my hand against his shoulder and shove with all my might. Crazy Dancer looked puzzled.

"I'm married. Can't you understand? I'm married."

"Yes," he agreed. "To me."

"Not to you. To someone else."

"But you can't. It's impossible. You're already married to me."

"I know we considered ourselves married. We were married, according to Iroquois tradition. But it's a marriage not recognized by Canadian law."

"What has Canadian law to do with you and me?"

"It sanctioned my present marriage. I'm someone you don't know anymore. I'm Mrs. Erich von Kerll."

"Von Kerll? German?"

"Austrian."

"What's the difference? He's still an enemy."

We stared at each other bleakly.

"I see how it is," he said in a low, toneless voice. "You love this other man."

"He's a very fine man, Crazy Dancer."

"He's a fool," he spat out, "if he loves you."

"Please don't hate me."

"Hate you? I want you to listen to me. I want you to come with me now. Now is the moment you leave your Austrian and come with the one who you married first and who loved you first. We will leave here and walk into the life we had."

"Crazy Dancer, Erich is a cripple. He only has one leg."

"That makes a difference? Then I'll cut off mine, both of mine. Come with me." With one light step he moved away from me. I stood rooted where I was.

He held out his hand. Mine was a heavy lump at my side. Another sudden movement and he was very close, but not touching. He spoke with controlled fury. "You called a Witigo to eat up your life. All that's left is lies, and faithlessness, and no love, no love at all. Throw out your guardian, he will not guard you any longer."

"If you are going to curse me, Crazy Dancer, don't hide behind guardians and Witigos. Do it yourself."

"Then I do, for throwing me away like a fish you don't want. For going against the promise of a life together, a promise made before my mother and my friends, a promise you tore in shreds and threw in my face."

"I have said all this to myself, Crazy Dancer. But when you think of me, besides everything you said, I want you to remember one other thing . . . I will be grateful all my life that you came back."

I turned away.

I half expected that with a glissade and a tour jeté he would land beside me. And if he did, I didn't know that I would have the strength a second time to walk away. Not like an unwanted fish. How could he think I would throw him away like that? A Witigo. Oh, dear God, I almost laughed. I knew from Elk Girl that a Witigo was a monstrous, hair-covered creature, who ate its young and lived below in an ice cave and had an ice heart. That's what he thought I had, an ice heart.

I didn't know where I was. I walked, taking streets at random. I sat in a little park. I sat there all day. I didn't think about Crazy Dancer and I didn't think about Erich. I watched a lady feeding pigeons, and children taking turns on a slide and rope swinging in tight circles. They called to each other in the quick voice pattern that is Canadian French. It was good to hear children play. I was glad for Anne Morning Light that her son was back. Would she also want a Witigo to attack my life?

I'd forced him to call the Witigo. I'd answered him in ways he couldn't strike back at or deny. "I'm married." I'd said it again and again. I used facts as my excuse, facts as my weapon. Fact: a husband. Fact: a ring. Fact: a legal marriage. Crazy Dancer used a different language. He spoke of love.

I watched the shadows of leaves as they danced on the walkway. I saw something surprising—a chameleon. Chameleons were not indigenous creatures in this climate, but they sold them at La Ronde. They came with a little gold chain and pin, to fasten to your collar. This small lizard had escaped the amusement park and lived here. As a result of his adventures he had only half a tail. Immediately I identified with him. I too had lost part of myself.

I went back to my room in the nurses' annex.

"Where on earth have you been?" Erich greeted me.

Fifteen

WE FOUND A small apartment. It was old French architecture and charming. Mme. Gosselin closed off three rooms of her home, and we rented them. There were no interior stairs, you had to go outside to get from one story to another. Erich had trouble at first, but by the third day had mastered the stairs. The largest room had been a library. There was a fireplace, and we curled up evenings in a Mackinaw blanket, the Hudson Bay kind with stripes of black and red, green and yellow. I didn't tell him about Crazy Dancer being alive, or that I'd seen him. I blocked it from my mind.

The bedroom was small. Once the double bed was in, there was no room for anything else. Erich was practicing his drafting skills and had a large drawing pad on the floor. It took up the entire space. He was able, with the aid of his crutch, to swing off the bed over the sketched plans to the bathroom, but I had to stand on the bed and jump.

I kept having flashbacks. Peering into fog, holding my end of a stretcher, not knowing where I was. . . . This kind of thing used to happen a good deal in the wards, it occurred in men who had seen combat. But it didn't have to be the war. In fact, it usually wasn't. Out of nowhere I'd hear his voice—"*I'll teach you to be an Indian.*" I knew it was battle fatigue, but having a name for it didn't make it go away. Even when I was at work—cranking up a bed, assisting Dr. Bennett, or checking a chart—*"Watch it!" and the three-wheeler turned over and spilled us into the bank. "The center of gravity is too high."*

The announcement of our marriage didn't bring things tumbling down around our ears as we feared. It was taken philosophically, and we were even congratulated. Erich was being considered for a position with an architectural firm, and had been in for a second interview, which we took to be a favorable sign. We were already putting by for our surprise visit to Mama Kathy. I wasn't very original: I kept the money in the sugar bowl. We figured in about three weeks we could buy the tickets. Erich was very good about saving. He'd heard how fine the Montreal Symphony was. Desiré Dufauw directed, and Erich very much wanted to go, but deferred it for the sake of our trip.

"You'll love Mama Kathy. She spent her honeymoon traveling by dogsled."

—Sometimes it was the gesture of his hand at the railway station. Or the hurt look in his eyes—

I revived my cooking skills. For years I'd eaten in the hospital cafeteria. But no more. Between dispensing medication, changing dressings, and starting an intravenous feeding . . . I planned menus. Tonight I would prepare saschlik, a Polish dish Mama Kathy learned from a trapper's wife: lamb and tomatoes—*Or that first moment when he framed my face in his hands and looked at me with trust and love*—garnished with onion and apple and poured over a steaming potato.

Hiroshima. The dropping of the A-bomb brought an abrupt end to the war in the Pacific. Did it bring an end to man's humanity as well?

The technological aspect fascinated Erich. "A new energy

source. Think of it! A teaspoon of U-235 will light the entire world. Submarines will be able to navigate the seven seas without needing to surface. The possibilities are unlimited."

One moment a human being, the next etched into cement like a trilobite. We had achieved world peace.

I ARRIVED HOME one evening to find Erich waiting for me on the stairs. He had a telegram in his hand. "I don't know whether it's good news or bad. It's from my mother. She's coming to visit us."

"All the way from Austria!" I ran up the remaining flight. "But that's wonderful, isn't it?"

"Of course it is. Only, the old life is so far away now. She'll bring it with her."

"Are you afraid she won't approve of me?"

"Nothing like that. Of course not. It's just that it was a lifetime ago I was her son."

"Yes, the Bodensee, the little boy in the sailor suit." I looked around at our three rooms. Each item we'd added had been a cause for celebration. The bud vase Egg gave us I'd tried in a dozen places—the table, the windowsill, by the kitchen sink. Finally it came to rest on the secondhand end table Erich had bought. Now I wasn't so sure—our home that looked cozy and just right, I saw with other eyes. Instead of being charming, its age seemed a defect. It needed paint, the ceiling flaked, and the walls were dingy. The bannister leading to the landing had buckled and the wood splintered. The wardrobes in his mother's home were undoubtedly larger than our bedroom.

"I don't think this place will be what she expects." And I don't think I will be either, I thought.

"Nonsense. You've done wonders with it. It's our home, pleasant, clean, comfortable—what else is needed?"

"Think of what she's used to."

"Remember, Mother's gone through a war. We don't know what she's used to."

"That's true," I said, relaxing a bit.

Erich laughed suddenly. "Of course if you mean it's not elegant, no it isn't."

His lightheartedness reassured me. After all, it was ours, brought together by borrowings, gifts, and castaways. Somehow it all fit together, and the result was warm and friendly. The china couldn't be so readily dismissed, two of the plates chipped and not all the same pattern.

Erich guessed my thoughts. "It isn't a crime to be poor and starting out. All Austrians have a touch of schmaltz in their nature, and Mother will think it romantic."

"It isn't only things, Erich. It's me. Your mother has never seen a First Nation person. Maybe she isn't prepared. Well, I am many skin tones darker than you."

"Once I get a good tan we'll be the same shade. Kathy, one of your amazing attributes is that you have no idea how beautiful you are."

"*Schön?*"

"*Sehr schön.*"

Now it was my turn to laugh at him. "I think the German language should be called *schön* talk. Everything with you is *schön*. *Sehr schön*, *bitte schön*, and *danke schön*. Any others?"

"Only you, *Liebchen*."

ELIZABETH VON KERLL was coming by air transport, which she had somehow managed with the occupation authorities. The same skies that only four months ago had been deadly now accommodated a first trickle of traffic. Imagine looking *down* and seeing clouds, and, when they parted, the ocean! Soon, we were told, there would be commercial flights. The map of the world had shifted. The islands of the Pacific, so bloodily fought for, whose every inch was counted in human lives, suddenly were worthless. The war had passed over them, removing yesterday's values. Now everywhere, everyone was making a new start. What if—But there would be no more what-ifs. I was grown up and knew how tragically meaningless they were.

Erich and I took a streetcar to Boucherville, seven miles outside the city. Our guest was coming in on the flying boat *Caribou*, at Imperial Airways. It was rumored they intended to expand and form a transatlantic mail service. How quickly the mindset of the country changed; this had been an embarkation point for Hudsons, Liberators, Flying Fortresses, Mitchells, and Martin Marauders.

"Suppose," I asked, facing a fear I'd been struggling with, "suppose she wants us to go back with her to Austria?"

"We take a return flight, of course." Then, shaking me by the shoulders, "Don't look so stricken, *Liebchen*. Don't you know that nothing, nothing could pry me out of here?" And his fingers interlaced with mine.

Just before our stop I asked in panic, "What shall I call her?"

This gave him pause. "I think Elizabeth. Elizabeth will be best."

When I saw her I realized why. Young, blond, and beautiful, she gave no indication she had been in the air thirty-three hours with a stopover in Ireland, another in Newfoundland, and a midair refueling.

She stood still, letting crew members stream past as she took in her son. She seemed to inhale him, then inventory him, taking in the man. She came toward us smiling, allowing herself to be embraced, and then, catching sight of me, she made an instant assessment. Coming a step nearer, she clasped my hand and drew me to her.

"Kathy," she said; and to Erich, "She's lovely."

Then, if I remember, they both talked at once. "And how is father—?" But he scarcely paused when she shook her head in the negative. "—And uncle?"

"They both send their love. And Dorotea and Minna."

"And cousin Arthur?"

And so it went. Family members, friends, and relatives, all with a message for him, all wanting to be remembered. I watched his face. It was animated, flushed, and eager. His mind was back there, home, where he came from.

She hadn't mentioned the cane he used. She knew, of course, but she didn't mention it. They acted, both of them, as though he were exactly the same as when he'd left. But he wasn't. He knew and I knew that he was a cripple, with all that entailed—physical limitations, need for frequent rests, pain, and pain medication. Into their mélange of greetings, endearments, nicknames, and remembrances I inserted how pleased we were to have her.

She nodded, smiled at me, and went on talking to Erich. Her English was fluent, with a trace of accent that set certain words off in a lilting manner. Her *th*'s tended to *z*'s. It was charming. Everything about her was charming. She wore a fox fur, which had probably originated here. I took in her nylons. Silk stockings were out, nylons were in. Her traveling outfit was an understated, tailored brown suit. Small diamonds were set in her ears, I knew they were diamonds because of the one in my onyx ring—they had the same shifting centers.

Once or twice she lapsed into German, but Erich answered each time in English.

Elizabeth stepped into the cab without a clue as to the hole it made in our budget. How else did one get from here to there? She was interested in the city, exclaimed at the sight of Mont-Royal, whose massive volcanic upthrust dominated the city, while the cross blessed it. Elizabeth was impressed by the well-to-do homes along its higher terraces, identifying Gothic revivals, French provincial, Tudor, and Queen Anne villas. It pleased her that there were so many parks and bridges, but in spite of an occasional French mansard roof and crenelated parapet, she thought the downtown looked gray with its massive fieldstone fronts.

"Impressive," she said of the city, "more English than French. And the signposts, all English. I had thought of Montreal as a French city."

"Actually," Erich told her, "it's cosmopolitan, bilingual, and wonderfully old." He ordered the cabbie to drive out of our way so he could show his mother the sights.

"There seems to be a church every few blocks," she observed approvingly.

Erich pointed out the Place d'Armes with its monument to Paul Chomedy, Sieur de Maisonneuve, founder of the city, and the great basilica of Notre Dame. Then southeast to the St. Lawrence with its immense docking facilities going on block after block. "Fifteen hundred ships at a time could load here."

But Elizabeth was more interested in the shops on St. Catherine Street. I kept stealing sideways glances at her. She seemed too young to be Erich's mother, hardly older than I. We came to the lower-middle-class suburb where we lived, and Elizabeth was immediately intrigued by the exterior stairs. She pronounced them quaint.

It wasn't until she was ensconced in our best chair, with her stole hanging in my closet and a glass of sherry in her hand, that she began what she had crossed an ocean to say. It involved an acknowledgment of Erich's condition. I will say for her that she faced it directly. "One would not necessarily realize—a limp is distinguished these days, the mark of a soldier. As to the cane, almost every gentleman carries a cane. You must believe me,

Erich, it is not that bad. I was afraid—one sees so much in the way of disfigurement among our veterans. Actually, I am quite relieved. I'm sure your rehabilitation is due in large part to the excellent nursing care you received." And she flashed me a brilliant smile.

I glanced at Erich. Usually, after he'd worn the prosthesis three or four hours, he would unstrap it and allow himself a period of relief. But with his mother here, he was determined to stick it out. The wound was still sensitive, and I was afraid of it becoming aggravated and inflamed. We had already gone through an ulceration, and I didn't want to deal with that again. But I couldn't say anything to embarrass him. Besides, seemingly he was tolerating it.

"Now tell me about Father," he said.

She shook her head. "Your father is in failing health. The war—at first we thought you were dead. Then the terrible financial reverses. There was so much for him to handle." She turned to me. "And now it must all be reassembled, the assets of the estate, everything, accounts in Switzerland, in the Caribbean, you've no idea. The bookkeeping alone is monumental. But," she added brightly, "not to burden you. You children have your own life. I can see how good it is. I see what a lovely wife you've chosen, Erich. Your home, so welcoming, so comfortable. I have a warm feeling when I look at the two of you."

When the sherry had been sipped, I suggested a rest for Elizabeth, which she was happy to take.

In this way I got Erich into our bedroom and helped him out of the prosthesis. The impacted area was inflamed, and I rubbed it with salve. This eased him, and he stretched out on the bed with a set of architectural drawings.

"Your mother is so pretty and so young."

He agreed. "One of the few people the war hasn't changed."

"Tell me more about your father."

"He doesn't capitulate. That's the main thing about my father. He belonged to the old Social Democratic Party. In your terms that would be the more liberal party. He didn't change when it became convenient not to belong to it, when promotions were going to the National Socialists. And he didn't change when it became dangerous to belong to it.

"During my teen years it got ugly. There were threats, there were incidents, I had fights at school. Things grew so bad that he resigned his commission. Mother wasn't happy about that. But he stood firm. He was like a rock around which waters boil and swirl. His convictions, that's all he knew."

Perhaps it wasn't as romantic as the Bodensee heritage, but it was, I thought, more substantial. And I pictured the old gentleman with side whiskers.

During dinner Elizabeth sketched in broad strokes the general tenor of her personal war. "Officially the war began in '39. For Austria it was 11 March 1938. I'll never forget it. They marched in from the east, through the Neusiedlersee Pass, which was still snowed in. Not only did they march, they skiied and trucked in, they came by rail through the Tyrol to Salzburg, and fanned out into Vienna and the farming districts, Bergenland, Steiermakki, Karnten, and Niederösterreich.

"Everywhere our soft-spoken melodious German was replaced by harsh Northern dialect. What a distasteful sound!" She shuddered. "They took over everything, of course, the chemical plants, the nitrogen plant in Linz, electrical power, crude oil, natural gas—but they aren't content with utilities—the National Bank of Austria is next, where, as you know, your father had a seat on the board. Fortunately, as it turned out, the commandant quartered on us was a career soldier, a gentleman of good family. It makes a difference. He saw to it that our larder remained full. We were not reduced to want, as so many of our friends and neighbors were. But our privacy was gone, our servants. We kept to our rooms while *they* had the run of the house."

She paused for a sip of port. "Then of course you were called up. You remember the initial euphoria. But a year and a half, two years later, the war news began to be punctuated, perhaps I should say *lacerated* by news that didn't fit. One heard things, a returned veteran, someone in hospital—delirious, of course, but . . . Here and there, it is rumored, a ship is sunk, and another—and then Russia . . . utterly defeated, we are told. Yet I heard a captain with the Hitler medal who had been at Stalingrad say our troops were starving, and winter would finish them. Nothing is official. It is all indirect. And from you, Erich, no more letters, nothing. But your father and I don't speak of it. Even with his connections, we didn't know are you alive or dead."

Elizabeth turned to me. "It is terrible to lose a child, an only son. Believe me, it is as bad not to know. To hope one day, despair the next, snatch the mail out of the postman's hands. It was then his father began to fail. I looked at him one day and saw an old man. But there—" She caught herself and turned back to Erich. "By a miracle you are returned to us."

Erich responded with a deprecating wave of the hand that took in his missing leg.

"What is that?" she said almost angrily. "You are with us, here, alive, when so many aren't."

"I feel that way too," I said, identifying with Elizabeth for the first time.

Erich was anxious to turn the conversation from himself. "The country," he asked, "will it recover?"

"Of course. Certainly. But it is heartbreaking. Half the railroads are gone, and the bridges over the Danube blown, in fact all bridges and roads are pockmarked by shells or completely destroyed. Life in the cities is just beginning to crawl out from the ruins. But," she said with resolution, "there are endless opportunities for someone with family, with connections, someone who was awarded the Iron Cross, someone like you, Erich."

"Not someone like me," Erich said firmly. "Someone who hasn't grown attached to a vast new country, someone who hasn't started a new life."

Had he wanted to say, someone who hasn't an aboriginal wife?

With a little laugh Elizabeth retreated. "Of course, you are quite right, my darling, to feel that way." Then, turning to me, "Your country is so large, so pristine and unspoiled. You must forgive me being stupid on the subject. But I know so little of it, and even less about your people. I did not even know that they are referred to as First Nation people. You bring such an exotic strain to our family, my dear. I must inform myself, I must learn something of your background, your fascinating heritage."

Erich intervened. "If you want to read up on Indians, fine. But Kathy can't tell you anything. With her, *background* and *heritage* are two different things. She was raised by a white woman, Katherine Mary Flannigan, and her husband, a sergeant in the Mounties. Her brother and sister are of French extraction, and she didn't know any Indians until she went to school."

I suppressed an impulse to tell her about the blanket ceremony and that I had married one of those exotic creatures known as First Nation people.

Erich must have felt uncomfortable too, for he declared we should leave the anthropology for another day. To another day also was left the question of his fealty. Was it, as his mother implied, to Austria?

Elizabeth continued to fill in the picture, emphasizing the very large hole Erich's defection made. His father, physically and mentally impaired, was no longer capable of attending to family interests. She herself, as she pointed out, was not a businesswoman. Yet she hesitated to rely on lawyers when so much was at stake.

Several days later, while Elizabeth was shopping, Erich and I had one of our private talks. "What would you think," he asked, "of going back briefly, for a fortnight or two? Just to straighten out the affairs of the estate, collect the proper documents, and put our claim for reparations before the new regime? Tidy things up, leave them in good hands?"

"It would certainly help Elizabeth out."

"How would you feel about it?" he persisted.

I countered this with "How would *you* feel about it?"

"What do you mean? I don't understand."

"I think you do."

"If it's that old obsession of yours about being Indian—"

"Erich, I *am* Indian. Your mother chooses to say 'exotic.' What about your friends, relatives, neighbors? The society your mother moves in? How will they see me, and how will they feel about me?"

"I fought on Hitler's side, simply because I am Austrian. Do you think that I or my family or friends have taken on any of his madness? That we believe in the special purity of the Aryan bloodline? Come on, Kathy."

Put like that it did sound stupid.

From then on it was assumed we were returning and would vacation in Austria. It did seem a marvelous opportunity, too good to miss. Especially as Elizabeth made it plain she was underwriting the entire trip.

I thought that perhaps, woman to woman, I would look for the right moment and confide some of my hesitation to her. That moment came as we walked through the Bio Exposition. I thought this exhibit was something she would enjoy. It was the second largest botanical garden in the world and housed, according to the brochure, twenty-six thousand different plant species. We passed thick rubbery stalks bursting with unlikely blooms and banked layers of savannah grasses where herds of papier-mâché elephant herds grazed, and came to a stop before delicate fan-shaped leaves with veins like those on our own hands. A zebra with a glass eye watched as I came out with it, asking if she thought that, once we got to Austria, I would fit in.

"Of course." And she gave me an impetuous hug. "Naturally you'll need a few things," she added.

My heart sank. There was nothing in our budget for clothes.

With wonderful intuition she guessed the problem. "There's a family fund that takes care of such necessities," she said, "so please, not to give it another thought."

But I did think about it and worry about it. Finally I asked Erich.

"Mother's right," he said. "There is a fund for such contingencies."

"Then it's all right," I asked, only half convinced, "to go shopping with her and let her buy me things?"

"You're my wife, aren't you?" And he dismissed the subject by kissing the tip of my nose.

Elizabeth had a list. From my feet to my head I was to be outfitted. We took a cab to St. Catherine Street. Next door to Eaton's department store we purchased a lovely pair of gray suede shoes with French heels. Inside Eaton's we looked at stylish suits and coats before settling on a black caracul. I refrained from looking at the price tag. Blouses and dresses went over my head in a small airless cubicle. I paraded them before Elizabeth for her approval.

On to Morgan's and then Simpson's. I liked a dirndl skirt cut on the bias, but Elizabeth dismissed it, insisting it did nothing for me—whatever that meant. I think it meant that I was totally lacking in taste, sophistication, and elegance.

When I thought we were through, we had merely stopped

for what she called tea and I called lunch. She dragged me past a Kik stand, where you could get an economy cola, two glasses for a nickel. I found myself instead in the Ritz-Carlton having brunch in the Oval Room. I would have much preferred a quick sandwich at Ma Heller's. Elizabeth, I saw, was at home among sugar tongs and, in the evening I suppose, candle snuffers. While we waited for our shrimp canapes and watercress rolls, Elizabeth described shopping in Berlin. "I'm talking of the old days, of course. Tauentzienstrasse, corner of Kurfürstendamm. Marvelous shops, especially for jewelry."

As the luncheon progressed, the various items we had purchased were gone over. "I thought you looked very smart in the Worth."

"The Worth?"

"Yes, yes," she said with a touch of impatience, "the suit we decided on, the Suez rose designed by Worth."

I remembered gazing at myself in the large store mirror with its gilt frame. Who was that slim, dark girl? She wasn't me. I was sure of that. She was the girl Erich and Elizabeth planned to bring back to Austria, to introduce to high-bred relatives and friends as Erich's wife. Perhaps that's who the girl in the glass was—Erich's wife. The Suez rose suit was very becoming to her, it somehow minimized the copper tone of her skin.

I tried to focus on what Elizabeth was saying. "And I thought the periwinkle blue exceedingly becoming. Schiaparelli is for you, *Liebchen*, long simple lines. Yes, definitely, he had you in mind."

How charming she was, how generous. A fortune had been spent on me. The coat alone was a year's wages. How fairy-tale it seemed, misty, charming, and totally devoid of reality. But that girl in the looking glass, that Kathy that I would turn into, belonged to the periwinkle blue and the Suez rose. I saw her beside Elizabeth, acknowledging introductions, shaking hands, exchanging pleasantries. She was wearing the white kid gloves we had just purchased. They came to the elbows and closed with tiny seed pearl buttons. What if—?

With a start I came to myself.

The excursion did not end with the shopping. Elizabeth must see the French quarter. Old habit held me and a world of what-ifs. . . . What if Kathy Forquet von Kerll captured all hearts in her furs and her chiffons and her gray suede shoes? Erich was proud as he offered an arm and escorted her onto the floor of the grand ballroom. I could almost hear the strains of a Viennese waltz.

Coming out of Duprez Freres we passed by a touristy window in which a dark-colored mannikin was decked out in deerskin dress and moccasins with quillwork. She had a feather in her hair. Elizabeth stopped and stared.

The packages were delivered the following day. That evening we had a grand showing. I modeled item after item. Erich watched silently. I began to feel apprehensive. I had allowed his mother to spend too much. But at the end of the show he kissed me. "You'll knock them for a loop," he said. He loved picking up slang. To Elizabeth he said more formally, "You did well, Mother."

He considered the money well spent. It seemed I was dichotomized into two persons. The old Kathy, brought up by Katherine Mary Flannigan, and the new me, the one about to step from the mirror and take her place in a what-if world. I hung my wardrobe carefully in the chiffonier, but I didn't throw out the boxes. Instead, I folded the tissue paper into them and placed them on the highest shelf, which they occupied with my wolf talisman.

That says it all, I thought. Could they continue to reside side by side as they appeared to be doing?

The end of Elizabeth's visit was approaching. She had what

she had come for. She had crossed the North Atlantic to bring us back with her. And we were going.

To make myself believe it, I went around after work to tell Egg. She looked up from her desk, and her face fulfilled its laugh lines. She was happy to see me and incredulous when I told her about a vacation in Austria.

"Such things don't happen to people I know," she said.

"It's wonderful, isn't it?"

She nodded that it was, but simultaneously made the sign of the cross over me.

I didn't phone Mama Kathy. I don't know why, except that she'd worry that I was visiting a country we had been at war with only months ago. Mama Kathy never worried about herself, it was just her kids. "Someday you'll know," she'd say.

I would write her, as I'd finally written of our marriage and our intention to visit. By return post she had answered with love and congratulations, but added that a civil ceremony such as I described seemed inadequate to her. It would be no trouble to arrange to repeat our vows in church with family present.

I spoke to Erich, and he was in agreement, he would be happy to do it. In large things and in small Mama was meticulous. One of the small, I explained to Erich, was saving foreign stamps. She used to save them for Georges. But I'm sure the habit was still with her, and she'd find some ten-year-old somewhere. . . .

In token of her farewell to Montreal Elizabeth decided we must have a suitable dinner, "at one of the better French restaurants." She had been reading the Divertissement section in *Le Devoir.* "The Chez Queux on Jacques-Cartier in the old French quarter sounds interesting. It says here, 'built on the fortifications of the original town.' According to this account, the chef has served the royal houses of France."

"He must be very old," Erich commented drily, "pre-Revolution."

Elizabeth ignored this. "And the same architect designed the palace of justice, the chapel of the Sacred Heart, and the church on Rue Bonsecours. We absolutely must dine there."

Later in the afternoon she slipped Erich money. That and the shopping expedition made me wonder if the family estate was in as desperate a condition as she depicted. But I dismissed the idea. Why else would she have made the crossing?

I dressed for the occasion in my elegant suit and felt like an Austrian aristocrat, until I saw a real one. Elizabeth took your breath away in a vaguely patterned, creamy material that gave the effect of sculpting her.

Erich's eyes passed from me to her. He bowed low but refrained from heel clicking, which he knew I detested. "What a privilege to escort two such beauties."

Snow White and Rose Red, I thought bitterly to myself.

As OUR CAB pulled up to the restaurant, a liveried attendant sprang for the door. A fringed canopy led downstairs to an underground palace. The maitre d' hurried to precede us through subdued lighting in which sparkled the crystal of chandeliers and goblets. I glimpsed elegantly folded serviettes lying on the laps of ladies who had been appareled in the boutiques I'd come to know. Flowers drooped toward a central fountain. I felt I was in a play or an opera.

Exchanging a few words with Erich in French, the maitre d' left, sending a sous-chef to our table. An enormously large bill of fare was placed in my hands. I saw immediately that my French was not up to the challenge of these dishes. I planned to say, "I'll have the same."

Erich and the sous-chef embarked on a lengthy discussion of the menu. I looked it over more carefully, and translated *prix du marche* to mean "price on request." Good heavens! They didn't print the price.

Another conversation flowed around me, this one triangular as Erich enlarged the discussion to include his mother. He turned to me. "It's between the entrecôte grillée aux trois poivres flambée au cognac, grilled steak in cognac sauce, or the Chateaubriand et sa suite, Chateaubriand for two with . . . with accompaniments."

"Accompaniments?"

"Soup, salad, appetizers."

"What are you having? Give it to me in plain English."

He laughed. "Filet mignon and potato pancakes in whiskey."

"Share the Chateaubriand with me," Elizabeth suggested.

I nodded, while Erich ordered from the wine list. A different waiter had appeared for this ritual. Kir Royals were decided on, to be followed by a Pinot noir Ramsey, and a Bordeaux la Grange Clairet. I was disturbed as I watched yet another waiter dutifully scribbling our preferences, a servant to the wines. But I had misjudged the profligacy of the establishment. Behind him, dinner napkin over his arm, was a second in command. His job was to listen, to smile, to nod approval, and, of course, the manual part of his job description, when the glasses arrived to set them on the table. I felt sad sitting there in Nile pink—no, no, Suez. It was Suez pink. At any rate I felt sad that a man should be a servant to a glass. But it seemed that if its contents had been pressed in the correct year the vintage was worth many times what he was.

The potage was served, bisque de crustace tuile parmesan, the salade d'endives au roquefort, avec noix. My champagne flute was removed and a wine goblet placed in front of me. A lightly smoked salmon in brandy marinade followed spiced duckling. I observed Erich carefully to see which of the array of forks he chose.

Elizabeth's color was heightened becomingly. They were speaking in English in deference to me, but of people and things I knew nothing of. "You remember Franz Werfel, he did many fine biographies. I read shortly before I came that he died. He was a Jew, you know. He escaped Hitler and fled to the United States."

"Yes, we played chess once. He beat me."

Then she was saying, "We lost the *Scharnhorst* early, so you would know about that. And the battleship *Gneisenau* in November of '39. And the merchant cruiser *Rawalpindi* in the North Sea. Each sinking was a blow to your father. Especially losing the pocket battleship *Deutschland* and the *Admiral Graf Spee*. Captain Langedorff's father was an old friend. You may remember him."

Erich had cast back his mind to the sinkings. "The focus was wrong," he said. "Time was wasted trying to produce an anti-radar coating for U-boats, using strips of aluminum as a decoy against incoming missiles. Nonsense like that, when they should have been concentrating on measures to counter the search radar on Allied surface ships. When the Allies began to detect, we began to lose."

I didn't know these things still rankled. Erich had never spoken to me about them.

"Of course," he went on, "the main problem for a sub is air. It was solved by a German scientist, Helmuth Walter. He developed a turbine propulsion system using oxygen generated from hydrogen peroxide. His demonstration model, the type XXI and V-80, was already built in 1940. But the High Command fooled around with that damn tin foil. We lost battles simply because we couldn't breathe. Three hundred and twelve Axis U-boats were sunk by aircraft—on the surface. If we'd been able to dive— Now, when it's too late, I understand we have the snorkel breathing system. Stupid, stupid, stupid," he murmured at his caviar Beluga/Oscietre.

"Still," Elizabeth soothed, "you saw the last of the really big actions."

"Do you want to know what a big action looks like? There are no heroes, believe me. We were running on radio blackout, total silence, when we were stove in. You don't see it, you hear it. Exploding showers of sound, and a high whistling bursts your head. The next thing you are conscious of is cold, a paralyzing cold. I'd been ejected with scraps of metal, bodies, and tinned goods into a sea of oil. I remember wanting to report to Command that their chemically heated, wind-resistant flotation jackets didn't work."

As I looked across at Erich Helmut von Kerll and his mother, I saw, not the panels of the restaurant, but the great hall of Valhalla. There sat Odin with his mead and ale. He feasted where warriors had fallen. There he was, the horn of plenty at his side, dining on joints of pork from a boar whose flesh never gave out. He kept a wolf on a gold chain, and eagles and ravens came to dine. Two ravens he prized above the rest. They were named Thought and Memory. He sent them far and wide to bring him tidings. He sent them also deep into the recesses of his being. What if? he asked them.

What if this Erich, the Erich who was fluent in French and English, at home among menus and headwaiters, this sophisticated, charming man of the world, was more Erich than the Erich who was my husband? My eyes opened wide like the eyes on a china doll when you've screwed off the head and put your finger in to flick the metal rod. I saw everything, Elizabeth as a Valkyrie, her blond hair in braids, wearing armored breastplate, a fierce battling female. She had come from the sky to bring her son Memory, memory of his home, of his family, of his duty.

She had come to take him back.

Him.

Not me.

Memory was with me too. Memory of Mama telling the twins, "Kathy is to be included." But there was no way I would be included in Vienna. It wasn't their fault. It wasn't mine. I just didn't fit.

I'd been through a war. There I was wanted, needed—not tolerated. There I did fit. The war had changed me. Just to be included was no longer enough.

Elizabeth never had the least intention of introducing an Indian girl to Austrian society. I was not an acceptable wife. I was not an acceptable daughter-in-law. She had come with one mission in mind, to make me see for myself how out of place it would be, how inappropriate. We belonged to different worlds, and she had set herself to demonstrate this.

How did she do it? With gray suede shoes, tucked out of sight under the table, with a Worth suit now hunched miserably in a chair, wrinkled, the material crushed. And by an evening such as this. He was at home, I was an interloper.

The final delving brought new torment. Erich had never spoken to me of his pain at the sinking of each U-boat, of his analysis of the war. How could he? I was the enemy.

Was I? Had he thought of me like that? I had considered him in precisely that way. I remembered my reluctance to go near him when he lay helpless in my ward.

I pushed myself from the table and stood up. The room swam, wineglasses were filled with swirling faces, with solicitous waiters, with flowers and a fountain, with the twin birds . . . what if?

"Kathy, what is it?" Erich asked.

"I'm going to find the ladies' room."

"Shall I come with you?" Elizabeth asked.

She was so sweet to me, so kind. What if I was wrong? Wrong about the braids and the breastplate? A waiter whispered to me the direction, and I turned toward it.

It was the last I remember. Like Erich I was shot out of the water, scuttled not by a depth charge but by a Bordeaux la Grange Clairet. How humiliating.

Had I actually fallen to the floor? Poor Erich. Poor Elizabeth. How embarrassed they must have been. I couldn't understand it. I had never fainted in my life. I hid under the washcloth on my forehead and kept my eyes closed.

Sixteen

ELIZABETH SAT BESIDE me for a long while.

"Don't worry," I said. "I'm not going back with you."

"Shh." She changed the wet cloth.

After a while her place was taken by Erich. "Are you feeling better?" he asked. Elizabeth was upstairs in the guest bedroom, packing—and repacking—her grips.

"I don't know what to say. It was the wine, I think, and the wonderful rich food, and—"

"You don't have to explain. It just happened, and I'm sorry."

"No, *I'm* sorry. You see, it was just too much. I'm not used to such—well, I'm not used to any of it. But I'm glad it happened."

He gave me a queer look. "What do you mean?"

"Erich, I'm not going with you."

"Of course you're going with us. Don't be ridiculous."

"Erich, I'm not."

"What are you talking about? It's our vacation."

"It's not. We both know it's not. We've all been pretending, you, Elizabeth, me. Once you are home in Austria, all this will fade as though it had never been."

He forced calm into his voice. Even so, it shook as he said, "You're crazy, Kathy. I don't know what you're talking about."

"You do. You know you do. And you know I'm right. I

wouldn't fit in, just like at the restaurant. I hated every minute of it. I hated my wineglass having its own servant. How can a human being think so little of himself? To me, Erich, it's affectation, a charade, to consult for twenty minutes how a dish is to be prepared, whether or not to add a truffle garnish."

"I had no idea you were not having a good time," Erich said stiffly.

"I'm not criticizing, Erich. I'm just saying—for *me*. You understand, for *me* it is not a way of life. I couldn't get used to it. I don't want to get used to it."

Erich was regarding me intently. "And if I give up the trip?"

I was startled that he would suggest such a thing, and touched. "I don't think I want you to do that. I don't think I want to be responsible for your life, cut off from everything and everyone you knew."

"Let me understand, Kathy. You want me to go?"

"Yes."

"And you stay behind?"

I nodded.

"And our marriage? It's over just like that?"

I compressed my lips in an effort not to cry.

"You've been unhappy all these months? You were unhappy with this place that we found together and fixed up? You never, never—" He turned away.

"I did! I do! Oh, Erich, it has nothing to do with loving you."

"But it was a mistake?"

"Yes." I couldn't look at him, but rushed on. "It's my fault, Erich. Totally, completely my fault."

"Let me understand. You're saying it's one of those things, a wartime marriage, a mistake?"

"A mistake, yes. Remember how it was, Erich? I didn't think it was significant then, but looking back, a lot of things become clear. Almost from the beginning there was chemistry. You liked me, flirted with me. But it wasn't until you were recovering from the amputation that you thought of marriage. That was part of your decision never to go back, to make a new life. I was part of that new life. I'm not part of the old. Neither one of us ever intended that I should be."

There was a long silence, which he broke at last. "We've been happy."

"Yes," I acknowledged.

"Kathy, it's not fair on the basis of one evening to condemn an entire way of life."

"Not condemn, I don't mean it like that. I'm trying to say I'm a fish out of water. I don't fit in and I never will. And I'm not willing to cut you off, not only from your obligations, but from all those who asked after you and love you. . . . I saw your face when you inquired about your father, your cousin—and it isn't just one evening. There's the dress by Worth and the caracul coat, and the suit Elizabeth kindly, and I mean *kindly*, bought for me. They were all new dimensions, like trying to make a balloon into a certain shape. You press here, it bulges there."

I could see he wasn't angry anymore. His gray eyes were again thoughtful. He was considering what I was saying.

"You've been honest with me, Kathy. I can see I have been less honest with myself. I believed it was a vacation. I believed I was coming back. But you're right about the obligation part. My family needs me. There is no one else. But you're wrong about life there. It isn't just social whirl and glitter. It's being a player in the reconstruction of my country. I could influence the direction it takes, make the whole scene more open, more democratic. My voice would count."

"That's what I've been trying to say. You'd never forgive me if I held you back from all that."

A minute ticked between us.

"I can't give you up."

"And I can't go with you."

We heard the front door. Elizabeth had come down outside, from the guest bedroom above. "I've brought you tissue paper to put between the folds of your suit."

Erich stood up and faced her. "Kathy is not coming with us."

Elizabeth remained very still, looking from me to Erich. She did a strange thing: she kissed me. Then, with a small flutter of a laugh, "In that case I'll use the tissue paper for my jasmine scarf. It will travel better that way."

In the morning the three of us chatted amiably about the hardships of travel, the difficulty of crossing time zones. Erich explained it as the disruption of the circadian rhythm. None of us referred to the fact that I was staying behind. He had thought about it all night. So had I. Morning did not change anything.

When they left, Elizabeth took my hand and held it. "My dear."

I smiled back at her. She understood.

Erich said, "If you change—"

I put my finger against his lips. "Goodbye, Erich."

In response he bowed over my hand in his most Germanic manner and clicked his heels. It was good he did that, it reminded us both. Irreconcilable differences, those were grounds in some courts.

Elizabeth left a note for me, in which she promised to try for an annulment. I set about transferring my things from the bedroom Erich and I had occupied to the guest bedroom. I gave the Schiaparelli dress, the gray shoes, and the Suez pink to charity. I am ashamed to say I kept the coat. Winters are so cold here.

In moving to the second bedroom I uncovered my old wolf talisman. It was a bit mothworn, not so bushy as it had been. But the Cree believe that age implies wisdom. Perhaps the wolf tail had grown in wisdom. If so, why had it imparted none to me?

Actually I think it had, and I hadn't wanted to listen. I

thought the loss of his leg would keep him here. I thought he needed me. It was I myself who had prepared him to leave, taught him day by day to be independent, to do for himself and not rely on me.

Had I known what I was doing? I think so. And yet I persisted. Day after day to care for the wound, to balance, to walk without crutches with only the help of a cane. And in mastering these physical impediments his confidence flowed back until at last he could face his family, his friends, and take up a career, take up his old life. He was the only son, and he was going home. In a way I was proud. It took good nursing skills and good psychological bolstering to accomplish what I had.

And what had it taken to undo a marriage, to break my vows? I stayed late at the hospital and after hours visited the little chapel. With a clicking of his heels he had shown me that he could leave me as easily as I could him. But it wasn't easy. It was one of the hardest things I'd ever done. It had made me sick. If I got up from a chair too quickly the whole room swam, just as in the restaurant.

I had always had perfect health. Mama Kathy used to say I was as strong as a little pony. What was this giddiness, this sudden faintness?

I was a nurse, and yet I didn't suspect. It didn't occur to me that I was pregnant. But a second missed period confirmed it, and thought disappeared down a black tarn.

I went to work. I changed the dressing for cot 4, checked that the acute dysentery case was responding, made a note that 12 was now urinating on his own. Suddenly I stood transfixed. I was going to have a baby.

That night I began my letter. *Dear Erich, . . .* I stopped. Dear Erich, what? Come back, we're going to have a baby? Remembering the final click of his heels, I wasn't at all sure he would come back.

What then? I've changed my mind, I'm joining you in Austria?

Austria was no longer the land of what if. It was as alien to me as the Martian plain or the ammonia atmosphere of Venus. Oh, God, what a mess! I stared at my blank letter with its standard opening—and tried to think. How had I come to make so many mistakes? I went back to the beginning trying to figure it out.

Katherine Mary Flannigan had done her best to ensure that my head was screwed on the right way. "Nothing should be worse because you were there," she'd told me more than once. And my sergeant Papa of the RCMP, what would he say of my impulse to leave things as they were, to not tell Erich? With a convulsive movement I took hold of the pen. We'd talked about having a baby. Later on, at some unspecified time in the future. He'd said a boy would be Victor after his father. I smiled because I knew it would be a girl and that she would be Kathy.

My hand held its position above the page. *It's his child. He has a right to know.* The child would be part of the fantasy. The question was—which fantasy? Would we go into the woods, trap and fish and live close to nature? That had been his first fiction. He caught at anything not to go home, not to let them know he was a cripple, a man with one leg. Why hadn't I seen as plainly as I did now that phase would pass?

The other fantasy was mine—Austria of the waltzes, the Bodensee, and the little blond boy in the sailor suit. I would no longer be Kathy, and of Oh-Be-Joyful's Daughter there would not be a trace. In their place a Rhine maiden sipping rare vintages from the *cartes des vin* with the servant of the glass assiduously pouring.

But what deterred me mainly was a child of mixed ancestry growing up in Austria, subject to what slurs, what discrimination? And if the Naziism in Hitler's homeland was festering beneath the surface? Did I want my child imbibing that atmosphere?

I put the pen down without writing a word. Someday, someday I would sing little Kathy the Austrian folk songs her father had taught me. I'd tell her of our marriage, a wartime marriage which held a great deal of love, but not enough to make it right for either of us. I would tell her. And she would make the decision. If she wanted to write him, she would. If she wanted to visit him, she could do that.

This was probably a terrible decision, I told myself, but for that night at least I didn't go on with the letter.

In the following weeks my waistband expanded.

I thought Elizabeth might send me a card. She didn't.

What if she had sent a card? Perhaps—perhaps then . . .

Mental paralysis seemed to have taken over. I needed to talk, confide, tell someone. Egg came immediately to my mind. But how could Egg counsel me? She had never married, never been faced with the prospect of a child. But there was someone else close to me who had.

It took only two days to arrange a temporary leave, book my seat, and once again be on the long, silver-flashing train. As mile after mile was consumed and I approached my old life, I wondered if I could find my way back into it. I wanted to be Mama Kathy's little girl, and Connie and Georges's little sister. Only there was no Georges. No Georges and no Papa. And my father—he was no longer that dark phantom shape, but I needed a woman. I needed my mother.

The silver and blue train sped on, swallowing the miles, swallowing the years. In Edmonton I left the Canadian Pacific and took a bus into the forests of Alberta. At the familiar crossroads I got out. There was no marker, not even a bench advertising the local mortuary.

Mama Kathy looked very small against the background of spruce and larch, yet somehow sturdy, timeless even, as she waved a bouquet of wayside flowers she had picked, tall lavender larkspur, fiery red paintbrush, and wild gold buttercups. She didn't exactly wave it, she shook it at me in her excitement.

I think I must have flung myself at her, for we rocked backward a moment, our arms tightly locked around each other. What we said was incomprehensible, because we talked at the same time, laughing, almost crying. She didn't notice I was pregnant. It seemed obvious to to me by now, but people didn't notice.

She had borrowed a neighbor's car for the occasion. We bounced along the narrow, overgrown road, Mama Kathy, me, my suitcase, and my flowers, talking all the while. Then there it was, the small house where we had all fit so snugly, the fields I had scampered across searching for arrowheads, the step I preferred to jump over, the porch where I played jacks with Connie—it all burst on me.

The past refused to be relegated to the past. It was here, present, overwhelming. Only because I had made the pilgrimage before, when Mama Kathy was in Vancouver assembling replacement parts for planes, could I bring myself to realize she hadn't always been here in the old familiar setting. She too had been part of the war effort, and her life must have changed as drastically as mine. It was exciting, she told me, but demanding. "I felt the pressure after a while. I'm glad to be back home. My own things, everything familiar. The pace of city life gets to you after a bit."

Mama Kathy looked older, her red hair somewhat faded, her

pretty face lined. "I suspect you're tired, Kathy, after such a trip. Your old room is ready for you. I'll call you for dinner, and afterwards you'll tell me what's on your mind."

I did as she said, just like the child I had been. And like that child, I put my shoes beside the bed and climbed under the quilt.

Oddly enough, when I began to talk, it was about Crazy Dancer. "He loved to have fun. He called me by my Indian name. And while I was with him I was Oh-Be-Joyful's Daughter. He rebuilt the toolbox of his three-wheel motorcycle into a sidecar, and we cracked up. He fitted out an old jalopy so it ran on kerosine. And he took me to an amusement park. When I was with him a kind of wildness took hold of me, and I was as crazy as he was. We sat on the moon, and afterwards he tied a handkerchief over my eyes, and I fed him ice cream."

Mama Kathy laughed, but when I joined in she looked at me sharply, and I realized my laughter had an edge of hysteria.

"He was a private. He drove trucks. When they sent him overseas, he asked me to marry him, Mama. And I did."

"Kathy . . ." The word was full of question.

"It was according to Indian ways, a Handsome Lake ceremony, an under-the-blanket marriage. We went to his mother, and she performed it, and neighbors and friends built a little tepee filled with boughs of leaves and flowers. Outside they left food and drink. It was beautiful. I want you to know that."

She rocked back and forth a few times. "But it wasn't a legal marriage? No priest, no church? It was not done in the sight of God."

"I think it was done in the sight of God. We made our vows to Him and to each other."

She continued to rock.

"We tried," I said. "We were going to invite you, and Connie

and Jeff. But when I telephoned, you told me about Georges."
My God, I was going out of my mind. I had mixed everything
up, confused what happened with Erich and my days with
Crazy Dancer. I burst into tears.

Mama Kathy reached for my hand and gave it a squeeze. "So
what about your young man? They took him?"

"Yes, they took him."

"Was he killed?"

"I thought so. I didn't hear from him. There was a telegram, I
heard the ship he was on was sunk."

"My poor Kathy."

"I've talked and talked, and haven't said it." I stood up,
walked up and down the small living room, and came to a stop
in front of her. "I'm pregnant."

In the silence I could hear Mama's intake of breath.

"And not by him," I said defiantly.

Mama's hand tightened over the arm of the old rocker.
"You don't have to tell me anything you don't want to,
Kathy."

"I wrote you. I married again."

"Yes, of course. That's why I'm so confused. But it's all right.
The child is your husband's," she concluded with obvious relief.
"The Austrian who was your patient, the amputee, is the
father."

"You have the picture, but not all the pieces. His mother,
Elizabeth Madeleine Hintermeister von Kerll, came after him."

"You mean, from Austria?"

I nodded. "She came to take him back."

"But—but—" It was too much for Mama Kathy. She started
again, "But he had a wife and child. . . ."

"He doesn't know about the child."

"What?"

I took a deep breath and explained all the counts on which the marriage didn't work.

"I don't know, Kathy," she said as she listened.

I finished and she continued to rock. "I wish I were wiser, but I'm not. My best advice to you is—stay here where you grew up and where you are loved. Give your heart a chance to heal. Eventually your heart will answer you."

"You think so? You think there is an answer for me? Oh, Mama Kathy, I'm terrified. I don't know whether I can go forward, I know I can't go back, and I'm stuck right where I am. I don't know what's best for my baby."

IT'S AN AWESOME thing to be in charge of someone else's life, to make decisions for them. So I didn't. Gradually I absorbed the rhythm of the household. The daily cooking, the cleaning, the gardening, the occasional shopping. Evenings we sang the old songs, the songs we'd sung with Papa accompanying us on his accordion, the one he bought from Old Irish Bill. Then one evening Irish Bill himself appeared, an ancient gentleman who led us in "Kevin Barry" and "Polly Wolly Doodle Wally Day."

Some evenings we updated our songfest with the radio's hit parade. Once I forgot myself and found I was singing in German, "*Röslein, Röslein, Röslein rot, Röslein auf der Heiden.*" Mama Kathy gave me a surprised and quizzical look.

For the most part I mused. I felt very well. Why not, I was full of life. Life swelled my belly, hard and round. I remembered Crazy Dancer's word for soul, *ahcak.* I wondered if the new little Kathy possessed one yet. When does it fly in? At birth?

Connie came. She and Jeff drove up in their Ford. It was a fire-engine red sports car, with a canvas top they kept folded down. Jeff was the same nice guy I remembered, but somehow I had expected her to be with Georges. We took our sister walk. We went off together, leaving Mama Kathy to explain.

"It should be like old times," Connie said, "but it isn't."

"No, it isn't."

"Jeff's great," Connie said. "I really love him."

But he's not Georges, I finished in my mind.

We walked down by the pond, where the ducks migrated each year. They sailed the surface, miniature galleons, their wakes streaming out behind them. Others, who had foraged further, flew in feet first, braking. We watched heads go down and rears come up and shake with the delight of their catch. We watched the males rise from the water, ruffle their feathers, and preen themselves.

"Do you notice," Connie said, "they go in pairs."

Like twins, I thought.

Staring at the mallards, not seeing them, she looked as Erich had when he realized he had only one leg. They'd maimed her too, when they'd amputated her twin.

"I knew," she said, no longer conscious of me, speaking to the wind. "The weight of the world seemed to crash down on me. I was buried under rubble. I died, Kathy. I died when he did, at the exact moment."

I believed her. It can happen that way.

"I love Jeff," she went on. "I love being his wife. But I'm a ghost, Kathy, not here at all. I watch them together, Connie and Jeff. And I smile because it's very sweet. But her heart is dead."

I didn't dare put my arms around her, I didn't dare touch her.

"The War Office sent Mama the standard we-regret-to-inform-you letter, and his things. He had so little. It was a challenge to him to do without, get by on the barest minimum."

My stomach knotted, remembering.

"He left a diary. Mama's going to read it to us tonight. We'll know what he thought, what he felt. It will be Georges talking to us, saying goodbye. I always thought if I'd had a chance to say goodbye, it would be easier."

"Perhaps," I said, "there are special messages for each of us. Or at least for you."

"You think so?" She caught at my words so eagerly that instantly I was afraid I'd stirred up too much hope.

That evening as we sat together, I told them about the letter I'd received from Austria. Not from Erich, not even from his mother. His attorney wrote that a petition had been approved by the archbishop and cleared with the Vatican. There would shortly be papers of annulment for me to sign.

Connie was momentarily pulled from the endless repetitive grief that mired her. While she didn't comment directly on what I'd said, she did talk about the baby. She said over and over how excited she was to be an aunt, and agreed with me that it was a girl, and that of course she was Kathy. But I knew what was on her mind.

Mama Kathy took the diary from the pocket of the old leather chair. Connie went chalk white as Mama opened it and began to read. Connie's hands were clenched, and she leaned forward as though to draw the words out more quickly.

I have come to think that Germany was not equipped to fight a major war. The outcome, I believe, was determined before the first shot was fired. In my opinion it was the state of technology and the decisions made regarding which weapon systems to develop that decided things.

The Germans began the war with a relatively small surface fleet, 57 U-boats, and the Z plan. This called for the building of

*29 U-boats per month. A shortage of materiel scuttled this plan.
As we discovered, it took them two years from the laying of the
keel to the commissioning of a boat.*

Yes, yes, I thought, glancing at Connie. Get around to the
family, Georges.

*At first, Germany had things pretty much their way. The
B-Dienst, the German intelligence headquarters, were success-
ful in breaking into our Naval Cipher No. 3, which we used to
send instructions to merchant shipping. The Jerries showed up
at every rendezvous.*

*In '41, however, there was an intelligence failure on their
part, one which they persisted in with true German thorough-
ness. This was the belief that a transmission of under 30 sec.
could not be picked up by our Directional Finder equipment. But
by then we were able to mount HF/DF equipment on escorts,
that allowed us to pick up a message as brief as 20 sec. From
that time on the tables were turned, we knew every move they
made. This invaluable device looked like a birdcage and was
mounted on the top deck of our ships in plain sight. German
agents in Spain took hundreds of photographs of it, but never
figured out what the birdcage was for.*

There was a grunt of satisfaction and a wry laugh from Jeff.
Connie's face was marble. A sense of panic began to rise in me.
She was waiting for that special word, she was waiting for
Georges to talk to her, and he went on and on about dry techni-
cal stuff that no one cared about now the war was over.

Mama had a sip of Coke and continued reading.

*Bletchley Park, the hub where I work, is the tracking room.
Our job: to detect U-boats. If I hadn't been so impatient, a similar*

transmission post was set up a year later in Ottawa. By that time we had established radio stations along the coast of Africa, the east coast of North America, Washington D.C., Iceland, Bermuda, and the Ascension Islands. At Bletchley we got so we could spot exactly who was transmitting. We even named them: Fritz had a strong even stroke, Hans was quick and nervous, and so on. Their styles are so distinct that we refer to them as fingerprints.

Georges went on to describe special buddies. Steve, whose digs he had been on his way to when it happened. Alan Turing was another, a somewhat remote figure, but the undoubted genius of the operation.

It's quite likely that Turing or at least one of them knows at least one of the opponents he battles in this silent game, where lives and countries and civilization itself are at stake. Both Stephen and Alan, at different times, talk of vacations in Austria and Switzerland. They frequently met up with young Germans hiking the same trails, or in a rest hut on the side of the Matterhorn or Mt. Blanc. They'd share a sandwich, trade stories, laugh together, and talk of their studies. I'm sounding now like sister Kathy with her What-ifs.

I made a gulping sound.
Connie jumped to her feet. "Don't read any more, Mama. I'd like to take it to my room."
"Of course," Mama started to say, but Connie talked through her words, "Did you hear what he said? Did you? He could have stayed right here in Canada. He said so himself. And done the same work. In Ottawa. Why didn't he wait? Why didn't he?"
Jeff started after her, but Mama motioned him to stay where he was. "They were very close," she said by way of explanation, and brought the diary in to Connie.

This worried me more because by now I was convinced that the word she wanted, the special thought for her, wasn't there. Georges had been caught up in the business at hand, fascinated by the deadly game he played for lives and ships and ultimately for the war itself. His twin was over here on the other side of the ocean. He'd kept his focus fixed. It was natural. It was natural for Georges, at any rate. And I worried.

I didn't sleep well. Too many dreams collided, broke apart, and couldn't be called back.

A faint sound disturbed what rest I had, and I found myself listening, not with my ears but with my pores. Something about it upset me, perhaps not being able to identify it. It came, I decided, from the living room.

I got up and very quietly stole across the room and opened the door. I don't know what Hell or Hades or any of those tormented places looks like, but it was there in front of me.

Connie was on her hands and knees, her hair falling in wild disarray around her. She searched through page after page of what had been Georges's looseleaf notepaper. The diary was scattered like a snowstorm. Scissors in hand, she was cutting out individual letters and pasting them on a large cardboard, her lips moving as she tried to press the letters into words.

The code. She was attempting to reconstruct the Twins' Code, like a psychic at a Ouija board, desperately trying to make sense of random letters, force meaning into them. But I could see they followed no pattern. Frantically she interchanged a letter here with a letter there. She was still working with every fifth word.

"Perhaps," she muttered, "perhaps I started in the wrong place. Perhaps I shouldn't have started at the beginning—" Her hands swept the letters lying in piles into new configurations.

"Nothing," she concluded. "He couldn't spare a word, a thought for me."

"Words, no. But thoughts—Connie, you told me yourself you knew in your own body the moment he died. What was that except his last, his very last thought? Be content with that."

She looked up. She hadn't heard me. "He could have stayed right here. He could have been in Ottawa the whole time."

I sat down beside her on the floor and began to gather the pages together.

"No, no," she said, stopping me. "It's here. I counted wrong. I'll start again. *I* is the first word. Count five. Second word is *that*. Count five. Third word is *to*. Count five. Fourth word is *The*. Count five. Fifth word is *determined*. So, it's 'I that to The determined.' But the capital letter in *The*, that's our signal to switch from words to letters. Every fifth letter. But I'm not sure whether to go on, or go back to the beginning. If you go on, it's *b, e, i, u, w, r.* That starts out a word, *being*, and if you skip ahead you get *n* and *g*, but the count is wrong. Go back to the beginning. *I, c, o, k, G* . . . " She looked at me hopelessly.

"It's not in the diary, Connie."

"But I haven't gone through it all. Maybe it's not all here. Maybe the censors got at it, tore out some pages at the beginning. We've got to start the count right and not miss a single word or letter. If you help it will go twice as fast."

"It's not there, Connie."

This time the words reached her.

She rocked back on her heels and looked at me.

It was a full minute later that I reached out a tentative hand and continued collecting the pages. She watched me put them in a neat pile and fit them back in the notebook. Then with sudden decision she began painstakingly to gather individual letters from the floor. She folded them in a blank sheet of paper and tucked them into the notebook. "You were always so sensible, Kathy. Even when you were a baby, you were a sensible baby.

I'm glad you said that, Kathy. I needed to hear it. If you hadn't said it just like that, so definitely, so positively, I think I'd spend all my life hunting through that diary for what isn't there. Why does there have to be 'last words'? That's kind of crazy, isn't it, to attach some special significance to last words. This is a diary. An ordinary diary. There's no code. It's just the day-to-day diary of a soldier."

I listened without saying anything as my sister put her life back. She was doing it methodically with grim determination, but she was doing it. I could do it too.

Connie and Jeff left in the morning.

Seventeen

WINTER MONTHS ARE deep and white and silent here. The snow lodges heavily in tree branches. When the sun shines you can see its structure, a honeycomb of crystals. I think I'd never taken time to notice before. Now things proceeded slowly, calmly, to a new rhythm. My baby grew, filling me. She would be born in the spring. That was when most new creatures arrive. I waited and watched for the first signs of budding.

One day Elk Girl came. Remembering her mysterious appearances at critical times in my life, I was not surprised to see her. She had left me on a stool eating eggs. I had been to war and come back, been married, and soon I'd have a baby. Elk Girl looked exactly the same. She had never been pretty, but from the time we were children, her face was filled with a great dignity.

She didn't want to sit and chat, but when she saw that tea and home-baked cookies would be served, she changed her mind. Elk Girl could always be moved by food. These days I was perpetually hungry and the smell of baking that so often filled the room was one of my pleasures. We sipped the green Irish tea Mama poured from the kettle with the cozy, and munched and talked, Mama inquiring minutely about her various friends on the reserve.

At last Elk Girl pulled back from the table. "Come to my house," she said. "I have to show you a few things."

"What things?"

She laughed and winked at Mama Kathy, who laughed back.

So I got my coat, put on my wool cap and muffler, pulled on mittens, fastened overshoes, and we started out. Any semblance of a road was obscured under snow, but we plowed through it. I knew I wouldn't flounder if I stuck close behind my guide.

Elk Girl neither paused or hesitated. It was as though she followed a broad avenue instead of trackless forest. The new life in me, instead of subtracting from my own health and strength, added to it. I had never felt so well, so alert to the day, the crisp weather, the gleam of an icicle hanging just out of reach. Life had doubled in me, and I took in more than my share.

Elk Girl had stayed on in Sarah's house after her death. That's where she lived. It was her house now. I was surprised, first to see a woman emerge from it, then on entering to find that in front of the cookstove a baby lay asleep under a beaver fur.

"Is he yours?" I gasped.

"Yes."

That was all, no other explanation. Whether he was hers biologically, or a foundling, or adopted, or simply acquired from someone who couldn't keep him I never knew. All I knew was there was no evidence of a father. If it is possible to share a lack, then it was a lack we shared.

"I brought you here to show you how to be a mother." She closed her eyes and went into her medicine place. "Your time," she enunciated oratorically, "is at the end of the popping of the trees. March. Or it could be when the leaves become large in the first part of April."

"I think that's right," I said.

"I will come then. I will bring *iskwao muskike*. That is a woman's medicine. It stops any bleeding."

"Good. Thank you."

"Now, about the baby. Do not wash it all the time. Use the oils that I will give you. And never wash it if it has fever, too much washing can kill it."

"My goodness," I said, thinking that Elk Girl and Mama Kathy were on a collision course regarding bathing.

"The kind of medicine you know was not the medicine that was here at the beginning. At the beginning medicine was made from natural things, things like maple sugar water mixed with pitch for a cough. And for a stomachache lard and charcoal with the head of the bullrush stirred in."

I thought of Mama Kathy's medicine chest: Smith Bros. cough syrup, milk of magnesia, and cod liver oil. I would guess the efficacy of the treatments to be about the same, if you excepted the washing. As a nurse I would also rate them as fairly interchangeable. I drew the line, though, at tobacco juice. It might, as Elk Girl firmly believed, be holy, but it did not stop infection as she claimed. There was a new wonder drug tried on the battlefield for that—penicillin.

Her baby smiled in his sleep.

"Such a pretty little boy. What's his name?" I asked.

She looked at me pityingly. "A baby is not named. A baby grows into its name. And when he is ready, I will make a blue sky trip and bring him a name."

"My baby's named already, even before she's born. Her name is Kathy."

Elk Girl considered this and then nodded. "There is a holy bond," she went on instructing me, "between named and namer."

"I know," I said. And it was true, I was beginning to know all manner of mysterious and unknowable things. Indian things such as Crazy Dancer dancing a path to the other world.

I went home with my head full of Elk Girl's remedies, chokecherry pemmican and camas roots dried in the sun then stewed. But the important ingredient she had given me was her friendship. That and pushing wide open the door to my Indian self.

The smell of him had come back to me . . . the first day I met him, grease and gun oil and sweat and outdoors. What if—? But it was not his baby I carried.

MAMA KATHY TOLD me it was an easy birth. Elk Girl, as good as her word, was there to assist, and I heard her and Mama Kathy in the kitchen, arguing about the *iskwao muskike.* I held on to Mama Kathy, to Elk Girl, to the sides of the bed as the rending and tearing passed the baby along the birth canal. I remembered a black-and-white illustration of the process in my student textbook, how logical the various stages, how mechanically correct. But when it happened in your body, too large a being squeezed along too small a passage raised the pain to an intolerable pitch.

It wasn't going to get born. I regretted my decision to have a home birth. I should have gone back to the city, had the baby at the Daughters of Charity hospital. They could have given me a spinal block. Why hadn't I done that?

It was too big, I was too small. Oh, God, I cried, picturing the wooden Christ on the cross above my bed in Montreal.

A final, impossible effort and it was over. Kathy was laid in my arms. I looked into my daughter's little wrinkled face. "Hello, Kathy. We're going to be great friends."

"Newborns know things no one else does," Elk Girl told me,

and it made sense. They are so recently here, just moments before on the other side.

The baby was white.

Elk Girl was disgusted. "You wouldn't know this child was Métis."

No, you wouldn't. She looked like Erich and like Elizabeth. Only her eyes indicated Indian blood, not brown but black. It was arresting in a fair face.

Mama Kathy was a typical grandmother. According to her the baby was beautiful and perfect besides, with a straight, strong back and well-shaped head—she could go on and on. When Kathy's black eyes met mine, I asked her, "Who are you, Kathy?"

Elk Girl also fell in love with the newest Kathy and forgave her for looking like Austrian royalty. She too fell under the baby's spell and oohed and aahed over her with Mama Kathy and me. Secretly she fed me roots of cranberry with an admixture of powdered bark so that my milk would be nourishing.

Of course I was modern and sophisticated and knew better, but I enjoyed playing Indian. For whatever reason, my milk was abundant and the baby throve. Elk Girl's little son was a toddler now, and, as spring grew warm, we sat outside on the porch, me with my baby in my arms, she with one eye on her little boy. The days were wrapped in a lazy, timeless glow. Then there came one, with Mama Kathy putting up jam in mason jars, and Elk Girl chewing tobacco beside me, a day in fact no different from the others, when a sudden energy took over. What was I doing drowsing away the afternoon? There was a whole world out there, and I wanted to give it to little Kathy with both hands. I wanted to take her to Belmont Park, show her the harbor, the ships and bridges, take her to visit evenings, when Sister Ursula played piano and the girls sang. I wanted her to see the lights of the city and the traffic flowing by, hear the caroling of Notre Dame's great bells.

I had come home to Mama Kathy. I had taken refuge in my old home. I had found my strength and composure. I had had my child. She was a whole and complete person. As she filled out and grew, she was becoming simply more herself. This Kathy was no ordinary little body. I looked into her face, and wide-spaced black eyes laughed back at me one moment, but how stormy they could become. How imperious, how demanding she could be if I was a second late offering her the breast. I was getting to know her. Happy and jolly yes, but definitely her own person and, I suspected, a complex one. How fulfilling to be her mother. She reminded me constantly that I was finally Oh-Be-Joyful's Daughter.

"We'll be going back to Montreal." The words blew about in the air like a dandelion gone to seed and fell into the mulch of the heavily pine-twigged earth.

"You're a fool," Elk Girl said.

But I knew how to handle her by now. "Tell me something I don't know."

Mama Kathy came and sat beside me on the step. "You're going back to nursing?"

I nodded.

"It's a wonderful profession, that and teaching—the helping professions. I've always admired them."

I sat a while longer and Mama Kathy ventured, "If you need someone to look after the baby while you work—?"

I knew she was getting ready to brave sin city and nominate herself. But I couldn't let her do that, knowing how she felt. This was the home she'd shared with Mike.

"Don't worry, Mama, I have friends back there who will help out."

I went in to start dinner and think about my decision. There were advantages to growing up in a small place like this, you knew everyone, and they knew you. Little Kathy would run freer here, but the mission school could not compare to a big-city school. I smiled down at my baby—I was getting a few years ahead of myself. But one had to think of those things. I saw little Kathy in a school uniform, her light brown hair neatly braided. Myself I did not see at all.

I considered briefly that I no longer had anyone to go back to. I was no longer part of Crazy Dancer's life, and I had sent Erich away. He might be part of my little girl's future, but he was no longer part of mine. Two men, I thought, whom I had loved. And who had loved me. But the war turned everything upside down.

I had a profession, one I was proud of and that I worked hard at. It tired me out often, but at the end of the day I felt good about myself. Besides, it was a means of making my way. I belonged to a new generation of women for whom that was possible.

There were fears, there were questions, and plenty of what-ifs—but I brushed them aside. I was ready for the fray. I could make it on my own.

THE LARGE GRAY slabs of rough stone that made up the facade of the Daughters of Charity of St. Vincent de Paul Hospital were familiar and welcoming. My heart beat fast as it had the first time I entered it. I carried four-month-old Kathy in a laundry basket; with it I marched into Egg's office.

She looked up. Her glasses slid along her nose to the turned-up end. "Kathy! And . . . ?!"

"Little Kathy," I said promptly. "I want to come back, and I'm counting on you. I need to work," I said, slipping into the chair opposite.

She didn't hear me. She reached for the baby. "Will you look at her. Will you just look at her!" Then, glancing at me and through me, "She's the image of her father."

I heard the question. "Erich returned to Austria."

"How could he leave this little beauty, this—" She stopped. She looked at me carefully. "He doesn't know?"

"No," I said in a small voice, "he doesn't."

Sister's lips came together in a straight line.

"There are reasons, Sister."

"I'm sure there are." But her mouth did not relax.

"He's needed at home. His mother came for him. His family . . ." My voice trailed off.

"A baby needs a father."

"A baby needs a mother. And I can't live there, Egg. It's not my world, and I don't want it to be hers. It's old, and over here we're new and full of energy, and finding our own way. I can take care of her. I can. If I can bring her with me while she's nursing and leave her for a few hours with whoever is off duty, it will work out. She's a good baby. She hardly ever cries."

"Absolutely not," Egg said. "One of the girls indeed! She stays right here."

I reached across the basket and threw my arms around my rotund friend.

I found a small apartment adjacent to the hospital. When I had told Mama Kathy I'd have help, I hadn't anticipated that from the first I would be inundated with offers. The girls vied with each other to baby-sit. Sister Egg wound up organizing the volunteers into shifts. Little Kathy was never without her devoted court. When I wrote to Mama Kathy that I was afraid she would be spoiled rotten, Mama wrote back, "Love never hurt anyone."

The hours were long and grueling, but there was unexpected

joy. Friends I didn't know I had rallied to support me. Emily was among them, an Emily no longer hesitant and unsure. She had never gotten over her habit of fixing and changing things. And in spite of it, or perhaps because of it, she had become Matron Norris's right hand.

Dr. Finch was an immediate ally. He said he didn't know how he had gotten along without me. "A surgical nurse is a rare and scarce item." I was part of the operating room team almost exclusively now.

At the end of the month I discovered my base pay had been increased. I felt it was justified. I worked with a will, and I was joyful.

Kathy was seven months, crawling into everything, dancing in her canvas swing with elastic attachments that allowed her chubby legs to push off from the floor.

It was Sunday, and after services we'd spent the day in the park. Kathy was asleep in her buggy, and I was weighing whether I was less apt to wake her if I bumped the carriage up the stairs, or lifted her out of it and carried her up. Occupied with this question, I didn't see him.

He stepped out of the shadow in front of me.

It was Crazy Dancer.

He kissed me before he said a word. "I've been wanting to do that for a long time."

There was a great rush of feeling in me that I didn't know how to give expression to. So I simply said, "Will you give me a hand with the buggy? I don't want to wake her."

"I'll go backwards. You lift up your end."

With two there was no problem, the baby slept on.

"I asked at the hospital. They told me you aren't married anymore."

"It was annulled."

"Kathy," he said, "I feel like I'm in a minefield. I'm afraid I'll say the wrong thing, make the wrong move."

"Come in," I said. "Sit down, and I'll fix tea. And jelly sandwiches," I added, remembering.

"I didn't die," he said, continuing the conversation we'd had more than a year ago, "because there was a sergeant waiting for me when I signed in. They put me on another ship. It turned out they wanted someone to look at these American torpedoes that had just been installed. They weren't firing accurately. For every hundred feet forward they fell about ten."

"Did you figure out what was wrong?"

"Not at first. We tried aiming higher, but all that accomplished was for the shell to hit the surface of the water before sinking. Then I thought—if they turn up the drive-planes to shoot higher . . . This worked short-range, but long-range— Oh, what the hell am I talking short-range, long-range? I want us to be together, Kathy. That's a real cute kid you've got there. Anyway, we went down off the French coast, and the Resistance saved my hide. I wrote, but I guess it was too risky, and they didn't send the letters."

"I understand," I said. "And you have to understand too."

"Right."

"So." I set the sandwich in front of him. "Were you able to diagnose the torpedoes?"

"Yeah. I found out from the gunner that to save money the Americans filled them with water for the test, instead of gunpowder."

"Water? You've got to be kidding."

"So what do you think?"

"About using water?"

"About us. You thought I was dead. Was the world supposed to stop on account of that?"

I sat on his lap and looked into eyes that mirrored mine. "Once you adjusted for the difference in weight, the torpedoes worked?"

It was a long warm kiss that turned time around.

"What did you say?"

About the Authors

BENEDICT and NANCY FREEDMAN live outside San Fran-
cisco, and are at work on more books that take the char-
acters of *Mrs. Mike* into the present day.